Cruel Legacy

Cruel Legacy

Heartless Heirs of Canyon Falls
Book 1

Dakota Lee

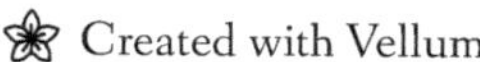 Created with Vellum

Acknowledgments

I can't believe it. This is my fourth book, and it feels like it's the first one all over again. I guess the nerves never really go away. First and foremost, I'd like to thank my children, for putting up with all the evenings when I ordered take-out, or made them find something microwaveable to eat, because I was too exhausted to cook.

I'd also like to thank them for putting up with my non-stop chatter about my writing process and story ideas, even when their eyes were glazing over.

I promise to find some book friends, I can talk story concepts and publishing goals with.

To the *amazing* BETA Readers who took time to read and provide feedback for this story. Thank you times a million. I'm still nervous, but your input helped me be a little *less* nervous. (Please see above... anybody wanna be my sounding board moving forward, so I can give my kids a break?)

And to the readers, thank you for picking up this book, and thank you for giving me a chance. I hope you enjoy your visit to Canyon Falls, and decide to stick around to see what happens next.

CONTENT WARNING

The following subject matter may be discussed in passing and/ or be described in detail on page:

Why Choose
Graphic Sexual Descriptions
Child Abandonment
Talk of Loss of Child
Student/ Teacher Relationship
Bullying (By Harem Members and Others)
Knife Play
Blood Play
Manipulation
Non-Con
Dub-Con
Somnophilia
Breath Play
Primal

Violence
Graphic Assault (Physical and Sexual)
Rape/ Attempted Rape

Your safety and well being is important to me. Please carefully consider these warnings before reading this book.

Bow down and plead

Before those who lead
Leave your will and moral compass at the door
Bleed and cower. Our rival devoured.

The Triumvirate. Legacy Born.

Prologue
Paxton Cox

"What do you think?"

I'm in the leadership room of my frat house with Garret Marques the fraternity recruitment coordinator. We both have stacks of papers in front of us with the names of potential candidates for joining Rho Beta Psi, our fraternity. It's a solid selection pool, but none of the names stand out as being exceptional.

We also have copies of the membership rosters and prospective candidates for all the other fraternities on campus. Without question, Rho Beta Psi is the best fraternity, yet our enrollment numbers have been down over the last two years, and it's not because we aren't accepting new members.

The Student Engagement Center sent out a campus wide survey, asking students how they view school life and extra-curricular activities. The results were less than flattering. Rho Beta Psi throws the best parties, we have the best booze, and the sexiest women shaking their asses; our philanthropic endeavors are widely reported, and our charitable donations unmatched.

Our alumni are judges, professional athletes, and world leaders, yet, the results showed less than ten percent of the guys who took part in the survey want to join our fraternity. A follow up question asked why, and those answers pretty much said the same thing. Why bother pledging when they know they'll get rejected, because we're too exclusive. *Too elite.*

I think it's a bunch of bullshit. Trash responses from people bitching because they know they wouldn't make the cut or we've already rejected them during pledge season. How can you be too elite? The more exclusive you are, the more prestige you get, the more power you accumulate. We'd lose credibility if we accepted everyone who pledges.

If it were up to me, I wouldn't be wasting my time with this batch of names or care that our numbers are down. We should only want people joining who genuinely want to be here. But the organization behind Rho Beta Psi doesn't see it the same way. Fewer prospects for our fraternity means fewer prospects for *them.*

The League of the Daggered Ravens. A secret society, *so secret,* you've likely never even heard of them. You'll never find their membership list, or see anything printed in the newspaper or online blogs about their existence. They're ghosts, not even whispered about, and yet they've influenced, erected, and decimated countries and careers; with a single call or swipe of a pen generation after generation.

I turn over another student profile and read the hobbies on the back. World politics being decided twenty years from now could very well be impacted by one of these names.

Garrett's still waiting for an answer to my question. I give him an answer he probably won't like hearing. "I think this assignment they gave you is a test. It's not supposed to yield prospects. It's the kind of task we all get from time to time. Busy work."

I've heard the rumors. Certain members of The League think it's time to expand our recruitment pool, but I don't really believe it'll happen. It shouldn't happen. The foundation by which the league operates has worked for centuries. Why change it?

Garrett sighs. I hear the frustration in his voice. "I've been at it all summer. Wouldn't they have told me to stop looking by now?"

Would they? It's hard to say. I've overheard a few conversations I shouldn't have and I know those old fucks have us doing a lot of things just to amuse themselves. "Maybe. It's possible whatever committee is spearheading this recruitment drive will start the pre-selection process, but something tells me no one you suggest will make it to the final ceremony."

I drop the profile I'm holding. "But by then, The League will have already learned all the applicant's secrets and taken advantage of whatever usefulness they have."

By the time the prospects are officially rejected, their families will be so indebted to The League they won't know how to untangle themselves from their clutches. This is how the council builds power. This is how members advance up the leadership ladder within the league and stay in control, well past their prime.

A council position isn't easy to win, and the governing term has the longevity of a Supreme Court appointment. I've only heard of two transfers of power over the last forty or fifty years. Those seats came up for grabs when the council members "retired".

In our world *retire,* is just another name for too cognitively disoriented to make sound decisions or dead. Case in point, the oldest councilman is eighty-three years old, and there's no reason to think he won't be healthy enough to do the job for another ten years, while he continues to cheat on his forty-two-year-old wife, with his twenty-seven-year-old mistress.

I'm not judging. If his saggy old balls give those ladies thrills, I say fuck their brains out until his heart quits. In our world, everyone has their thing and with power comes opportunity. It's been drilled in my head from an early age, whatever I want in this world is mine for the taking, and I. Want. It. All.

I look back down at the stack of folders in front of me. If helping Garrett go over a list of names to help bolster our fraternity numbers gets me in the council's good graces, I'm happy to do it.

I see the intensity on his face as he pours over another application. He wants to find that gold ticket prospect and is desperate to please the council members. To be recognized. To prove he's an asset to the organization.

There are two phases to joining The League of the Daggered Ravens. Pre-selection screening and initiation. If you make it through pre-selection screening, you become a Prospect. An official member of the initiation group. Similar to a pledge at a fraternity or sorority. Prospects are called Wrens and it's all most initiates really care about. If you're a Prospect, you're on the council's radar and a *friend* for as long as you live. Friends get perks, although the relationship is never on equal footing. Prospects will always do more for The League of the Daggered Ravens than The League will ever do for them.

The prospect period lasts as long or as short as the selection committee decides. Anyone selected to initiate when the prospect period ends, will write their ticket in this world.

Not every member in Rho Beta Psi is privy to the existence of The League of the Daggered Ravens, and not every Prospect or Initiate advances through the steps at the same level. I'm a legacy born, which means the men in my family have been members of The League of the Daggered Ravens since its inception. It also means the hoops I have to jump through are multi-faceted.

One day, when I've done everything they require to prove myself, I'll embrace their oath, swear my allegiance to their ranks, and be reborn a full-fledged member. On that day, the initiate pin I'll wear will turn into a brand signifying a bond that cannot be severed or forsaken.

My life, my loyalty, will belong to The League, and theirs to me in return. We'll be an unshakeable, powerful force. I can't imagine anything better.

So even though I think this screening process is a waste of my time, I dig back in. There's a bigger picture here and I do my part to support The League.

Chapter 1
Theona LaReaux

I'm on the side of the road, standing on a narrow stretch of asphalt that's supposed to be a safe pull-off by mile marker two sixty-six. It's so safe I'm staring over the side of the cliff. The embankment is a steep drop of at least fifty feet and I'm hovering over it like there's a steel guard rail to protect me from falling. There isn't. In fact, there's no sort of railing at all. Not even a hazard sign, cone, or construction barricade to warn you about getting too close.

This is definitely not the road to speed along after having anything to drink. In the daylight, it's treacherous. At night bathed in pitch black nothingness, it's probably deadly. There's nothing below me but jagged rock, and yet I see the majestic beauty of this cliff and feel as calm as I would be if I were sunbathing on a tropical beach.

My heart rate spikes as I lean over a little further, a laugh falls from my lips. There's nothing better than the feeling of adrenaline pumping through my veins. If this were any other day, and I had my stuff, I'd scale down the side to see what's at the bottom beyond my line of sight.

Unfortunately, I *don't* have my gear. I'm short on time, and I have at least another hour of driving ahead of me. I need to get moving if I want to reach my destination before it gets dark. I close my eyes once more, inhaling deeply, committing this feeling to memory before returning to my car.

My shoulders deflate as soon as I'm settled in the driver's seat. I doubt there's any room for fun and excitement where I'm heading. If the stilted calls, texts and emails I've received from my aunt and uncle are any clue, I'd say they don't believe in fun.

I start the car, my gaze sliding over the envelope on the passenger seat. It's the letter from my social worker officially discharging me from the Nags Creek Independent Living Program.

Independent Living is the post placement program for foster children who have technically aged out of the system. As long as you work, are attending school or some type of training program, or have a medical disability that prevents you from being able to do one of those things, the state continues providing medical coverage, employment assistance, a small living stipend and subsidizes your housing to help you transition to adulthood.

I was all set to start paying the rent on my own in eighteen months, but my case worker threw me a curve ball and sprung this aunt and uncle into the mix. After years of being on my own, here come some people I don't even know wanting to take me in. I roll my eyes at their "generosity". *Now* they wanna help, when the hard part is done and I no longer need it.

I was planning to tell them to stuff their helpfulness up their asses but Mrs. Sprout, my social worker, made it a point to tell me over and over again how this move was a great opportunity I couldn't pass up. It provides me with a chance to graduate from an Ivy League College without owing a mountain of debt.

For that reason and *only* that reason I packed up my two-bedroom apartment and loaded everything I own into the back of the moving van my aunt and uncle sent.

My things shipped last week, and I opted to drive instead of using the airline ticket they wanted to buy. Flying would have been faster, but I needed these endless hours on the road to convince myself this move was a good idea. Spoiler alert... I still need convincing. I've turned this rental car around at least three times already, but I've never gotten more than a few miles down the road before turning around again. My nine-hour drive is heading into unlucky hour number thirteen. My favorite ring tone cuts in over the music playing on the radio. I stab the button on my corded microphone to answer. "Sup, girl?"

"Well, since you answered, I guess this means you're still not there yet. Are you still sitting outside the truck stop on the edge of town?" My best friend Sasha knows me so well. Because I did spend thirty minutes at the truck stop before getting on the road this morning. I wait until the background noise on her end dies down before answering. "I've got another thirty minutes or so before I make it to the last rest stop, then the navigation system says it's another ten minutes to the turnoff from there."

"And fifteen miles to town." She says repeating the directions I told her last night and this morning.

"Yup."

"And you said you won't have cell reception?"

"The map says this place is surrounded by mountains and dead air. Shit, girl, I'm already out of range for my prepaid plan. I'm shocked I've even got a signal right now. But I paid for two months of service just in case. It might be spotty with hella roaming charges, but you know there's no way I was gonna risk not being able to call you when this shit goes sideways."

"Now Thea, don't be like that. We're expecting good things to come from this."

I roll my eyes at my bestie's expectations. I appreciate her trying to put a spin on it, but I'm less inclined to believe this move is the answer to all my unspoken prayers. Shit, I don't *have* prayers because I stopped believing they'd come true long before I wound up in the system.

When you have no clue who your father is, and your mom's

known as the town drunk, you quickly learn there's no such thing as the Tooth Fairy, Santa Claus and Happily Ever After.

My friendship with Sasha is the only thing that's endured my many moves and school changes. We met when we were seven, at one of the first foster homes they sent me to. That was about six months before her grandparents came and got her. I spent another year in the home before my foster mother had a heart attack requiring me to move to a new home.

I went back to my mom a little bit after that and Sasha and I wound up in the same school. Then the cycle started. Mom would be sober. Things would be good. Then she'd meet some asshole and the minute things didn't work out, she'd spiral out of control. First, she'd stop going to work, so there would be no money for paying the bills and no food in the house to eat. Then she'd trash the place the moment the landlord confronted her about the unpaid rent, and let's not forget my personal favorite... moving us in the middle of the night like the hounds of hell were on our tail.

I guess I can consider myself lucky I'm an only child and learned to make do with the situation. I rationed out food when it was in the house, or swiped an extra lunch from school, but if there had been another kid around there would've been way more days I'd have gone hungry.

I zone out while Sasha yells at one of her cousins. She still lives with her grandparents, who took in three of their other grandchildren. It's always a full house over there.

Sasha is happy and loved, but I know she's waiting for the day she has enough money to move out on her own. She's crashed with me plenty of times, but we never made it official since it was against the rules for Independent Living to have anyone live with you. We had plans to get a place together just as soon as I turned twenty-one and finished the program. We still might, if this relocation doesn't work out.

When there's a lull in the yelling, I say, "Still busy around there, I see."

"Girl, yes. My cousin Casey is here with her man and they've got shit everywhere. It's like I can't even get a minute of peace. And since they're a couple, Alicia and I had to move into the room with Ellie. We're standing on top of each other."

"I thought Ellie was moving out?"

"She is. Her departure date for basic training got pushed back another month, but she's going."

There's a scuffling sound, then Sasha groans. "See this is-"

Whatever else she says gets cut off when my phone signal drops. I crank the radio up, letting the music keep me pumped during this boring ass drive. I'm in the middle of my road trip concert, when the Australian voice on the navigation system cuts through my harmonies. *In two miles, take a right at the fork.*

I glance down at the screen and see I'm getting closer to the rest stop. The sun dropped out of the sky when I was talking to Sasha, but even with my headlights on to brighten up the ink black road, I can't make out any signs or landmarks.

A right, in two miles. Okay, I can do that. I scan the right side of the road, looking for my turnoff.

In a quarter mile, take a right at the fork.

I squint into the darkness and still can't see where the roads diverge.

In one thousand feet, take a right at the fork.

I'm leaning forward over the steering wheel trying to make out something in the dark, but all I see are the white highway lines in front of me, and trees on my right. I turn down the volume on the radio and slow my speed.

In five hundred feet, take a right at the fork

Take a right at the fork.

I almost miss it. I *guess* you could call the tiny sliver of road, a fork. I cut the wheel sharply, giving the car's shock absorbers a workout as I bump along the road. I look down at the navigation screen again to make sure I'm on the right path. The little line is as steady as can be. With each bump, I get closer to my destination.

I'm glad the GPS system is confident I'm heading in the right direction, because the poor excuse of the road in front of me has me worried I'm about to run into one of these trees. They're dense as fuck, no moonlight coming through. I flick on my high beams. I still can't see more than a few feet in front of me.

I'm driving slower than a student driver, riding the brakes as if a deer might dart out from the trees. I'm not usually this slow, but the car's a rental and I don't have money to reimburse my uncle if I get into an accident. I check to make sure the navigation system is still getting a signal. It's been quiet since I Tokyo drifted onto this road and I'm pretty sure I should have seen the rest stop by now. Maybe I took the wrong turn.

Just as I'm about to turn around and head back the other way, the electronic voice tells me to turn left in half a mile.

I drop my speed, preparing to find another non passable passage through trees. I'm right. The left-hand turn is more like a dusting of gravel thrown along a patch of dirt, in the middle of a forest of trees. I spot a structure in my rear-view mirror. It's a Rest Area sign with a red "Closed" sticker slapped across it. Good thing I don't have to pee.

This road is a little better than the last one, and after another ten minutes, I come across a weathered sign telling me Canyon Falls is five miles away. I take another right when the navigation tells me to, and cross an old wooden bridge. It creaks and groans with every thump of the wheels.

I drive over a set of railroad tracks, and past the dilapidated sign that reads Canyon Falls Township, established 1869. The streets are quiet and eerily deserted for a Friday night, which only reinforces my earlier prediction. This place is gonna be the opposite of fun.

I shake the tension out of my hands and shoulders, and crank my radio back up now that I'm on an actual road. I glance down, fiddling with the tuner to find a station, and look back up ten-seconds before a thump hits the car. I slam on the brakes, my heart in my throat, as I briefly lock eyes with the guy who just slid over the hood of the car like some kind of action hero. *Where the hell did he come from?*

He readjusts his backpack and pulls his hood lower before running off into the trees on my right.

What the hell?

I'm still staring at the tree line, trying to make sense of what happened, when my phone alarm goes off. It's the alert I set for the time I wanted to arrive at my final destination. The GPS says I'm twelve minutes away from the house.

I'll be staying on campus at Canyon Falls University. Move in day was on Tuesday, and classes started yesterday, but my aunt and uncle insisted I spend a few days with them so they can help me get settled in my new town and dorm. I rolled my eyes so hard when they said that. I've never needed help settling anywhere before.

I can hear Mrs. Sprouts' voice telling me to stop bringing my negative past into my positive future. *"Every day is a new day that something amazing can happen."*

She's genuinely one of those perennial sunshine types, but I've heard her threaten to cut a bitch.

I turn onto the street the GPS has directed me to and slam on my brakes for the second time tonight. This time, it's because I'm sitting at the bottom of a driveway. At the top of it, there's a massive gate blocking off a group of houses which can easily take up an entire block in my old neighborhood.

You can't always trust technology. The roads were deserted and the navigation seemed suspect the last hour of my drive. I felt like one of those penguins in that commercial, wondering if I should just ignore the GPS and follow my instincts. I do a final route check to make sure I'm in the right spot. A big red blinking dot marks the spot, confirming I'm in the right place.

I ease off the brake and creep forward. Good thing there's a call box since nobody gave me instructions on how to access the gate.

The gate slides open before I even get my window down. I drive the winding road, looking for the house number. Thankfully, it's not the third house on the left. I've seen the movie with that title and don't need that bad mojo around me.

Pulling to a stop, I gawk up at the mini-mansion in front of me. There's no other way to describe it. There's this mansion you can rent for parties in Vegas, that Sasha and I went to once. This house is smaller than that mansion, but way fucking bigger than any normal sized family home I've ever seen. I suspected these folks had a few spare dollars in the bank, but to be confronted with this...

I only have to look to the house next door to know they get fancier the further up the hill you go. My phone still doesn't have a signal. They're probably on private towers out here.

I don't care how many miles I just drove. I'm still toying with the idea of fending for myself. This is not my scene. Yeah, *fuck this*. I'm going back home. Before I can throw the car in reverse, the front door to the house opens. Shit. So much for running. They obviously know I'm here, and with the way they keep opening doors and gates, they seem hella anxious to get me inside. I kill the ignition and climb out of the car, taking my time to grab my duffle bag from the back seat.

When I've stalled for as long as I can, I straighten up, sling my bag over my shoulder, and close the car door with a hip bump. I make a point of walking around the front of the car before crossing the driveway to get to the stairs. I count four steps between the ground and the top landing.

I'm greeted by a stern-looking woman with her bun pulled so tight it's pinching her eyes back and lifting her brows so she looks like a surprised cat

"Finally," she says before I'm halfway up the steps.

Whatever nerves, doubt, or awe I was feeling evaporates in the face of her rudeness. "Excuse me?"

"We expected you four hours and seventeen minutes ago."

"Uh, huh." Who's this bitch? I've seen a picture of my aunt. This isn't her. "Are um, Moira and Scott here?"

"They are not. They were called away unexpectedly for a business meeting, but will return tomorrow to make sure you're ready to begin classes. In the meantime, I've been tasked with getting you settled in for the evening, and as I said, we expected you hours ago.

As it is, everyone has retired for the evening." She frowns, "But I suppose I can get someone up to fix you dinner if you haven't eaten."

"I ate a few hours ago."

She gives me a curt nod and says, "Then you should be fine until morning." She turns and crosses the huge entry way, moving towards the stairs. I guess she senses I'm still rooted in place, because she says, "Come along. I'll show you to your rooms. Please pay attention, so you don't get lost and wander into any off-limit sections of the house."

I close the door and follow after her. "Off limit?" I ask when I catch up with her on the stairs.

"That's what I said." She doesn't offer any further explanation about it.

I listen as she points out wings and quadrants, but none of it makes any sense. Her pace quickens when we reach the third floor. She leads me down the hall towards a set of white French paneled doors which she unlocks with a silver key.

My mouth hinges open when I step across the threshold. I was expecting another hallway, but we're standing in the middle of a large sitting room. I don't have much time to take it all in, because we're still on the move.

She opens another door that leads to the bedroom. She gives me a brief explanation about the individual temperature control for the thermostat, tells me I have direct access to the servant's wing by dialing zero on the phone or tablet on the dresser, shoves the keys at me, and leaves.

Minutes pass and I'm still standing in the same spot, trying to figure out what the hell is actually happening. I've spent my whole life struggling for basic comforts, but my aunt and uncle live like *this*?

Mrs. Sprout never actually explained how these people found me, or went into much detail about them. She assured me they were properly investigated and their relationship to me has been confirmed.

Scott is my mother's cousin, but they grew up together like siblings, hence the aunt and uncle title. He told Mrs. Sprout my constant moves made it harder for them to track me down. If it weren't for me finally getting my own place with utilities in my name, the PI would still be collecting a check.

I check my phone. Still no bars. Walking over to the sliding glass door that leads to the balcony doesn't help. The first order of business is to find a new prepaid cell phone provider, because there's no way in hell I'm staying here without a way to send an SOS to my best friend.

I built this day up in my head for weeks. Now that I'm here, I'm not sure what to do with myself. The adrenaline from the drive and my Red Bull is wearing off and my body is stiff from sitting for so many hours. A nice, hot shower should fix that.

I open the door to what old sour puss called a private *en suite*, which I know is just a fancy name for bathroom. My mouth must have a loose hinge joint because it's open. *Again.* This thing looks like a spa. A huge ass soaker tub sits in the middle of the floor.

The oil rubbed bronze fixtures match the faucets in the Jack and Jill sinks, and the four shower nozzles protruding from the walls in the walk-in shower which is big enough for three people. That's in addition to the rain shower head suspended from the top of the ceiling. There's a half frame tinted glass enclosure, a bench butts up against the glass. I can't wait to test the heating capacity and endurance level of the hot water tank in this house.

I hurry back to the bedroom and fling open the door to the biggest closet I've ever seen. It's as wide and as deep as the bedroom, with a sitting area in it, as well as a full-length mirror. It's giving off serious dressing room vibes. I walk forward and turn left. Walk the length of the aisle, then turn right, like I would in a store. Dresses hang on the middle racks and there's an entire wall of shoes on the farthest wall, a dresser on my right.

I open the top drawer and find it's full of bras and panties. The next drawer has t-shirts, and the one below it, socks and pjs.

Seeing this stuff reminds me I didn't see the boxes with the things I sent ahead. Whose room is this? From what I know, Scott and

Moira never had kids, but that doesn't mean there's not another niece out there who uses this room when she comes to visit. I hear Sash's voice in my head telling me not to overreact. My stuff has to be somewhere in this house, and they probably haven't gotten around to getting these things cleared out. I walk back into the bedroom and fling my duffle bag onto the bed. I always carry two extra sets of everything with me, so I have a change of clothes and something to sleep in no matter where I go.

I grab my body wash and loofa and snag a towel from the warming rack on my way to the shower. The water heats quickly. I'm used to taking fast showers but tonight, I take advantage of not having to jump out before the water gets ice cold, or skipping the hair washing routine because there's a line forming outside the bathroom door. There's no line, and nobody's waiting, so I wash and rinse everything twice, including my hair.

After I'm clean enough to be the guest of honor at a virgin sacrifice, I wrap the fluffiest towel I've ever felt around me, and stand in front of the bathroom mirror while I detangle my hair. I put it in two French braids and grab another towel to lay across the pillow to help soak up the last bit of water in my hair.

I slip on the basketball shorts and t-shirt I'm sleeping in, and climb onto the bed with a notebook in my hand to make a list of things I need to do before I move onto campus. I write the same thing twice before finally admitting I'm too tired to focus. I climb under the covers and close my eyes, my hand holding tight to the object I never leave home without, and let exhaustion win.

Chapter 2
Pax

I make my way through the trees and bushes to the meetup spot. I'm early, but I know the guys are already on their way. We never travel together for these things, to throw people off our trail, making it harder for us to be followed. Other groups don't have the same philosophy. They think teamwork means doing everything together, every step of the way, even though I think we've proven to them ten times over it doesn't.

As I approach the end of the shrub line, I spot a figure moving in the shadows on the right. That'll be Holden. Wherever we go, we usually arrive within minutes of each other. Unless it's the library. He's there hours before anyone else, including the head librarian. I think she gave him a key and uses his early bird status to her advantage.

He crouches down beside me, keeping hidden from the street as we wait for our third. I scan the street. Movement halfway down the block catches my eye. Finn is on the roof, flipping and jumping from building to building, like it's his personal parkour course. He's not at all stealthy about it either, like the last thing he's worried about is someone following him. I guess he has a right to be cavalier about it. It's hard as fuck keeping up with his free-running ass.

I check the time on my watch. We're still ahead of schedule. Tonight's mission is simple. We should be in and out before anyone notices, and back at the dorm laughing, while the other teams are still trying to pull a plan out of their asses.

We've all been given the same coordinates, but my boys and I are sure to come out of this game on top. We've got the perfect team. Finn with cat burglar type skills, Holden the puzzle solver extraordinaire, and me... I take point on damage control and risk assessment. I'm also usually the man with the plan. The other team's plans. They need to get better at guarding their secrets if they ever want to beat us.

Finn's almost to us, now. He's hanging from the top rung of a fire escape and then lets go, free falling five stories before grabbing the next one, and swinging through the side of the ladder rung. I turn to say something to Holden, when a squeal of brakes drags my attention back across the street just in time to see Finn leap into the air, tuck and roll off the hood of a car, then land on his feet, before disappearing through the trees, like that shit didn't just happen.

Holden and I share a look. We're thinking the same thing. Who the fuck is in the car? We creep through the trees to meet up with Finn, my mind going over the possibilities of what just happened.

"What the hell is a car doing out here tonight?" Finn asks, glaring in the direction of the car, which is long gone by now. Whoever it was didn't even stop or get out to see if the person they hit was okay. That could be a good or bad thing.

Holden asks, "Are you hurt?"

I do a quick look to make sure Finn's not bleeding. It's not as if that shit matters to him. But it would be a problem for our mission because he'd be leaving DNA all over the scene.

"Fuck no." He waves off Holden's concern. "I'm pissed. Whoever it was messed up a sweet ass aerial landing I've been working on all week."

I scoff at his answer. Of course he's mad he didn't stick his landing. "Did you get a look at who was driving?" I ask, working through this little hiccup.

"Nah. I didn't bother to look."

That's smart, because we're supposed to be sneaking around. Making eye contact is a surefire way to be identified.

"What do you wanna do, Pax?"

I turn, heading deeper into the foliage, and say, "There's only one thing we can do."

We trudge into the dark bunker. The lights are on an automatic switch. It flips on or off when the door is closed and the locks engaged. This side of town was left to waste a long time ago. It's ignored and avoided, which makes it the perfect place to work out of. The bunker looks like shit on the outside, but inside it's a state-of-the art, smart home. Our very own impenetrable fortress.

Last night's job took longer than expected. After Finn's run-in with the car, we had to make sure we weren't being followed. No one drives across the railroad tracks to enter or leave town.

The road shut down when my dad was a kid, after they paved the new highway on the Northeast end of town, and made it a major artery between here and Palisade Shores.

So what the hell was someone in an Audi doing coming from that direction? I'm sure it's overrun with trees and dirt by now. Then, there's the mountain terrain you have to drive up. Nobody's foolish enough to drive up it in the dark. That makes the car being there suspicious as fuck, and we had to lie low to make sure we weren't being set up.

Even with our delay, we still made out better than the other teams and came in first. We're *always* first. Years of living, playing, and training together make my friends and I an efficient team. We were first to complete our mission, but it wasn't without its challenges, and the second-place team was close behind us. So close, I know I'm going to have to answer questions about it.

I put my gear on the shelf, lock the trinket we procured in the safe, and grab my cellphone from the charging station. We never take our cellphones, because these games call for no distractions. The team in last place is still out there, running in circles. Someone hacked their cells and sent them in the wrong direction.

Finn, Holden and I know this city inside and out. If there's anyplace we're unfamiliar with, we use paper maps. You can't hack paper. I look over at our tech genius. "How much longer should we leave them out there?"

Okay, so we're the ones who sent them the wrong directions.

Holden shrugs. "We're done. There's no reason to let them continue to wander around other than for the laughs." I give a quick nod and he taps a few keys on the computer. "Done."

I don't know the particulars, but what he's done is send them the correct instructions and coordinates to complete their challenge. We finish gathering our stuff and head to our cars, powering up our phones, when we're clear of the bunker. We have jammers inside so no one can track our signal, but you can never be too careful. The first part of the challenge is to grab whatever thing we're sent to retrieve. The second part is hanging on to it.

DAD

Home

The one word text greets me as soon as my phone powers up. It's nearly one in the morning, and I'm dead on my feet, but my bed will have to wait until after my debrief with my father. This is another reason the guys and I take separate cars. I never know when I'm gonna be called away on some bullshit.

On the drive to my parent's place, I go over what happened last night. My father will want a recap about everything we did, starting from the moment we got the details for the challenge.

My body screams in protest as I drag myself toward the front door, but I shake off the sore muscles and fatigue. I know better than to show any signs of weakness in front of him. The house is quiet when I walk inside, but I know where he'll be. In his office, a glass of bourbon in his hand, and a lit cigar in the crystal ashtray in front of him.

I knock on the closed door and wait for him to invite me in. He's behind his desk, his sleeves rolled back and his tie undone. This is as close to casual dress as I've ever seen him, outside of the golf course.

He points to the seat across from him. I take it and wait. It's all a game to him and I've learned no matter what I say, he'll never start the inquisition any faster than he wants to. It's not just me, he does this to. Making people wait in awkward silence is an effective tactic. One I've adopted. People spill their secrets to fill the silence.

"You did well las night." He says, immediately putting me on edge. Dad's done two things out of character. Spoken before the ten-minute mark, and paid me his version of a compliment. "Even with the delayed start, you and your team performed admirably."

Of course, he knows we didn't start at the same time as everyone else. It's hard to keep secrets from him, but that doesn't stop me from trying. "Thank you, sir."

I'm ready for him to flip out and demand to know why we were late getting to the final starting point. Instead, he continues to act like he's been body snatched. He smiles, pleased I haven't left my manners at the bunker. I watch as he sips his drink, takes a tote of his cigar, and then sets the full weight of his stare on me. "It's late, and I know you have a full day of classes tomorrow, but there's been a development."

"What kind of development?" It could be anything, but it's probably someone complaining the teams are unevenly matched. There's been talk about splitting me and my friends up, but so far nothing's come of it. If tonight is the night they pull that card, this little visit's gonna get real bad, real quick. I'm prepared to fight with everything I have to keep us together. Consequences be damned.

"In the next few days, you'll be getting a new resident at Vale Tower."

Not where I saw this going, but I prefer this to answering any other questions he might have.

"This guy. You want me to guide him towards Rho Beta Psi?" If dad's interested, it's the logical thing to do.

"It's a female, and I want you to keep an eye on her. Report back everything she does and says. No matter how small or unimportant you think it is."

A girl? He wants me to babysit and report back on a girl? "Who is she?" I ask, trying to get more information. At the same time, I'm thinking of who I can farm this job off to.

"We really don't know yet. We were only just alerted she's starting in a few days and they've put her on your floor."

My eyebrows shoot up and he smirks at me. It's the first hint of emotion I've shown. But he's gotta cut me some slack. Vale Tower is a legacy building. Priority goes to descendants of the Legacy Twelve. The twelve families who initially donated money to have the school built. Your room and floor assignment depends on the amount of the initial donation, and how many generations of your family have attended Canyon Falls University since the beginning. We live like kings and queens in that building. It even has a small store on the first floor. Someone popping up out of the blue and getting luxury accommodations just doesn't happen.

He continues, "It could be nothing. It probably *is* nothing. Just a glitch in the dorm assignment, but I want you to handle this personally and provide me weekly status updates."

"Understood, sir."

He doesn't have much more use for me. After an obligatory conversation about maintaining my GPA (which doesn't really mean shit in our world, but it's just one more thing for him to brag about), he dismisses me.

I'm fuming on the drive back to campus. With everything else I have going on, the last thing I need to be doing is stalking some chick because some screw up put her on the wrong floor, in the wrong dorm.

Chapter 3
Thea

I've lain in bed for as long as I can. I tossed and turned all night, unfamiliar with the sounds of this house. I hate that I can't get a good night's sleep anywhere new, because foster care and group homes have conditioned me to always be on high alert at bed time. There's always some idiot wanting to test the new girl in her sleep. More often than not, their attempts to surprise me gave them a personal introduction to Clint, the butterfly knife I've had since I was ten.

Some kid was flashing it around one day at the playground, bragging about all the cool knives his pop owned. I won it off of him in a race and never thought twice about him having to explain to his father where it went. If there was any fall out, I wasn't around to hear about it, because I used the knife to defend myself against one of the bigger kids in the foster home, and got shipped off to a new location that same night.

I strain my ears, listening for sounds of other people. The house is just as quiet as it was last night. I roll out of bed and smooth the comforter down before heading to the bathroom to wash my face and brush my teeth, then put on my change of clothes and retrace the path sourpuss and I walked last night. I get turned around a few times, but eventually find my way back to the foyer.

She mentioned off limit areas of the house, but all I care about is figuring out where my stuff is. I'm on a mission to find a garage. Do rich people even store their stuff in garages?

I walk outside and around the left side of the house. A set of stairs lead down to a pool, and then continue down to a beach with pristine white sand and the bluest water I've ever seen.

The map was misleading. It didn't make it seem like the town was this close to the water. I'm itching to go down there and get in, but I'd have to swim in my clothes. Until I find my things, I need to treat my outfits like they're made of the finest silk.

Continuing around the path to the other side of the house, I find the garage. I jiggle the handle on the door, and find it's locked. There's some type of key pad on it. Sourpuss didn't give me any passwords or alarm codes, or keys to the house. Now that I'm thinking about it, I'm pretty sure the front door had an electronic lock too. Great. I've locked myself out.

I don't want to be rude and wake the house by ringing the doorbell, so I decide to wait it out. It's a toss up between walking the beach and lounging by the pool. I settle on the latter and head back around the path, taking the stairs to the pool. I settle onto the chair closest to the middle of the patio because it gives me the best view of the beach. There are houses on both sides of us, but I can't see over the gates or hedges.

Something's moving along the shoreline. At first I think it's the shadow from the sun creating a weird glare off of the water, but it's getting closer. The blob is two yards out from the bottom of the stairs when I realize it's a guy running on the beach, shirtless.

His body's toned, with defined muscles. The guys from my old neighborhood are trim and athletic because they spend their free time playing basketball at the playground or flag football in the field behind one of the churches or schools. Some spend time at the boxing ring. They wouldn't be caught dead *running*, unless it's from a Rottweiler they've antagonized or the cops.

A noise behind me draws my attention away from the hottie on the beach. The glass door, which I hadn't noticed next to a huge bay window, slides open. I jump to my feet and hurry towards the door, trying to make noise so I don't spook the woman who just walked out. "Hello."

She looks up from where she's putting folded towels in the cabinet and says, "Miss LaReaux, Good Morning. I didn't realize you were awake." She finishes with the towels and closes the cabinet doors, heading back into the house.

Miss LaReaux? Nobody, other than the judge at my court hearing the day I got caught riding in a stolen car, has ever addressed me as Miss LaReaux. I've been called miss thang, miscreant, and a *mistake*, but never Miss LaReaux. I'm uncomfortable with the formality and sound of it.

"Uh, you can call me Thea." I say, following her into the house.

"I'm Cora."

I give a cursory look at the room we're traveling through. It's some kind of bedroom, but it doesn't look like anyone slept here last night. I follow her up a small flight of stairs and turn left down the hall that empties into the kitchen. It's a stunning combination of white, black and chrome. Clean lines and angles and empty.

She's starts pulling things from the pantry as I take a seat at the huge island counter in the middle of the room. The scraping of the stool must remind her I'm still here.

"Oh, Miss. You must be starving. I'm sorry I wasn't up when you arrived. You can wait in the dining room, and I'll have your breakfast brought out to you."

I ignore the Miss part, and my stomach chooses this moment to growl. "A bowl of cereal sounds great, but I can eat it here."

A voice behind me snaps, "You most certainly cannot eat it here."

I roll my eyes so hard, I literally feel them bouncing around in my skull, before turning to look at Sourpuss. She looks just as dour and unpleasant this morning as she did last night. "Oh, you're here."

"Of course I'm here. I'm your uncle's assistant." She says as if she's repeating it to me for the tenth time, when the truth is this is the first I'm hearing about it. Last night, she never actually introduced herself or told me what she does.

"*Right.*" I turn back to Cora. "Like I said, I'm fine eating cereal here. No sense going through all the trouble of bringing it to the dining room."

"It's no trouble at all," Cora says. "Your aunt and uncle prefer a formal set-up."

I arch my brow at her. "Well, they're not here, and I prefer not to sit at a ridiculously huge table alone, when this counter is just fine." I settle myself more comfortably on the stool.

Since Sourpuss is Uncle Scott's assistant and seems to know so much, maybe she knows where my stuff is. I turn to face her. "Um, did my shipment arrive?"

Cora drops something on the counter when the stuffy witch says, "It did."

"Cool." I wave my hands around, indicating the walls and doorway she's standing in. "Care to point out where in this big ole house I would go to find it?"

"You won't find it anywhere in here."

"Okay. Then where is it?"

"Closest landfill most likely," she says, walking over to the coffee pot.

I rub my ear to make sure there's no water in it. Nope, there isn't, so I heard her correctly. "Excuse me?"

My voice bounces around the cavernous kitchen, sending it out in stereo. I fly off my chair and stalk towards her. "What the hell does that mean?"

I don't have much in this life to call my own, but what I do have I packed up and sent here, trusting it would arrive and be waiting for me. Now she's telling me they threw it out like garbage?

"That was my stuff. What gave you the right to throw it out?"

"What in god's name is going on in here?"

I spin around, coming face to face with my relatives for the first time. They look more uptight in person than they do in their pictures, but they've got impeccable timing. *Today.* The rest of their timing was bullshit, since they were about ten years too late for showing up to make a difference in my life.

"What's going on is your assistant was just telling me she threw my stuff in the trash." I glare at her before turning back to them. "You told me I was welcome here, and this move wasn't meant to disrupt my life. But somehow, I don't have my clothes or any of the things from my old life. Everything I owned was on the moving van and now it's just gone!"

My aunt looks at her husband, before taking a tentative step towards me. She looks freaked out. I get it. You open your door to someone and your first interaction is her going off. But they had no right to trash my stuff.

"Theona, I'm sure it's all a big misunderstanding."

"I understood the words *landfill* just fine."

She looks at her husband again, before saying, "Ms. Mercer has a unique sense of humor. We had the crate with your things put in storage and the unit sustained some water damage."

I glance over my shoulder at the witch. That's not at all what she suggested, and if landfill was a joke, it wasn't even remotely funny. Redirecting my gaze to Moria, I ask, "So everything got wet?"

"I had our insurance adjuster go there. He's still working on the claim. If anything is salvageable, it will be brought here, and if not, then you'll be reimbursed for the cost of what was damaged."

I feel my anger deflate. "Well, she could've explained that."

"Yes, um, we meant to talk to you about it ourselves, last night when you arrived, but we were called away on a business trip at the last minute."

"*That* part she explained."

Aunt Moira's gaze is fixated on a spot over my shoulder. "Is that your breakfast?"

Oh shit. I don't wanna get Cora in trouble for doing something I asked. "Yup, and don't be mad at Cora. I told her I'd feel more comfortable eating here than at a big formal table alone." I hurry to retake my seat.

"Oh, yes, of course," Moira says, as she grabs the seat beside me. "I think we'll join you. Right, Scott?"

Scott looks less enthused about the idea, but sits on the stool next to my aunt, anyway. Cora puts a plate in front of me. It's not the cereal I asked for. Looking around the room, I'm guessing they don't have that in this house. It's cool. The bacon, eggs, and flapjacks will do.

I'm enjoying my food, ignoring the awkwardness of our first official meeting, waiting for someone to say something. Uncle Scott breaks the silence first. "Your aunt and I apologize for not being here when you arrived, but we expected you early afternoon."

I stick a forkful of pancakes into my mouth and suck down some coffee before answering. "Yeah, about that. I was on my way and turned around a few times. I would've called, but my cell phone stopped working."

A worried expression crosses my aunt's face. "Oh dear. That's awful. We could send it to get serviced. Who's your provider?"

I wave my fork dismissively. "Oh, it's not that. The reception dropped off. It's prepaid, so I knew the service carrier probably wouldn't reach this far. I'll just find another one around here and try to keep the same number, that way-."

My uncle cuts in, "A prepaid plan won't be necessary. We'll have all of your new electronics delivered to you by this afternoon."

My aunt nods, then says, "Oh, that reminds me. I can't wait to show you the car."

The two of them lob things off their to-do list at each other while I'm still processing the words electronics and car. I cut in when they get to *clothes and allowance.* "I'm sorry. What's happening right now?"

They continue talking as if they didn't hear me. I put my fingers in my mouth and whistle the way Antonio Vega taught me the first time we snuck into a high school football game.

The conversation stops, and I ignore the look on my uncle's face to address the seemingly more approachable person at the table. His wife. "Can someone please explain what you mean by *Theona's car and electronics?*"

"There's nothing to explain. We'll be providing you with the latest smartphone, laptop and tablet, and a car." Scott says, as if it's already decided.

All of that sounds expensive. I have some money left in my bank account, but until I get a job, I can't afford to be paying for any fancy new shit. No sense in pretending otherwise. "I appreciate you making arrangements for me to have those things, but we're gonna have to put a pin in it until I find a job."

"Why would you need a job?" He's hard to read. I can't tell if he's appalled or amused at the idea of me being employed.

"Because working is a sign of maturity and is the way I take care of myself. Don't you work?" I mean, I'm assuming he does. But maybe he inherited all this and just sits home all day or plays golf.

"What your uncle meant was we don't have any expectation for you to get a job until you've finished school."

And I don't have any expectation of depending on anyone for my basic needs. "I like working and I'd need to pay to use all those things you mentioned."

Moira cuts her eyes at Scott. Why does she keep doing that? Does she need permission to talk or something?

"I see, but uh, these things are gifts, and we're happy to provide them to you. You don't need to reimburse us."

"Why not?" I squint my eyes, trying to get a read on her. Nothing in life is free. Especially state-of-the-art technology and a car.

My uncle's voice is terse when he says, "Because we're your family and we've assumed responsibility for you."

I lean forward to look at him. "That doesn't mean you *have* to do it. If those words meant anything, then the foster care system wouldn't have kids there who were cast off by *family* members who are *supposed* to be responsible for them."

Moira places a hand on mine. I look down at it and try not to snatch mine out from under hers. I'm not used to people touching me so softly unless they want something or are up to something. She must feel the distrust rolling off me, because she quickly pulls it away. She sounds sincere when she says, "You're right. We don't have to, and I realize you're used to taking care of yourself. But you're here, and we'd like to provide these things for you."

"So I don't have to take it."

Scott's voice is clipped when he says. "No, you don't. But things will be easier for you if you do."

This dude is working my last nerve. I fold my arms against my chest to keep from hurling my plate at him. "Easier how?"

He lowers his fork, fixes his gaze on me, and says, "The high schools in this town are very tech heavy. Canyon Falls University won't be any different. All the students use laptops to take notes, and most of the teachers have gone paperless. You'll need a device to access and submit your work."

"And the car?"

"I'm sure you're used to walking and public transportation, but there isn't any way for you to get here from campus without us sending a driver, you catching a ride, or having a car. We thought you'd like your independence and a car would be a better fit."

I like how he lays it out. It makes sense, but I still think it's too much of an investment in someone they don't know, and I can't help but see strings and expectations. I can't be owing anybody anything.

"Let me see if I got this straight. You bought me a car, so I'd have a way to drive here from school?" I don't add the other part I'm thinking. What makes them think I want to come here and visit?

She ducks her head, but not before I see her face turning red. Is she blushing? "No, I um. I had my old car spruced up a bit for you."

Yup, she's embarrassed, but her statement gets my attention. If it's not brand new, I'll feel a little better about maybe using it. Sometimes.

"Would you like to see?" I give a curt nod. She pulls up a picture on her phone and passes it to me. "It's in the shop getting some minor repairs and then it'll be cleaned and detailed. I hope you like it."

I look down at the picture and back up at her. "This was your car?"

"Many, many, years ago. Scott wanted me to get rid of it, but I couldn't stand the idea of parting with it, even though it's been sitting in the garage untouched all this time. Then when we tracked you down, I knew it had to be yours."

I look at the picture again. The 2006 Pontiac Solstice is definitely something I'd pick for myself. And I guess if I need a way to get around, I can use it. *For now*. I need to make sure there are no expectations about them owning me or me owing them a kidney. "This would just be a loaner. As soon as I can get my own stuff, I'm giving yours back."

A vein throbs in my uncle's cheek, but my Moira nods, agreeing to my terms. Sourpuss Mercer comes back into the kitchen, taking Uncle Scott's attention off of me. "Sir, it's time for you to head out."

My aunt looks over at the assistant, the happiness on her face disappears. Huh, guess I'm not the only one who thinks the woman's abrasive. When she looks back at me, I can see she's struggling to keep up the cheerful act. "I'm sorry Theona, we have another meeting to go to."

I shrug, handing her phone back to her. What do I care if they work all the time? But at least they can get my name right. "It's Thea. I prefer Thea."

"Yes. Of course." This time, her smile is more genuine as she climbs off the stool. "We'll be back tonight. In the meantime, make yourself at home."

"Uh... about that."

She pauses, her body stiffens, waiting for me to speak. I guess she remembers me saying I make no promises about how long I'm staying. "There's stuff in the closet in the room I'm staying in. I know I got here late, so is there a different room I should sleep in tonight? I don't want to take up someone else's space."

Her shoulders relax, but I can see she's still a little on edge. "Oh. Those things are yours."

"Mine?"

"Yes. I thought you might need a few things since your stuff was, uh, damaged, and I wasn't sure if you'd just be arriving with the clothes you were wearing. Are they not the right size?"

She was worried I wouldn't have any extra clothes, so she went out and bought a bunch of stuff? My skin feels itchy. I don't like people paying my way. It took *years* before I was okay with Sasha and her grandparents, making sure I had a new outfit every year for my birthday and Christmas.

"I honestly didn't check. I thought they belonged to whoever else stayed in the room before me."

"No one else has ever stayed there. It's your room Thea."

My uncle rushes her along. She exits the kitchen mumbling something under her breath about it always being my room.

When Moira and Scott said they wanted to make sure I got settled with everything I'd need on campus. They meant it. First off, I have a single room that's bigger than the last open bay group home I lived in. It's not just the size of the room. It's the huge ass kitchen, fully stocked fridge, the pantry full of snacks, the bedding, the bathroom decor, and the wardrobe full of clothes.

I didn't even bring a quarter of the outfits Moira made me get when we went shopping over the weekend. I'm talking frilly shit, fancy shit, and snotty preppy shit. I was sized, and measured, and boob cupped within an inch of my life.

Thankfully, when the custom fitting and tailoring was over, and she'd dressed me up like socialite Barbie to her satisfaction, she let me buy normal clothes. FYI I have way too many of them too.

Sasha would freak if she saw all of this. Hell, I'm freaking out because of it. I tried to tell Moira not to waste her money, but she didn't listen. She said it wasn't a waste, and she always wanted someone to shop for other than herself. Then she ran for the door after telling me to have fun and enjoy this time at school, because it was about learning and self-discovery.

Uncle Scott didn't give a huge speech when he left. He just shoved an envelope at me with a wad of cash and three different credit cards inside and told me to talk to Sourpuss if I needed more. At the car, they both told me to call them if I needed anything.

The words sounded nice. I guess it's what you're supposed to say, but they kept staring up at the dorm building with these apprehensive looks on their faces. When I mentioned to Sasha that I think they're already regretting the decision to take me in, she said it probably wasn't regret I saw, but worry. An emotion I hardly recognize because it's been so damn long since anyone gave a shit about me.

I stashed the money and credit cards, I won't be using, in the wall safe hidden behind a panel in my closet. I've still got a bit of money in my checking and savings accounts, and as soon as I get situated with my classes, I'll be getting a job. I meant what I told them in the kitchen at breakfast. I believe in paying my own way.

Moving into the dorm didn't take long since Moira insisted on helping me unpack and decorate, while Scott went to make a final payment at the business office. Now, I've got nothing to do on my last day before I start classes.

Scott *suggested* I tour the campus, read the school handbook, have an early dinner and be back in my room before the sun goes down so I can get a good night's sleep. What am I, twelve? I *will* be taking a tour, but of the town just outside the campus gates and a little beyond.

This place seems nice and all, but it's not me. I need to find out where people like myself hang out, because there's no way I'll be able to tolerate partying with these proper, pretentious folks. I'm not throwing shade. The observation is built on years of experience.

Sasha and I have crashed plenty of college parties and I've learned one thing. They have the good booze and anything you want to smoke, snort, mainline, or swallow, but when the cops show up or shit goes sideways, people like me are always the first people questioned.

That shit gets old real quick, so I prefer to party where we're all considered menaces to society and nobody's pointing fingers at anyone else.

We don't call the cops. If there's a dispute, we handle it between us and keep the party going. Things get scary sometimes and the minute I see a gun, I haul ass, but the fights, I stick around for those. Even when I'm not the one throwing punches.

With one last look around the room, I grab my new phone and the key fob for my door. The electronic lock is coded to the fob programmed with a pin number I selected. I thought it was a bit much when a regular key works just fine, but Moira seemed happy with the added security layer. I ride the elevator alone and walk past the lounge area towards the sliding doors. Once outside, I take a moment to bask in the sun, letting it warm my skin.

I take off towards my right, which leads to the middle of campus. Canyon Falls' University is huge. The campus grounds are bigger than Nags Creek community college and its satellite centers combined. I'm loosely following the campus map, just so I know where all my classes are, and to get a feel for my surroundings. I won't tell Uncle Scott, but his suggestion was spot on. I always make sure I know several ways to get to and from the same place.

It's the middle of the day, and the campus is bustling with more activity than I expected. I know everyone has their own schedules and they don't all match up, but I figured if no one's in class, they'd be in bed sleeping, or watching tv. Doing something other than hanging around like sitting ducks, with all their sparkly shit, just waiting to be robbed. I shake my head, reminding myself things are different here, and I'm not in Nags Creek anymore. Flashing your valuables might be safe to do around here, but it's still obnoxious as hell.

It's been a little less than an hour on my tour. I've scoped out the longest and shortest routes from to and from my dorm to my classes and Rockford Dining Hall. The brochure I picked up from the Welcome Center says everyone calls it The Rock. A second dining hall with grab and go meals is over by the gym. I give The Rock a cursory glance, and head towards the hiking trail on the back half of campus. That's where I'll probably be spending most of my free time. According to what I've read, this trail runs from campus to the neighboring town.

There used to be another part of the hiking path that went to Canyon Falls, where my aunt and uncle live, and down through the valley between the cliffs and into the Santa Monica Mountains, dropping you off at Brunson Canyon. From there, you could make your way to the Hollywood sign.

That's a long ass hike. One I'd be happy to attempt; camping out along the way. The problem is, I keep coming across the same articles and blog posts, which say the old hiking trail was closed over forty years ago. None of the articles mention where the entrance to the trail was located. I love nature and a good mystery, so it's safe to say the only thing I'm excited about since coming here is finding that damn trail.

Chapter 4
Holden Sullivan

I tune out the conversations around me, focusing on Paxton's movements and facial expressions. I'm trying to get an idea of what might be going through his head. He's never been big on sharing his feelings and is always careful about what he says out in public. The vein in his jaw is throbbing the way it does when he's clenching his teeth. Whatever he's thinking can't be good.

We won our challenge and so far there's been no mention of Finn's almost hit and run, so I'm betting the accident isn't the source of his anger. Only one other thing stresses him out, his father, Malcolm Cox. He's probably not ready to talk about it, but that doesn't stop me from trying to get him to open up. "Did you see the old man this weekend?"

Pax is leaning against the wall outside of the school store, staring across The Circle. The area on campus that branches out to five different directions. "Thursday night, after the job."

That's not unusual. His dad usually touches base with him after a job. "And?"

He pushes off the wall. "I'm going to the gym."

I let him walk away, knowing that's about as much as I'm going to get out of him, but it gives me some insight into how he's feeling. He's going to the gym, which means whatever his dad said was just an annoyance. If he would've said he was going for a drive, that means he's trying to outrun whatever's on his mind.

Pax and I have been friends for so long I don't even remember a time in my life when we weren't. Finley came along when we were in junior high. He's from a legacy family, but they didn't live here when we were in elementary school. Something to do with his father's job overseas. They moved back right before seventh grade.

Finn thought he was a big deal because he spoke French, Italian, and Japanese. The girls loved it, but Paxton and I thought he was a pussy. We got the shock of our lives when he showed up at one of the legacy families' mini vacations.

That weekend was a camping excursion with a bit of wilderness survival training and obstacle courses. We just knew his scrawny, sonnet reading ass wouldn't make it through the first obstacle on the course. Not only did he make it, but he came in a fraction of a second behind Pax. Until then, Pax and I had always flipped between first and second place, and nobody ever came close to matching our scores.

We were ready to call it a fluke, but when Galen Prescott went to square off with Finn in our makeshift wrestling ring, we learned Finn had so much more to him than a love of languages and poetry. He was quick and strong and had Galen on his ass in the third round.

Finn won. That should have been the end of it. But Galen had always been a sore fucking loser.

Coming back from swimming one day, he rushed Finn, trying to catch him off guard. The clothesline he received for his trouble was fucking amazing, but the flash of the knife against his crotch... now *that* was how I knew Finley Jefferson Rhodes, the Third, was not someone to be fucked with.

Everything in our world is a competition. The parent chaperones didn't give a shit about side fights and squabbles, but weapons weren't allowed.

Galen came in fourth on the scoreboard and tried to tell one of the parents Finn pulled a weapon, hoping to get him sent home for the rest of the trip. His buddies backed him up about seeing a knife. The parents did a thorough search of Finn and his stuff. They didn't find anything. To this day I have no idea where he hid the knife.

One thing you can count on with him, there's always at least one blade on him, we just never know where.

Throughout the years, Pax, Finn and I have fought *with* each other and *for* each other. We've created an unbreakable bond. I'm sure whatever's troubling Pax, we'll face it together.

My thoughts are still swirling around our childhood and how our normal experiences are mixed in with some shit no kid should be subjected to, unless you're training for a post apocalyptic lifestyle, or to get away from a kidnapper. I shiver at that last part. I know first-hand that it's not out of the realm of possibility.

Wilderness training was fun when we were searching for land-marks and animals. Using those skills all the time to track people and artifacts belonging to other fraternities, not so much. The games on campus are a tradition. No one knows who's in charge of them. It could be several people affiliated with each organization or one person running the whole thing. All members of the fraternities and sororities get anonymous texts, and invitations in our mailboxes, and we do whatever the instructions say.

The pranks and risks keep getting bigger and bigger. What I do know, is when Pax, Finn and I get the invites, we can't refuse to participate, because no matter how large or small the task, we're working to prove ourselves to a society of people who live in the shadows.

Each year, I feel the pressure from my family. From all of our families. The constant reminder that soon, we'll be doing more for and within The League, and yet we can't let our grades or our status at school slip. Be aloof, be charming. Make the right friends, impress the right people. *Be. The. Best.*

There are so many expectations. Sometimes it's hard to live up to them all. But I can't admit that. To anyone. So I push through. Do more. Learn more. My brain never shuts down. Not even when I'm trying to sleep. Fuck, what I wouldn't do to shed the weight of these expectations for just a little while. To get more than a few stolen moments of peace.

The alarm goes off on my phone. Those moments won't be today. I have a class to get to.

Chapter 5
Thea

I've found the greasiest, most obnoxious smelling place around. Starting with their burgers and fries and ending with the motor oil under some of these dude's nails. The women are wearing various items of leather and lace and smell of flavored cigarettes and cheap beer. I inhale deeply, feeling the tension loosen around my shoulders. This is my kind of place.

My dorm is nice. Fancier than any dorms I've ever been to, and I love having a room to myself, but it's too shiny. Too pristine. *Too much.* I'm uncomfortable with all the splendor.

My apartment wasn't a dump or anything, but it wasn't in the richest part of town, either. It had a living room/dining room combo. A kitchen with a dishwasher, and two bedrooms with a shared bath. I had AC. It was safe, clean, and mine. That was more than enough.

Being in the dorm makes me feel like I'm pretending and if there's one thing I hate, it's posers. So I looked up dive bars, slipped on a new pair of ripped jeans and my favorite jacket over a band tee and drove here to immerse myself in an environment that's gloomy and messy, and real.

I can't imagine any of the kids I've seen on campus coming here.

It's perfect. The bartender doesn't bother carding me. Wouldn't matter if she did. I've had an ID that says I'm old enough to drink since I was sixteen. I thought about leaving it behind, but it'll be another eighteen months before my driver's license catches up with it. I'm glad I kept it. I *really* need this drink.

I down my warm up shot and take my first sip of beer before I spin around on my bar stool to take in the rest of the establishment. There's a jukebox in the corner and tables placed in a semi-circle around the floor to create a dance area. There are people standing and lingering around. Some are even swaying, but I wouldn't actually call what any of them are doing, dancing. The biggest attractions, as far as I can see, are the dart board, pool tables and the mechanical bull in the corner.

I'll be trying out the bull just as soon as I finish my beer. I figure it can't be much harder than staying on a motorcycle while doing wheelies, which I perfected two years ago.

I'm heading over to get in line for the bull ride, when someone grabs my attention. He's sitting in the back corner of the bar at a table by himself. His cream Henley stretches across his broad shoulders and chest. The color is out of place in a room of denim and leather. It's unbuttoned, the sleeves pushed up to the middle of his muscular forearms.

He's wearing one of those hemp bracelets with seashells on it, on his right wrist. I glance down at his feet, making note of the dark brown Chukkas, then drag my eyes back up over his dark blue jeans and thick thighs.

His caramel brown hair is styled haphazardly, as if he couldn't be bothered to do more than run his hand through it. He's watching the bull riders with detached interest. He's easily the hottest guy in here and he looks like he smells good.

New plan. Why ride the fake bull when I can feel this specimen between my thighs? I tell the bartender to send him a drink and I watch his reaction as it gets delivered. When his gaze slides to mine, I tip my drink towards him, slide off my stool, and make my way to the pool table area. If he likes what he sees, he'll follow.

I've just finished putting all the balls in the triangle when he comes over. He's still holding the beer I sent. That's a good sign. Standing under the archway, he looks even yummier than he did before. He's tall as shit. At least six, three or four. I'm five six myself. I'm definitely gonna have some fun climbing him.

"Lag for the break?" I ask, pointing to the table. He's here. I assume he's willing to play. He walks over to grab a cue stick from the wall rack.

The pool stick I usually play with, is in the storage place with my other stuff. I hope it survived the flood. It's worn and used, but I know exactly how to work it to make my shots. The one I'm holding is comparable in weight. It should be good enough to do what I need it to do.

I gesture towards the table, letting him go first. I watch as the cue balls hits the back end of the table before returning towards us, stopping about three inches from the edge. *Good.* I hate when guys try to let me win. On my turn, the ball stops half an inch behind his. He's won the right to break, since his ball is closest to the edge.

I step back from the table, shamelessly eye fucking him while he takes his turn, trying to imagine what he looks like underneath all those clothes. One thing's for sure. He's got a nice ass. One that's just begging you to dig your heels into it.

The sound of balls dropping in their slots pulls my attention back to the table. He's good. Almost as good as the guys who hustle Vegas tourists back home.

When it's finally my turn he mimics my stance, obviously checking out my ass, as I size up my shot. He's standing so close I can feel the heat from his body. He smells as good as I thought. Like a mixture of cedar and cinnamon and a touch of leather.

"What should I know about you?" I ask, after I drop the first two solid balls in their slots.

"Nothing, except I'm gonna beat your sexy ass in pool."

His voice is warm, soothing, and a bit husky. Like smokey whisky sliding down my throat. I round the table so I'm facing him and lean forward, setting my cue stick between my fingers.

I'm preparing to take my shot, when he asks, "What about you? Is there someone waiting for you to come home tonight?"

Interesting way to phrase the question. That could mean my parents or my man. The answer is the same either way. Glancing up at him, I answer with a question of my own. "Does it matter?"

He joins me on my side of the table and crowds me against it. His hands firmly on my waist as he presses against me. There's still a little space between us, so I can move if I want to. I *don't* want to.

He lowers his body, his chest leaning lightly against my back, his lips against my ear, and says, "Depends on whether or not you'll be in trouble when you come home walking funny."

Cocky. I like that, but only when they can back it up. "I won't be."

His lips graze the shell of my ear, sending a shiver down my spine. "Well, this escalated quickly." I say, straightening up and leaning into his hold.

"I think we both knew where this was going the moment you sent me that drink."

I point out the flaw in his thinking. "A drink is just a drink. I could've sent it to anyone."

"But you didn't, and now here we are. Ball's in your court."

He's right, the drink was an open invitation because I saw him and decided I wanted him. I press my ass against him, because where we are isn't nearly as far as I'd like us to go. He pulls the stick from my hand, placing it on the table, and turns me in his arms. Our game is quickly forgotten as we sway to the music piping through the speakers in the corner of the room.

I don't like wasting time and I know what I want. When he leans forward, I meet him halfway, our lips joining in a kiss that tastes like bourbon, cheap beer, and reckless decisions. It's exhilarating. An adrenaline rush. One I've been needing since I drove into town.

I'm not big on relationships, but I don't bed hop either. At home, I had someone I'd casually hook up with to keep the edge off. This night will have to hold me over until I can find someone to fill that role. It won't be him. Once I do this, I'm not sure I'll ever come back to this bar again. It's over an hour away from campus. I hope he makes this memorable.

He backs me into the wall across from the pool table and hoists me up. My legs immediately go around his waist, my ankles crossed against his lower back. He devours my neck, his stubble brushing against my skin.

We're pressed close, his erection nestles perfectly against my clit. I rock against him, pulling his mouth to mine again. Just as I'm settling into the kiss, he lowers me back to my feet, grabs my hand, and pulls me through a door on the back wall. It leads down a hallway and out the back door of the bar into an alley.

Before I can adjust to the change in scenery, he pulls me into a small alcove on the right and maneuvers me backward.

His right hand is braced on the wall near my head, his left is on my hip as he studies my face, waiting for me to change my mind. Cute. But I've got no hesitation about this.

Fisting his shirt, I pull him in for another kiss. His thick tongue sweeps into my mouth as I reach between our bodies and flick the button open on my jeans, shoving them down to my ankles, and slip off a shoe. I pull one leg out of my pants before moving to work on his next and push my hand into the opening.

A shudder runs through me when I grip his shaft. It's dark, so I can't make out what it looks like, but his dick feels divine in my hand. Thick and heavy. Velvety warm. I stroke him until he pushes my hand away, breaking our kiss. He takes a step away from me, but his gaze never leaves my face. I hear the foil tear, but when he moves in close again, I still do a quick check to make sure he's really rolling the condom on. I've had guys try to fool me before and I'd hate to end our fun before it really begins.

His fingers press against my damp panties, his thumb brushing against my clit. This time, it's my turn to push his hands away. I'm ready. There's no need to prolong this. I move my panties to the side with one hand and use my hold on his dick to bring him closer, lining him up against my opening. He flexes his hips, slowing pushing inside. The burn and stretch as he enters me feels so good.

He pulls out a little, then pushes back in, seating himself deeper. Just that small movement has me panting. I haven't had new dick in such a long time. I almost forgot how exhilarating it is. That first joining with a new partner. The heady combination of nerves and lust.

It pains to to say, but sometimes the anticipation of the act is the best part of sex for me. His strokes are sharp and precise. Hitting me at an angle which has me quickly spinning out of control. I won't be disappointed tonight. He clearly knows what he's doing.

"Yes, yes," I chant, when he picks up speed, my inner walls flutter around him. I shift my hips, trying to take him deeper. He readjusts his legs, pinning me so tightly against the wall. All I can do is hang on and take what he gives me. A shiver runs down my spine as I free fall into bliss sooner than expected. I drag my fingers through his hair, patiently waiting for him to finish.

He swirls his hips on the downstroke and squeezes my right tit through my shirt even though we're well past the foreplay stage. The twinge of pain sends another shockwave through my cunt. He hums and pushes my shirt up, popping my tit from my bra. I bite down on my bottom lip as he drags his thumb across the nipple.

There's a weird twitch in my clit. I'm not multi-orgasmic. Not without using my toys on myself, and even then it takes a while for me to work myself up again. But the way he's working his dick feels so good. With a little more time, I think I could cum again. I would totally love to be the girl to say a guy made her cum twice on his dick.

Sasha would be so jealous. But he has to be close, too. Right? As if sensing my inner thoughts, he hoists me higher, holding me with one hand and flicks his thumb against my clit. "Come on, sweetness, give me another."

The words are endearing, but there's a bit of edge to his voice like it's a command. One my body instinctively wants to obey. But my mind overrules my body. I don't do well with commands. I tense up and fight it. Tensing up has the opposite effect from what I'm expecting. Instead of cooling my libido down, my walls grip him tighter. He feels even bigger at this angle. The niggling in my clit grows stronger.

He drags his dick out, almost to the tip, then surges back in. "Be a good little girl and show me how good my cock feels."

"Who said it does?" I pant, biting down on my lip to muffle the groan building its way up my throat.

He skims his hand along the inside of my thigh, pulling it away and shoving his fingers in his mouth. "The evidence is running down your legs. Yet you're still so tight. Warm. Sucking me in. *Fuck,* I could get lost in this sweet pussy and be happy never to resurface."

I'm clamped down around him, lost to the sensation of him spearing me with his thick cock and his filthy words in my ear. I'm *so* close. The sensation of being on the precipice of a second orgasm while being stuffed with his dick is new, and a little scary, but damn, I want it. I silently plead for him to keep going until I come again.

"That's it, sweetness. Guide us to the place we both so desperately crave."

He hooks my leg over his forearm, spreading me wider. His thrusts are sharper, harder, rougher. I'm cracking apart from the inside out. A delicious warmth starts in my stomach and spreads through my body. Strands of my hair cling to my forehead. I don't care about my hair or the fact that anyone coming by will hear and see us, because I'm too caught up in what feels like the biggest lead up to the most epic orgasm I've ever had.

"I wanna feel you flooding around my cock. Right. *Now!*"

There goes that command again, and before I can even think about refusing-*not that I plan to*- he tugs on my clit. *Holy shit.*

I lose control of my limbs and my vocal chords. Every sound I've been holding back comes out at the same time. His hand clamps across my mouth, muting my cries as I detonate. It feels like something opens in my vagina. Like a pressure release deep inside. *What the fuck is even happening?*

Whatever it is, I can't stop it. With preternatural speed, he yanks his dick out of me and hoists me higher, clamping his mouth around my pussy, catching every single drop of the projectile liquid that comes gushing out. I'm on the bottom wave of my orgasm, still trying to wrap my mind around whatever *that* was, when he lowers me to the ground and turns me to face the wall, before sliding back inside me, resuming his brutal pace.

"Fuck, sweetness." He grunts against my ear. "You were so perfect, squirting for me." He pulls out to the tip and says, "Now I'm gonna cum for you."

He slams in twice more and growls like an animal who's been denied food for too long. It's the sexiest sound I've ever heard, and I mentally pop my collar, damn proud of myself that I made him do it.

When he finally pulls away, I take an extra second to catch my breath and get myself together. I won't tell him, but that shit was epic. I'm still a little shaky, but I move fast. I shove my foot through the pants leg, tug my boot back on and button my jeans.

While he's still fiddling with the condom, I step forward, pop a quick peck on his cheek and take off towards the end of the alley. I'll be in my car and long gone before he even finishes tucking his stellar dick away.

Chapter 6
Thea

I'm well rested, still coasting the high from Sunday night. My body is achy, but in the best way possible. I've never had someone be so physical during sex before. It was just the right amount of athleticism and act of rebellion I needed to remind me I'm alive.

It's like the time Sasha and I snuck into the high school and painted Reed Turner's locker pink with glitter epoxy. We were determined to do it even though we knew we might get caught by the guard patrolling the school.

Scratch that. It was more like the time when we were fifteen and stole Reed's dog. Actually, we stole his daddy's car. The asshole had left the poor dog in it, in the middle of the summer, while he was fingering Betty Richards on her back porch. We took the dog and the car to Marco's chop shop, earned some cash and saved a pup. Good times. So yeah, sex with the mystery man was an adrenaline rush and feel good moment all rolled into one.

I hold up my hand to block out the sun glaring in my eyes. I've walked this campus twice, so I know where all the important buildings are located, but I still take one final look at my schedule to make sure I'm where I'm supposed to be. Statistics, the Hawthorne Building. *Yup.* This is the right place.

Students sporting fancy watches and diamond earrings the size of my fingernails walk by, happily chatting with friends, reminding me my lack of jewelry makes me stick out around here.

I grip my schedule tighter. My Archaeology class is in the building across from this one. This is why I've agreed to come here. Attending Canyon Falls University puts me closer to my career goals.

People get weirded out when I say I want to be an anthropologist and spend my life traveling the world, working on archaeological digs. They think it's all about digging in dirt to find bones, but it's so much more than that. It's about reminding the world of the many civilizations that have died out, and about shining a light on those being erased. They deserve to have their stories told. To not be forgotten.

As someone who's spent the majority of my life being treated like I'm invisible, like I'm an inconvenience, someone who doesn't matter; I can sympathize with these cultures, the lost societies, the forgotten people. I want to give them their voices back.

With that reminder, I grab the metal door handle and step into the Hawthorne Building. It doesn't take long to find my class and I'm happy to see there's an empty spot in the middle of the class next to a window. I need to have an opening to a door or a window near me, otherwise I feel like I'm trapped. And when I feel trapped, I react. *Badly.* I should've had at least five assault charges filed against me last year alone, and those are just the ones where people needed more than a bandaid and ice pack to fix them up.

I exhale, sending a lock of hair swirling out of my face. *No fighting.* It's the promise I made to myself when I decided to come here. I won't mess this up. I'm doing it for me, Sasha, and anyone else who wouldn't have the chance to come to a school like this without selling a pair of major organs or blackmailing a politician.

I take a second to look around the room. The class holds twenty-five people, but there are a lot of empty seats. I guess statistics at eight in the morning isn't for everyone.

"Fifteen minute rule is in effect, right?"

I glance over to my right to see who's talking. The guy's wearing blue chinos, boat shoes, and a shirt unbuttoned by one button too many. I shrug, not agreeing or disagreeing with him. I don't even know what the fifteen minute rule is.

I catch on quickly, when the other students start shoving their stuff back in their bags. A few are even on their feet heading towards the door.

"Sit down." The professor says, as he comes into the classroom. "It's only been fourteen minutes and seven-seconds."

The professor is short, wearing a brown tweed jacket, and huge square framed glasses. He looks just like Rick Moranis. I'm staring at him. Hard. I might even be drooling a little. I swipe my mouth just in case.

I want to take a picture of him so badly, and send it to Sasha, but I can't do it without someone seeing. We had a huge crush on Rick after we saw Honey I Shrunk the Kids, back when we were going through a science phase.

Sasha outgrew it. Me, not so much. Call me weird, but I like 'em rugged and reckless and I like them smart with a vocabulary that includes more than monosyllabic words.

I suppose that's why it's never bothered me that I haven't had a long-term relationship. I need a whole lot of different types of guys to make up the perfect boyfriend.

I settle in to listen to the guy who looks like my childhood crush talk about the importance of organizing, analyzing, and evaluating data. Maybe this school won't be so bad after all.

"Brutal, wasn't it?"

Class just ended. The guy in the chinos is hovering over my desk. He's too close and I have to remind myself about my no hitting rule. I stand before gathering my things. I don't think he's intentionally trying to intimidate me, but I don't know him and I'm not about to start our acquaintance off, with him in a position of power over me. I'm a big dog in a woman's body. Plus, letting him stand over me will make it harder to fight back if he tries something.

In answer to his question, I say, "It was a lot of information thrown at us for it to be my first day of classes."

His head bobs up and down. "And the syllabus is crazy. I don't know how he expects us to keep up with all the reading on top of the homework and projects."

"Mmm." I say, heading toward the door. This guy's worried it's too much work, and here I was thinking I might need to ask for extra work so I don't get bored. My academic advisor wouldn't let me take two maths this semester. *Fucker*. Chinos follows me out of the building. I move ahead of him on the path, thinking we're done, but he jogs behind me to catch up, and says, "Damn you move fast."

"Don't wanna be late for my next class."

"You have time."

I stop walking and turn to face him. I don't have time. But I'm not about to let him follow me around all morning. I look past his preppy attire. He's cute, in a boat loving, polo playing kind of way. Sun kissed tan, golden locks and blue eyes. He's a walking Ken doll.

I notice the girls eyeing him as they walk by, and the giggly, "hellos". To his credit, he responds, but not in an overly flirtatious way. He wants something. It's better if he gets to the point, sooner rather than later. "Who are you, and what do you want?"

He laughs as if he's not put off by my bluntness. "My name's Austin. Austin Kincaid, and I don't want anything. I figured since we're in class together, I'd say hello."

That shit's a lie. Everyone wants *something*, but I don't have time to explain id, ego, or superego to him. Instead, I pull some manners out of my ass and say, "Hello, Austin, nice to meet you. I'm Thea, and I'm about to be late for class." I turn back the way I was heading, tossing over my shoulder. "Good luck with your homework."

I weave in and out of the bodies, on the sidewalk, making note of the groups and cliques that I'll definitely be avoiding. I make it to my next class and slip into a seat in the seat closest to the door, since the chairs in the back are already occupied.

This is why I wanted to get here early. To pick out a good seat. Talking to Austin, cost me valuable time. I won't let him hold me up again. I'm pulling my laptop out as the teacher comes in and announces. "Hope you read the study material I mentioned last week. Time for a pop quiz."

The students groan and I stifle a chuckle. Pop quiz on the first day in my history class. This should be fun.

Chapter 7
Pax

Canyon Falls University is a private university, but we have one of the biggest campuses in the state, with a lot of undeveloped space. The buildings are grouped together by type.

All athletic and extra-curricular buildings are on the South side of campus. Arts and Humanities to the North. The Science and Math buildings are West, and the Administration Building and Business Center are smack dab in the middle of campus, with the dorms dispersed along the perimeter.

The East edge of campus houses the faculty apartments and their entertainment center, which is basically a small movie theater and bowling alley. The school built the entertainment center to give the faculty a place to unwind where they won't run into students. I'm not sure how many people use it. Everyone knows the best places to hang out are in town.

The Academic and Administration buildings have a designated traffic pattern students are supposed to follow to prevent bottlenecks in the hallways or stairs. It's supposed to help you get where you're going faster, but it doesn't.

Having to walk all the way to the end of a hallway to reach the stairs you have to use to travel up or down is a nightmare, and so is the requirement to only use the pedestrian walkways to get around campus. That means no cutting across the grass or darting between buildings.

It's a stupid rule, but we follow it. *Correction*, the other students follow it. Me, I have my own way of getting from place to place. Like the staff elevators, and the underground tunnels around campus that connect the buildings together. Those tunnels also have golf carts that the administration uses to get around. I have access to the keys to the restricted hallways, which house the elevators and stairs leading to the tunnels.

I'm heading to one such hallway now. My head down as I read the latest message on my phone. I'm following the bullshit traffic pattern and don't bother looking up to see if anyone is in front of me. I don't have to. The students know to get out of the way when they see me coming, so I'm confident the path in front of me is clear.

"Oomf."

"Hey! Hey, asshole!"

I lift my head and look around to see who is calling whom an asshole. There's a girl on the floor, on her hands and knees, glaring at me. I look around again to see who's involved in the drama. She couldn't possibly be talking to me.

"That's right. I'm talking to you neanderthal," she says, climbing to her feet.

I guess she is talking to me. I don't have time for this, but there are people in the hall and the last thing I need is for them to think it's suddenly cool to talk to a legacy this way, especially not one of The Trium.

This girl, *whoever she is*, has lost her fucking mind. I can spare a few minutes to remind her of her place. Glaring at her, I ask, "You wanna try that again?"

"Sure."

She pauses as if she's waiting for me to say something. When I don't, she holds up her hand and ticks off options for me. "You can start with excuse me, sorry, or my bad. All those work when you knock someone down."

"You know what else works? Getting the hell out of my way when you see me coming."

"You came from behind, asshole. I don't have eyes in the back of my head."

"Grow some." I snarl, then continue towards my destination, already forgetting about her and this irritating little spat.

"I'll get right to work on that." Her voice drips with sarcasm. "Let's say we meet back here for a progress meeting next week. I'll show you how far I've come and you can show me you can pull your head out of your ass."

Is she fucking with me right now? Is this a sorority prank? It has to be, because no one in their right mind would do this without being forced into it.

I snap at the people standing around. "Get to class."

They clear the hallway, knowing if they stay around to watch any longer, they'll feel my wrath too. Stepping towards her, I take in her outfit and hair. She doesn't look familiar, but it doesn't matter. In thirty-seconds, she'll fall back in line.

"If I were you, I'd be very careful about the next words coming out of your mouth. In fact, if I were you, I wouldn't say anything to me ever again." I make sure the threat can be heard in my words and seen on my face.

She shakes her head, a smirk tugging at her lips. "*Anng.* Wrong answer. If you were me, the next words coming out of your mouth would be... *Fuck. Your. Warning. Asshole.* And if you don't want to hear my mouth, try apologizing for the illegal block in the back."

This girl. Whoever the hell she is has just sealed her fate. Finn and Holden emerge from around the corner. Without even asking what's going on, they take up position, forming a triangle around her. I'm in front, Holden's on her right flank, and Finn is on her left.

She tries to take a step backward, but we press into her, crowding her, making sure she has nowhere to run.

"You'd do well to tame that pretty little mouth of yours, Pet," Finn soothes in the voice that usually gets what he wants. "Before someone does it for you."

"The only *pet* around here is this junk yard dog. I'm assuming you're the one who let him off his leash. Feel free to yank his chain and take him for a walk."

Her gaze flicks to Holden before turning back to me. Her deep blue eyes hold enough defiance to fill a stadium. I know we're all thinking the same thing. We're going to make her regret her life choices, right here and now. As a unit, we take another step towards her. I'm thinking a trip to the shower might be what she needs.

"Oh boys, I'm so glad I ran into you." I look up and see Mrs. Banks, the head librarian, clearing the last step of the stairwell across from where we're standing. "I was wondering if I could get your assistance with some things."

She doesn't wait for us to answer. She just continues past us like we're not in the middle of something, her heels ticking quickly along the tiled floor. "Come along boys, I don't have all day."

If it were any other teacher or faculty member at this school, we'd ignore her. But Mrs. Banks has been at C Falls U, longer than anyone else. She was working here when our parents were students. Plus, Rho Beta Psi sponsors the school library. All frats and sororities are required to select a school organization or a department to sponsor, and raise money for them during the year. We have the library and a literacy campaign for the public schools.

I'm not complaining. I'm happy to raise money for the library, and Holden takes point on most of the stuff. But today, Mrs. Bank's timing couldn't be worse. Or maybe for this girl it's perfect. Because we were definitely about to fuck up her day.

We peel off behind Mrs. Banks. With one last look at the girl, Finn says, "See you around, Pet."

She holds her middle fingers out, pointing them towards us, then rights them so she's flipping us the bird. That's the last thing I see before I exit the side door of the building.

Chapter 8
Finley Jefferson Rhodes, III

Pax is looking grumpier than usual, and it's fucking up my vibe. So is the lack of power behind his punch. He's distracted and not hitting as hard as he usually does.

Most people wouldn't want the behemoth that is Paxton Cox hitting them with the full force of his fist, but I do. I like to train as if I'm fighting an actual opponent, and Pax is the perfect sparring partner. He's taller than me, thicker than me, and has a mean left hook. Fighting a southpaw ups my skill level by a million percent, but today, I might as well be punching a heavy bag for all the response I'm getting.

The timer dings ending our training session. Pax goes to the other side of the room, while I plop down on the floor to work on my abs. Holden's in the corner meditating or some shit. He's a wall of muscle too, and lifts super heavy, but he's all graceful and shit because he likes to do yoga.

It's hard to reconcile the way he looks with his nature loving, tree hugging personality. He used to get so much flack about it. Now, he doesn't share that side of himself with anyone anymore.

I say fuck all the haters, but underneath that brain, and all those muscles, he's a sensitive soul.

Pax finishes his set of bicep curls, then moves to the pull-up bar. "We have an assignment," he says after his first set of ten reps.

Holden cracks one eye open and says, "I didn't get a text alert from the frat."

"It's not Beta Psi business."

The only other place an assignment could come from is The League, but it's too soon for that. Unless they're upping our timeline. Or about to punish us for what happened during the last prank night. I'm certain it's the latter, so I ask, "How much trouble am I in?"

Pax drops down and looks over at me. "None. I didn't mention what happened to my father."

"That doesn't mean they don't know."

He nods and says, "This assignment came from him, but he didn't bring it up that night."

I let out a small sigh of relief, but Holden loses his chill. "According to Chapter twelve, subpart seven paragraph three of the bylaws, no member of The League of the Daggered Ravens may assign tasks to members of their bloodline, without the express agreement of the entire council. The council hasn't sent us a summons to appear. So whatever assignment this is, is against the bylaws."

Pax wipes the sweat off his forehead with his shirt, then jumps up to do another set of pull-ups. He finishes ten reps before dropping down and replying, "This is more like a favor."

"Then we don't have to do it."

Holden's right. We don't have to but, the look on Pax's face says he's not so ready to dismiss his father's request. He scrubs a hand through his hair and says what we all know to be true. "If we don't do it, you know he'll find a way to make us regret saying no."

And that would be a problem. We're not Initiates. We're barely even prospects, but we know better than to alienate the people who'll be issuing our tasks and deciding if we progress to the next level.

"What does he want us to do?" I ask, as I climb to my feet and walk over to the where I left my water bottle.

"The top floor is about to get crowded. He wants us to keep an eye on our new neighbor."

Somebody's getting fired. Everyone knows only direct descendants of the top four donors to the school can live on the tenth floor. The residents are usually the oldest children of the current generation, except in Pax's case, he has a cousin who's two years older than him. It's a good thing she went to a different school, or he'd be on a different floor, or sharing a room.

Family representation from the fourth bloodline has been absent for fifty something years. That fourth room is basically a reminder of what was and a status symbol of what could be.

At any rate, I think we've all assumed the room would remain empty. Which is why we're known as The Triumvirate instead of The Quadrumvirate.

"This guy, what's his deal? He pledging a rival fraternity or something, and your dad approved him to live next door so we can get some dirt?"

"I do not know what her deal is. It's definitely some kind of mix-up with the dorms, but he wants us to report back on her, anyway."

"Her?" Our new neighbor's a girl? This is a favor I can get behind. I've grown bored with the girls from the summer, and Eloise, my future wife, and I are still doing our own thing. We're not due to get back together until the spring.

There's nothing like a new project to celebrate the start of the school term. I can have some fun, while keeping an eye on the lower level legacy baby, whose family has clearly slept their way to the top floor. Hopefully, she's learned a few cool bedroom tricks along the way.

Pax told us about his father's request yesterday, and we spent all night brainstorming ideas about how to get the information we need on her. I'm still trying to wrap my head around the idea that someone else will be living in the fourth dorm room.

We like being up there alone, not caring about the amount of noise we make or having to worry about a lot of people coming and going on our floor.

I'm also on edge because we don't know if The League knows about the car incident last week. We're operating under the assumption that they don't, but that could change at any minute.

I'm not paying attention to where I'm going, so it's no surprise when I end up missing the street for the movie theater I'm heading to. I've come off campus to watch a movie.

I could've played a DVD in the entertainment room in the lounge, or in my dorm room, but there's nothing like seeing a movie on a big screen with massive surround sound.

They're playing a midnight screening of one of my favorite movies, Takers. I've seen it like a dozen times, but there was no way I was passing this up.

The theater's relatively empty. That means I get to stretch my legs out on the back of the seat in front of me while I watch the movie and eat my snacks.

I'm just about settled in my seat, when a pair of tits catches my eye. It takes me a second to place her. She's the girl from the hallway. The one who was giving all sorts of attitude to Pax.

I didn't get a good look at her before, since I was in alpha mode. Tonight, she's sporting baggy jeans and a hoody with the brim of a ball cap sticking out of it, looking like some kind of B-Boy.

I wait until she grabs a chair in the middle of the row ahead of me, then gather up my stuff. I know how cool I look when I hop over the chair and slide into the seat next to her.

She checks me out, trying to mask her interest behind this whole, I'*m looking but not looking,* facade. I'm used to it. I stretch like I'm getting comfortable, letting my shirt ride up to expose my lower abs. Girls love abs.

The lights dim, and she says, "If you're a talker, move the fuck over right now."

She grabs the popcorn off the chair next to her with her right hand, and pulls something from the pocket of her hoody with her left, before slouching down a little in her chair.

The light from the movie screen glistens off the flask in her hand. The distinct scent of spiced rum hits my nose. I watch as she pours a measured shot into her cup, gives it a little shake, then takes a sip.

Shit, why didn't I think of that? Booze is exactly what would make this movie experience better. The movie's about to start, but my gaze keeps drifting to her pocket where the flask is, and she's staring at the licorice whip in my hand.

I wave it around and point at the flask. She pulls the licorice from my hand and passes me the tiny silver bottle.

I pour a generous amount in my cup. Her brow arches when I go to hand it back and she snags another licorice. I guess the amount of rum I poured was worth two of them for payment.

We sit through the movie in silence, but I can tell she's just as into it as I am. She's biting her lip, her eyes flick around the screen, and she makes this weird little noise when the protagonists come on screen.

Her body's damn near vibrating with excitement. I've seen this movie dozens of times, but I'm hyped too. It's an amazing movie and if I were cast in it, I'd be the guy in the Fedora, playing the piano. I definitely have his charisma and charm. But I'm also wily, like the guy jumping off buildings and over turnstiles, avoiding the cops and shit.

I reach my hand down and hit the empty bottom of my popcorn

bucket. Shit. I must've been eating it faster than usual, thanks to the salt craving that accompanies me drinking rum and coke. The girl's still got half of the jumbo size. She must sense me looking at her. She turns her head a little while still trying to keep her eyes on the screen.

"What?"

I shake my bucket. "Share?"

"No."

Now there's a word I'm not used to hearing. That's because no one ever uses it with me. I tell people what I want. They give it to me willingly, or I take it. But she's new around here and sometimes I have manners, so I say, "Please."

"Nope."

She doesn't just leave it with a no. She grabs a kernel and makes this huge production about bringing it to her mouth and exaggerates her chewing.

When she goes to do it again, I snatch her hand, bring it to my mouth and grab the popcorn from her fingers. Licking all the butter and salt off of them.

I take advantage of her shock and dump a bunch of the buttery crack into my bucket, then turn my attention back to the thieves on the screen. If she wants to take this popcorn back, she'll have to reach between my legs to get it.

I shift in my seat. If she does *that*, we'll be sharing something else that goes pop.

Chapter 9
Thea

*W*ell, *there goes an hour of my time I can't get back,* I think as I push through the heavy auditorium doors and step into the stifling hot air.

New Student Orientation was just as useless as the online orientation I did last month. At least that one explained school rules and where to find resources around campus. Today's orientation seemed like a poorly coordinated excuse for the various school organizations to talk about themselves.

I make it three steps before a commotion behind me has me turning back around to see what's happening. If shit's popping off, I need to know, so I can catalogue the trouble makers and know how fast I need to move to a safe location.

"Amazing, isn't it?"

I glance over at the girl standing next to me. I can't help but notice she's got a bit of drool on the corner of her mouth. She's staring at the guys who've just exited the auditorium.

They're basically standing in the middle of the walkway, forcing people to wait or go around them. I recognize them right away and refrain from sharing my opinion about them.

"They're *sooo* hot." She says, in a dreamy voice.

Admittedly, they're attractive, but I have to deduct about fifty hot points because of the shit they pulled in the hallway the other day. Bringing them down to only slightly above average in the looks department, which solidifies my assessment that the stranger in the bar is still the hottest piece of sex on legs I've ever seen.

Locking that thought and memory back away, I ask, "Who are they?"

She's staring at me like I'm a sideshow act. "What do you mean, 'who are they?'"

Am I supposed to know? Sasha, says celebrities and children of influential people are enrolled here. If they're famous, it would explain why they're walking around like they think the world revolves around them.

"Are they like reality tv stars or something? I never really got into watching those things."

"Reality tv? Girl, that's Holden Sullivan, Finley Jefferson Rhodes the Third, and Paxton Cox." She says, pointing each one out.

After our run-in, I'd say the cock part fits. He's a certified dick. "I'm still not tracking."

"They're The Trium."

I still have no idea what she's talking about and shrug. "The Triumph? Is that the school's football team, or something?"

"The Tri-*um*, or Triumvirates. The top three legacies on campus." She looks around, then leans in close, lowering her voice. "And they're Wrens."

When I still show no sign of recognition, she explains. "They're prospects for The League of the Daggered Ravens. The secret society was founded on campus but they don't really operate on school grounds anymore."

Okay, now we're getting somewhere. College fraternities. Not my jam *at all*. "If this boy's club is a secret, how do you know about it, and who's in it?"

Her brows furrow, like nobody's ever asked her that question before. "I don't. Well, not concretely or anything, but I heard Paxton's great grandfather was a member and things like that are passed down through the families, so he'd be expected to join. It's safe to say Finn and Holden would, too. If they were joining some other organization, they wouldn't be friends anymore."

I study her face while she's talking. She's serious about this. "You're saying this fraternity makes you ditch your friends?"

"It's a *society* and yes. I hear they're very particular about who they interact with. It preserves the sanctity of the membership and its secrets."

"Seems to me if you choose some new people and their secret handshakes over your old friends, you were a shitty friend to begin with."

She nods, though I'm not sure she agrees. Just one more thing that's different around here. Loyalty means a lot where I come from and dickheads who dump you for notoriety are the worst kinds of back stabbers.

Everyone's just standing around ogling them, but I'm over it. I turn my attention back to what I was doing, heading to lunch, and walk down the path that leads to the dining hall. I leave her to stare and drool at asshole one, two, and three in peace. After sitting through that useless assembly, I'm starving. The shuffle of feet on the sidewalk behind me gets my attention. The girl's following me. She's slightly out of breath when she finally catches up. "Geez, you walk fast," she says, as she struggles for air.

I know I do, and I don't apologize for it. There have been plenty of times when I've had to make a quick exit. Sometimes running draws too much attention, so I learned to speed walk away from some messy situations. Although, I don't think I was walking *that* fast.

She's about my height, with curves to die for and dark brown skin with wide almond set eyes, and a wide mouth with the kind of lips girls pay good money to achieve. Her hair is parted in the middle and falls in soft waves against her shoulders. She's gorgeous.

We're one of the first ones to make it to the cafeteria. Another bonus to not waiting around with the masses is I can strategically choose a table to sit at and I'll get the first wave of food. I order my food and fix myself a cup of coffee while I wait for my order.

By the time I get my tray, I've scoped out where I want to sit. It's on the back side of the room, near the doors which lead to the outside patio area. It's the one spot in the dining hall with the best sun exposure.

I head there and lower my ass towards the bench, when the girl who seems to have attached herself to me shrieks. I drop my tray on the table, ready to fend off an attack, but there's no one else around. She's staring at me with a horrified expression on her face.

"What?"

"You can't sit there."

I look down at the seat to make sure I didn't miss the sign that someone was holding this seat. There's nothing here and I don't see any stains that might ruin my clothes. "Sure I can. It's open."

"No, um, I mean you can't sit there, because it's in *their* territory."

"*Whose* territory?"

"The fraternities, sororities, and organizations. Basically, all the popular and powerful people. This is the area where they all sit."

She points to the left. "The jocks and cheerleaders sit there." And sweeps her arm right. "And the entertainers and social media influencers sit there."

Then she points to another table. "The Trium sit there. They each have their own tables, and if you're not a member or a prospective member, you can't sit on this side. Didn't you see the rope?"

"There was no rope."

She points and I turn to look behind me. There's a red rope coiled on the floor under the next table. "Looks like they forgot to put it back when they cleaned. At any rate," she says, looking over her shoulder as if she expects someone to jump out at us. "We can't sit here."

She looks really spooked, and I'm too hungry to argue with her, so I pick my tray up and move to another table. "Is this good?"

She gnaws on her lip, then nods. But she doesn't look any less stressed. "What's wrong with this one?"

"Nothing. It's closer to them than I usually sit, but it's not off limits."

"Great." I plop down and take a sip of my liquid energy. With this girl I'm gonna need it. "So listen, you wanna tell me your name before you interrupt any more of my breakfast hour?"

"Oh!" She looks away with a nervous giggle. "I didn't introduce myself. Did I?"

"No, you didn't."

"I'm Layla-Jean Breland."

"Thea." I thrust my hand out, which she takes, giving it a tentative shake. I bite into my toast and ask, "What's your deal?"

"My deal?"

"You singled me out in front of the auditorium this morning, and now you're sitting here. Are you this friendly with every stranger you meet?"

"Oh. Uh. Not usually. No."

"So, how did I get to be so unlucky?"

Her face falls. Agh, *shit*. I wasn't trying to make her feel bad. It's just the way my brain works. I'm sarcastic as fuck, and I forget not everyone can relate to it. I've gotten so used to Sasha understanding my personality.

"Hey. I didn't mean anything by it. I'm grateful you stopped me from sitting at the other table."

"You are?"

"Sure. I don't usually care about pissing people off, but I don't need the drama today, so thank you."

She beams at me like I just made her year. It makes me uncomfortable. I don't like being responsible for anyone's feelings but my own. But here I am, getting ready to try this *new thing* called being social, because Sasha said I can't spend the next two years living like I'm on an island of one. I disagree. I can totally survive on my own.

Been doing it damn near my whole life. But I promised. To try. This is me, *trying*.

I'm half listening as Layla tells me about herself, and what she's majoring in. I follow the conversation enough to ask the appropriate questions, but I'm also watching the room. That's how I'm the first one to spot the three amigos when they walk in.

Since I'm no longer in fight mode, and don't have the sun glaring in my eyes, I can finally get a good look at them.

The leader, Paxton, has massive shoulders. Like he spends all his time doing shoulder shrugs in the gym. Or maybe it's the way they're hunched up to his ears, like he's trying to distance himself from the world. Who knows? I'm spit balling his height, but I'd say he's about six feet. Six one if I'm being generous. His dark hair is styled to perfection, and his boots look like they've been spit shined for a military inspection.

His eyes are the most alluring thing on him. Jade green like this ring I saw once. When he turns and his face catches the light, I get a glimpse of some blue in them. They're aquamarine, like the dual colors of the sea. That's hot. I can totally picture myself staring into eyes like those while riding someone like a bronco at the rodeo. Too bad they belong to him.

The guy next to him. Holden? He's a little shorter than Paxton, but still tall as fuck. That means I need to reassess my height assessment. I'd definitely put Holden at six one, giving Paxton another inch on him.

Holden's mouth is the first thing I notice. Or rather, the shiny lip ring he's wearing is the first thing I notice. The one in his eyebrow is next. He's got dark brown hair, cut close on the sides, a little longer on the top. His skin is flawless. A dark natural tan, and his eyes are storm cloud gray.

He's a tank too. He's sporting a short-sleeved shirt and shorts. The exposed skin suggests he's hard muscle and angular lines. I'm too far away to make out the pattern of the ink on his arms. Holden looks bored with everything and is gripping a book in his hand.

Too bad he hangs with Paxton the Dick or I'd invite him to read to me at night.

The last guy. The one with all the letters of the alphabet in his name is a popcorn thief, and he seems the happiest out of the group.

He's smiling and laughing as he makes his way to their table. He's thinner than the other two, but I can tell he's still solid under his ripped skinny jeans and heather grey t-shirt.

The tips of his curly brown hair peeks out from his beanie and brushes against his forehead. His light blue eyes hold too much mischief.

I remember the way he called me pet and how he seemed to enjoy saying it even more when I called him out on it. He's definitely the jokester out of the group.

When his gaze sweeps over my table, his smile widens. I dismiss him with a flick of my eyes and turn away.

We were at the same movie; I let him have some of my rum, and he stole my popcorn. That doesn't mean we're suddenly buddies or anything, and I don't need Paxton Cox and his buddies thinking I'm seconds away from falling at their feet like everyone else seems to be doing.

I might be on the hunt for steady dick, but those three are the last people I'd ever want to hook up with.

Chapter 10
Pax

My dad's orders were clear. Keep an eye on our new neighbor. It hasn't been as easy as it sounds.

She must've stayed off campus this weekend. There were no sounds coming from her room. Not even a muted television or flushing toilet.

Dad gave no details or identifying features about her. She could be any one of the girls who walked by me this morning. Monday would have been our first chance to get eyes on her.

She's in the same early morning statistics class as Finn and Holden, but they skipped because we were still dealing with the incident from our last challenge.

A street camera a block away from the scene captured the license plate of the Audi. Holden worked his magic. We know it was a rental car, now we're working on finding out who was driving it.

For the third time in almost as many days, I wonder if the near miss with Finn was a test.

The South side of town is basically abandoned. The land development board and city council decided they wanted better control of access points in and out of town when we incorporated. As the years went on, the cost of homes here grew. Business was booming, and the town went from an affordable quaint town to a thriving beach front city, owned and operated by the independently wealthy.

The land and property taxes increased for everyone. The lower-class families were hit the worst when the mines, their primary source of income, dried up. They found new jobs that required a longer commute, using the canyon pass as an access route, but the accident at the mouth of the canyon was the final blow.

The road and bridge were deemed a safety issue, and traffic was rerouted through the new highway system. The one with a high ass toll fee going to and coming from LA.

The South-siders couldn't keep up with the property taxes on their crappy houses and eventually moved to Palisade Shores, which despite its name, isn't as affluent as it sounds.

The bar, the hotel, and a few other businesses on the East side of town by the pier are the only small businesses in town that are still family owned and operated.

They sit on some pretty coveted acres of land, but the families have all agreed they'll never sell to the city. They formed a conglomerate to make sure no one could be forced to back out of the agreement.

Individually, they're just business owners. Together, they're pretty powerful. They've been holding out against the council for a long time, but the current owners are getting older, and their children and grandchildren aren't interested in taking over. Not when the jobs on the North side of town come with more money, better benefits and prestige.

The city council and land development board know this. They've been biding their time, building up fancier new shit, while the older establishments lose money, or close because they can't match the amenities and draw of the newer businesses.

They're waiting for the old folks to pass away, and fully expect for the family members to sell off the properties for pennies on the dollar, compared to the amount the city will make when they rebuild.

I walked in on my dad on a call once. The council wants to turn Canyon Falls into the West Coast's answer to The Hamptons and Martha's Vineyard.

I pull my weighted jump rope out of my gym bag and start my warm up. I do ten minutes of jump rope, then move on to upper body, then legs, abs, and finish off with one final round of jump rope before getting on the ground to stretch out my calves. I grab a towel off the rack to mop up the puddle of sweat I left on the mat and toss it in the laundry bin on my way to the exit.

There's a gym in our dorm, but this one has more weights. I never shower here. Not since the time my shit got stolen by a rival fraternity as a prank.

It took me three days to track down who did it. My retribution was swift and embarrassing, with just the right amount of flair. I chuckle, remembering the look on Tyler Stuart's face when he found out his car was missing.

We taped a note to the windshield, which was the only thing left in his parking spot. I know for a fact he never found all the pieces to the car, because his steering wheel is in the bunker.

I pushed myself hard at the gym. My post workout high has me in a better mood when I get back to the dorm. After a nice hot shower, I'm feeling human again. More in control.

I grab a banana and a bottle of water from my kitchen before heading to breakfast. The food in the cafeteria is amazing, but we never know when Rho Beta Psi business will interrupt our meal, so I always try to put something in my stomach before I go there. Most of the time, Finn does the same. But Holden... sometimes he gets so caught up in his head he forgets to eat even when there's nothing going on. We try to keep granola, nuts, or fruit snacks in our cars and backpacks for him to snack on.

I stroll through the side door of the cafeteria and see the guys are already at our usual table. I head to the line and place my order before joining them.

We never wait for our plates at the counter. There's literally a line out the door of people willing to serve us, even if it means they won't get to eat their own food.

I've barely settled into my seat when the scent of roses assaults my nose. Someone's sprayed perfume so heavily it's making my nose burn and my eyes water.

I grimace, looking up at the source of the offending odor. Her makeup job isn't much better. She doesn't look familiar. I'm guessing she's a freshman. One who's reinvented herself at college, because if she was practicing beauty tips in high school she'd know nobody wants someone who's bathed in perfume and wearing obvious layers of makeup.

Even I know you're supposed to blend that contour shit in. I lean back and let her place my tray in front of me. "End seat," I say before digging into my food.

If you're lucky enough to deliver our food, then you're allowed to sit at our table for that meal. We decide where. Sometimes it's right next to us, and other times we pawn you off on someone else at our table. Either way, you're seen in our company, which immediately elevates your social status. Maybe someone will take this girl under their wing and tell her to tone that shit down.

Holden's sitting across from me, his head in a book, as usual. The spot in front of him is empty. Either he didn't go to the food line to order something, or no one brought his tray, and because he's distracted with whatever he's reading, he hasn't noticed.

I glance over at Finn, who has no trouble deciphering my look. He says, "It's on the way. He ordered an omelet with mushrooms and spinach, but insisted they use the ingredients he brought."

Holden's a picky eater. He's growing shit on his balcony, and when he harvests something, he makes sure it's used. We all have those things we use the power of our names to get. Holden uses his name to make sure the chefs in the back cook his food just the way he wants it.

It takes a while to get used to his quirks and mannerisms. Because of it, he's treated differently than me and Finn. It's not always obvious he's being ostracized.

Nobody's stupid enough to come right out and say they think he's weird, but we can tell. Just like now. The girls at the table are going out of their way to talk to us. Even going so far as yelling down the table to get our attention. But the two girls next to Holden aren't paying him any attention.

It's their loss, because he's a walking contradiction. He looks like he can bang nails into boards with his bare hands, but he's so fucking smart it's scary. I mean it. Some of the shit he knows, like how to dismember a body with the least amount of blood loss, or the best way to access a secure server and make it look like someone else did it, really used to worry me.

What twelve-year-old knows that shit? But Holden did, and he remembers everything with perfect recall. He's got a photographic memory and an insatiable thirst for learning.

I'm not too proud to admit a huge part of the success of our team is because of him. He plans our missions, including contingencies. But he's also able to guide us when we have to improvise, and when we throw down, he's a bruiser. Holden's actually a better fighter than I am. You know, since he knows exactly how to incapacitate you with one blow.

A guy approaches with his tray, looking nervous. It's one of the chefs. Another of his quirks is he prefers the person who prepared his food to bring it out to him. That way, if it's poisoned, we know who to destroy.

While Finn and I are relatively certain nobody's slipping poison into our food, Holden isn't as trusting. An incident when he was seven has made him distrustful of people in general. The way he's been treated by girls since high school has him weary of women in particular. That's why he doesn't care that none of the giggling sluts at the table are throwing themselves at him or trying to get his attention.

"Eat, man," I say, letting him know his food is here. He stabs his fork in his eggs, without looking up from his book, and holds it out to the girl on his right. I stifle a laugh. That's the only hint he gives that he's been paying attention to what's going on around him.

The girl that mumbled, "Why am I stuck sitting next to the freak," just got nominated to be his official taste tester.

"Why are you giving me this?" She asks, confused, since nobody else is feeding the other girls at the table.

He turns the page in his book at the same time he says, "Because if it's poisoned, there will be one less bitch in the world. Now eat it, like you've got a mouth full of my cum sliding down your throat. Don't even think about spitting it out."

It's a soft command, but you can't miss the bite on the end. She must've been saying some other shit before I got here. She looks around the table, quickly realizing no one's gonna intervene. Slowly, she opens her mouth and wraps her lips around the tines of the fork, trying to take the smallest of bites.

Holden's as quick as a python striking. He shoves the fork all the way in her mouth, the way he would shove his dick down her throat. From the way she flinches, I'm sure he's scratched the roof of her mouth with it.

He pulls the fork out, unwraps a new one, and sets the timer on his watch, digging into his food when five minutes pass without her turning blue or foaming at the mouth. That's what I mean, about being so quick to dismiss him. He's as cruel as he is kind. I wouldn't want to end up on his bad side.

While I'm eating, I'm scanning the cafeteria for signs of anyone giving off suspicious vibes. We're always on guard. The frats and sororities are constantly trying to out-prank each other, and students at the bottom of the food chain are always looking for a way to reach the top.

My gaze clashes with Steven Lane's. Football hero. Total prick. He's leaning back in his chair as if it's his throne. A girl I vaguely remember hooking up with once or twice last year is sitting in his lap. I think she's a congressman's daughter. I didn't ask too many questions.

The cocky ass grin on Steve's face is one that says he's got one up on me. He doesn't. I might not remember whatever the girl and I talked about, but I *do* remember my friends and I stretched her holes out like a misshapen sweater.

As soon as he realizes that, he'll toss her to the side. He's looking for that perfect prospect. *A future wife.* One that will catapult him to the top of the food chain. I turn back to my table, dismissing him. He can keep trying. He's in a rival frat. His daddy might be some big shot lawyer, but nothing he's done so far has earned him a second look by The League.

Unless he gets an in, that rise to power. True power is never gonna happen.

Chapter 11
Deacon Wolfe

Today's the first day of a new Physical Enhancement class. I used to get excited about the start of the semester, but now it's just another day on the wheel. About fifty students sign up for the course. That number's usually cut in half by the end of the first week. More than forty percent of the drops are girls, and I'm okay with it.

The future wives and mistresses of the top ten percent of the countries, one percent think flashing the waistband of their underwear, or sometimes even the whole damn thong, and a bit of skin is enough to get me to fall into bed with them. You'd think after three years word would have finally gotten out that it won't. Just like their gender won't get them out of having to do the same exercises as the men. There is no slow or easy pace for this class. Even some of the guys drop after the first week.

We do calisthenics, weight lifting and martial arts. The workouts get progressively harder and tougher. There's a reason for that. On the other side of campus, behind a security fence guarded by a para-military organization and enough jolts to make your hair stand on end, is the Military Science and Tactical Strategy Command Campus.

MISTIC, is Canyon Falls University's answer to West Point. Some students take my class to prepare them for the physical assessments they have to take each quarter as part of the MISTIC program.

Others use it to augment the physical training and conditioning programs they're getting at another fitness facility or gym. There is no beginner class. Everyone does the same thing.

Today is probably the easiest workout they'll have all semester. It's admin day and the first class of the semester follows the same routine.

I give my speech about attire (because I don't need or want to see nipples and ass cheeks); I pass out the liability waivers (don't want mommy or daddy suing me for injuries incurred in the course of training), and I do a cursory assessment of everyone's endurance level by administering a physical fitness test. It's like the one they give out in high school. Real easy.

I'm lingering in my office, giving time for stragglers to walk in. This will also be the only day students beat me to class. At the ten-minute mark, I exit my office and step into the gym. I'm on autopilot as I walk to the front of the class, my welcome speech tumbles from my lips, and I ignore the excessive perfume wafting through the space, and the tittering of the girls trying to get my attention.

Everything is following the usual routine. I tick off the boxes on my checklist, not that I need it, but it's a power move. It lets them know I'm being precise and detailed. Phones aren't allowed in my class, so I look up to make sure no one's holding a device, and that I've got their attention. That's when things go sideways.

I pride myself on being able to maintain my composure. It's served me well in and out of the ring, and when dealing with the more difficult aspects of teaching here, but I almost lose my shit when I come face to face with the blue-eyed sex kitten I haven't been able to stop thinking about since Sunday night.

How the hell is this even happening? The whole reason I was

drinking two towns over is because I wanted to avoid running into anyone I knew. Fucking people you work with will mess up a good thing at work. So will messing with a student.

I feel things tilting. An unexpected feeling of vertigo, like I just got my bell cleaned by someone wearing cement gloves. It doesn't matter that I didn't know she was enrolled here. Now that I do, I'm quickly evaluating my options. Is she even legal? It's a valid question. We have some fifteen-year-old juniors here.

I pull up my roster and start calling attendance. The list is in alphabetical order. It makes it easier for me to match names with faces. I ignore the sugary sweet way the girls say here, or present, and the extra bass the guys put in their voices. I quickly drop my gaze back to my clipboard once I match a face to a name.

"Theona LaReaux?"

"Here, and it's Thea."

I don't want to look up. I don't *need* to look up, because I know it's *her*. Her voice is etched in my brain. The sass, the passion, the way she screamed when I made her come. But if I don't raise my head and acknowledge her, it'll look suspicious as fuck. I lift my head, barely looking in her general direction, before quickly averting my gaze.

I finish calling out the remaining names and put the class through a series of jumping jacks, pushups and sit-ups, before sending them out to run. This initial test will be what I compare their scores to throughout the semester to show them how much they've improved.

My gaze slides over her, again. She's looking at me like she doesn't recognize me. Maybe she had too much to drink that night, or has poor vision. Doesn't matter. I'm happy to ignore her and pretend like I don't know her too. With any luck, she'll show up on my drop list before the week is over.

Cruel Legacy

Thea

I've been enjoying my classes so far, even though the way the material's presented is a little boring, but I guess that's part of the stuffy vibe of this school. Posh professors, for a posh environment. My Physical Enhancement class starts today. A whole one and a half hours of working out every day. I'm here for it. When I step into the gym, I see there are mats on the floor in front of the mirrors.

There are more girls than guys here. They're dressed in lycra tights and sports bras, or midriff shirts. Some are wearing cut off booty shorts or track shorts, which leave little to the imagination. Their hair and makeup on point. They look like they're about to run errands, not work up a sweat.

I hope this isn't like a Pilates class or yoga class or something. There's nothing wrong with those forms of exercise. I actually love a good yoga session, but when I looked at the class description, it mentioned lessons in wrestling and martial arts.

I'm looking forward to knocking someone on their ass. It's been a while, and I really need to work on my grappling moves. I check out the guys standing off to the right. They're a mishmash of shapes and sizes. I could probably pin about half of them to the mat with no problem. The other half, I'd have to work for it. *Please don't let this be a yoga class.*

The whispering and giggling on my left draws my attention back to the girls. Why the hell are they fluffing their hair? A voice cuts through the noise.

"Good afternoon class. I'm Coach Wolfe, and I'll be your Enhanced Fitness Trainer for this semester."

Coach Wolfe finally comes into view. If I had enemies, right now - *this very second*- would be the perfect time for them to launch a sneak attack on me. I'm so shocked at what I'm seeing that I'd be too slow to react and defend myself. It's *him*. The stranger from the bar.

I've been dreaming about that face, and those hazel eyes staring at me, while he did delicious things to my tits. The voice that felt like it was burrowing its way under my skin as he whispered filthy things in my ear.

Those eyes sweep over me now, as if I'm not even here. That brings me back to the present. Maybe he doesn't recognize me. That's a good thing, because this shit's embarrassing. I was counting on never seeing him again.

I'm an adult and I've been in awkward situations before. Since he doesn't seem to know who I am, it'll make pretending like it never happened easier.

I ignore the topsy-turvy feeling swarming around in my stomach, and focus on what he's saying. He's talking about class expectations and proper gym attire. News flash, your stomach, tits, and bikini line have to be covered.

I'm wearing yoga pants that come to mid-calf, and a sports bra. The shirt I'm wearing over it hits the top of my upper thigh and I have my zip up hoodie on. I always dress in layers at the gym, removing my hoodie after my warm up, and eventually my shirt the deeper into my workout I get. I'll be sure to wear a tank top since it sounds like the sports bra look is frowned upon.

Coach Wolfe paces in front of the class, his walk slow and commanding, every bit the apex predator his name implies. If I had to fight him, I'd have to work for a win.

My warped mind flashes to an image of being pinned underneath him as he uses the thing in his pants to try to force me to submit. I unzip my jacket, the temperature of the room is suddenly hotter than it was seconds ago.

Okay, Thea. He's your teacher. He doesn't remember you, and you're happy about it because it's one and done. And because he's your teacher, so. Yeah. There are probably school rules forbidding it.

"If you signed up for this class because you heard it was an easy A. You were lied to. We work out and work hard. There will be days when you will feel like you have to throw up, and days when you probably *will* throw up. Expect bumps, bruises, and an occasional black eye. Your safety is important, but accidents happen." He waves a stack of papers. "And as such, each of you must read and sign the liability waiver. Wet signatures *only*."

My mind blitzes out again, remembering what he did when I was wet. Then it shifts to him, swallowing that wetness like it was a cool, refreshing drink. Damn, that was hot, and... *no, no, no.* Focus. He's my teacher, and he's still talking. I force myself to listen.

He concludes his speech with, "If you're uncomfortable with that, your pampered asses have until Friday to withdraw from the class without penalty."

This school is dickhead central. For the cost of this high ass tuition, they should pay me to have to put up with this shit. He's talking to the entire class, but it feels as if that last statement was specifically for me. Am I gonna drop this class just to avoid seeing the guy I fucked in an alley? I square my shoulders and slap a bored expression on my face. Not a chance.

My first full week of class is in the bag. There's some kind of faculty holiday, on Monday, so most of the students have gone home or to the beach. Or their homes on the beach. *Whatever.* Aunt Moira said I was welcome to come to the house. I declined. I'd rather be here acclimating myself to my surroundings and doing what I'm about to do right now. Explore the woods behind the campus in peace.

I fold the map so the trail I'm looking for is topside up and run my finger over the squiggly line, making note of the way it winds through the trees. It's not to scale or an actual image of the path, but I like to know which way my body should be going, and as long as north is always north, I can figure out where the hell I am. I have my compass in my pocket, a hat on my head, my jacket, plenty of water and snacks in my bag, and my portable charger in case my battery dies before I get back.

I fold the map smaller and tuck it into the side pocket of my backpack. With one quick look to make sure my shoes are tied, I step through the trees, ready for my first Canyon Falls adventure. Technically *second*, but since Coach Deacon Wolfe is a jerk, I'm pretending the whole bar scene never happened.

An hour into my hike, I see something that's not on the map. It's a path that veers off the main road. In the horror movies you're not supposed to deviate from your route but this is real life, and I've learned sometimes the best way to explore is by veering off. So, I mark a tree with my knife, then take the path less taken. Literally. As thick as the brush is, I doubt anyone ever comes this way. I have to duck down under low hanging tree branches and prickly foliage as I pick my way along.

Finally, about a hundred feet in, it clears. I walk another fifteen minutes, then come to a stop, a squeal tumbling from my lips. This is why I don't feed into Urban Legends. Smack dab in the middle of nowhere, I've stumbled across a stream. It's tucked away back here like a secret oasis.

It's hot as hell today, and a sheen of sweat already coats my skin. I take a seat on one of the fallen logs and sip some water, as I watch the gentle ripples in the stream. I wish I had a bathing suit, so I could swim. If I were in Nags Creek, and this was the high school's swimming pool, I'd jump in. But hiking with wet clothes isn't my idea of fun. Then again... I'm in the middle of nowhere. Alone. This would be one of those times when Sasha calls me insane. I stand, pulling off my clothes and wade into the stream, sighing as the water cools my skin.

I don't know how people do it. Work jobs that keep them cooped up in stuffy, artificially oxygenated buildings all day. A desk job would literally eat away at my soul. I'm a nature lover. I belong outside.

I swim a little distance from the shore, then flip over on my back, floating as I look up at the sky, peaking through the canopy of trees. One day I'll come back here to watch the sunset. I can imagine how beautiful it looks.

There's a rock jutting out of the water. I swim over to it and climb up on it, letting the sun warm my skin, lazily dragging my hands down my body. I brush palms against my nipples before gently squeezing them, biting my lower lip as I give them a tug, then move one hand lower, gliding it across my hip, over my thigh, between my legs, dipping my finger between my folds, and rubbing my clit, alternating between slow lazy circles and dipping my finger into my slickness, gathering some of the wetness before rubbing my clit again.

I find a steady rhythm, working my pussy over, pushing myself toward release. It's not as good as a thick cock, but an orgasm is an orgasm and I need one. It's already been too long since my last one.

A week might not seem like a lot of time for some people, but for me, it is. I've been too busy getting settled and haven't taken time to please myself. It's perfect that I'm doing it now. Out here. Where I feel free and the sexiest I've ever felt. I'm not quiet about how good I'm making myself feel, letting my moans and whimpers join the chorus of the wildlife in the trees.

"Fuuuck," I pant as my release ripples through me, easing the last bit of tension from my body. When my breathing steadies, I slip back into the water, to rinse off, and swim back to the bank. I would love to stay out here longer, but I've got more ground to cover on my hike. Sighing, I pull myself from the water, and brush the water droplets from my skin as best I can. I take a few minutes to finger detangle my

hair and braid it in two French braids while the blistering sun dries me the rest of the way.

I've finished putting my shirt on and I'm bending over to retrieve my boot when a branch snaps behind me. I whirl around and see a shadow dart behind the trees. *What the fuck?* Is someone perving on me? Did they see me on that rock? It's far enough away that you couldn't make out my features, but close enough to know I was naked and what I was doing. I slip Clint out of my other shoe and yell, "Don't hide now! Come out here and I'll give you a closer look at my tits."

I won't, but whoever is out here doesn't know that. On bare feet, I pick my way over to the tree across from the one where I saw the shadow. When I rush behind it, it's empty. I scan the path, searching for anyone or anything which would explain what I saw. There's nothing suspicious around, but that doesn't mean there wasn't something or someone here. I go back over to the fallen log to finish dressing, then make my way back to the original path, with Clint tucked into the waistband of my shorts instead of in my pocket.

If someone *is* out here creeping on me, I'll be ready.

Chapter 12
Pax

It's another stellar morning here at C Falls U. I stifle a yawn. I need a few more hours of sleep to feel human. Everyone around me looks like they're dragging ass, but our reasons aren't the same. They probably partied from the time they left campus on Friday until early this morning.

I was at home attending charity dinners and the opera with my family in LA. I drove back last night but stayed up late finishing a paper which is due this morning. I slept maybe three hours before my alarm went off. As tired as I was, there was no way I was skipping the gym. Now I'm sitting in the first floor lounge area of the dorm, killing time before heading to breakfast.

Finn likes to watch what he calls the Society Princess Lingerie Show. It's basically the girls on this floor running from one room to the next, or to the showers, in their underwear. It's not until you reach the fourth floor and above that you get a shared bathroom with your quad mates.

On the sixth floor and seventh floor, it's a three-bedroom apartment set up. There's a lounge, game room, and laundry room on the eighth floor. The gym and pool are on the ninth.

The top floor, the tenth, has four full sized two-bedroom apartments. There are only two elevators that take you all the way to the tenth floor, and you need an access code for that to happen. One of them is an express elevator, disguised as a utility closet on the other side of the building. It goes from the secret tunnel in the sub-level of this building and only stops here on the first floor and the top one.

"Who's that?" Someone snickers, drawing my attention to the elevator doors. I shift in my seat. I've been keeping an eye on it, since it was called back to our floor, waiting for it to make its slow descent to the lobby. I swear it must've hit every floor on its way down.

Our school has average enrollment numbers and class sizes compared to other private universities, so there's no way for me to remember all the names and faces of people I see or meet, but I recognize the girl from the hallway as soon as she gets closer to the lounge.

It's hard not to notice her. She stands out like a sore thumb, and I'm not just talking about the indigo and purple-colored hair. She moves differently than the other girls here. Like she's trying not to make noise with her shoes. Her head is facing forward, but her eyes shift around, never settling on one thing for long. It's sketchy behavior. I should know, because it's how I scan an area before we pull a prank.

"What's our pet doing here?" Finn asks, tracking her movements.

"It's her." Holden says.

I tilt my head to the side. "You sure?" There are other women getting off the elevator too. Any of them could be our mark.

He nods once, passes me his tablet, then turns the page in his book. Finn stands and walks over to a group of girls standing in the middle of the lobby. He drapes his arms over two of their shoulders and leads them out the door. It looks like he's just escorting them because he's a big flirt, but he's following her. That's the assignment we were given, and we've been taught to take all tasks, no matter what they are, or who they're from, seriously.

The girl is gone by the time Holden and I join Finn on the sidewalk in front of the dorm. He smiles at the girls tucked under his arms, and sends each of them off with a kiss, before turning to me and asking, "What we got?"

I hand him the tablet so he can see for himself. "We've got nothing. It's definitely a dorm mix up."

He looks up from what he's reading and asks, "What makes you so sure?"

I gesture towards the device in his hand. "It's all right there. Theona LaReaux, born in Marshall Springs, Louisiana. Single mother, unknown father. Bounced around a lot until she and her drunk of a mother landed in Nags Creek, Nevada. Population, 10,931.

She was in and out of foster homes and groups homes from the age of seven through twelve, at which time her mother disappeared, making her a permanent ward of the state. That's where she was right up until she got here."

I pull out my phone and send a text to my dad, letting him know I have eyes on the girl, before finishing up my assessment. "Like I said, it's a mistake, and this assignment will be over sooner than we thought."

Holden cracks his knuckles and says, "That's an optimistic view. Sometimes the easiest tasks are the hardest." He always takes an opposing view, just to make sure we're considering all angles.

This won't be one of those times. It's pretty cut and dry to me. "Her tuition is covered by Moira and Scott Hughes, who I have never even heard of, have you?"

They both shake their heads. "Right, and think of all the parties we've been to over the years. I'm pretty sure we've met every daughter, niece, granddaughter and cousin of all the legacy families." I point to the dorm. "You were in the lobby. Nobody spoke up about knowing her, or vouched for her. If she were someone, *anyone* with half a drop of blood relation to a legacy, someone would have recognized her."

We all have family members we don't like or don't trust, but we make sure we account for everyone, no matter how distant the blood relation. You never know when that relationship can be exploited. I finish with one final thought. "And on the off chance she is related to a legacy, she'd still be on the wrong goddamn floor, because the fourth bloodline died off a long time ago."

Finn nods in agreement, while Holden types away on his tablet again. When he looks up, he's got his math whiz face on. Whatever he just read can't be good.

"What is it?"

He flips his tablet over again. Our new project is also the driver of the Audi.

Chapter 13
Thea

Somehow I've made a friend. I wasn't trying to, but it happened. Ever since that day in the cafeteria, when she stopped me from sitting at the wrong table, Layla-Jean Breland has been like a shadow that never fades and a song that never ends.

I never knew someone could talk as much as she can. It's been a bit of an adjustment for her and for me. Too many times to count, I've hurt her feelings without even trying. She doesn't say anything but her face is so expressive, it's easy to tell when it happens.

"LJ!" I've called her name three times already, and she hasn't answered. I pinch her to get her attention.

"Ow, Thea." She rubs the spot on her arm. "What was that for?"

"I'm calling your name and you're not listening."

"You are?"

"Yes, LJ. I am."

"Well, that explains it. Since you didn't say Layla-Jean, I figured you were talking to someone else." She mumbles the last part almost to herself.

"Well, I'm talking to you. Does everybody use your whole name like that all the time?"

"Yup."

I give her a look that says, *give me a break*. "Layla-Jean is a lot to get out. How did you go this long without a nickname?"

She shrugs. "I guess it just never came up in my family. My grandmother said your name is your identity and you don't want people getting used to using a cutesy version you can't grow out of, because it distorts their perception of you, or something like that."

"Well, no shade to your grandmother, but I disagree. I don't think the name you're given at birth dictates how people see you in life. Your actions do. Now I know you have the manners of a southern bride, but I don't. I say what I think and feel in the moment. Five seconds after you introduced yourself, I felt like your name was just too damn long for me to be saying it all the time. It's like the way I cringe whenever someone calls me *Theona*."

She works through what I'm saying. When it clicks, she nods and says, "Oh, I get it now. Sure. You may call me LJ."

"Was already doing that."

She chuckles at my flippant response. When her laughter dies off, she says, "Can I ask you a question?"

I pause before responding. I don't generally like answering questions. "Depends on what it is."

"Where did you go to school before you moved here?"

"Nags Creek Community College." I know she's never heard of it, so I give her a better reference. "It's in Nevada."

"Oh? How far from Vegas?"

"The town is about an hour's drive from Vegas, if you break the speed limit. Ninety plus minutes if you don't." Where I come from, speed limits are basically suggestions. I guess that's why so many people's licenses were always suspended.

That prompts her to tell me a story about a group trip a bunch of kids in her high school took to Vegas. She stops talking, mid story, along with everyone else. The entire cafeteria gets quiet. I don't hear an alarm or some kind of public service announcement, so the instant hush seems odd to me. "What's going on?"

"It's them." She whispers, before putting her finger to her mauve painted lips to silence me.

"Them, who?"

Before she can answer, *they* come into view. "These pricks?" I say it loud enough to earn some dirty looks. I glare right back at the girl on my left. I know what I know. Forgive me if I didn't drink the fucking Kool Aid.

I look around to see if maybe somebody else important, like a faculty member, is coming through the door. Nope. It's just the three jack holes from the hallway who tried to... well, I don't know what they call themselves *trying* to do. Scare me? Whatever they hoped to accomplish didn't work. I've been cornered by way scarier guys than them.

"LJ, why is everyone acting like someone flipped the off switch to their brains and mouths?"

"Because today is the day."

"Wednesday?"

"No. *The day.*"

That makes even less sense than the first time she said it. "How about you talk to me like someone who doesn't know what the hell you're talking about, because she's new here? Oh wait, that's exactl what I am."

"Today is the day the sororities and fraternities announce beginning of pledge season. But first, Holden, Pax, and Finn going to name two new people to sit at the Legacy table and tially move into the Rho Beta Psi frat house, permanently."

"There's like ten empty seats over there. Why are th picking two?"

"Because they lost two people over the summer an replace them."

"Say what now?"

She shushes me again, seconds before dickhead number one, *Pax,* starts talking.

"I know you all heard we lost two of our table mates over the summer. I won't go into details, but know their dismissal is permanent. We now have two slots to fill. We've reviewed everyone's application and have made an interim decision."

Application? Interim decision? To eat at the same table with these assholes? God, this is so pretentious. I understand filling an opening for your crew, when someone with a certain skill set gets pinched, but the criteria for joining isn't something any of the gangs in Nags Creek would ever put on paper. Doing that's just asking to get caught. You go by reputation and word of mouth. What dickhead number one is saying sounds a lot like a job interview.

He calls out the first name and I see someone from the jock table stand up. He high fives and fist bumps people as he walks to the center of the room to stand next to the guy, Finn. Today he's wearing red beanie to match the red and white sneakers he's wearing.

A second name is called, and that person comes from the influ-
and actors' table. He goes to stand next to book guy, Holden,
all file out of the cafeteria. As soon as the doors swing
ind them, the conversations starts up again. That's it?
on pins and needles for that shit? Talk about anti-

explain to me what just happened? They called
Why is that even a thing that needs a huge

f the most exclusive fraternities on campus,
points to the one near where they were
u it's the legacy table?"

he legacies. To do that, you have
ily or be invited, and the only
whose family can be an asset
Leo weren't sitting with them

already. They're Rho Beta Psi members as of last year, but they aren't legacies, so they couldn't eat at their table, and there were no rooms in the frat house. Now that they've been picked, they'll eat at the legacy table and share a room at the frat house for the next thirteen weeks. This could change their lives."

"Okay, so jack hole one, two and three live in the frat house?" She's giving me a look. "What?" I ask, lifting my brows.

"Did you call Pax, Holden, and Finn *jack holes*?"

"So?"

"So nobody disrespects them behind their backs."

"Oh, don't worry." I say, rolling my eyes. "I've already done it to their faces. I'm just covering all the angles."

Now she looks like she's swallowed a lemon. I circle my finger in front of her face. "What is wrong with your face?"

"Thea, please tell me you're kidding."

"I'm not. The reject boy band and I had a run in last week, and I was happy to tell them all to fuck off in the most posh way possible." I give her the double salute to demonstrate.

"You *didn't*."

"I did." I laugh at how scandalized she looks. "Now you were saying they live in the frat house, so this little show was to make people feel even shittier than they already do for not being picked first for dodge ball?"

She shakes her head and says with a dreamy sigh. "They don't live in the frat house. The Triums live in Vale Tower."

"Really? I've never seen them there." I've obviously said something else wrong, because she's doing that thing with her face again. Geez, I need an instruction manual around here.

"Oh god, Thea, please tell me you're not trying to hang out over there."

Now it's my turn to give her a weird look. "Yes, I hang out there. Every night from dusk til dawn, as a matter of fact."

"You need to stop. Don't go back there." She says in the sternest voice I've ever heard her use.

I lower my parfait cup. She looks nervous and scared. "Hey, LJ? What's happening here? Why are you freaking out?"

"Whoever invited you to Vale Tower must be up to something. I don't want you to get in trouble or hurt for breaking the rules."

"Okay, one, I'm not scared of anyone hurting me. I'll give as good as I get. Two, I don't know what pretentious ass, self-made rules I could be breaking. My dorm assignment is Vale Tower."

"That's impossible. It's reserved for legacies."

I pick my parfait back up and spoon out another scoop. "I don't know about any of that." I say, waving my spoon in the air. "Sounds like more bullshit and rumors, to keep people fawning after those assholes. My aunt and uncle paid my tuition and room and board. The school gave me a shiny key fob for all the doors, and it works. I've been entering and exiting and sleeping there for two weeks now."

She still doesn't look like she believes me, and not that I have anything to prove, but I decide to put her mind at ease. "When we're done with breakfast, I'll prove it to you."

Chapter 14
Holden

"Enchante."

I roll my eyes at my French-speaking friend. Finn loves to pull out his language skills when he meets new girls, and they eat that shit up.

"The three of you, walking around campus, together. Now that's not fair. There should be a rule about it. How am I supposed to decide which one of you to hook up with?"

They giggle and do various versions of hair flipping and trying to look seductive. If this were a contest, none of them would rank higher than a three on the originality scale.

"Isn't it hard, Holden?"

The sophomores he's talking to exchange nervous looks. They can relax. I'm not about to ask for their numbers. Why would I? In the five minutes we've been standing here, I haven't heard any of them say one thing of value. I grunt a response, letting them take it any way they want.

When I was younger, I was told I talked too much about things other kids weren't interested in. Now people think I'm weird, because I don't talk. Sometimes, I think *they* think I *can't* talk, despite having the highest GPA in school. There's nothing wrong with my ability to communicate. It's everyone else's limited knowledge about a vast range of topics and their lack of comprehension skills that's the problem. So I've stopped trying to engage them in conversation.

I tilt my head towards the building, letting Finn know it's time to get to class. We're already later than I want to be, because he made me wait for him while he polished his favorite knife. Most of the students are already in their seats. His delay throws off my routine. Next time, he's walking to class alone.

Finn grabs a seat closest to the window, and is staring out of it before I'm even settled in my chair on the opposite side of the room. We rarely sit together. Finn's a talker and he knows I like complete silence when I'm working.

The door squeaks open, drawing everyone's attention to the front of the room. Our new neighbor, Theona LaReaux, rushes in with seconds to spare. I was so lost in my head I didn't even notice she wasn't in class. Austin gives her a wave, which she returns before plopping down in the chair. Right. Next. To. Me. No one does that. The other students would rather sit on the floor to avoid having to be near me.

Theona's fumbling around in her bag looking for something, cursing up a storm. I can honestly say I've never heard that string of profanity before from a woman. Maybe not even a man. It's amazing how she uses fuck as a noun, adjective and verb. Finally, she stops muttering to herself and straightens in her chair.

We're supposed to be following along with what Professor Roberts is saying in our workbook. This is one of the few classes where we have actual textbooks to use because the teacher wants to make sure we understand the work and aren't relying fully on computers to get the answers. I'm glad she's done. Her mumbling was distracting as hell. I'm engrossed in what the teacher is saying, which is why I don't notice her leaning in until she bumps into me.

"Is there a reason you're crowding my space?" I infuse every bit of annoyance I can into my voice. It's not hard. I *am* annoyed.

"Yes." Her eyes flick to the front of the room to make sure Roberts isn't watching us. "I was running late, and I left my workbook. I'm taking notes, but I need to see the example to understand what he's talking about, and since he said work in teams to check each other's work, I figured we'd do it together."

I missed that part. Or ignored it, because nobody works with me. Except Finn and it's usually via text, after I've explained the project or lesson to him.

I turn my head slightly, and ask, "You want me to team up with *you?*"

Her violet-blue eyes narrow into slits, her irises constrict. Her pouty lips part. I can tell she's pissed off before she even opens her mouth. "And what the fuck is wrong with me? Or does the little boys' club you're in not let women work with you? Is that against your club rules or something?"

She says it like it's a tree fort and we've posted a sign that says no girls allowed. I have my reasons for wanting to work alone, none I'm willing or interested in sharing with her, and explaining fraternity and sorority dynamics to her isn't my job. She can pick up a campus brochure and read all about it. She pushes the paper she was writing on towards me, and says, "I started the first equation."

Does she not understand I'm saying no? Out of a morbid sense of curiosity, I look down to see how badly she butchered the problem. "You understand the lesson?" I look back up and wait for her answer. You can tell a lot about a person's intentions by looking at their face and blocking out their words. Her features transform from an impenetrable fortress to a look of understanding.

"Of course. Um, I can explain it to you. I know probabilities can be hard in the beginning."

I dismiss her offer to help. "I don't need an explanation. I can do the work."

"Oh yeah? Prove it."

I don't need to prove anything to her or anyone else, but I like solving complex problems, so I pull out my pencil and work the next equation with her, watching over my shoulder the whole time, waiting for her to say something about my weird brain, and how I'm not doing it right, since I'm working the problem backwards. But she doesn't. She just watches.

When I sit my pencil down, she's staring at me with this weird look on her face. "You worked it out in your head?"

I press my molars together. Here it comes. She'll ask me to do her classwork or homework in exchange for being her boyfriend. I fell for that scheme when I was in high school. It took me a minute to realize the dating part of the agreement wasn't real.

Theona's just like the other girls. She'll use me until she gets an A, and I won't get any boyfriend perks. This is why I don't talk to the girls around here. What did Finn say? Someone slept their way into a legacy dorm? Sounds about right. I sit back in my chair, waiting for her pitch.

She's studying the paper and catches me completely off guard when she says, "That was awesome," before pulling the workbook back towards her. I watch as she tries to work the next problem in her head the way I did. She makes it through the first half of the equation before she uses her paper and calculator again.

When she finishes, she pushes the book back over so I can do the next one. A light breeze of air drifts over my hand when she asks, "How long did it take for you to learn to do that?"

It sounds like a genuine question, so I answer it. "I was doing algebra at seven or eight."

"And you didn't test out of this math?"

"My dad thinks it's important that I actually attend classes." Shit, why did I tell her that?

"Fuck that. If *I* was a math genius, I'd be up there teaching, and not back here learning shit I already know."

My neck feels itchy so I reach up to scratch it. "Um. I'm not a math genius."

She snorts and says, "I bet that's what all math geniuses say. Hey..." She puts her hand on my arm. My gaze snaps to hers. "No hogging the workbook. It's my turn."

My eyes drop to where we're touching. Not a fake touch. She has a real solid hold on me. But it's her words that affect me. She wants me to let her do her own work. I set the book between us and stifle a groan when she starts talking to herself while working through the next problem.

This is why people think I'm weird. Because I love math, science, and all things learning related, and she's right. I *am* a math genius. Or rather, I have genius level intellect. But the requirement to be able to survive, and make alliances in our world means I have to play the part of a normal college student. I have to *socialize.*

"Agh. Tricky bastard. You're not gonna stump me."

I watch her as she works the problem. Her head's tilted forward, her leg bouncing under the table, and then she giggles. She's having fun. I see all that, and my dick does something it hasn't done in class since I was in tenth grade. It gets hard for no goddamn reason.

Time passes quickly, and before I know it, the instructor is dismissing us. Theona slides my workbook back toward me with a dejected sigh. "I thought we'd get them all done before the end of class, but that final problem was playing hard to get."

I nod, even though I'm only half paying attention.

"Thanks for letting me borrow your workbook." She says, as she climbs to her feet. I'm still sitting, watching as she hurries out of the room.

Finn stops at my desk to wait for me. "You okay?" I hear the concern and anger in his voice. He knows what I've gone through with girls and classwork.

"We had to partner up." I don't know why I said that. He knows this. He's in the class, but I didn't check to see if he was doing the work too.

"Shit. I'm sorry, man."

I climb to my feet and grab my stuff, walking away from him on autopilot. He's sorry, but there's nothing to be sorry about. It's not his fault the teacher made it a joint assignment. Our friends are already at The Circle when we arrive.

"What took you so long?" Pax asks as we get closer. He takes one look at my face and knows something's off. Nobody else would be able to tell, but Pax knows me, he knows my tells. "What happened?"

I'm still trying to work that answer out for myself. I tell him, "Theona sat next to me in class."

"What?" He bellows loud enough to draw attention.

Finn knows how to mute or hide his anger behind a jovial smile and flirtation. It's what makes him so dangerous. He pulls you in, then eviscerates you. But Pax is a bomb detonating in the middle of a crowd without remorse.

I motion my head towards the edge of The Circle to put some space between us and the people listening to our conversation before explaining what happened. "We had to team up on a class assignment."

"I'll take care of it." He pulls out his phone. "The professors know the only people you're supposed to get paired with are members of the fraternity."

Finn chimes in, "I'll be sure to give the teacher a personal reminder next class, and use the new neighbor as a visual aide."

I know they're saying these things trying to help, but I don't need it. I never need it. They've just gotten into the habit of speaking for me, since I choose to keep to myself. As volatile as Pax is, he's still the safer choice when it comes to dealing with these types of issues. Finn's reminders get bloody and mine get illegal. But in this case, the outrage is uncalled for. I don't care that we had to work together. She didn't do anything out of line except... "She made my dick hard."

That stops Finn's tirade. He turns to stare at me, mouth gaping open. I've made him speechless. Can't remember the last time that happened. Pax, however, still has control of his tongue. "What did you just say?"

I look over at him and repeat, "She called me a math genius and made my dick hard."

"What she did was try to manipulate you into doing her work." Pax turns to Finn. "Didn't you go to class today? How did you let this happen?"

The accusation gets Finn's mouth moving again. "First of all, I was on the other side of the room soaking up some rays and the teacher didn't announce a group assignment until after our neighbor had already taken the seat beside him. Second of all, I don't see what the problem is. She made his pecker woody. If it's still standing at attention and he needs to blow, he can go back to the dorm and rub one out before his next class. Or do you want me to hold his hand while he does it?"

This is a new development, but Finn's right, I don't see the problem either. It's not like she actually asked me to do anything. "I'm fine Pax, she never even asked me to do her work, and Finn, I'm not rubbing one out before my class."

"I would, and if you needed me there for support or whatever, I'd supervise."

That's Finn, in a nutshell. No shame, no remorse, with impulse control issues. He would totally rub one out and wouldn't necessarily go to the dorm to do it. "I'll take a raincheck for making you feel inadequate."

He shrugs, unbothered by my inference that my dick is bigger than his.

"You're sure you're okay?" Pax asks, bringing my attention back to what he's really upset about. Finn has impulse control issues, but I guess I do too. Only, when I need a pick me up, I usually hack into something I'm not supposed to, find dirt on someone, and leak it to the masses. The last time I did that, I got dangerously close to outing someone in witness protection. I wasn't even sneaky about it. The feds questioned me and threatened me with jail time. Thanks to some calls being made, to an FBI bigwig who's a league member, and a little keyboard stroking to help him access a server he couldn't get a warrant for, I dodged a bullet. Barely.

I don't want to put the guys through that again, so I assure them both, "I'm totally in control."

Chapter 15
Thea

I study my face in the mirror, swiping on some mascara and making sure I don't have creases in my eye shadow. The smoky liner and shadow really make my eyes pop, without clashing with my hair. The plan was to stay in and get some studying done, but LJ's been begging me to go to this party, and Sasha convinced me I could use some fun. She had a point. I mean, free booze. Why pass that up, am I right?

LJ's sitting on her bed watching me get ready. "Are you sure you don't wanna wear something... dressier?"

I take in her outfit. She definitely looks amazing in her short sequined dress and glittery heels, but I'd never be comfortable at an outside party wearing something like that. I need to be in my jeans and boots in case something pops off. That might not be a problem here, but old habits and all. "Nah, I'm good with what I'm wearing. You said it's in the woods, right?"

"Just behind the athletic stadium."

I slide some coral pink lipstick on my lips and give one last look at my outfit. "Okay, can't get any better than this," I say, meeting her gaze in the mirror. "You ready, LJ?"

She's nods and climbs to her feet. It took a few days, but she's finally gotten used to her nickname. We ride the elevator down to the first floor of her dorm and step outside, heading towards the back end of campus.

We fall in with a group of students walking towards the sports stadium, and I marvel at LJ's ability to navigate the uneven terrain in those heels. We walk for about ten minutes after we hit the trees behind the building, then come to an area someone has cleared out. There's a fire pit set up, a drink table, and a sound system. There are people already here, but by my calculation, we're still on the early end of the arrival spectrum. That's fine by me. It means we can scope out a good spot to sit. LJ's heels are killer, but her feet will be trash if she has to stand on them all night.

I lead us over to the drink table and peruse the selection. "What you in the mood for, LJ?"

She eyes the drinks and says, "Whatever you're having is fine."

What I'm having is a jolly rancher, since they have all the ingredients to make one. I want to be nice, not drunk, so I mix my drink with a little extra splash of the cranberry juice, then do the same for her. I pass her the cup and watch as she takes a sip. The grimace on her face says it all.

"LJ, is this your first time drinking?"

"It's my first time everything-ing." She says with a flourish of her hand. "I've never even been to one of these things."

"Then why are we here?" This was her idea to come.

"Because I want to be the girl that comes to these things, it's just..."

"Just what?"

"I don't fit in with the girls I went to school with."

I give a pointed look at her outfit. "Trust me. You fit in."

She tugs at the hem of her dress. "These are just clothes. I'm talking about fitting in with, you know, normal high school and college stuff. Eloise and the girls she hangs with we were all friends in junior high at our all girls' school. Then we got to high school which was by the boy's campus and they bloomed and I didn't. "

"Again, not following, since I'm literally staring at your tits."

"It's about more than the physical changes, Thea. Eloise and the others they started doing *stuff*, and since I haven't, they stopped hanging with me."

Stuff? She's looks uncomfortable with the topic, and I'm starting to get a clearer picture. "LJ, are you saying they stopped being your friends because you're still a virgin?"

She looks around like she's afraid someone heard me. "Yeah. That. I guess you've done it with someone before?"

Scanning the crowd, I say, "Several someones." I refrain from telling her I'm looking for someone to do it with right now.

"Oh."

I grab her arm and pull her over to the log I've been keeping an eye on. More people are showing up and if we want the best seat, we need to claim it now. When we're settled, she asks, "Are you mad?"

"About what?"

"That I pretended to be cool and you're finding out I'm not?"

"LJ, what I think shouldn't matter. You are what you feel. So if you feel cool, you are cool. But no, I'm not mad that you don't have party experience, or haven't done whatever ridiculous thing you think you're supposed to have done already. You're no different from anyone else. It doesn't matter where we come from or how much money a person has. We're all faking who we are until we figure out who we're not."

She's staring at her lap when she asks, "Does that include you?"

If she only knew the life I came from. "Especially me. College is the perfect time to reinvent yourself. To try new things, to fail horribly, and then try again. I think that's part of the fun."

She still has a pensive look on her face. "Look, I don't care if you've never had sex before. I'm not the president or owner of a sex club and I don't select my friends based on swapping fuck stories. So don't give too much energy to that, okay?"

"Okay." She gulps her drink this time and coughs and grimaces at the taste.

I laugh, patting her on the back. "What I do care about is you learning how to take a proper drink. We'll work on that."

Pax

The first bash of the school year is in full swing by the time we arrive. I'm pleased with the turnout. There are a lot of people here, but the night is still young, and I expect a lot more to show up. Namely, people from the other fraternities and their sister sororities.

Everything is a competition. Those other organizations will want to see what we're doing and hope they can do it better. They can't. Tonight's party is just us getting warmed up. The appetizer of things to come.

Most of the guests are on one side of the fire pit, closest to the drink table. It's also closest to the line of trees they used to get here. The guys and I used a different path. One that emerges from an underground tunnel, deep in the woods. Sometimes, like now, we come from that entrance just to watch what's happening when we're not around. It's how we found out the two members we lost over the summer were working for a rival fraternity.

I don't know how they thought things would turn out, or why they even thought they could defect from Rho Beta Psi and be promoted to a leadership position in the other house, taking our secrets and followers with them.

It was a stupid plan. One that failed miserably and now they don't have a frat to belong to at all. The one they were working for knew we'd never stop attacking them if they let them join. Nobody wants our full focus on them. We're easier to deal with when we spread mayhem to all the frats on campus. The sororities have their own rivalries going on. So those two idiots are now strays. Belonging to no one, and nothing.

Finn, Holden, and I make our way across the dirt towards the place where we always sit, speaking to people we know. I look to the left side of the fire pit, and my steps grind to a halt. "You've got to be kidding me."

Finn comes to stand beside me, a curse tumbling from his lips. Holden is quiet, but I can tell he's assessing the scene, trying to figure out why there are people sitting in our spot. Two people. A girl whose name I don't remember and our new neighbor. The bitch from the hallway. *Theona LaReaux.* She might be new here, but her friend isn't. She sees us glaring at them and taps Theona on the shoulder, trying to get her attention.

Is she really this clueless? Anybody with working eyes can see the other guests are avoiding this area. When her friend taps her again, and says, "I think we should move," Theona finally looks our way, only to dismiss us.

Finn steps forward first, all smiles and good intentions. "Hey there, Pet."

"Hey there, asshole."

He takes that in stride. Name calling never bothers him. "Your friend is correct. You've come too far past the boundary and need to head back over to the other side of the fire." He explains, ever the diplomat.

"Why?"

Why? Because we fucking said so. It's a good thing I'm not the one talking to her. Finn's better than me and takes the time to explain. "Because this area is reserved for legacies, which you are not."

"Thank god, for that." She snorts. "My life hasn't been perfect, but if being pissed off all the time and only being allowed to sit in one place is what it's about, *not* being a *legacy* sounds like a blessing to me." Her voice drips with condescension, like she's too good to be a legacy, and we should be happy to be in her presence.

Being nice isn't going to work with her, and we're drawing an audience. I can't let people see her trying to talk back to us *again*. I edge Finn out of the way and stand over her. "Get. The. Fuck. Up."

Her friend says in a hushed tone, "Thea, we should go. I don't want any trouble."

She ignores the warning and says, "I don't want any trouble, either. I just wanna finish my drink while you rest your feet before we get out there and dance. I didn't ask for them to come over here, and if they think standing like a brooding little boy band is gonna turn me into a crying little mouse, they've got the wrong girl. In fact, I wish they hadn't come over here at all, because they're messing with my vibe."

She's not far off about that. We are used to a certain type of girl. The type that falls to their knees to get our attention. Her sitting here, broadcasting to everyone that she's not intimidated or interested in us, is definitely sending the wrong signals to the people standing around.

I watch as she crosses her ankles and sips her drink like she's on a beach in Maui. Holden's hand on my shoulder stops me from hauling her to her feet and pushing her through the fire.

"Really, Thea. I'm done with my drink now so we can go dance."

With an exaggerated sigh, she stands and helps her friend to her feet. Then smooths out her shirt, dusts off her ass and says, "Fine, but only because they're playing my song."

They don't go far. They're right on the edge of the crowd, twirling and spinning. When the bitch catches sight of us watching, she tosses her hair over her shoulders, swirls her hips, and flips us off. Someone should break those fingers since she doesn't have any better uses for them.

"Is it me, or did it seem like she wasn't flattered by my attention?"

Finn asks as the other legacies take up position on the logs and canvas folding chairs behind us.

Glaring at her over the fire, I say, "She might not have wanted it. But now, she's going to get it."

"We're gonna do more than watch her?" Holden asks.

"That's right. We're gonna teach her, her place and what it means to find yourself on a legacy heir's bad side."

It'll take some time to come up with the perfect punishment for the bitch in suite C. Luckily, I've got nothing but time on my hands. The assignment to watch her will actually come in handy. It'll give me the data I need to shut her up for good, and it'll send a message to anyone who thinks backtalk and disrespect of a Trium will *ever* be tolerated.

Chapter 16
Pax

Most people look forward to their lunch and dinner hour to decompress, but coming to the dining hall makes me feel like I'm on display. It doesn't help that the table we sit at is in a roped off corner of the room with pretentious clubs led by some of the biggest asshats enrolled here.

It's one thing to sit as a group because you want to, and another to sit with the same people every day because you *have* to. I like my frat brothers well enough. We get along and have a decent time. I can tolerate the legacy heirs. We've been thrust together at various functions and events over the year and we're all just carving out our spot in the world. It's the other shit that gets on my nerves.

For instance, the Future Wives Club. Don't ask me who came up with that ridiculous title. It sounds a lot like the *First Wives Club* and believe me, it's close to being true. There are a lot of first and second marriages in our world.

The men marry young and trade their brides in for younger models when crows feet develop, and women toss their husbands to the side because they don't learn to not get caught with their dick's in their secretaries' mouths until they hit their forties.

Either way, there is a very real segment of the female population at this school who are all focused on snagging a husband. There are two tables set aside just for them.

I don't know what the joining criteria is, aside from having fucked a legacy, but I do know it's supposed to be exclusive, so not just any used pussy can sit there. I think Finn mentioned there was a point system. Double points if you've fucked a Trium.

It's a new school year and the tables are relatively empty. Until just now, it didn't even occur to me that a lot of the girls who sat there last year were seniors. That explains the number of save the dates I got in the mail over the summer.

For some, marrying up is wishful thinking and for others, it's not *if* it'll happen, but *when*. For the last two years, the head of this little group of future divorcèes has been Eloise Faulkner. She's one person who knows her union to a Trium is a sure thing.

Her father has been in negotiations about her marriage to Finn since we were twelve. There are some names in the hat for me, as well. Holden is the only one out of our trio whose family is having trouble finding him potential matches. It says a lot when the guy with a knife fetish gets a bride before the genius, doesn't it? But it's all about status and appearance, and people mistakenly think Holden's social skills are lacking. He doesn't project the right amount of showmanship, the charisma, the schmoozing, the *bullshitting*, Finn and I do. He's too methodical and analytical for all that.

The League has already decided he'll be one of the players behind the scenes because he's ineffectual at networking and won't be able to make deals and alliances that benefit the society. Holden doesn't care. He's perfectly happy to sit behind a desk and send emails, or smash some heads in if required.

He's not off the hook, though. Eventually, a bride will be chosen for him. One the high council approves of. None of us waste our time thinking about a love match. We know the true purpose of a marriage is to create a legitimate heir. That works out fine for me. I push aside all thoughts of loveless marriages and babies. I'm twenty-one and the average age of marriage in my family is thirty. Who they pick for me to settle down with is a worry for another day.

I drag my attention back to what's happening at my table. My seat gives me a view of the front and side entrances to the cafeteria, and it's far enough away from Finn and Eloise, who's sitting over here today. She's sitting so close to him she's practically in his lap. I scan the room for the girl he's been hooking up with since the Fourth of July. She's on the other side of the room looking like her entire world is going to shit. Ah, that explains it. Playtime with his latest fling has ended. He's probably using Eloise to send the message.

I don't know why the discarded Trium tramp looks upset or surprised. This is what Finn does. One minute he and Eloise hate each other and he's off fucking other people. Then, they get back together. They're like the poster children for dysfunctional dating habits. He says he'll have the rest of his life with Eloise, so there's no reason to limit his options now. Makes total fucking sense if you ask me. And if my dad settles on someone before I'm done with school, I might start fucking around more than I already am, too.

My gaze drifts over to Holden. He looks up from his book as if he can sense me watching him. Before he can ask what I'm thinking, something near the door draws his attention, causing him to stare. I turn to see what he's looking at. *Her.*

She's sitting alone, acting like she's oblivious to everyone and everything that's going on around her. No. That's not the right word. She's bored. Disinterested in what's happening. Like she's better than it all.

It's been three weeks since school started. Anyone else would have made more than one friend by now, but not her. The only person I ever see her with is the girl from the party. Everyone else is avoiding her. I'm sure it has something to do with our altercation.

We haven't said anything yet, but the student body knows her mouthing off has painted a target on her back. It's just a matter of time before we start lobbing arrows at her. I turn back around to see

Cruel Legacy

Holden was watching me the same way I was watching him. He asks, "What's that look about?"

"Just brainstorming ideas for what to do about our new neighbor."

Chapter 17
Holden

I slip into my seat in statistics while opening another file on my tablet. I'd rather be reading a book right now, but sorting through these records is more important. Now that we know who our neighbor is, we need to find out everything we can about her.

We're all suspicious of new people and Pax always thinks people are playing an angle. Most of the time, he's right. The dorm situation is probably a mix up. There's a code input each year to show the fourth room as unavailable, but this wouldn't be the first time they accidentally assigned someone to it because of a computer glitch. The school usually catches their error before they issue a key.

Pax's father knew Theona was moving in before the night of the prank, so that's what I'm focusing my energy on. If he knew, then someone else must've too. I'm trying to find out who she's been in contact with and who would have told her to drive through the south side of town that night.

If she were quiet, and blending in, we would probably just overlook both instances, but every time we see her, she's giving us shit. Nobody talks back to us the way she does. If someone were trying to distract The Trium, or knock us off our game, these insidious little moves would be the perfect way to do it. I hypothesize it's one of the other frats.

I'm on research duty. Pax is busy plotting her demise, and Finn can't quit talking about wanting to bite her ass. It's a nice ass, and the only reason I know that is because I'm paying attention to her in a way I haven't looked at girls in a really long time.

I can see her as more than a set of organs and limbs inhaling oxygen and dispelling toxins. I want to dissect her eye color, evaluate the width of the cupid's bow on her lips, measure the size of the two tiny freckles under her left eye. But I have to ignore my curiosity about her, because nothing and no one comes before my brotherhood.

I rub the small scar on my palm. I've sworn loyalty above all else to Pax and Finn, and it's an oath I intend to keep.

Finn decided he's sleeping in today, so for the next ten minutes, I have the class to myself. I like to read the intro to the lesson or review my notes in peace before the other students show up. Some would say I don't need to prep, since I have perfect recall, but the process is comforting and keeps my mind from wandering onto things it shouldn't.

The door squeaks open and *Thea* walks in, a disposable coffee cup in her hand.

The class is empty. There are plenty of seats for her to take, but she sits down next to me. I watch her arrange her workbook on her desk, so she's not here to ask to share mine again.

At the party, never once did I jump in and tell Pax to back off. There's no way she can think I'm an ally or that I want her anywhere near me. Even if I sort of do.

I can smell that she's drinking a dark roast from the cafeteria. She's sipping on the watered-down version of caffeine like it's the nectar of the gods. I like coffee, but I make mine in my dorm room. No way in hell I'm drinking that pre-ground crap.

She doesn't speak. She just slips her earphones in and opens her workbook and laptop. It looks like she's reviewing the material, just like I am. I don't have much experience with seeing other people actually study.

I'm not talking about a cram session in the library the night before a big test or paper is due. I mean methodical studying and taking notes to make sure they understand *and* retain the information long after the test is over. The kids we went to private school with didn't study. They didn't need to when their parents could pay to have their transcripts show whatever grades they wanted.

I'm hunched over my side of the table, trying to maintain a bubble of space between us. I startle, sitting upright in my chair when her leg bumps against mine.

Intellectually, I know touching is natural. That it happens when you're standing or sitting too close to someone, but I'm used to people going out of their way to avoid touching me, as if intelligence is contagious. They could be so lucky.

"Sorry." She mutters, snatching her leg away as if she's been burned. The look on her face isn't horror, like I've got a communicable skin disease. It's unease. I guess her friend explained what happens when you cross a legacy. Good. Maybe she'll survive this school after all.

The other students trickle in, and she shifts her bag and body further away from the aisle. The move causes her arm to brush against mine. My skin feels warm where she touched me. She's closer now and I catch a whiff of her scent. Are girls supposed to smell like warm apple pie if they're not eating it?

My left hand twitches. I suddenly find myself fighting the urge to grab her hair and shove her face into the desk just to put some space between us.

If Finn were here, he'd be smooth and charming to get her to move. I don't have the patience for it, but I need her *gone.* "Why are you sitting here?"

My voice is gritty, like I haven't used it in a long time. She tilts her head to look at me, but doesn't answer. "There are plenty of other seats in the classroom. I suggest you move to one of those."

Her eyes flick to my lap before she drags them back up my body. "This seat seems like the best in the house. If you don't like sharing, you can move."

"I was here first."

"And I'm here now." She turns back toward the front of the class. "Now, zip it, pretty boy. I'm trying to hear the lecture."

My mouth opens. I'm forced to close it when no sound comes out. She wants to hear the teacher and did she just call me, *pretty boy*? I know I'm attractive. My face is well proportioned. I've got these exotic grey eyes and big muscles.

Objectively, I'm what many women call hot, but they don't say it to my face. Not anymore. They reserve all those niceties for Pax and Finn, who respond appropriately and reciprocate in kind. My resting fuck off face scares them away.

I settle back into my seat and try to focus on the lecture as well. It's hard to do with her sitting beside me, scribbling notes and nodding and highlighting stuff in her e-textbook on her laptop.

She's enthralled with what Professor Roberts is saying and when I glance over at her work, I can tell she truly understands it. This time, I'm hit with an overwhelming urge to bend her over the desk and listen to her recite the orders of operation for the Pythagorean Theorem as I rut her from behind.

She smirks at me when she catches me staring. Like I've somehow played right into her hands. As soon as class ends, I bolt out the door to find Pax and give him an update on my theory about Thea.

I wasn't sure this morning when she first sat down next to me, but I am now. Something's off about her and when we find out what she's up to, it'll make whatever punishment we come up with that much sweeter.

You never start a game with the Trium that you can't win. Spoiler alert. We *always* win.

Chapter 18
Finn

Holden's on edge. I don't think I've seen him this distraught since Stephen Hawking passed away. But here he is, keyed up to a hundred, because of my new little pet.

From what I gather, she sat next to him again and did her own work. Controversial, right? I guess for him it is, because there's a history of people trying to get him to do their work for them. I ask for his help from time to time, but only after I've missed about a week of classes. If I'm actually in attendance, I can do my own work.

I'm also not carting around an awesome rack and a bite-able ass, which is why I think he's really freaking the fuck out. Oh, and because the girl he's got a boner for is also the girl who almost turned me into road kill, but I'm willing to forgive and forget all that frogger shit.

Thea's a lousy driver but a great movie companion. I close my eyes, remembering the taste of salt on her fingers, and how excited she was watching the movie.

I have a feeling she's an action junky like me. If she is, I'm sure she'd be really sorry if she knew she nearly ran me over and interrupted my landing. She'd be all apologetic and offering to let me play with her tits while pumping my dick in and out of her cunt to make it all better.

"Are you listening, Finn?" Pax is staring at me, disapproval written all over his face.

"Yes, kill, maim, destroy. Turn her into a blubbering mess. Got it." Or at least I think I've got it. These types of things always end the same way. *Us* standing over someone and *them* realizing they can never show their face in public without reliving the humiliation again. We usually let the women handle the women, but my pet is getting special treatment. Not the kind of specialization I think we should give her, but Pax is taking the lead on this, and since it's tied up with the job... oops sorry... *favor,* we're doing for his dad, we're letting him do this his way. I just hope his way leaves room for improvising.

Does she like heights? If so, I can take her to my favorite cliff and push her off, then dive in after her. She'd be so scared, she'd cling to me and spill all her secrets. Then we could have hot sex under the cool waterfall. Or sneak into the pool one night and fuck hanging off the end of the diving board.

Holden and I have this theory about sex, fear, and adrenaline. I'm thinking twenty feet above the pool is a safe way to test out how hard girls come when suspended over the edge of a cliff. Tuning back into the planning strategy, I ask, "So, what's my role here?"

Pax answers, without looking constipated, so I know I haven't missed that part of the plan yet. "Right now, we're just on recon. Holden's doing the digital searches, but I think we should also follow her around and find something we can use against her."

Righto. Stalk her. Got it. "And what about your dad?"

"We feed him information just like he wants us to, but we'll keep our little plan to make her life painful to ourselves."

Holden sends us all a copy of her schedule. We both have a free block of time today, before our last class. Perfect. I'm always up for practicing my ninja skills.

Thea doesn't do much on the break. In fact, she doesn't do anything at all. She sits outside for a while, talking on her phone, then goes to the library where she checks out a bunch of books on parks and nature.

I'm bored out of my mind. This job would have been better for Holden. He's the sit in the library surrounded by dusty books guy. I'm the go to the bar or club guy. If you want fun, hit me up. You wanna be smart? Holden is the way to go, and if you just want to be ignored, Pax is a sure thing.

I have a paper due next week and I'm trying to take advantage of this library time to work on it, but I'm bored, and it's hard for me to concentrate on what I'm supposed to be doing.

One of the sophomores I met last week walks through the front door with a guy from the football team. His arm's around her, and she's staring up at him adoringly with those innocent doe eyes. He's strutting around like he's won the lottery. That can only mean one thing.

I pull out my phone and send her a text. Her gaze darts around as she tries to figure out where I am. I send her a clue and tell her she has three minutes to come find me, before moving to the alcove between the stacks.

It takes her two and a half minutes to track me down. She looks nervous. This alcove isn't all that hidden. Anyone coming up and down the stairs behind us will see us. Not my problem. If I'm gonna be stuck in the library, then I want to study how deep down someone's throat my cock can go.

"Hi." She blushes like just speaking was the hardest thing for her to do.

Awe, isn't she precious? "Hi."

"You said you needed my help?"

"I do chèris."

"Okay, what do you need help with?"

I trail my finger across her jaw and press my thumb against her lips. "My dick is dry and cold. I need you to warm it up for me."

I point to the floor, showing she should kneel.

"Um?"

"Don't overthink it, chèris. I'm a Trium. Sucking my cock will be the best thing you do all year. And if you're really good at it, I'll let you be my special friend and do it again tomorrow. Don't you wanna be my special friend?"

Of course she does, but she's trying to pretend she doesn't. I tip her chin up. "Damn, you're so beautiful. When I stopped you and your friends, it was because I noticed you."

She smiles, eating up my bullshit. "I know this seems sudden, but I felt this connection to you when we were talking. I thought you felt it too. You felt it, right?" I nod my head up and down, and she unconsciously does the same.

When they start mimicking your body language, you have them where you want them. I grasp her shoulder firmly, then caress her face again while I pull my dick out of my pants. "Chèris."

I don't even have to tell her what I want again. She attacks my cock, gagging as her untrained mouth tries to stuff me in. Her earlier hesitancy and coyness long forgotten. It's amazing what the power of suggestion can do. "That's right, you don't need to breathe. Just suck me down."

"Connie!"

She goes to pop off my dick when the guy she came in with yells her name. I can't have that. I look him in the eye and smooth my thumb across her cheek. She moans and goes back to taking me down.

"You fucking slut. I knew you were full of shit when you gave me that six date rule."

I understand why he's miffed. He's going home with dry balls and I'm about to flood her throat. In her defense, her six date rule probably wasn't bullshit, but I don't have time to be jumping through those kinds of hoops, so I used a little neurolinguistic programming to speed things up. Her friends are just as primed as she was. She just happened to be in the library when I needed an outlet.

"Don't worry. I'll be done in a minute, then you can have her back."

I empty my load, then tuck my dick back in my pants and move to another area of the library. My brain feels clearer now. I should be able to bang out a few thousand words before my time is up.

The rest of the hour passes with nothing to report. Whatever Thea was working on required a map. She sets the books to the side and shoves a map back in her bag, then exits the library.

I follow behind her as she heads towards her next class. She walks through the door and I send off a text letting the guys know where she is, before continuing to my class in the next building.

"Hey baby!"

I groan as I slip my phone into my pocket. I've been having such a good day. Nothing spectacular happened, but any day I'm not dealing with Eloise, my so-called fiancé, is a good one. There's no way for me to reroute, so I'm gonna have to deal with her and her friends for the next few minutes.

Looping her arm through mine, she says, "I was hoping to run into you before my next class."

"Oh yeah? Why's that?"

"Because, baby, I haven't seen you all day. I waited in the lounge this morning, but you must've left early."

She pushes her bottom lip out. Like her pouting is going to make me feel bad. It doesn't.

She's absolutely correct, though. I left early so I could avoid *this*. Her pawing at me and hanging onto me like we're a couple. This stupid arranged marriage bullshit has us paired together. Everyone knows it's happening, but we agreed to see other people until we have to settle down.

We don't have any claims on each other. I stick to my end of the bargain, and she does shit like this when she's between men. I heard someone say she's got her eye on a senior. Hopefully she'll wear him down soon and I'll have another few months of peace.

She's so close, I feel her tit pressing against my arm. I reach up with my other hand and drag my thumb over her nipple.

Despite how I feel about being told who to marry, Eloise's body is banging, and she's good in bed. But that's kinda the problem. She likes to limit shit to the bed. Hence the reason I'm looking for someone to help me with my aerial projects. I could body hack her, but then I'd have a different problem to deal with. It would be too far out of the parameters of her personality.

I use Neuro Linguistic Programming to give them a push. Make them more comfortable about doing something they already want to do, the same way a pretty poison shot would, without the chemical hangover.

With Eloise, it would be like an entire personality transplant. People would notice, then my secret would be out.

When I started studying NLP, it was because I wanted to learn more brain chemistry and lowering or controlling inhibitions without pharmaceutical interference. I guess it was a sort of self study, trying to understand why I am the way I am.

The more I read, the more intrigued I became, and I couldn't very well practice these techniques on myself, and I would never use it on my friends. That leaves everybody else. The only time I use it is when something needs to happen in an accelerated time frame.

"I had to make a run this morning."

"Oh, so you didn't spend the night out?" She tries to make the question sound all casual and shit since her little girl squad is listening in.

I've been too busy getting acclimated to being back on campus and preparing for this year's pledge season to find a new steady hook up. But that's none of her business. It'll never be any of her business unless I want it to be. "Is it your fucking place to ask me that?"

She chuckles, like I'm a comedian. I'm not. "Oh, come on, Finney. I'm just saying, if I would've known you were in the dorms last night, I would've come to you. You know I'd never leave my man wanting and unfulfilled."

Whoever her man is, she needs to go fuck off and be with him, because what I want is someone hanging upside down Houdini style while they blow me. Or is this innuendo filled conversation her way of saying she's decided to explore more? "You'd do anything to make me happy?"

"Of course, silly."

I grab her hand, pulling her away from her friends, and taking the path to the right. "Where are we going? Wagner Hall is that way."

I steer us towards Edgewick Manor, where the Dean lives. "Fuck class, let's spend these next two hours together."

"What are we doing here?" She looks around, afraid someone's gonna see us. I drag her behind me around to the back of the house.

The Dean's bitch ass son is a sore loser. I know he's the one who placed the anonymous tip about Pax's last race. We were on the strip for an hour being questioned by the cops. He thinks he's got big dick energy, hiding behind daddy's name, but I'm about to have my dick and cum all over his sheets.

With my hand still locked in hers, I march us right up to the back door. "Finn..." I glance over my shoulder, waiting for her to say whatever she has to say. "I'm not sure breaking into The Dean's house is a good idea."

I step closer, smiling to put her at ease. "I understand your nerves. Your first daytime B&E is a big deal." I pull her close, rubbing soothing circles on her back, and trailing kisses along the shell of her ear. Before grabbing her ass to pull her against my erection. She gasps, looking up at me with hooded eyes.

"Finn..."

I drag her hand to my groin. "You said you wanted to fulfill my every desire, right?" She nods, taking over, rubbing my cock. "My desire is to go in this house and rub my dick all over little Arnie's bed, while you eat my ass."

"Wh-What?"

I nod, letting it sink in. Watching as she balks at the idea. "I don't."

"Don't what? Wanna break in, or don't wanna eat my ass?" It doesn't matter what answer she gives, my response is going to be the same.

"Baby, I just-"

I'm done with the false endearment. I'm not about to beg her to fuck me when she's the one who sought me out. "In or out, Eloise?"

We both know I've backed her into a corner, but she still tries to turn this around. "I wanna do this for you, Finney, but think about the consequences. You're a Trium. You'll get a slap on the wrist, but if I get caught doing this, I'll be punished. Think of how my family will react to the scandal."

A scandal sounds like fun. God, what I wouldn't give to fuck someone who's not so worried about appearances all the damn time. "You're right. I should never have asked you to do this with me."

She smiles like she's just won something. "I'll just find someone who really wants to do *anything* it takes to please me."

I hop the hedge and leave her standing there while I access the service tunnel next to the pool house, and use one of the Dean's golf carts to get me to class on time.

Chapter 19
Deacon

The drop deadline for class has come and gone. I'm down fourteen students, most of them girls, but the one I hoped would quit didn't.

Now I'm stuck watching her bend and stretch. Listening to her puff out air through the workouts, which sound a lot like pants and sighs, and pretending not to notice the way her sweat-soaked clothes cling to her body.

It's the worst kind of torture.

"Damn, she has a nice ass." The class is finishing up on a run, and the two guys from the basketball team were the first ones finished. They're standing behind me, watching everyone else complete their last few laps.

Thea came in fourth on the run, and is bending over, stretching out her calves. I should've continued with the lesson in the syllabus today, but I couldn't.

Yesterday was torture enough. I had to watch her partner put his hands on her lithe little body as I taught them the first set of wrestling moves.

It wasn't a complicated hold, but it takes work to learn the right foot and hand placements, which means when the opponents are mismatched in height, there's a lot of accidental touches to the wrong parts of the body.

A few of the female students have already asked for extra tutoring. I told them I'd be happy to arrange it. I watched as they walked off, chatting excitedly and casting flirty looks my way.

They're gonna be sorely disappointed when they realize tutoring for my class is peer tutoring, just like every other subject. If they want me to personally guide and train them, they have to pay and show up at my gym.

The last student crosses the finish line and I clock their time before blowing the whistle to signal the end of class. "Make sure you stretch out before leaving," I yell to the students already making a dash towards the locker rooms.

My head is down and I'm staring at the school issued tablet, reading the error message I'm getting trying to work in this new digitized grade book.

This Prospectus software program they insist we use integrates with student's email, financial records and social media platforms. It's a one stop shop for future employers and schools to see what a student did in and outside of class.

Grade inputs *could* wait until later, but I'm intentionally avoiding eye contact with the female students walking by. I ignore the pair of shoes that stop in front of me, waiting for them to walk away. She doesn't.

"Coach Wolfe."

"What?" I bite out. I hate that she's making me talk to her, because whenever I hear her voice, all I can think about is how it sounded when she was moaning in my ear.

"I heard some of the other students saying you have a gym and teach classes for mixed martial arts?"

"Yup." Clipped answers are the easiest way to run off co-eds. She should be walking away any second now.

"I was wondering if you're taking on new students?"

I have a few openings, but I don't give those out to just anyone. "My classes are intense and take discipline. It's not a beginner class and we don't pull punches. It takes heart, stamina, and you have to be fearless, even when a guy twice your weight and height is pounding the shit out of you. If your boyfriend sent you to ask me if he can sign up for classes, then I already know he's not a good fit."

"I'm asking for myself."

I grit my teeth. She didn't dispute the boyfriend comment. She lied when she said nobody was waiting for her. My classes are definitely not for women who pick me up in a bar and fail to disclose they're undergrad students at the school I teach at. "Liars aren't a good fit either."

"What the hell is that supposed to mean?"

My gaze snaps to hers. "This is college, LaReaux. If you lack basic comprehension skills, you shouldn't be here."

"And if you lack basic manners, you shouldn't be a teacher."

"I'm *not* a teacher. I'm a fitness trainer."

Her eyes are defiant little slits when she hisses, "You're dealing with students, so it's the same fucking difference. I asked a simple question, a *no* would suffice, instead of acting like you've got small dick syndrome."

One step is all it takes to close the distance between us. "You thinking of my dick is not the way a student thinks of a *teacher*, and I don't recall you complaining about the size when your drenched cunt was clenched around it."

"If you remember *that*, then you remember I can take a beating." Her eyes shine bright with her challenge.

My dick perks up because, yes, she took the pounding I gave her and something tells me she could have taken more. Her chest is heaving, her hands clenched at her sides, ready for a fight. Fuck, she looks hot like this. All stubborn and ready to go toe to toe with me. I'm one step away from pushing her behind the bleachers and testing those words.

She smirks up at me as if reading my thoughts. Shit. This is getting out of hand. I already have to deal with her in my class. There's no way I'd be able to maintain my professionalism if she's working out in my gym.

This little interaction we're having is testing my resolve more than a naked stripper on my lap ever could. I take a step back, regaining my composure. "Like I said, my class isn't a good fit for you."

"Understood, sir. Then can you recommend a gym and trainer that you think *would* be a good fit?"

I know some good gyms, with great trainers. I think about her asking them for extra sessions, and how those lessons would lead to extra touches and lingering looks.

I also know each of those guys would fuck her with no hesitation. They'd be more than happy to test every boundary and see how much of a pounding she can take in and out of the ring. *Fuck that.* She can learn martial arts from a YouTube channel.

"No!" I growl, turning my back on her and walking away.

When I get back to my office, I pull out the flask I keep in my bottom right desk drawer and take a drink. I can't believe I let her bait me like that, or that I'm having trouble separating my feelings about what happened between us from my job as her *teacher.*

God, I really hate that term, because I'm not a teacher. I don't teach. I train, coach and mentor. Teaching requires a soft touch which I don't have.

I churn out winners and fighting machines. I find weaknesses and push folks to the breaking point, grinding them down to dust, then build them up to be warriors. I don't have time to babysit and hand hold pampered prince and princesses, and I definitely don't give a damn about embarrassing them in front of their peers.

There is a separation between Deacon Wolfe, the coach, and Deacon Wolfe, the man. Thea LaReaux barely met the man, so I shouldn't be struggling with being her coach.

It has to be because I didn't fully release that night. My stress, not my load. Sex was the plan. Fucking in an alley wasn't. I thought maybe I'd go back to their place and have a few hours to work through my pre-semester routine.

I wanted to decompress from the shitty month I had before the start of school and thought I'd do that in some pussy.

Maybe I need to go out and pick up someone new. That way, she isn't the default setting in my brain for the last time I got my dick wet.

I take another drink and check the incoming text on my phone. I have a scouting session tonight. My plans to empty my mind and my load between someone else's legs will have to wait.

Chapter 20
Thea

I scowl at the car that barely tapped its brakes at the intersection. I was nowhere near the street, but I'm still pissed about it speeding through the light.

I'm also moodier and more irritable than usual. I knew this would happen. Sitting around doing nothing makes me antsy. I've always had way too much energy. Even as a kid. It was easier to control when I was outside playing. Or doing favors for cash.

I've got anger issues. I knew this about myself before any shrink ever pointed it out. *Hello,* mom was the town drunk and more times than I can count, she let her relationship drama and love affair with alcohol affect our home life. I had no home at all once the city got involved, so you're damn right I'm angry.

In the last three years, I've found some coping mechanisms that help and I've taken up hobbies that won't land me in jail. This week, I've been walking more and practicing meditation, but I'm still on edge. The best way to calm my urges would be in the sack or the ring.

I tried to do the responsible thing and ask Coach Wolfe about working out in his gym. He didn't give an explanation for why he said no, but I caught the subtext. Girls can't fight.

Or at least that's what I *thought* he was getting at until I looked up his gym and saw the pictures of him posing with various students. Some of them women. There are even pictures of him at some of the biggest fights in the country and ding-ding, you guessed it. He's hugged up with women fighters.

He obviously knows we're badasses in the ring, so why the hell was he so dismissive of me?

It's bullshit that Deacon Wolfe is the guy that could help me out in either of the ways that'll mellow me out, and won't, or can't.

I didn't ask about a second round of sex, and *wouldn't*, knowing he's my teacher. I'm sure that crosses a line. But even if I was willing to risk it, his body language and attitude clearly says he's not interested.

At first, I had convinced myself that he didn't remember me, but he definitely knows who I am. I can't believe he tried to throw our hookup in my face. So fuck him, *I'm* not interested.

I'm researching gyms in the area, since he couldn't even be bothered to recommend one. Until I find one, my next best course of action is to just keep moving.

Today's walk is through what the students call Canyon Falls proper. The university is in Canyon Falls Annex. I didn't get to see much the night I drove into town or when Aunt Moira took me shopping, so today I'm taking it all in.

The division of wealth hits me as soon as I pass the downtown area. The sleek office buildings, fancy hotels, and sky scrapers end and then there's just a traffic light, and an abandoned lot on an empty street.

I walk half a block down the empty street, which curves to the left, before another building comes into view. I stand in front of it, taking in the worn shingle and awning. It reminds me of one of those houses on Bourbon Street that you see all the time on television. The one's with clapboard shutters, where people stand on balconies watching parades go by.

The building next to it isn't much better. I walk to the end of the street and stop in front of the first building that looks halfway decent. It's hard to make out the sign, but I take a picture, because I'm curious to know what it used to be.

Across the street, on my right, there's a parking lot butted up against a building with a mural painted on it. I cut through the lot, then dart through the small alleyway until I reach the front of the building.

A laugh bubbles up out of me when I spot the beach. How did I not know that the town was actually below the street level where my aunt and uncle live? I squint, trying to make out houses on either end of the beach, but I'm too far away to see any.

"Hello, there." The greeting draws my attention back to the front of the building.

"I'm sorry," I say to the woman, decorating a chalkboard behind me. "I didn't realize I was blocking the entrance." I'm standing in front of a restaurant and there's a hotel right next door. There's a whole stretch of businesses on this cute little boardwalk, going as far down as I can see. I think I just found my new favorite place. Turning back to the woman, I ask, "Are you open?"

"Oh, yes! It's a little bit of a lull between the breakfast and lunch crowd, so it's mainly staff from here and the hotel next door eating, but it's gonna pick up soon. Come on in."

I follow her inside, taking in the sea scape decor, and salty breeze coming from the open windows. She settles me at a table where I still have a great view of the beach. As soon as she walks off, I pull out my phone to take a picture and send it to Sasha. She's gonna flip. We've always talked about going on vacation together some place where we can see a view like this.

"Here's a menu, hun."

"Thank you," I say, taking it from her hands and scanning the offered items.

"We're setting up for lunch, but you can still order off the break-fast menu if you'd like."

I'd been walking around for a while, and now that I'm sitting, I realize I'm famished. Everything sounds good and I'm having a hard time deciding.

"You wanna hear the specials?"

"Sure." Maybe hearing them will make it easier for me to choose.

"For breakfast, we can whip up a short stack smothered in chocolate syrup, strawberries and whipped cream, with a side of eggs to order, bacon and biscuits. If you want lunch, today's special is a turkey club and sweet potato fries, with a slice of our famous peach cobbler."

"Everything sounds good. I think I'll go with the turkey club, and can I get a lobster bisque soup, please?"

"Absolutely, that lobster bisque is my favorite. And how about I bring you the strawberries with chocolate syrup too, but I'll hold the pancakes?"

That sounds rich and decadent and perfect. I agree with her suggestion. A part of me really wanted those strawberries drizzled in syrup.

"Alright hun, my name's Mel. You just yell for me if you need anything."

She looks older than my Aunt Moira, but her sun kissed hair swings from a ponytail at the crown of her head, like it belongs to a perky cheerleader. I'm used to the waitresses in Nags Creek having attitude problems because they work long shifts for no money, and get stiffed on tips.

Mel seems genuinely happy. I guess I would be too, with this view. The door opens and a few more people come in. A girl with a maid's uniform, and an older couple.

Mel waves at them, and I watch as they seat themselves, with the older woman facing me. She's got salt and pepper hair and a kind face. Her companion says something, and she throws her head back and laughs. It's a loud, heavy, happy sound.

Her laughter dies off, and she catches me staring at her. *Shit.* For the most part, I mind my own business, but when I see older women,

I always try to figure out what their story is, and if they've had a good life.

I have no clue why I'm compelled to do it. Maybe it's because my only experience with women over the age of twenty-five is my mother, Mrs. Sprout, and the people in charge of the foster homes and group homes I've lived in.

Good is not how I would describe the lives they were living. Carefree laughter and fun were often missing. Living in Nags Creek was hard and stressful for a lot of people. I duck my head, and when I pick it up again, the woman is looking at me.

She offers a small smile before turning her attention back to her friend, and I go back to staring at the beach and its inhabitants until Mel comes over with my food.

I abandon my people watching in favor of stuffing my face. I pay for my food and leave Mel a generous tip before heading out to explore the rest of the boardwalk. I grab some saltwater taffy and a gelato, then find a spot on the beach where I can dip my toes in the water.

After I've rested with my toes getting wet long enough to prune, I crawl under the boardwalk to get out of the sun. Before I know it, I'm reclining back, listening to the crashing of the waves, then laying down on the warm sand, and finally I drift off to sleep.

Chapter 21
Thea

I pull the mail out of my box and unfold the paper that was sticking out of the side. It's a flyer, reminding students of the rules and responsibilities for Mayhem Night. I show it to LJ. "What's this Mayhem deal?"

She looks at the flyer, then pulls me towards the elevators. "So you know, how I told you last week was the start of pledge season?"

"Sure."

"Well, this... Mayhem Night is like the final bash."

"So, it's another party."

"Oh, no." She shakes her head hard enough to make her ponytail swing. "It's a campus wide shut down. There's an official changing of the guard. The week leading up to it, the fraternities and sororities battle it out in some kind of prank war. At the end of it, new leadership gets inducted and then it all culminates in Mayhem Night. The next day is when we find out who the new members are. The fraternities and societies will be doing the craziest shit to... well, I have no idea what they do, because nobody's ever gone deep enough into the woods to find out."

"Too afraid of the dark?"

"Too afraid of not coming back out, the same way you went in."

I laugh at her answer. "That sounds like something you hear when people are telling bullshit ghost stories."

Her eyes widen as she chews her thumb nail. "I guess, but my cousin said two years ago, this couple snuck out and followed a group from the Ironside to see what pranks they were pulling and came back all bruised and bloodied. The couple broke up, and the boyfriend left school, because of whatever happened."

"What do people think happened?"

"It depends on who you ask. Some people say it was a fight club type thing, others say he was tortured. Whatever it was, he never talked about it."

"And this girl? What happened to her?"

"She got shipped off to an institution in a catatonic state. I'm telling you, Thea, whatever happens on Mayhem Night is bad. So unless you're invited, you can't even leave the dorms."

"You're telling me the school just lets these clubs terrorize people and have run of the campus?"

"Yes, as long as it doesn't spill over to the admin buildings and destroy any property. The frat houses and sororities are all technically off of school grounds and the woods are like neutral zones. They can do whatever they want in those areas on Mayhem Night."

"And nobody tries to crash any of this?"

She hands the flyer back. "That's right. There are smaller events leading up to Mayhem Night. Anyone can attend those, but this last night, the only people participating are members, alumni, and special invites."

I crumple up the flyer and toss it into the trash on our way out of the building.

She turns to look where I threw it. "You didn't want to keep that? The other events were listed on the back of the paper."

"Nope, I'm good. I'll leave all these club activities to the social types. I prefer to just chill and do my own thing. Clubs and organized circle jerks aren't for me."

She's quiet and has what I call her thinking face on. That thinking face means she's trying to convince herself to say something that might be taken as controversial. For LJ, controversial is her disagreeing with anyone. She sucks at it, which is why I love to encourage her to do it.

"How do you feel about these clubs?"

"I think they could be fun. At least it looks like they have fun when pledge season is over, but I won't get invited to join, so it doesn't matter."

"You mentioned before that it was an application process."

"It is for most of them, but some are invite only."

"And let me guess the invite only ones are the best ones?"

"They are, and the only way to even get your name out there is to show up to as many events and mixers as you can before the application phase ends. I still wouldn't get picked, but it might be fun to see what happens, right?"

We've talked about this before. Her wanting to put herself out there more and I've agreed to go as her plus one, just until she makes more friends, or gets comfortable enough to go alone. "We can go to some of these things. Just tell me which one's interest you."

"Really?"

"Sure, and then we can do something I want to do."

"Absolutely."

I chuckle because she's so eager. It's cute and dangerous. "Lesson number two LJ," I say, pushing her ahead of me on the path, "Never agree to something, without knowing all the details."

I'm on my way back to the dorm, having just finished a quick after-dinner walk and my daily phone call with Sasha. I'm tucking my phone into my back pocket when I see one of the Coxsuckers over my shoulder.

He was outside the science building when I came out this afternoon and left the cafeteria at the same time I did at dinner. Now here he is on the path to my dorm. I try to think nothing of it, since this is a college campus and we all live here, but it still puts me on edge having people behind me for extended periods of time. I'm not sure if I'll ever learn to let my guard down on an empty street.

I hurry into the lobby of Vale Tower, finally able to breathe, and slip into the only elevator that goes all the way to the top floor. I enter my access code and wait for the doors to slide closed.

The reject band member, which one is he again? Finley something roman numeral? He gets in too, and moves to put the wall at his back, much like I'm doing across from him.

I shift my body to the left so I'm standing in the corner where the two walls meet. I hate blind spots and having any of my sides exposed. "Why are you following me?"

He looks up from his phone and tugs one of his earbuds out. "Excuse me?"

"You've been *behind* me for thirty minutes, and now you're in my dorm. Why are you following me?"

"I haven't been behind you." His gaze drops down to my feet, making a slow return to my face. "But we could definitely talk about that happening."

"I'm not imaging things. You've been following me all day. I'm gonna call security."

"Relax, Pet. No need to call the useless security force, unless you just feel like paying the fee for an unmerited call. I live here."

LJ mentioned that, but I thought she was mistaken. I've been here for almost three weeks, and I've never seen him before. Not that I think I've seen everyone who lives here, but he would stand out.

I take in his dark brown hair. The ends curling along his forehead, sweeping his brows, and those ice-blue eyes. I imagine he could restart the ice age with that stare. And then, of course, there's the part where he's a card-carrying member of the asshole coalition. Yup, I'd definitely remember seeing him here.

Maybe he spends his time in another dorm, with a hot young co-ed he's giving it to, and only comes here occasionally to pick up laundry and condom refills.

The car stops on the second floor. More people get on. It stops again on the third floor. There must be something happening in the dorm this evening, because they all get off on the fourth floor, leaving us alone in the elevator again.

He doesn't have on workout clothes or a bag of laundry in his hands. There are only three more floors he could live on. I close my eyes for a second, finding my peace. The keypad beeps.

I crack an eye open. "What are you doing? Stop pushing buttons before you get us stuck between floors."

"I'm putting the car in private mode to take us all the way to the top. Or do you prefer to stop on every floor?"

Okay, so first off I didn't *know* it had a private mode, and two... "That's stupid, since you need to get off on the sixth or seventh floor."

"What makes you think that's my destination?"

"Because there are no living spaces on the eighth and ninth floors. You don't have laundry with you and you're not dressed for the pool or gym."

He smiles, making my stomach flip. He's boyishly cute, but when he smiles, it's sexy and disarming. A combination of sweet and seductive. Devil and angel. His smile hints of a secret. The promise of *something*. I know what he's going to say before he even opens his mouth. "I don't do bottom or middle, Pet. I was born to be on top."

The elevator dings, depositing us on the tenth floor. The doors slide open, filling me with a sense of dread. I hurry toward my door, groaning on the inside every step of the way, praying we don't share a wall. Something tells me he's an obnoxious neighbor. Or maybe he's bullshitting me. Three weeks is a long time not to have seen him. Maybe he's visiting someone, and he's hijacked my code to get up here. What if it's a girl that ghosted him? Oh well, not my problem.

Still, I find myself asking, "If this is your floor, how come I've never seen you?"

"Because I was having some work done in my room and temporarily relocated. It's all finished, so I'm back home now."

He presses his key fob to the door of Suite B, which is directly across from mine, and flings it open. "You can come over and try out my new toys, if you want."

"What, like your GI Joe and race track? I'll pass."

"I put away kid toys when I learned there are adult games that are much more interesting."

"I definitely don't wanna see your sex toys."

He gives me that stomach flipping smile again. He really needs to stop doing that. "I never said what kind of toys, but it's interesting *that's* what you're conjuring up when you think of me."

"I don't think of you."

"No?" He pouts. "That's hurtful, Pet. "Now I rescind my offer to let you hang out with us."

I never heard an offer, and who is us? As if summoned from the depths of hell, the doors to the elevator slide open again, and I watch the other two stroll towards us.

"What's going on here?" Pax asks, glowering at me.

I straighten to my full height and scowl right back. Finn pretends not to hear the animosity in his buddy's voice and says with a cheerful grin. "Just saying hello to our neighbor."

Our? No, no, *no!* This can't be happening. But it is... I watch Pax walk over to the door next to Finn's. A is definitely for asshole, and Holden is standing in front of Suite D, which is the one next to mine. "All of you live on this floor?"

"That's right," Finn says with a wicked gleam in his eyes. "We can't wait to welcome you to the neighborhood, properly."

I swipe my key and thrust my door open, slamming it closed behind me. I lean against it, trying to catch my breath. There are only four rooms up here.

How did I wind up being the only girl crowded in on all sides by *them?* Some would call it a blessing. I think it's a curse. I'm not averse to being the only woman on a male dominated floor. I just don't want to be neighbors with them, because I foresee bloodshed in our future. I wonder what the process is for changing rooms.

I cross my living room to the sliding glass doors. I love my balcony. It overlooks the back of campus, where there's nothing but trees as far as I can see. I love being able to sit out here and just enjoy the fresh air and sunset. It helps me relax.

I step outside and inhale deeply, letting the stress and the revelation that I'm boxed in by those jerks melt away. I can handle it. They stay away from me, I'll stay away from them. Easy.

The soft swish of a door draws my attention to my left. Finn steps out and slides into the hammock he has hanging across the balcony. He's shirtless, wearing board shorts and rocking a pair of sunglasses.

His thumb flies across the screen of his phone. Seconds later, death metal comes blaring out of some unknown location, ruining my tranquility.

I scowl at him as I climb to my feet. I'm pretty sure he knew I was out here. I go back inside and pray I don't have to deal with Holden blasting music through the walls. I liked being up here with limited access and no nosy, giggly neighbors.

In the span of fifteen minutes, they've ruined it for me. I go to my bedroom and close the door, dragging a pillow over my head to muffle the noise I can still hear from the balcony.

Fucking Coxsuckers!

Chapter 22
Holden

I keep to the trees and remain quiet while I watch. The first time I found her here, I could hear her laughter before I reached the end of the trail. I stomped through the brush, intent on running the trespassers off.

Then I saw who it was, and what she was doing. Our neighbor, the girl with the serious attitude problem, the one who makes my dick take notice, was skinny dipping in *my* lake.

No one hikes this deep into the woods unless there's a party or a paint ball game going on, and nobody takes that path because it looks impassable. I even dragged extra tree branches and sticks over to cover the ground and planted shrubs just to make it look like an over-grown jungle. You have to actually go deeper into the woods, on the left -where there's no trail at all- to find a clearer entrance. Yet somehow she's found my oasis and claimed it as her own.

I've come out here twice since the first time I saw her. She was swimming naked each time. I've learned to stay quiet so she won't see me, and I watch. She seems to love nature just as much as I do. That's hard to find around here.

She dips down into the water, swimming a few yards before

surfacing again. From here, it's hard to see the water droplets on her skin, but I imagine they're clinging to the pointed tips of her dusky nipples. She stretches, arching her back, her tits pointing towards the sky. Rotating her neck, she grabs her hair, pulling it over her shoulder to press the water from it. I quietly make my way over to another tree to get a closer look.

I love that she's totally comfortable with her nudity. She's finishing up her swim so she'll be leaving soon. Once she starts getting dressed, I'll hide deeper in the woods until she goes.

If this were anyone else, I'd erect a security gate to prevent them from coming here, destroying the ecosystem. Thea's very careful about where she steps and doesn't move anything from where I have it set up.

She climbs out of the water and walks towards the log where she dropped her stuff. She's much closer now. I can see the dark patch of hair between her toned legs.

My mouth waters as she bends over to pick up her shirt. It's been a long time since I've watched anyone like this. Most of the time it's for a prank, or to do a job for someone. It's never for me. Never for fun. Even now, I'm supposed to be documenting what she does so we can report back to Malcolm.

Does he really need to know she swims naked and that sometimes she flicks her tongue against her own nipples and fingers her pussy on the rock in the middle of the stream? I'm certainly not taking pictures of it.

It's mandatory that we follow orders and I'll report she went for a hike through the woods behind campus. But maybe *this* could be my reward for all the shit I put up with. This could be my secret, just for a little while. I'll tell Pax and Finn eventually, but just for an escape from all the things I have to do, this can be just mine.

She's putting her jeans on, so I drag myself away, waiting for her to continue her hike. It's hard to focus when my cock is hard and throbbing in my pants, begging for relief.

Trailing Thea has it on high alert. I'll take care of it when I get back to the dorms. I wonder what she'd do if she knew I was following her. Stalking her like the prey she is. Would she hold her ground and order me to stay away? Call me degenerate, like I've heard whispered so many times before? Or simper in fright and run?

Confronting me would be the safer option, because the thrill of the chase... I'd catch her and the things I'd do to her would leave her broken at my feet. Finn's in your face with the way he tests your boundaries. Pax leads with his temper. But I'm quiet. Reserved. Always fighting for control.

This woman tempts me in ways she doesn't even know. I've been mesmerized watching her flit from one emotion to the next with her friend and the guys brave enough to approach her when she's out in town.

She's witty and flirty, with just a little too much mischief and stubborn defiance in her eyes. I could make her yield. Submit. I groan as I think about the different ways I could go about it. If only playing with her wouldn't end in disaster.

If I gave in, I'd destroy her. There's no coming back from it. No amount of money anyone could throw at the problem to make it go away. My dad's job would be in jeopardy. The league would ostracize us. My family is depending on me to keep it together. I can't let the dark thoughts win.

As we're heading back through the trail to the main part of campus, I take hold of my thoughts and shove them all back into the box I keep them in. Locking it down tight.

It's harder to do than it usually is, because I don't want to lock them up. For the first time in a long time, I want to bathe in them. Feel them. Let them drag me down.

That's why she's dangerous to me. The way she looks at me in the morning when she walks into class, or on the rare times when I interact and answer a question about the lesson everyone else is working on. I know she likes that. Likes that I'm smart.

It's been too damn long since anyone has thought that was an attractive quality to have and not want to exploit it.

We've made it back to the dorm and I wait until Thea goes in before I circle back around to the library. It's impossible to spend 24/7 watching her. I have homework I need to do. Hopefully, it'll be enough to distract me from my spiraling thoughts.

I text the group chat, letting them know where I'm going.

Chapter 23
Thea

My aunt's been hounding me to come for a visit since the day they dropped me at the dorms. I finally agreed to show up for an awkward family dinner.

I drive up to the gate that closes off this block of houses from the rest of the street and wait as it opens for me, just like my first night here. I'm assuming there's a guard with a camera hiding in one of the nooks and crannies, granting access, because I doubt it's programmed to open for everyone. That would be a waste of a security gate.

I haven't asked about a gate code. That would give them the false belief that I plan to spend a lot of time here.

I park the car at the top of the driveway, walk to the door, and give two quick stabs to the bell. The person who answers the door isn't Carla. This must be one of the standby staff she mentioned.

The look on this woman's face says it all. I look nothing like the dinner party guests she's used to serving. I can roll with that sentiment since she's nothing like the waitstaff I'm used to seeing in diners. She escorts me into the living room where my aunt and uncle are sitting.

"Thea, you're here." Moira says, standing to her feet.

"I said I would be." We just stare at each other. Yup. Awkward.

She finally tells me to take a seat. When I settle on the couch, she asks, "So, uh. How's school? Do you have any friends?"

Small talk? They asked me to come to dinner so we could talk about stuff she could have asked over the phone? Not that she'd get an answer. My personal life and friendships are none of her business. "School's fine."

"Do you like all your classes and your professors?"

I relax a little. I can talk about what I'm learning and about the teachers all day. Nodding, I say, "I do. I'm really loving History of Eastern Culture and I think my statistics class might be my favorite. But if I had to pick the one that's most challenging, it's probably ethics."

Fitness training too, but I don't mention that since my issue with the class has to do with me having fucked the teacher.

Uncle Scott looks over at me and asks, "Why is that?"

"Because I feel like my teacher is biased."

"How so?"

"How can you teach ethics when you make it known the only acceptable viewpoint is the one that aligns with your personal belief that decimating a civilization or empire to make yourself rich is fine?"

He tilts his head to the side, considering my question all of five-seconds before saying, "Darwin would say that's just the way evolution goes."

He's one of those? Great. Lemme correct his misinformation right now. "Darwin was talking about the *natural* evolution of things. Unless he was a psychic, he didn't foresee creating weapons and wars to take over entire continents and steal artifacts to sell to museums."

Scott swirls the drink in his glass. "So you would have suggested what?"

"The same thing anyone with something valuable would suggest when presented with the opportunity to lose it. Pay a fair compensation to acquire it."

"And who decides what's fair?"

"The person in possession of the item."

He stands, crosses the room, and sets his glass down on the bar cart. He turns back to me with his arms folded across his chest. "Given that model, how do we prevent price gouging?"

"Nobody's worried about that shit now. So I doubt it was even a thing back then." He gives me a funny look. "I can see you don't agree. It's cool, neither does Dr. Schmidt. So if I flunk this class, at least you know why."

"You're flunking?" Aunt Moira asks with a worried look on her face.

"I said if. *If* I flunk this class." The thought makes me sick. I've never gotten a failing grade before, but I won't pretend to agree with something I don't, just for an A. "Don't worry, I'll pay the money back if I do."

Uncle Scott bypasses the *if* part and acts like a failing grade is a done deal. "Why would you risk a poor grade rather than dropping the class?"

Is he serious? "Why would I drop the class and deprive the other students of an alternate viewpoint? That would be selfish of me."

I brace myself for whatever he's gonna say next. Aside from asking about my grade, Moira didn't say anything during our exchange, but she's on his side. She's his wife and all. Maybe I should've invited LJ as backup. But then again, why subject her to this shit show?

Someone clears their throat behind us and announces dinner is ready. Great. The sooner we sit down to eat, the sooner I can go. If I do the old *move it around your plate trick*, I can pretend to be full, faster and speed up my departure time.

"I enjoyed hearing your viewpoint, Thea. It was a well though out argument." Scott says, breaking to the silence.

"You did?"

He settles into his seat before he answers. "Yes. Healthy debate is good. And I agree people should be free to express their views even if they're in disagreement."

"You don't care if my views cause me to get a failing grade?"

"We want you to do your best, and I'm sure you'll pass, as long as you're answering the questions on the test according to the source material in your textbook or lecture notes."

I dig into my plate as soon as it's placed in front of me. We eat in silence for a few minutes and then it's back to making small talk. Moira's fixated on this friend thing. "You didn't answer earlier, Thea. When I asked about friends."

I humor her, divulging a little bit about LJ. "I have one person I guess you'd call a friend. And I'm friendly with people in my classes, but I'm not planning any vacation trips or shopping sprees with anyone just yet, if that's what you mean."

"What about the dorm? I heard they upgraded the lounge area. Are they still doing the dorm movie night on Thursdays? Or the floor wars?" She chuckles. "I remember that used to be a big thing."

My aunt seems to know more about Vale Tower than I do. "I don't spend time in the lounge or on the other floors. If there's some kind of dorm competition, my neighbors are definitely participating in it without me. Maybe I should knock on their doors and invite myself along next time." I scoff at my own suggestion. "Actually, they'd probably just announce they won without even competing."

"Your neighbors... so you've met them?"

"Sure have." I look at my watch. "I'm sorry I've gotta go."

"You're leaving. Already?"

I ignore the sound of sadness in her voice. I came. I ate. What else did they expect? "Dinner was great, but I promised LJ I'd meet her at The Circle for one of those sorority mixers or whatever."

I could be imaging things, but I think they both look uncomfortable at the idea. Me too, folks. Me too.

"Look, I know it's not my style, but I guess the only way you can get an invitation to pledge one of these silly little clubs is if you put your face out there. Right now, LJ's face is hidden, and some of that might be because of her association with me. I figure I owe her one. She didn't ask to be caught up in my conflict with the Coxsuckers."

Moira and Scott share a look. "Coxsuckers?" Her lips move like she's having a bit of trouble saying the word. She'll need to get used to me cussing if she insists on me coming around.

"My neighbors with the idiotic club name. The triumphant-whatevers."

"The Triumvirates?"

I snap my fingers. "That's them."

Her eyes widen. I guess their reputation precedes them. "You had a run-in with them?"

"Nothing I can't handle."

"Thea."

I wait for her to finish, but she doesn't. She just shares another one of those loaded looks with her husband. "What's the problem?"

"If you've had issues with The Trium, maybe you shouldn't go to this event tonight. It's best not to put yourself in their path for a while. Just until things die down."

"You're suggesting I flake on LJ because they might be there? Not gonna happen. I'm not sitting at home because some entitled pricks have decided they don't like me." You'd think I just let it rip from my ass, the way they're looking at me. "*What?*"

Moira clenches her napkin. "Thea. I. *We* understand you're used to looking out for yourself and making your own decisions, but on this, you need to trust that we know what's best. Those boys. They're trouble. Stay away from them."

"Trouble?" I laugh. "I can tell you that you're probably the only person who feels that way. They definitely don't think anyone should stay away, and judging by the way those boys -as you've called them-eat up the attention, they're all for an audience. Even the teachers and staff kiss their asses just as hard and wet as everyone else."

I can tell by the way Scott's looking at me that he didn't appreciate that imagery. So I double down. "I'm talking tongue flicks and nibbling all up in that puckered flesh. Whole tongue, French Kiss deep in the-"

"Thea!"

I chuckle, waving off Scott's tone and the throbbing vein in his temple. "Relax. I don't want anything to do with the golden boys of Canyon Falls U and their not so secret society. If they stay away from me, I'll stay away from them."

I shoot off a text to LJ, letting her know I'm on my way.

"What do you know about that?"

I look over at Scott. "Uh, about what?"

"The society."

"I don't know anything about it. My friend LJ was talking about the fraternity Rho something or other and then mentioned that the top asshole and his minions are part of some supposed secret society because their rich daddies are. I don't know how true it is. I've asked a few people if it's secret how come average people know about it, but nobody has an answer for me."

I tap my phone against my palm. "I'm betting it's all made up, just to convince people to join row, row, row your boat. I know how effective exclusive marketing can be."

"Is that why you're going tonight? To enter pledge season or to be tapped by a society?"

I give Moira a look to let her know she's fucked in the head. "Of course not. We're just going to party. I have no interest in joining any clubs or groups unless it's hiking. Besides, I figure if this subversive branch of fraternity life exists, and it's *secret*, it can't be good."

"That's very sound reasoning there, Thea." Uncle Scott says, lifting an au gratin potato to his mouth.

I finish my drink and jump to my feet. "Don't wanna be late. Thanks for dinner."

"Thea." My aunt stops me when I get to the door.

"Yeah?" They keep holding me up and I'm getting irritated, but I try to hold it back, preparing myself to hear her say something about just leaving in the middle of the meal or whatever. I mean, I did say thanks for the meal. And it was good, so I ate it all.

"Thanks for coming to dinner, and um, be safe and have fun tonight."

She gives me a quick hug, then backs away. The shock on her face must match mine. Because I can't believe she did that.

"Sorry. I know you have boundaries. I just. I'm sorry."

I shake my head, as if that will help me wade through what I'm feeling. I haven't broken her arms for touching me. Huh. Progress.

"It's fine." I say, and I mean it. I'm fine.

"It is?"

I quickly dash the hope in her eyes. "It *was* fine, but let's not make this a thing."

"Right. Of course. It won't happen again."

Chapter 24
Finn

I dart across the street towards the entrance of the movie theater. This new movie is supposed to be full of car chases and explosions.

I check the time on my watch as I wait for the cashier to finish printing my ticket. Good, I've still got enough time to get my snacks before the trailers start.

I'm pulling open the glass doors when I see a familiar reflection in the glass, and hold it open wider, so she can walk in ahead of me.

I'm such a gentleman. "Hello there, Pet."

"I'm not your, Pet."

I roll my eyes at her response. Why does she keep saying that? "You are what I say you are."

She wheels around to face me. "Look, I came to see this late night viewing *alone,* because I like to watch my movies without a bunch of yapping. Just because we're neighbors and here at the same time doesn't mean we're together. We're *not* together. I suggest you find somewhere away from me to sit."

"I'm hurt, Pet. You don't want to sit near me?"

"Hell no. I remember the last time I sat with you, you tried to steal my snacks."

I grip her shirt, tugging her towards me. "I don't have to steal, because if I ask nicely, you'll give them to me."

She pulls my shirt, yanking me even closer. She's strong for a little thing. "Begging with words isn't the flex you think it is. If you want me to share, think of more creative things to do with those lips."

I'm still holding her shirt. With my free hand, I tug on her ponytail, forcing her head back, and lean over, my mouth inches from hers. "We can skip the movie if that's what you want."

"I don't want anything from you. I'm just letting you know it takes a little more than *pretty please* to get anything out of me."

She lets go of my shirt and pries my fingers off of hers. I release my hold on her hair, and allow her get in line ahead of me at the concession stand. She gets an extra large bucket of popcorn, just like before. I buy my usual snacks too and a drink, then follow her into the theater, waiting for her to pick out her seat.

I ignore the annoyed sound she makes when she sees I'm behind her. It's a late night showing of an action flick. She can't possibly think I'm going to let her sit alone in a dark movie theater so some dude with a tiny dick can sit next to her and steal her popcorn. I take my seat and press the button so my chair reclines.

It takes her a few minutes to settle all her snacks just the way she wants them, then reaches into her pocket and pulls out the flask. She shakes her head when she sees me eyeing it. "I'm not sharing."

"Pretty, please."

"I already told you that doesn't work."

Is she serious with the no? Does she really want me to use my mouth more creatively? I tuck her hair behind her ear, then lean over, tracing my tongue over the shell of her ear. "Be very careful what kind of challenges you put out there, Pet. I like games and I like to win."

She shifts her head to look at me, likely trying to decide if I'm willing to back up my threat. I pull my own bottles out of my book-bag. "I've got apple vodka and cranberry juice. Wanna trade?"

I do nothing to hide the smug look on my face. I saw her devouring jolly ranchers at the party. So okay, maybe I packed this, maybe hoping I'd see her here, but also because I like the flavor combination.

"Fine, we can trade. I'll have a little of yours and you can have a little of mine."

We pass the bottles back and forth, and finally get everything situated in time for the first movie trailer. By the halfway point of the movie, we're both reclining back and curled against the shared armrest. It's almost like curling up on the couch at home. Maybe next time I'll pack a blanket.

When the movie ends, Thea walks towards the exit like she's trying to escape me. "Are you trying to race me home, Pet?"

"I-" She looks at me over her shoulder, then darts off towards the parking lot across the street.

I let out a whoop and take off too. Jumping over cars as I go. She's parked a little further away than I am, but that's on her. I'm not about to wait for her to reach her car before taking off.

I gun the engine and peel out of the parking lot. Her headlights flash, showing she's right behind me. I stab the button on my radio, turning on my highway mix, letting my own personal action sound-track pump through the speakers as I navigate the streets of Canyon Falls Annex. They're deserted this time of night. We both ignore the posted speed limits.

I make it over the railroad crossing just before the arms come down. When I hit the highway, I open my engine full throttle. A quick check in my rearview shows the road is empty behind me. Too bad. She's gonna lose precious minutes waiting for that train to cross.

I'm about to let up on the gas when I spot a car zipping up the on-ramp ahead of me. I cackle when Thea pulls into the lane right next to me.

We drive the next few miles, her slightly behind me. She makes her move to overtake me, but I cut her off, pulling over to the off-ramp. She's right back alongside me when we reach the street. The backend of her car drifts when we take the left-hand turn that leads to the road to the main gates. I slow down to make sure she doesn't spin out or crash. She handles the car like a pro and is back in the race. *Dammit.*

Around and around the curves we go. The last half a mile is a straight shot. I push my car faster than I ever have before. Pax would be proud. We're neck and neck when we enter the gate, but she doesn't slow. She heads straight to the student parking garage. I have a private space on the third level. She's out of her car and walking towards the dorm before I put mine in park. This is where I get an advantage and give her a lesson in competing against me. You don't stop until you've made it all the way to the end. I said race home. That meant the dorm, not the parking lot.

I've run through this garage more times than I can count. I don't even bother going to the first level. I jump over the wall on the second one, landing in the grass in a crouch, then take off down the side of the building, and across The Circle towards Vale Tower. She's almost to the courtyard. She turns and sees me coming, then takes off running, head down, arms pumping.

I overtake her, running through the doors and reach the elevator before she makes it to the lobby. I stab the button for the elevator, willing it to hurry.

She reaches the doors before the car arrives, and grabs my shirt, trying to pull me away. The doors open and she rushes inside, trying to close the door so I can't get in, but I put my hand out to stop them from closing.

We're both breathing hard. My chest hurts. A combination of exertion and laughter. Her chest heaves, drawing my attention to her tits.

She's bouncing on her feet, waiting for the car to stop on our floor. I'm ready too. As soon as the doors open, we rush into the hall, running towards our doors. Her key fob is already out. She waves it at her door, and the lock flashes green. I snatch her off her feet before she can turn the handle. "

I win, Pet."

"How? My door is unlocked. I won."

I carry her across the hall, open my door and walk inside, closing my door with my foot. I'm still holding her when I drop down on the couch. "I won, because you never stepped foot in your room."

She shifts around so she can face me. "You dragged me in here. That's cheating."

"That's winning at any cost." I trail my hand up her back. "So where's my prize?"

She gnaws on her lip, then says, "We didn't bet any prizes. This was for bragging rights."

Bragging rights? Just to tell people you won? I don't get it. "Do they do that a lot where you're from? Just walk around saying, 'I won' and people believe them?"

"Yes. Sometimes there are witnesses and sometimes there aren't. But if you claim the title, you have to be ready to defend it at any time, so most people don't just say they won without the ability to back that claim up with a new challenger."

I think about that. I like winning. I like people knowing I'm a winner. But I also like knowing people's secrets, and this is like a combination of both.

It's a secret we were at the movies together and raced home and *I* won. I'm okay with not sharing that info with anyone.

My hand's on the back of her neck, massaging the tendons on the side. She shifts against me, making my dick hard. "So what now, Pet?"

I apply a little more pressure, pulling her towards me, and rock my hips so she can see what I think should happen next.

She tries to climb out of my lap. "Now, I need to get to bed."

I pull her down against me, grinding my dick against the seam of her pants. "I have a bed." Though we don't need to go there. I can do everything I'm thinking right where we are.

"I meant, mine." She puts her hand against my chest and pushes back. I release my hold on her and let her climb to her feet. My eyes drink in the shape of her ass as she walks over to my door. She doesn't even say good night when she steps into the hall, closing the door softly behind her. I drop my head back on the couch.

I had a shitty day. I can't name one thing that made me feel that way, but I've just felt kind of off. Like I've been dragging around, uneasy and heavy in my skin. That's why I went to the movies tonight. I was hoping the adrenaline rush from the screen would work its way into my body and lighten me up.

I'm in a better mood, but I know it was a combination of the movie and the girl I sat next to.

Thea

LJ and I are hanging out tonight. This is the first time she's been to my room, even though I've invited her over before. She kept turning down my offer, afraid of what the other residents would say. I finally convinced her nobody will care enough to say anything.

When we reach my door, she says, "Tell me again how you wound up with a room right next to them."

I swipe my key against the access panel and look over at the door across from mine, staring at the handle as if it's gonna swing open at any minute. "Just unlucky, I guess."

"Girl, everyone and I do mean *everyone* would kill to live next door to The Trium."

With a flourish of my hands, I say, "Let the bloodbath commence. I'd be happy to swap places with the winner."

LJ heads straight for the balcony when we get inside. I know what she's probably doing. Looking over the side, to see if she can catch sight of them. I don't need to go out there, because I know there's probably some bullshit going on.

I thought things couldn't get worse after that first night with Finn and his music, but I was so, so wrong. Now, I avoid my balcony when he's home.

"What's Finn doing? Is he cleaning knives?" I shrug, even though she's not looking at me. "Holy shit. Is that Holden? How did I not know he's this *hot*?"

I grunt a response. How did she not know? The piercings and muscles are the first thing I noticed about him. The second was how smart he is. That hot brainiac combo makes me weak in the knees.

Today was definitely one for the books. The teacher was doing a recap of last week's lesson and we were all assigned a problem we had to teach to the class. Holden was called on first.

I couldn't tear my eyes away from the way his shirt stretched across his back while he was writing on the dry erase board, or the look on his face when someone asked a question. Those piercings, those eyes and that voice. Soft, deep and a little scratchy. Like his vocal chords are fashioned out of gravel. Dude is sexy as hell when he's in teacher mode. I kept zoning out of the lesson because I was imagining him making me stay after class for extra credit.

I shake off the memory. It's girl's night and torturing myself with lust filled thoughts of men I can't have. Correction, men I *don't want*, is a waste of time.

The semester's just starting and going to these pre-pledge events with LJ is the perfect opportunity to find someone to use for a little pillow party.

Once I do, the Holden lust haze will fade away. Okay, so *maybe* I have a little Finn lust happening, too. He's annoying when he's with his buddies, but he's also fun. Racing back to campus? Come on, there was no way I could say no.

"I mean, we all say he's cute. They all are, but I kinda thought he was just shy all the time." LJ continues to ramble on, even though I haven't answered. "But here he is, walking around with no shirt on like its nothing."

He's shirtless? That's new. But nope, not. Gonna. Look. A few seconds later, she squeaks and gasps. I look up in time to see LJ leaning forward, balancing on her hips and teetering over the edge of the railing. I hurry out the door to grab her before she slips into the space between our balconies and gets stuck or plummets to her death. Big mistake. I should've let her fall out of the nest, because now I'm in range of what I didn't want to see.

Finn is really putting on a show. He's gone from buffing his blades to showing his ass. As in, he's not just shirtless. He's in the doorway, completely naked.

There's no way he didn't know LJ was watching. Because he can see out the patio door just as easily as we can see in. Despite my good intentions, I look down. Is that a shadow on his leg or is that his dick?

Holden's standing next to him. He's still got his pants on, but he is definitely missing a shirt. Is that a nipple piercing?

I drag LJ back to safety and into the apartment. She keeps looking back over her shoulder, so I close and lock the door, and draw the blinds shut. We do not need any problems.

She flops down onto the couch, her eyes darting to the door. "What do you think is going on over there? You know, I heard orgies and stuff are part of being a Wren. Do you think that's what's happening?"

Where does she hear this shit? For someone who's not a part of that world, she sure knows a lot about what's rumored to happen in it.

"Whatever they're doing is none of my business."

It's really not. I don't care what they're up to. Although I am a little disappointed about Holden's participation in an orgy. I liked that he seemed a little anti-social like me.

I should know better than to build someone up in my head. The reality of them is usually a huge disappointment. "Did you want popcorn?" I ask, changing the subject, and refocusing LJ on why we're here.

"Ooh, yes, and do you have caramel topping?"

I make two batches of popcorn. One with extra butter, one with caramel topping. I settle next to her on the couch, an amused smile on my lips as she tosses chocolate candy bites into her bowl. She must have a great dentist to combat all the sugar she consumes.

We're just settling in to watch the movie when I remember I tossed my phone on the patio chair, when I thought LJ was falling to her death.

I slip outside to grab it. I straighten from bending over and freeze in place. Finn is outside on a massage table and he's not alone. The three of them are lying on their backs, with nothing but a towel draped over their hips, getting rubbed down by women wearing barely there bikinis.

The women are working their lower halves and it looks like they're on their way to happy endings. I scan my eyes down their bodies, taking note of the intricate ink patterns on Holden's left forearm. Pax's entire body is a canvas of tattoos from his neck to his hip. Finn has the least amount of tattoos.

These guys are ridiculously hot, and I'm going through a drought. That's the only reason I'm standing here watching them get rubbed down in oil.

I drag my eyes from their pecs and abs, back up to their faces. They're all leaning on their elbows, looking at me. *Shit.* I just got busted perving on their bodies.

I'm getting different expressions from each of them. Amusement from Finn, curiosity from Holden, and contempt from the head dick in charge.

I give them a look of my own. One accompanied by me holding my thumb and pointer finger close together to show I'm not the least bit impressed with what they're working with.

I saunter back inside to watch my movie. They're obviously doing this shit on purpose to keep me trapped indoors. I need to come up with a plan. I'm done letting them run me off my own balcony.

Chapter 25
Pax

I watch as Holden tugs at his collar. Tonight, we're attending a mixer at the Sandstone Social Club. Thursday night mixers are reserved for Initiates and League members. I look over at my father, trying to gauge his reasoning for bringing us here. Is this when they spring it on us? Reveal that they know about the car incident the night of the museum prank?

I keep my face neutral, so no one suspects I'm nervous about being here. Not much makes me nervous, but my father breaking routine always puts me on edge, because he rarely does it. We follow him through the front door of the club and across the massive foyer, into the ballroom. I get the impression we're the last ones to arrive. My father acknowledges a few people we pass, but his face gives nothing away. I can't tell if us arriving later than everyone else was just happenstance or intentional on his part. Probably the latter. Malcolm loves to be the center of attention.

We move to the center of the room, falling in beside a few prospects I recognize from last year's graduating class. Carlisle Inglewood, who's running for mayor, is standing on a platform at the front of the room. He's a lower council member with very little political experience. Still, his campaign fund is bigger than the current incumbents. I look around to see if Mayor Boeman is here. He's one of the older league members who should be relinquishing power but refuses to do it.

"Gentlemen." Inglewood says, "Welcome to kickoff night." I share a look with my friends. They're just as clueless as I am. "It's a longstanding tradition that the prospects be tried, tested, and proven before they join our ranks. We have thrown this little get together, to celebrate our young men and women being one step closer to that milestone, and to recognize the start of a new pledge season."

When he says women, the doors open behind us, and my confusion increases as some of the wives and daughters enter the room, accompanied by a few other women I'm sure are professional entertainment.

"We have a fine selection of treats for you tonight. Any item you may desire. And as always, we leave the negotiations up to you."

My father steps away to talk to a league member, giving me and the guys a few minutes to talk.

"Is this what I think it is?" Holden asks.

Finn waggles his brows. "If you think it's a sex party, then yeah. It is."

We've heard about these events happening. But why are the wives and daughters here? "We don't have to..." My statement gets cut off when an elder approaches us with a drink in his hand.

"Gentlemen. It's good to see you among us tonight." He's smiling at us like our presence is the best part of his day. "I hear you're doing amazing things on campus and currently rank higher than anyone else ever has in those little games."

Finn responds, "Appreciate that, sir."

He waves his hand at the room. "Your first kickoff night?"

I answer confidently, "We throw a party on campus for pledge season."

He cracks a smile like he's humoring me. "Ah. Yes. Many Rho

Beta Psi traditions are influenced by The League. But I'm sure you'll see that nothing is quite as good as the real thing."

"We're just happy to have been invited." I say, because it's expected.

He looks down at our hands. "Where are your drinks?"

"Oh, we weren't planning to drink tonight. We have classes tomorrow."

He laughs, and his smile brightens. "Nonsense. Everyone participates." He waves a server over and passes each of us a glass. Raising his in the air, he toasts, "To be reborn."

We do the same and take a drink. His eyes light up. Then next thing I know, we're surrounded by women. "I leave you in capable hands."

I'm looking around the room, trying to take it all in and figure out just what the hell is going on, when Finn chuckles. I turn back towards him, giving him a questioning look. He tips his chin towards the door. "Isn't that..."

"Miss Griffin. Our tenth grade biology teacher." Holden says, finishing Finn's statement. We watch as she walks up to one of our classmates, drapes her arm across his bicep, and leads him towards the exit.

I watch a few more people get escorted away. The reality of this night settling in on me as I watch Sarah Withers. Someone who is maybe four months past her eighteenth birthday, smiling up at Councilman Heart. His smile is lecherous and nausea inducing. His eyes fixated on her breasts. I shift my gaze over to her parents. When Sarah takes a step back, putting some space between herself and the councilman, her father all but pushes her into the creeps arms. She's a legacy daughter. Last year her father was in negotiations to have her marry some acne faced runt. He isn't a legacy, but his father is influential on Wall Street. I thought the deal was all but done. So what's going on here? Sarah glances nervously over at her parents, before pasting another smile on her face and letting Councilman Heart lead her out of the room.

My dad walks back towards us, motioning for me to join him away from my friends. I hate talking to him away from them, but I can't cause a scene. When we reach the hallway, he opens a door and ushers me inside.

"I won't keep you long. It's your first kickoff night. You should experience everything it has to offer."

"Thank you, sir."

"I wanted to touch base with you on the student on your floor. Tessa Lawrence wasn't it?"

"Theona LaReux."

"Right. LaReaux. What have you learned?"

I don't even know why he's wasting his time on this. He's got more pressing shit to concern himself with. For example, the incident that happened after last year's induction ceremony. The council put this year's induction planning on hold, pending the outcome of the investigation.

Whoever is in charge of finding answers is dragging their feet. I'm sure everyone knows what happened, and they're just looking for an appropriate pansy to pin it on. They need to get an official statement out soon, before someone, the *wrong* someone, starts digging into it. Until they close this review, nobody can move to the next stage in their indoctrination. The second years can't become thirds, and the prospects can't become official first years.

But instead of focusing on the thing that'll hold us back, he's got me shadowing the bitch. "Truthfully sir, I've got nothing."

His eyes slit. That's not the answer he wanted to hear. "It's been weeks. How don't you have a single drop of intel you can share, outside of what she eats for breakfast?"

"The information I've given you is all we've been able to find." His face says it all. I'm such a disappointment. "It appears it's as I thought. Her dorm assignment was a mixup. One that can't be changed until next semester, unless you think it's prudent to make some calls. I'm sure there would be no problem getting her room changed should an alumni express concern about it."

"I can't make any overtures or get involved."

Bullshit. He loves to get involved. He likes to butt his nose into everything. "I don't understand why not."

He stares at the wall, then faces me with a pensive look on his face. "I didn't want to say anything until I knew more, and perhaps this conversation is a little premature, but after what I've learned, I think you should know. It's why I wanted to speak to you alone."

"Okay."

"What I'm about to tell you is of the most sensitive nature. Do not share it with anyone. Not even your Trium until you get proof."

"Understood, sir."

"There have been whispers all summer. Really, as early as last winter that there are some unaffiliated parties looking to infiltrate The League. Of course, we've heard these stories for years and nobody's ever been able to do it, but..."

"But you think it's finally happening?"

"We're a solid society. It's hard to come straight at us, but an incendiary tactic would be to elevate someone to a position they are not owed or deserving. Placing them in our midst and having them form alliances with future league members and their companions."

"You think Thea is this person?"

"I think it's quite strange that the school would make such a grievous error and do nothing to rectify it or compensate the families who suffer from their mistake. The fourth room in Vale Tower is a symbol of a previous power structure. It's the holy grail for legacy families hoping The League will one day appoint a new line to that position. You don't just put people in that room like it's overflow."

"Agreed."

"Good. I knew you'd understand. So dig deeper and be vigilant. If she's part of this faction we've been hearing about, she's dangerous and can't be trusted."

He stops me when I move towards the door. "There's one more thing, son."

"What's that?"

"You never let the fox stay in the henhouse while waiting to prove it's a fox."

"You want me to push her out?"

"You're head of your Trium, and the people on your team are lead prospects. If I have to explain everything, then the position is wasted on you."

With that parting shot, he walks out of the room first. It's always a power play with him, but he's a powerful man, respected and successful. He's smart and good at making deals. He's shit at communicating with me as his son, but he's not wrong in what he says.

If Thea is a part of this threat, she has to go. We can't let her stay in Vale Tower or our school and risk disrupting the tradition that our community is built on.

When I step into the hallway, I can see Finn and Holden have drifted closer to the door. I walk through it and catch their attention, letting them know I'm ready to leave. They reach me, but as we turn to exit, our escape is thwarted by Kristoff Johns, my father's heart mate. The guy he was paired with when he was a second year prospect. Your heart mate is your primary confident, a perfect opposite to your strengths and weaknesses. I've called him Uncle Kristoff for as long as I can remember, but I haven't seen him much in the last few years.

"There you boys are." He says with a genuine smile on his face. I allow him to pull me into a hug and wait while he shakes Finn and Holden's hand. "What do you think of all this?"

"I imagined The League was too busy running the world to throw parties." I say sarcastically.

"The world running is still going on. Within this room, at this very minute. Sometimes people are more agreeable to terms when they're in a friendlier environment." He levels me with a look. "Which is why I came over here. You three should not be hiding in the corner. This party is your first introduction to our social setting. Even though kickoff night is usually reserved for second-year prospects and above, we've decided to bend the rules a little this year."

That explains it. They've pulled back the curtain for first year prospects to get a view. To get us excited about the future, and I would be, if I would've been more prepared.

"Mingle," Kristoff says. "Have fun. There are all sorts of things around the building. Something is sure to catch your attention."

Everything is telling me this is a bad idea. One thing my dad has always taught me is never to go into anything blindly, and this is the definition of it. "We weren't sure if we should."

"Of course you should. You wouldn't be here otherwise." He clasps me on my shoulder and steers me across the floor. "In fact, there's someone who's dying to meet you."

We have no choice but to go with him, through a side door and into a room occupied by a woman I highly doubt has been waiting around to meet us. Is she expecting someone? Undoubtedly, but I don't think it's anyone in particular. She has a job to do and will do it with anyone.

She gets to her feet walking over to Kristoff, a hungry look on her face. He swats her ass and says, "Show these boys a good time. They're our future."

As he's walking out, two more women enter the room, closing the door behind them. I share a look with Finn and Holden. We know we're not getting out of this room without being serviced by one of these women.

This is it, the start of it all. I look over in the corner and see it. The small camera that's probably in every room in this club. We're here for one reason and one reason only. To prove our desire to join The League of the Daggered Ravens. Tonight will be the first of many nights they'll use to obtain leverage over current and future members.

My gaze slides to Holden. Finn and I can do this with no problem. Holden's the one who's gonna have to suffer through being unsatisfied. Finn's already pulling his jacket off and unbuttoning his pants.

"What do you like, boys?"

Never one to drag things out, Holden barks, "We'd like you to shut the fuck up and get on your knees."

They comply, eager to please. Finn doesn't waste time. He spits on his hand, rubbing it over the latex he's already rolled on, then moves to position himself behind one of the women and plunges into her cunt.

There's no way she's wet and and he doesn't give a shit if she nuts or not. He's known to be selfish like that. We all are. Holden sits down on the couch and motions for the one closest to him to work her throat.

He watches as she frees him from his pants and waits until she's got him hard, before closing his eyes. To anyone watching, I'm sure it looks like he's letting himself go, enjoying the moment. But I know better. He's fixating. Concentrating on staying in control. Locking his urges down. Since we were blindsided about tonight's events, this would be the worst time to let his demons out to play.

I hear the scrape of metal and turn my attention back to Finn. He's much more forthcoming with his interests. His knife is like an extension of his arm. A crutch.

He twirls it through his fingers, before dragging the tip of it down the woman's arm. The noises she was making suddenly stop. Her eyes widen as the sharp point presses against her flesh. I can taste her fear in the air.

He's barely touching her, and she starts crying, begging him not to hurt her. I roll my eyes at her dramatics. Finn puts the knife away with a heavy sigh, before pulling out of her hole. He goes to stand in front of her to get off the way Holden is doing. He takes her mouth to shut her up.

I grab the last remaining girl and drag her into my lap. Turning my head away when she tries to kiss me. That's not what this is about. I pull my dick out, roll on a condom, and shove my cock into her ass.

If she's not ready, that's not my fault. This is all transactional anyway. This is just a fuck. Another task set for us to prove our worth.

I zone out too, letting her bounce on my dick, unbothered by the fact that someone somewhere is recording this. We aren't the first and won't be the last people to be serviced by professionals.

Chapter 26
Thea

Weekends aren't nearly long enough around here, especially when my first class is so early on Monday mornings.

I stayed up late last night going over my map and missed my alarm. That means I had to skip breakfast this morning to get to class on time. I take my seat in the middle of the room, next to Austin. My favorite teacher isn't here yet, so I still have a few minutes to review my notes.

Austin and I are comparing our homework answers when two of the three Coxsuckers walk in. Instinct tells me to avert my gaze, but I ignore those instincts, focusing all my attention on Finn and Holden as they walk towards me, then past me to their seats.

To everyone else, it may look like they're just their usual stuck up selves, but I recognize a predator when I see one. There's an air of tension around them like they're seconds away from pouncing. They have their guard up and so do I.

Just as I'm about to relax, Finn comes back to Austin's side of the aisle. He stares at me and points to the chair next to his. "Move."

I snort, then promptly ignore him. They're on edge. No way I'm sitting anywhere near those assholes today.

"What was that, Pet?"

Austin leans back in his chair, kicking his feet out and crossing them at the ankles. "Sounds to me like that was a *no*."

Finn tilts his head to the side, considering that answer. "You can move voluntarily or we go to option two."

What's this shit? Since when do they even talk to me? I look over at Holden, who's in his usual seat, watching our exchange. I can't tell if he's in on this or not. His emotionless face always looks bored. Like he's checked out on life around him when more than one or two people are around.

It doesn't matter to me what he thinks about this anyway, 'cause I'm not letting Finn order me around. I shrug, unperturbed by the threat.

Austin chuckles and says, "I'm pretty sure she's choosing option two."

Finn steps away as the teacher comes in, sing songing "Option two is my *fa-vo-rite*," as he takes his seat. I exhale and give Austin a smile. I'm glad my bluntness didn't completely turn him off that first day. He's the only other person I know who has an issue with these legacy brats running around like they're in charge, making stupid demands -as if they're some kind of gods- instead of students like the rest of us.

At the end of class, Finn slips by me, chuckling at something on his phone. He shows it to Holden, who gives a curt nod, before they disappear through the door.

I get some weird looks in my next class, but I ignore them. Whatever's up their asses, has nothing to do with me. I'm heading towards The Rock when some chick steps in my path.

"What's this I hear about you trying to sit next to a Trium?"

Oh *god*. I knew it wouldn't last. I've been to enough schools to know the popular kids always have groupies, and there's always one bitch that thinks she's in charge of the horde of them, laying claim to the hottest guys. I've been lucky enough to avoid them, until now.

"Don't."

"Don't what?" She asks, brows furrowed in confusion.

"Don't know you, what you heard, or give a fuck," I step around her, leaving her to work through it on her own.

This is gearing up to be a headache inducing day. I would skip out to my room or the library, but since I woke up late and didn't eat, I'm starving.

When I reach the checkout counter after ordering my lunch, I'm told there's an unpaid balance on my account that has to be cleared before I can access the dining services. I try to tell the cashier whatever she's reading isn't up to date, because all my fees were paid in full, but she doesn't listen and moves on to the person behind me like I'm not even here.

I pull up my account on my phone and see she's right. It shows an unpaid balance that equals my time on campus so far.

I stalk off and call the finance office. They tell me it'll take seventy-two hours to review my account and resolve the discrepancy. I'm glad I have food in my room, so I don't have to waste money on takeout.

For the rest of the day, I feel people's eyes on me as I walk around campus. I hear them whispering about me not having money to eat. Pointing out that I'm obviously living above my means or trying to defraud the school, bouncing checks.

When my last class lets out, I can't get to my dorm fast enough. The only reason I don't run there is because I won't give these gossiping twits ammunition like that. I walk at a leisurely pace, letting them know I don't give a shit about what they're saying.

LJ is waiting for me outside of my dorm, with bags at her feet. "What's all that?" I ask.

"Uh, just a few things I picked up on my break."

"Do you need help carrying them over to your dorm?"

She shakes her head, biting down on her lip. "They're for you."

She rushes along and says, "Don't be mad, but I heard a few people in my English Lit class talking about what went down in the dining hall. So, um, I got you some groceries."

Her English class is nowhere near the dining hall. "God, is everybody on this fucking campus a gossip? Why can't people mind their own fucking business?"

Her face deflates at my outburst. "Look LJ, I appreciate the sentiment, but you shouldn't have wasted your money."

Her lip quivers. "It's not a waste, Thea. I was worried about you starving in the dorms and I know Austin is the only other person you talk to, but I wouldn't trust that he'd feed you."

I'm feeling properly chastised. "I'm sorry about my outburst. It's just been a whole day with people whispering about this. I've already talked to the finance office. It's just gonna take a few days for them to correct their computer glitch and I won't starve because I actually have food in my fridge. My aunt and uncle are not having financial problems or bouncing checks or whatever else you may have heard."

"Oh. The way everyone was talking..." She gives me a sheepish smile. "I guess I'm no better than them, believing what I heard without investigating. God, I'm so sorry, Thea."

"You believed them?" I don't know why that stings.

"There were so many people talking about your meal card being declined and since we've never really talked about your aunt and uncle... Look, it wouldn't matter to me if any of it was true. You're right. It's nobody's business. I just wanted to make sure you'd be okay."

I digest what she's saying. She heard people talking and without a second thought, she went out and brought me food just in case it was true. Sasha would totally do the same thing, but she'd have called me to get the entire story while she was shopping.

I look down at her bags. "Any good snack foods in there?"

She smiles. "Only the best."

I grab a couple of bags and walk through the door. "Okay, let's go upstairs and see what you got."

"Yeah?"

"Yeah. You went through all this trouble, so the least I can do is make you dinner."

I've been waiting for a package. It's three days after the expected delivery date and I finally got ahold of customer service, who says it shows as return to sender.

By the time I tracked down the postal service, they confirmed they have my package, and when I asked why it was there, the customer service agent said all my mail is being returned to the post office as undeliverable with no forwarding address, and if I don't collect it by close of business today, it's going back. They're welcome to keep or trash the junk mail, but I need this package for a school project.

I make my way down to the student parking lot and head over to the spot where my car is parked. Where my car is *supposed* to be parked, only to find an empty spot.

I knew it. I *knew* this town wasn't perfect. I look around at all the flashy vehicles. Whoever stole my car did so because it's an older model. Easier to take. Less anti-theft measures. If I were just boosting for parts, I would've taken it too.

I hurry over to the campus police station, which is a ten-minute walk from campus, to file a theft report. The front desk is empty. I ring the bell waiting for service and after five minutes, someone comes strolling out the back.

"Can I help you?"

"Yes, I'd like to file a theft report."

"And what was stolen?" He asks, flicking his gaze over me. The look on his face says he can't possibly imagine that I'd have anything worth stealing.

"My car."

"Your car?"

"That's right. It's a 2006 Pontiac Solstice. Silver convertible with a black Ragtop." He's still looking at me like I'm here as some sort of joke, so I spout off the license plate number and the VIN. It's not until I pull out the copy of the insurance card that I have in my wallet that the expression on his face changes. "What are you doing?"

"I'm about to call my aunt's insurance company and file a claim to make sure I have all my bases covered. Hopefully, you'll have the police report number ready to go by the time I'm connected to an agent."

He starts typing something into his computer and asks, "What's your name?"

"Theona LaReaux."

"And your student ID number?"

I recite it and pull up the screen shot I have of my parking permit number in case he needs that for his report, too.

"Silver Pontiac Solstice, you said?"

"Yup." I'm connected with an agent who asks who she's speaking with. "Hi, Charlene. This is Thea LaReaux." Then I spout off my date of birth and last four of my social security number as requested.

Just as I'm about to tell Charlene the nature of my call, the cop says, "It's not stolen. It's been towed."

"I'm sorry, Charlene. One second." I put the phone on mute. "What do you mean, towed?"

"The system showed it was towed at ten twenty-five this morning during a security verification. The officer on the scene ran the plates and permit pass through the school and the DMV. The driver's license you put on your permit application is suspended." He looks back up at me. "You'll have to prove you have a current license and pay the impound fee in cash to get it released."

"Charlene? Yes, I'll call back."

Clenching my phone in my fist, I say, "My license isn't suspended, and I don't know what check was supposedly done, but I can't show a suspended license in California because my license was issued in *Nevada*."

"That's not what it shows here. Your parking pass has a California license and picture."

I pull out my driver's license. "Does whatever you're looking at look like this?" I ask, thrusting it at him.

He shrugs. "Nope. But I have to go by what's in the system."

"Your system is wrong."

"You're only allowed to have one license and if you live here, you're expected to change it within ten days, if you're a resident of the state. So the fact that you didn't turn that in or do it isn't proof of anything. You'll have to go to the DMV to straighten it out. And remember it's seventy-five dollars per day for storage on the tow lot."

I refrain from explaining that, as a student, I'm not required to change my license. I haven't registered to vote here. So Nevada is still my state of residence. "What about my original application? Won't that prove what I registered the car with?"

"Yes, but the copies of those applications are at our central office. It's closed until Tuesday. You can put in a document request. That'll be thirty-nine, ninety-nine and you have to allow six to eight weeks for delivery."

Someone comes in behind me and he moves over to help them. I huff out a frustrated sigh, certain I'm not going to get any further with him. I'm working out a plan and scrolling through my phone, trying to find the number for the central office, when I see the time. I have a little less than an hour to get to the post office. I pull up a ride share app, hoping someone is close by.

Thankfully, there is, and I make it to the post office with twenty minutes to spare.

It's not until I'm back on campus that I really start to think about the string of bad luck I've been having lately, with computer systems. It can't be a network error if I'm the only one affected. These are targeted attacks. Finn's words come back to me. *Option two.*

He couldn't fuck with me in class, so he's messing with my privileges on campus. I'm gonna murder them, *after* I walk the ten flights of stairs, since my elevator code isn't working. I'm in a pissy mood and feeling stabby when I bang on Finn's door.

He answers, wearing nothing but a towel. I force my gaze to stay on his face and not his perfectly sculpted abs or that deep delicious V.

"Hello, Pet."

"I'm giving you one warning. You've had your fun. Now stop fucking with my shit." He frowns, feigning confusion. "Oh, cut the innocent routine. You suck at it."

He smirks, proving me correct. I'm going through all of this because they've somehow messed with my student file.

"Have you learned your lesson, Pet?" He asks, tucking a strand of hair behind my ear.

I slap his hand away and warn, "This is a courtesy visit, Finley. Back off."

"Or what?"

I step into his space, waiting for him to look down at me. I walk my fingers up his chest. He catches his bottom lip between his teeth, thinking I'm suddenly ensnared in his gaze.

I pull his door closed with my other hand, and step back, taking his towel with me. I hear the lock engage and twirl the towel around in the air. "Keep fucking around with me and find out."

Chapter 27
Thea

It's been a hellishly weird week. I got my car back yesterday, with an apology from the campus police department about the mix-up, and an email a few days ago saying my meal account was corrected. I still haven't gone to the dining hall to find out. I've been living off the groceries LJ brought me and basically avoiding the whispers that have been following me around school.

I don't give a shit about gossip, but there's nothing like eating a meal in peace. I've cooked for us most of the nights, not wanting to use her food solely for myself when I didn't need it. Plus, I like hanging out with LJ in my room. She seems to like it too, seeing how she doesn't have a kitchen, and I do.

I would've cooked tonight too, but LJ had a study group. Rather than hang out at the dorms, I decided to take my aunt and uncle up on their dinner offer.

The chicken parmesan was delicious. I'm scraping the last bit of sauce and cheese off my plate, wondering if I can get Cora alone to ask for the recipe. When dessert is served, my aunt pushes her chair back and stands, going to grab something from the corner of the room. She comes back over, dropping a glittery pink box on the table in front of me. It's really pink. And *glittery*. I lean away from it, feeling a rash coming on. "What's this?"

"Open it."

I do, trying to avoid getting glitter on me. My eyebrows inch up as I look over at my aunt.

"I, uh, noticed your favorite jacket is leather, and worn, so I got you a new one."

The jacket was my moms. I always loved to see her in it as a kid and when she took off, she left it behind, along with some other clothes. I kept them and started wearing them when I got big enough for them to fit. It makes me feel connected to her. Stupid, I know, since she didn't give a shit about our connection, but girls want their moms. Or so the shrink said.

"It's nice." I close the lid and move the box to the side. "But the one I have is fine."

Uncle Scott disagrees. He's always got some slick shit to say when I graciously turn down a present. "The leather's scarred and the underlining is showing through in some places in the back. It's time to retire it."

"The way your assistant retired all my other shit?"

They said it was in storage, but I haven't heard a peep about it since that first day, which makes me think she was telling the truth about throwing it out.

Moira cuts him off before he can respond. "The insurance adjuster is still working through it. He says there are a lot of old items and he's having trouble assigning a valuation to it. Do you maybe have receipts? That could help."

"Some of the clothes, like my jacket, are my mom's things. I wasn't around when she bought it, and she wasn't big on paperwork or organization. The sporting gear is second hand stuff I brought at a flea market or thrift store. So no, I couldn't tell you the *monetary* value of it."

"I can't imagine how hard it was for you growing up. That's why

I'm glad you came here. We're going to give you the life you deserve. The one you should've had."

She continues talking as if I'm not even sitting here. "I don't know what Hailee was thinking, and then to have you put in the system. That's not what was supposed to happen. She was supposed to keep you safe."

She looks at me with tears in her eyes. "I'm sorry you had to grow up the way you did. Without a parent you could depend on. Without someone who held you and comforted you. It's no wonder you're averse to touch."

Is she saying she wants to pretend my life before I came here didn't exist? I mean yeah, mom made life choices that sucked but she doesn't get to judge her. Because mom was there. It's these Jack and Jill come lately's that are just getting to the party.

Buying me shit doesn't change the fact that they turned their backs on us, and my issue with touch has nothing to do with mom. It's the life I led after she stopped being able to hug me that's got me like this. And tell me one person who wants to be touched by strangers without permission. Go on. I'll wait.

She waves a hand over her face, drying her tears, and gives me a watery smile. "Now that you're here, well... you don't have to ever worry about anything again. That life's over now."

She sniffles again, and I lose it. "How. Fucking. Dare. You." Moira jumps back as if I bitch slapped her. She's lucky I didn't.

"Theona!" My attention snaps to my uncle.

"It's Thea! You'd know that I hate being called *Theona* if you hadn't just showed up five-seconds ago."

I turn my fury back to my aunt. "And I don't know what you *think* you know about my mother, but you have no right to talk about her like that. Did she hide in booze and fall off the face of the earth? Sure, but neither of us know why."

I point to Scott. "She's *your* so-called sister. You knew her longer than I did, so why don't you try having a little compassion for the woman when she did it all by herself for as long as she could. Tell me,

Aunt Moira." I say the word like it tastes bad in my mouth, because it does. "Where's the outrage for what my dad didn't do? I don't even know that prick but I'd say he deserves some of your vitriol too, since the only thing he left behind was his jizz."

Scott's voice is razor sharp when he says, "We have brought you into our home. Show some respect."

Does he think he's about to chastise me? Fuck that all the fucking way to hell. I don't care if he's pissed, because I am, too. I point an accusing finger at the both of them.

"I didn't ask to come here. I told you I didn't *want* to come here, because I knew what a disaster it would be. But you kept hounding and begging me. So here I am. In all my flawed, unpolished glory. You want some respect? How about you show some goddamn respect for the situation I was in, and the woman who gave birth to me? Despite how you feel, Hailee Murphy was my mom. Sure, it was fucked up when she crawled into the bottle, but you weren't there. You don't have the right to judge her, and you certainly don't have the right to push your guilt over not being around onto me."

I shove away from the table and slam their phone and car keys on it. "If being here means you get to be total asshats or think you own me, you can take all this shit back, and I'll take care of myself. Like I've done for all these years."

I'm out the door and out the gate before they can stop me. I don't have any cash on me to catch a bus and since I gave the phone back, I can't call a ride, which means I'm walking to town. I hope Mel is at the diner and will let me use the phone.

It takes me an hour to get to the diner on foot, only to find out it's closed for a special function tonight. If it were earlier, I'd have no problem with walking the fifteen miles to campus, but now, without my tunes, it feels like a bad idea.

I step over to the end of the boardwalk for a moment just to listen to the roar of the surf. The sound alone soothes the rage boiling inside me. After a few deep breaths, I no longer feel like I'm about to erupt. Maybe I can camp out here under the stars tonight.

"Hello."

I turn towards the sound of the voice. I delve into my memory, trying to remember where I know the older woman from. She tucks her hair behind her ear, then it clicks. She was at the booth in front of me the first time I came here for lunch. Stepping closer, she asks, "Are you okay?"

"Yeah." I look over at the diner's sign. "Thought I'd stop in for a bite, but it looks like they're closed."

"They're catering an event tonight."

"Oh."

"If you're hungry, though, you can come in and grab a bite. I'm sure there are leftovers in the fridge."

"You have keys to the diner?" I ask, making sure I heard her correctly.

"Of course." She says, like it's common knowledge. Hell, it probably is. I'm just not hip on the inner workings of this town. "Well?" She asks, when I don't respond.

"Well, what?"

"Did you want me to grab you some food?"

"Oh, uh. No. Thank you. I actually ate before I walked here, but the pie..."

She smiles, knowingly. "The pie is incredible. We don't have to go into the diner for that. I happen to have some in the hotel. Come with me."

I'm not in the habit of blindly following people, but for some reason, I find myself marching after her into the hotel lobby. It's warm and cozy and feels a lot like one of those quaint bed and breakfasts you see on television, rather than a glitzy hotel. I immediately relax.

She leads me to a cute little nook where there's a beverage and snack cart set up. "Oh wow. This is quite a spread." I say, staring at the selections.

"We like to have some treats on hand for our guests if they want to sit by the fire or out on our patio to watch the sunset."

"You take debit card, right?"

"Everything you see is complimentary for the guests."

"Right, and I'm not a guest, so...."

She gives me a curt nod. "I see. Well, I invited you inside. That makes you my guest, so I can't take your money." She cuts me off before I can give a counter argument. "But if you feel like you need to pay, we're about to hit an evening rush with check-ins and I'm short staffed. I could really use someone to answer phones for about an hour. Think you can handle that?"

"For one slice of pie?"

"For a slice of the best damn pie in California."

"The pie will cost me $3.25. Seems like you'll be getting off cheap on the labor."

"I'll throw in all the drinks you want."

"Water is free."

Her lips twitch. "Two slices of pie and coffee?"

I can take the pie with me, and probably use the phone to call a ride. "Sold." She nods, and I gesture towards the desk. "Show me the ropes, boss."

"It's Evangeline, but everyone around her just calls me Van."

"Thea."

I'm glad she doesn't try to shake my hand or anything. She just leads me across the lobby and stops in front of the desk, motioning for me to step behind it.

"It's real simple. Read the script." She says, pointing to the laminated paper on the desk. "Most of the calls will come from inside the hotel. Jot down any messages or complaints, and someone will come by and collect them."

"What if someone is calling to verify their reservation? Is the computer on?" I ask, stabbing at a button.

"We print out our reservation list a week in advance, so you can look it up in this book." She points to a green leather-bound binder.

"If it's further out then that, just press two on the phone to transfer the call over to guest relations." I look over to the other desk, which must be guest relations. "All set?"

I nod. Easiest way to earn pie. "Got it."

"Okay, then I'll see you in an hour."

It's two hours later, before I get relieved. The girl Van was waiting for came in, but the phone was ringing off the hook, so I hung around a little longer to help. It was an efficiently run madhouse.

On the outside, you wouldn't think this place does as much business as it does, but I heard it's booked solid up until the holidays. I'm tired when I finally plop down in a chair near the patio. It felt good to be busy doing something useful.

Since it's later in the evening, I opted for tea to drink with my pie instead of coffee. Van is sitting next to me and we're discussing how I like the town so far.

I shrug. "It's not that it's boring, but it's a little too upscale for me."

She nods at my answer. "It's changed a lot since I was your age, a lot of people have moved away. We had a lot more independently owned and operated businesses back then. A lot of them were sold off, and then shut down. The landscape of the town is changing."

She gives me a tight smile. "Newer and better, that's what young people want, right?"

I shrug. I don't think new is always better. "Why didn't you move or sell?"

"Because Canyon Falls is my home. My history is here. My husband and I run this business. I couldn't walk away."

"It must be nice to have that type of attachment to a place."

"Don't you miss Nags Creek?"

Do I? I shake my head. "I miss my friend Sasha and a few of the hangouts, but not the town. If I'm being honest, I guess it never felt like home. Maybe I'm not designed to get attached to places since I moved a lot."

"You're young, and no one expects you to put down roots so soon."

"I want to be an archaeologist. I'll probably never put down roots."

Her brows lift. "Traveling the world? Going on digs?"

I brace myself for the conversation. I've heard it enough times. "I know that doesn't sound like a glamorous career or a moneymaker."

Her face lights up and she says, "Oh no, Thea. I think that's fantastic. Where do you want to go first?"

She seems like she's really interested in hearing my answer, so I tell her my dream destination and before I know it, another hour has passed. Looking at my watch, I say, "Oh my god, I totally lost track of time. I didn't mean to talk your ear off."

I feel bad that I've been holding her up when she has a business to run.

"Nonsense." She waves off my concerns. "I was enjoying our conversation. As you can imagine, running a hotel keeps me busy, and it was nice to just sit and talk for a while."

"It was nice to talk to you too, Van."

We both climb to our feet. She pushes me toward the cart. "Take two slices to go, and if you're ever back this way, drop in and say hello. Get home safe."

Shit, I forgot to make my call. "Uh, I'm sorry. Can I borrow the phone, so I can call a ride?"

"No need dear. I'll have the hotel shuttle drop you off at school, or wherever you need to go."

"I'm heading to campus, but I don't want to take your shuttle out of service. What about the guests?"

"Our driver actually has a pickup at the mall near campus, so this is perfect. He'll be waiting out front." She gives me another smile and rushes off towards the back.

Just as she said, the shuttle is waiting for me. The driver doesn't try to engage me in conversation during the ride and I'm happy about that.

I take the time to reflect on this weird ass day. The folks I should have had a nice cozy interaction with pissed me off, and an absolute stranger made me feel more seen and validated than any adult other than Sasha's grandparents and Mrs. Sprout has in a long time.

Chapter 28
Thea

The day after our disastrous dinner, Moira and Scott had the phone and car delivered to me back on campus. I had three voice messages and two texts of apologies from Moira.

I'm using the phone, but I'm leaving the car parked in the student lot. While I was waiting to straighten out the towing mess, I found out the school offers a shuttle that drops you right in front of the post office. I came here last weekend and I'm back again.

Three blocks over from where the shuttle dropped me off is the warehouse district. It's deserted this time of night, with a lot of what I assume are abandoned buildings. Nothing exciting to see, but I'm still mapping terrain, hoping to stumble across some hidden gems.

Academics aside, I'm drowning at Canyon Falls University. I feel too exposed when I walk through campus. I need some place I can hang out without drawing too much attention. The grungier the better.

I cross the street to where a guy is standing on a corner. He's only stopping guys and I pick up on what he's doing. He's a promoter. They all have the same purpose. To invite people to whatever event that's happening, but they only target certain people. Hot girls for clubs which bring in the guys who spend money on drinks trying to get laid. Or tough guys and men in suits who might want to bet on a little action.

I walk right up to him and hold out my hand. "Do I make the cut?" He gives me a once over, taking in my clothes and my tits.

"Yeah, you make the cut." He hands me a flyer. "Bring your friends."

I look down at the flyer. I've got one friend in this town and before I bring LJ, I need to check things out myself. "Where is this place?"

"Red Canyon. It's halfway between here and Palisade Shores."

Palisades Shores. That's where the bar is where I met Deacon. It's about an hour west of here.

"Cool." I leave him to try to drum up more patrons and continue my walk through town, It's teaming with students from school, walking in groups, laughing and talking, sharing meals together. I ignore the looks I get since I'm alone. It doesn't bother me. I like it this way.

I treat myself to dinner and a movie, and force myself not to think about Finn sitting with me the last time I came to a movie. That's back when I almost thought he'd be halfway decent to hang out with. Turns out my first impression was the right impression. He's an ass and not worthy of my time, thoughts, or energy.

It's almost eleven at night when the movie lets out. Now I'll really get to see what this town's all about. There has to be a club around her somewhere.

I cut across the side street next to the movie theater. Another block down, I see people walking and cars that look like they're double parked. I can also make out flashing neon lights against the street. That's the sign of a club or a bar, if I ever saw one.

All of this activity is happening on the street parallel to the one I'm on. I decide to cut through an alley behind what looks like an old warehouse instead of walking around the building.

I'm halfway through the alley when the rusty squeak of a hinge drags my attention to the third story of the building. Someone climbs out of a window and makes his way down the fire escape. A thinner guy follows soon after him.

I ignore them. Maybe I was wrong about the building being empty. They must have repurposed the warehouse into one of those chic apartments or something.

That thought doesn't stop me from looking again. There are no lights reflecting from any of the windows and they have graffiti on them. There's something suspicious about what they're doing. There's no way an upscale apartment building would leave the windows vandalized like that. I pick up my pace. Whatever they're up to. Not my problem.

The guys jump down off the fire escape and walk over to the dumpster, where they do the stupidest thing they can. They start talking about their score. *Fucking amateurs.* Just yammering without checking their surroundings.

They keep talking all excitedly, when someone yells, "Zeus, what the fuck are ya'll doing?"

Their heads pop up and I know they've spotted me. I keep walking, pretending like I didn't see or hear them. A hand lands on my shoulder. I shrug it off. I just need to make it a few more feet. The hand grabs me again and I acknowledge the fact that there's no way I'm getting out of here without having to deal with this shit. I spin around ready to defend myself, but stop when I see Michael Pearse, from my Physical Enhancement Class in front of me.

"Theona LaReaux." He says with a low whistle. "I didn't think you ever left the campus."

"And I didn't know what I do is any of your business. Or are you watching me, hoping to learn some new defensive moves?"

"Whatever, little girl, I'd own your ass in that ring."

"The way I remember it, Coach Wolfe is very selective about who he pairs you up with. Good thing too. You might be quick on your feet, but you're like a dull hammer smashing things. All brawn, no finesse. There'd be too much paperwork to fill out if everyone was knocking you on your ass, like Torrance did when he caught you with that sloppy ass roundhouse the first week of class."

His friends exchange a look. I get the feeling he's not completely honest with them about the losses he takes in class. "He wasn't supposed to be kicking, and you know it."

"What I know is you lost that round. I heard there was some type of wager attached to it. Did you really have to watch while he fingered your girl, and she came so hard just by his hand that she dumped you?"

The skinny one says, "I thought you said *you* broke up with her?"

"This bitch doesn't know what she's talking about."

I shrug. He's right. I don't know shit about what happened. I'm making it up as I go along, but it's funny, and I'm trying to distract him, because I've stumbled onto some shady shit and need to get out of here.

"What are you doing here, *Theona?*"

I grit my teeth. He's heard me tell Coach Wolfe and the other students that I don't answer to that name. "Taking a piss. You? Don't tell me... You're letting slim over here, tickle your tonsils? Sorry to interrupt. I'll just be on my way."

"Yo, Mike. I found it. I can't believe this building doesn't have an alarm." Someone yells from above.

How many more idiots are still in the building? Michael's eyes snap to mine. I'm playing it cool, but thinking about my exit route. I'm closer to the end of the alley I was heading for, but I'm facing the way I came. His buddies are moving closer. They're almost behind me and I have no way of knowing how fast or slow they are.

"I'm gonna ask you again, what are you doing here, Theona?"

"Stargazing. Minding my own fucking business."

"In an alley?" He squints, sizing me up. "This is a pretty dangerous place for a girl."

"Can't be too dangerous if you're hanging out here."

The skinny guy steps closer, looking me up and down. "You know, you got a real smart mouth on you."

His buddies agree. The one who just climbed down off the fire escape says, "And a nice ass."

I recognize the tone in his voice. I've heard plenty of guys comment on my ass, seconds before they have the stupid idea of touching it. Time to go. I try to move around Michael, but he steps into my path. "Move."

"Make me."

His buddies have a good chuckle about that. Little do they know, I'll have no problem doing just that. I move to the other side and he gets in my way again. "What's your hurry, *Theona*? Stay. Hang out with us."

"Yeah. Hang out with us." Skinny says. He's now closer than I want him to be. He pops me on my ass. I knew it was coming. Too bad he can't say the same thing about what I'm about to do. I turn around and punch him in the nose. "You, *bitch!*"

"Takes one to know one." I shift my feet, settling my weight. Preparing myself to fight my way out of here. "Anybody else interested in making a love connection with my fist?"

The last guy to exit the building stalks forward. "You got a lucky shot off on my friend. But like Mike said, stick around and have some fun with us. We're in the mood to celebrate."

"I suggest you get the fuck out of my way."

"Or wh-"

He doesn't get to finish his statement. I chop him in the throat and take off down the alley towards the neon lights.

"Get her!"

I'm almost to the end when a hand snatches my ponytail, forcing me to a halt. Arms band around me, lifting me from the ground. It's bad luck for the guy who moved in front of me. I kick him in the nuts. One of the other guys grabs my legs and they drag me back to the middle of the alley putting me right back in front of Michael.

He grips my chin in a punishing hold. "I was just trying to have a nice conversation with you, but you wanna get all mouthy and shit. Start throwing blows. I heard all about you mouthing off to The Trium. They don't know what to do with a bitch like you, but I do, so I'm gonna do what they can't and teach you some manners."

His friends push me to my knees, holding onto my shoulders to keep me from getting up. That doesn't stop me from letting Michael know what I think about his threat to teach me anything. "Better women than you have tried."

He looms over me and snarls, "I'm about to show you, I'm all fucking man." He fumbles with his pants, and I take a steadying breath.

I don't know what I stumbled across, but a court case my first month here was *not* how I expected this new chapter of my life to go. But you know, a girl's gotta have healthy boundaries, and being forced to my knees in front of this prick, is well outside those boundaries. I guess Clint is about to come out of his short lived retirement.

I snake my hand inside my shoe, grab hold of the handle, and slowly drag it from its hiding place strapped to my ankle. There's a shuffling noise behind me. I can't turn to see what's happening, but I watch as Michael's face pales. He pauses with his small ass dick halfway out of his pants. I'm seriously doing him a favor by chopping it off.

"Well, well, well. What do we have here?" I stiffen because I recognize the voice. *Great.* It's an asshole convention.

"What are you doing here, Finn?" Michael asks, casting a worried glance over my shoulder.

"Oh, I'm just out for a little late night hell-raising." Finn steps closer and asks, "What about you? What you got here? A new pet?"

I grit my teeth. I've already told him not to call me that. "I'm not his pet."

Finn smooths his hand down the back of my head. It's quick, yet unmistakable. The asshole just petted me, like I'm some kind of dog. "Course not. I meant *mine*."

"Listen dumbass-"

"Quiet!" Michael's buddy -what did he call him Zeus?- hisses at me and yanks my hair. He's about to meet the business end of Clint too. I'm okay with leaving them all bleeding from various points on their bodies. The thought makes me smile.

"Whatever I've found is mine." Michael says, dragging my attention back to the conversation.

Finn is now standing next to him, taking in the scene. "Righto. Finder's keepers and all that."

Thing one and thing two are still holding me down, and skinny is off to the side holding his nose. Finn's eyes flash with something when they land on my shoulders. Then just like that, his face is impassive once again. He turns back to Michael, and says, "You know I'm a reasonable guy. How about we trade?"

What is this shit?

Michael snorts, "Trade? What do you have that'll be better than the blow job I'm about to get from this bitch?"

These fucktards are *not* about to barter over me like I'm not even here, so I answer. "How about your pathetic dick remains in one piece?"

Finn's gaze snaps to me, an exasperated look on his face. "Quiet, Pet."

"Eat my ass, Finley."

"Now *my* dick is hard." He mutters to himself, but he's close enough that I hear him. He turns back around and says, "Old friend, you sure you don't wanna trade?"

"We're not friends, *Finley*." Michael says, mocking my use of his name.

The gasp Finn makes is dramatic as fuck. I can't hold back my snicker at his theatrics. "Well, you can't say I didn't try to be diplomatic about it."

He drops the teasing tone. His voice is like steel when he says. "Now we'll take *her and* whatever fun trinkets you have on you."

Michael stammers. "Wha- What?"

"You heard me. You're down here, and Zeus has on his trusty little backpack. That means you were out on frat business. We'll take whatever your challenge item was, and you get to go back to school with considerably fewer bruises than I'm currently planning to inflict on you."

Michael sweeps his gaze across the alley again. "What we? It's just *you* Finn."

The flash of fear I saw is gone, now that he's confirmed that whatever he was looking for isn't here. My guess is he was checking for Holden and Pax since they're usually tied together at the dick. Sensing Finn is no threat, he pulls himself up taller. It's comical. Real easy to be a tough guy when he and his friends outnumber his opponent.

Finn sighs, "Yes, and that's too bad. *For you.* Because that means there's nobody here to rein me in."

There's a flash of steel, and for just a second, I'm impressed with how quick he is. It's like he summoned his blade from thin air. It lands right at Michael's feet, and somehow he's got another one at his throat. "Don't for one-second think that I won't gut you before your boys even have a chance to make a move. Before you're even done bleeding out, I'll have made a call to deal with anyone or anything that may question my version of events."

The blood leeches out of Michael's face. There's clearly some underlying meaning behind Finn's words. Mike grabs the bag from Zeus and starts pulling stuff out of it, shoving it against Finn's chest.

Finn looks over at the two meatheads still behind me. They realize they're no longer in control of this situation, and back up, giving me space to get to my feet.

I leave Clint in my shoe, since it doesn't look like I'm gonna need it tonight. But that doesn't mean these jerks are getting off easy. I stalk over to them, hands clenched at my side. I'm gonna give them matching nose jobs. Before I can deck Zeus, I'm snatched off the ground and dragged away.

"Come along, Pet, you're making me late."

"Call me, pet, one more time." I say, as I wrench myself out of Finn's hold, turning to confront him.

He stalks forward, probably expecting me to back up. I don't. I stand my ground and crane my head back to look him in the eye.

"*Pet.*"

I strike out to punch him in the face, but he ducks and spins me around so my back is to his chest, my arms pinned to my sides. "Now I'm *really* hard."

He grinds against my ass, proving his point. My eyes flutter closed. I have to bite my tongue to keep from moaning. I don't want him to think what I'm feeling has anything to do with him. I'm only reacting like this because it's been a minute since I've had anyone pressed against me, and all that knife wielding was hot as sin. It's the circumstances that have me horny. Not the person.

I've seen Finn's dick twice. He likes to hang out naked on his balcony, and despite what I say, it didn't look tiny. Feeling him up against me just confirms it.

Before I get carried away, I remind myself that we're in an alley. Not that I care about the location. *Hello*, best fuck of my life was in an alley. But I do care that Michael and his goon squad are still here, and I care that it's Finn grinding against my ass. That part especially. He's one-third of the Coxsucker trio. Unworthy of my lust.

Finn walks me towards the wall and presses me against it, nuzzling my ear. He lifts his head and says, "Leave boys, before I decide not to be so understanding."

I hear them running away and expect Finn to back up when they're out of range. He doesn't. I squirm, trying to put space between us, but he presses even closer.

"Do you mind?" I huff, trying to get myself out of his hold.

"Not at all. I love the way your ass is rubbing against me." He grinds his thickening cock against me and breathes out, "Do it again."

I'm tempted to, but I refuse to give in to the urge. "I meant you need to move."

"Do you really want me to? I can show you some of those mouth things we talked about before." He nibbles on my neck and damn if that doesn't send sparks shooting through me. Fighting and fucking, goes together like PB&J.

His phone rings, and he steps back with a groan. "Sorry, Pet, we'll have to finish this later. I really do have somewhere I need to be."

He links his hand in mine and drags me out of the alley, then down the street, depositing me on the corner in front of one of the pickup spots for the school shuttle. There's a bus already here loading.

"Go back to campus and stay out of trouble."

I turn to tell him to fuck off, but he's already gone. Disappearing as stealthily as he appeared in the alley.

Chapter 29
Holden

Finn sent us a text, telling us what he stumbled on, and that he ordered Thea to go straight back to campus. She didn't listen.

A traffic camera showed her walking away from the bus. A second camera caught her going into the nightclub on South Street. She stayed there for hours and was definitely tipsy when she left the club with Austin and that Breland girl.

I don't know what's going on with her and Austin, but they're getting closer. He's the only guy on campus that she allows to touch her. I press my hand to the panel on the wall that gives me access to her room. She doesn't know the shelf in the back of her closet is actually a door connecting our rooms. Only the current and previous Triums know it's here.

The shelf slides open. I leave it ajar because I won't be here for long. I step into her room, staring down at her sleeping figure. She's barely coherent.

It's supposed to matter. Her inability to defend herself is supposed to mean something to me. It doesn't. I like that she can't hang on to a thought long enough to argue, or lift her hands enough to fight back right now.

At first I was only watching her in the daytime. Now I do it when she's asleep. She's a light sleeper and has a thing for aromatherapy. She keeps a candle on the night table beside her bed. I heard her tell Layla Jean that she uses it every night. I swapped out the candle a week ago, with one I made. It has a little something extra in the wax. The dosing is low. Just enough to put her in a deeper sleep.

I step forward, staring down at her. She looks so beautiful, with her mermaid hair fanning across the pillow. The first time I came in here was after forcing myself to participate in the sex room at the league party. I needed a moment where I could really feel like myself.

I knew she was at the library when I let myself in and used the time to go through her things, trying to see if she was hiding something.

She came back just as I was finishing up, and I stood in the wall between our rooms listening to her get ready for bed. I had every intention of going back to my room then, but I waited until she was asleep and came out of my hiding space.

She tossed and turned until she finally got comfortable. I can relate to finding it hard to fall asleep. That night started something. I've come in here almost every night since. Whoever put her to bed tonight left her clothes on her. That's unacceptable. Thea doesn't like to sleep with clothes on.

I pull off her jeans. Her shirt is next and then her bra. Her tits settle on her upper ribs when I release them from their confines. The cool air puckers her nipples. I slide my thumb across my tongue, then spread the moisture on her tight tip. Dragging it back and forth in lazy strokes. The action calms me. Her brows furrow, her mouth opening, as she releases a soft pant of air.

"Feels good, Rey?"

She clamps her legs together, and rolls onto her side, with her hand wedged between her thighs. I roll her on her back again and guide her hands into her panties, dragging her fingers through her folds, then pulling them out. I lower my head, taking them into my mouth.

She tastes better than I imagined. The perfect combination of tart and sweet, like my favorite drink of strawberry lemonade.

I want so much more than just a taste, but there are too many unanswered questions surrounding her appearance. She looks like such a fragile thing sleeping peacefully in the middle of her bed. It's in stark contrast to the way she walks around campus.

She moans, dragging my attention down to her hand, which is back between her legs. "What are you dreaming of, little temptress?"

My dick thickens as I watch her pleasure herself in her sleep. She rubs her clit with small circles before dipping her finger into her slick heat. Circle, circle, circle. Dip. Circle, circle, circle, dip.

She picks up the rhythm, her body arching off the bed. I move closer, palming my dick through my jeans. My free hand clenched into a fist. She has no idea of the danger lurking over her bed as she seeks her release.

"What a needy little cunt you have. Is that why you're always pleasuring yourself? Tempting me with your sinful little body?" I shove my pants down, freeing myself, and pump my cock in time with the roll of her hips. "Fuck that hand, Thea." I hiss. "Make yourself come all over your fingers."

Her breath ticks up, a short moan tumbling from her wicked little mouth. I slide my hand along my length, base to tip. My nuts tighten, my back tenses. She goes to roll over, but I halt her movement. Holding her down, forcing her to stay on her back.

"Don't be a dick tease. Let me see it."

I release my hold on my dick to part her legs, giving me a perfect view of her hand moving inside her panties.

"What's that? You want me to fill this dripping cunt?" I slide my hand across her thigh and whisper, "I could own you. Hurt you. Bleed you. Would you enjoy that? Or would you look at me like a monster the way others have?"

I hover my hand over her throat. Pleasure coursing through me as

I imagine how hard I'd have to squeeze to snap her neck. I've been trying to be good, but every time she sits next to me in class, or skinny dips in my stream, or hikes through my woods, it fuels the part of me that sees her as something to possess, and toy with.

I fist my dick, pumping harder. My skin is on fire. I'm shaking with the effort it's taking me not to touch her. Not to hold her down and drive into her. To not give in completely to the monster living under my skin. I slide my hand against my length with punishing strokes. Taking everything I feel out on myself.

Her leg bumps against mine, sending a jolt through me. I bite down on my tongue to keep from making noise as I blow my load. I do my best to catch everything in my hand, but it spills over, dropping onto the sheets. Her thigh. The back of her hand.

The tightness in my chest eases, the scratching at my soul, abates. My dark desires settle. For now, I'm okay. Just those few moments hovering over her, knowing she was at my mercy, were enough to satisfy me. I tuck myself back into my jeans and slip back out of the room.

I didn't go too far tonight. I maintained control.

Chapter 30
Finn

I lean back on the couch and respond to the text message confirming my appointment with Babette today at three. Babette has magical hands and I always look forward to her putting them on my body. I don't know why more people don't schedule appointments for regular rub downs.

I've missed the last two weeks, and my body feels like one big ball of tension. Massages are my self-care time. I've tried to get Holden and Pax involved, but they usually turn me down.

That's why I was surprised when they joined me at my last session. It wasn't until we were already on the table that Pax confessed they joined in, because it would be the perfect way to annoy our neighbor.

Thea and I have this little routine going. She walks out onto her balcony every night, sits in her chair and breathes deeply. I let her get three or four deep inhales and exhales out of the way before going out onto my balcony. Without fail, she takes off as soon as she sees me.

I knew her little friend was watching me love on my knives, before I stripped for my last massage, and I took advantage of that shit. The nosy little cherub almost fell over getting an eye full.

I thought we'd seen the last of the both of them when they went inside, but Thea came running back out and caught the masseuses with their hands in the cookie jar, so to speak.

Most girls would've looked away, or pretended to be embarrassed, but not her. She didn't blush or pretend not to look. She drank up our bodies, took a second look and then told us we had tiny dicks. It's a lie. We have really nice sized penises. Bigger than average according to what I've read and what I've seen in the locker rooms.

At any rate, she liked what she saw. I could see it in the way her tongue darted out, and her pouty little mouth popped open when she was eating us up with those shimmering blue eyes. Points to her, she didn't look at any one person longer than the next.

She took equal amounts of time eye fucking each of us. That doesn't happen often. People take one look at me and think I'm the soft one, since I'm not as jacked or as inked up as Pax and Holden.

I'm not soft. I'm just as dangerous as they look. Maybe even more so, since my knives are like my Amex card, I never leave home without them.

A fact that I had to remind that idiot Michael of. I was out on a mission of my own when I stumbled across him and his buddies in the alley. I would've kept walking, but I heard Thea's voice, all bitchy and promising pain. I had to get closer to see what was happening.

Her on her knees with that short dick fucker about to slide between those lips made me feel homicidal. I scrub my hand through my hair. The one time none of us are trailing her and she gets her ass in trouble. Good thing I got there when I did. If she's gonna be sucking anyone's dick, it'll be mine.

I'm in the lobby, waiting for Pax and Holden to show up. This morning's lingerie show is a bit of a drag. It's like they're not even trying to impress me. I'll have to have a talk with them.

The elevator door slides open and out pops the woman I was just thinking about. She's wearing a sun dress today, with a man's button-down shirt over it, like it's a jacket.

I feel a pang of jealousy, wondering what asshole left his clothes at her place. Then, I remember she must've had the shirt before she moved here, because there haven't been any men in her room. There won't be. Nobody's crazy enough to come up to our floor without getting our permission first, and that shit's not happening. Our floor has a three dick maximum.

I take another look at the elevator. I don't know what's taking the guys so long. They'll just have to walk together, and I'll escort my lovely pet to the dining hall so I can make sure she's okay after her horrifying ordeal.

I jump to my feet, and follow her outside. She's standing in front of the building like she's waiting for someone. I do a quick perusal of the sidewalk to see if anybody's coming our way, fully prepared to send them off. *Alone.* It's empty. What's she waiting for? It takes a second for me to realize she's just soaking up the sun.

"Good morning, Pet." I purr against her ear. I make note of the slight shiver that runs through her before she stiffens and turns to face me. It's the same reaction she had when we were pressed together in the alley. Her face and mouth say go away, but her body says come closer.

"Do I know you?"

I squint my eyes, trying to figure out what she's playing at. "Oh, I get it. You're trying to pretend the other night didn't happen. There's no need to be shy. Rubbing your ass against me was a totally natural reaction. It doesn't have to be weird or anything. In fact, I think it'll make our next movie date even better."

"I'm not pretending anything. I just don't want to deal with the second hand embarrassment of being seen talking to someone with so little to offer."

"Little?"

She flicks her eyes towards my waistband. "That's right. They should warn a girl in orientation that this school is full of little dick men."

I flash her a grin. "Oh, Pet, you were simply standing too far away when you saw me. I promise objects are much bigger than they appear." I slip an arm across her shoulder. "How about we run back upstairs and I show you?"

She looks around and says, "There's nobody out here with a magnifying glass to spy on us. I think it's safe for you to whip it out right now."

"Right, here?"

"Yup."

"Right, now?"

"Absolutely."

Oh, my little pet has no idea what she's just dared me to do. I'd have thought the incident in the alley with Mikey might have traumatized her. Made her wary of seeing any more dicks any time soon. I guess I was wrong.

I give her another minute to back out. I know public exhibition isn't a lot of girl's thing. She just stands there, waiting expectantly. I drop my bag and unbutton the fly of my jeans. She still doesn't freak out or tell me to stop. I get to the third button and flick the sides of my waistband down to make the opening level with my cock.

The doors to the dorm hiss open behind me and Pax's voice, cuts into my fun, demanding to know, "What's she done this time?"

"Nothing, yet. Hopefully, we're about to change all that and the answer will be me."

Thea's looking at me, still waiting, like we're playing chicken and she thinks she's gonna win. My boxers are exposed. I gesture towards my junk. "Shall I go on?"

She pulls out her phone, flicks on the flashlight, and arches her brow, silently communicating for me to continue. Thank, god. I want to flash her so badly, I can taste it. Then I'll let her taste it.

"Knock it off, Finn." Pax snaps, coming to stand next to me. He scowls down at her, trying to scare her off. "We've got shit to do."

"Can't it wait? This is way more fun." I really wanna see how far she's willing to take this.

"No, it can't."

Uh, oh. I know that tone. I look over at my friend. He's sporting his pissed off at the world frown. There's no way I'll be able to enjoy this moment with him sucking the fun out of the air. With a heavy sigh, I rebutton my pants. "Sorry, Pet. We're gonna have to finish this later. Tonight at one am work for you?"

She blinks, trying to keep up with the topic shift. "Uh, no."

"You're right, we should get started earlier, so we have time for round two. I'll see you at midnight." I fall into step with Pax and call out. "Don't wait up. I'll just let myself in."

This is a great start to the day. Why's he in such a funky mood already? "What's up with you?"

Pax turns the question back on me. "Me? What's up with you? We always meet in the lobby if we don't ride down together and today I come down and find you outside with her. Stripping."

"Nothing wrong with getting a little naked."

"There is when the person you're getting naked with is *her*."

I shrug, dismissing his grumbling. I was waiting. They took too long. Geez. Dramatic ass. "I was just having a bit of fun. You should try it. You don't have nearly as much fun as you used to."

"We'll have fun once we're initiated into The League. Until then, we have work to do, and that doesn't include flashing our new neighbor. We're not here to make friends with her, Finn. We're trying to find out her secrets and break her. Holden, back me up on this."

I glance over at our quiet friend, who says, "Pax is right. We have to stay focused." Of course he sides with him. He always does.

"But Finn may be on to something. We have to follow her. What better way to keep tabs on her, then to be in her face? So far, messing with her student accounts doesn't seem to bother her. Maybe we're going about this the wrong way. If Finn's working his charm she'll never suspect that you and I are deep diving into her life, to find out why she was on the South side that night, and why she's even on our floor. This is probably our best shot at finding some personal information we can use to tear her down. It's all intel gathering and it doesn't have to be done in the dark."

That's right. Everything doesn't have to be done in the dark.

Some things could be more fun with the lights on. Like watching a certain neighbor's eyes as I do delectable things to her body.

"You're not even listening to me." Pax says, forcing my attention back to him.

The disappointment is heavy with this one. "I heard everything, but Holden and I, out voted you. I'll become her friend and get all her juicy details. Good?" I give a definitive nod, agreeing with myself. "Good."

Now I won't have to follow her around and sit through endless hours in the library. Getting her to open up should be easy. We've been doing our movie thing, and I saved her from Mikey and his minions. Gaining her trust should be easy.

Chapter 31
Thea

There's a soft breeze blowing across the hotel patio. I set my cup on the corner of the stack of papers I printed, and hover my pen over the one I'm holding ready to mark it up. A familiar voice grabs my attention.

I figure I must be hearing things, but I turn around anyway, and spot Uncle Scott coming around the corner with Van. He sees me right away. I slowly climb to my feet to meet them in the lobby.

"Thea, what are you doing here?" He asks when I get closer. It's posed as a true question and not a subversive way to scold me.

"I work here."

"Since when?"

"Since around the last time I told you, I can take care of myself." I see him thinking back on that day. I'm confused when he gives a heavy sigh. He had to have known I was serious, right?

"I suppose this is the reason you haven't been using the credit cards or the car."

He would be right. This job and the cash I already had in my bank account have me sitting pretty flush.

Van cuts in. "What's going on here?" She looks between the two of us, her brows furrowed, like she's caught us doing something wrong. Uncle Scott's a cutie and all, and I'm sure plenty of girls would go for the silver fox look that he'll eventually be rocking, but *eew*.

"Van, it's not what you think. This is my uncle." She quirks a brow and I clarify. "Not in a *-he dates my mom-* kind of way, but in a he's an actual relative and him and his wife are responsible for me as much as anyone can be responsible for a grown woman under the age of twenty-one kind of way."

I cast my gaze to Scott. "Translation, I don't need a babysitter."

"You don't? Then stop acting like a child. Translation, an adult wouldn't be trying to hide the fact that they're employed. They'd come right out and say it instead of blindsiding me with it." He retorts, mimicking my head tilt.

"She's your niece." Van says with a tone I can't quite place.

I ignore it, even though I probably owe her an explanation about why I didn't mention having an affluent benefactor when I convinced her to let me pick up some shifts here. I'll explain it later, but right now, I've got to deal with Scott's shitty attitude.

"I know this isn't the uber posh sky scraper you work at, or whatever, but this is a solid and reputable business. I would appreciate it if you don't bring our family squabbles here."

"I agree." He says before I can say anything else.

"You agree to leave?"

"I agree this is a solid and reputable business and I wouldn't think of having a family squabble in plain sight of the guests."

"No?"

"No." Van cuts in. "Because those we generally handle out back."

"Don't you mean in the back?" Scott asks, like a general smart ass.

Van is still assessing me with her newfound knowledge of my ties to the stuffy suit. "No, son. I mean in the back, by the trash dumpster."

That's right, *son*, I think cosigning on Van's joke. "Okay, so if you didn't know I work here and aren't about to get me fired, why are you here?"

He holds up a basket. "I came to have lunch with my mom."

My gaze flicks back over to Van. Shut the front door. *Son*, as in real son. I quickly flip from shocked to mad. Now I'm glaring at Van. She's been withholding vital information from *me*. Did she know who I was that first night? Did he tell her to make sure I got back to campus? She must see the suspicion on my face.

"Thea, I'm just as shocked to learn of Scott's connection to you as you are his connection to me." She soothes. "I had no idea Scott and Moira had found you, and that you were here."

My head whips back over to my uncle. "You didn't tell your mother?"

"Moira and I have been busy, and I thought this was a discussion to have in person, for obvious reasons."

I don't know what those obvious reasons are, but Van must because she's nodding like what he says makes sense. She's Scott's mother. Moira's mother-in-law. Does that mean she knows who my dad is, too? If she was like a mom to her, that means she must've confided in her, right? I wanna ask her, but not with Scott standing here.

Van and Scott share a look and she says, "Why don't you join us, Thea?"

"Nah, that's okay. You enjoy your mother-son date. I was just about to head back to campus, anyway. I've got a lot of homework to do."

She nods, and I appreciate her not being pushy about it. "Oh, Thea..." she calls out before I've taken more than a few steps. I turn slowly. This is it. I'm about to be fired. "Make sure you check with Marguerite about next week's schedule before you leave."

"I still work here?"

She snorts. "Of course. Just because Scott works at an uber snooty skyscraper or whatever doesn't mean I'm giving up one of the best workers I have."

I stare at Scott, waiting for him to object. He leans forward, kisses his mother's temple, and says, "Thea, this hotel has been in my father's family for generations, and I'm glad you're working here. Get back to campus safely."

There's no trace of sarcasm in any of that. He actually means it. Will wonders never cease? Maybe this will be the common ground he and I can find to stop sniping at each other.

"Thank you, and um, enjoy your lunch."

My mind drifts as I wait in line. I think about Van and Scott being related, the good morning texts I've been getting from Moira, and how I'm completely turned off by the men in this school. Austin, being the exception, but I only see him as a friend.

That thought segues to Finn, who's giving me whiplash. Two weeks ago, he and his buddies were fucking with my accounts, and now he's threatening to strip and prove he's packing.

He was trying to call my bluff and I was prepared to call his. I had no intentions of stopping him, but then the fun police interrupted us. Party poopers.

I haven't seen any of them in two days. Finn hasn't even been on his balcony. Thank, god. I've missed the feeling of peace I get from watching the sun set. After my run-in with Michael in the alley I was desperately needing those moments of inner reflection staring out at the trees.

Today is my third day back in the dining hall. I'm in line waiting for my food when a familiar silence engulfs the room. I know without turning around that the Coxsuckers have arrived.

When the talking resumes, I take it to mean they've made their way to their seats. There's a scuffle behind me and I'm jostled around so hard that I'm almost pushed out of place. Pax and Holden come into view.

Seeing them tells me everything I need to know about what the shoving was all about. They were pushing people out of the way to get to the front of the line. "Fucking. Assholes."

The guy in front of me shoots a look over his shoulder, but doesn't agree or complain about them cutting the line. "You don't agree? We've been standing here for like ten minutes and here they come getting food without having to wait. That's cool. Pretend not to see it. My eyes work, and I say they're *fucking assholes for cutting!*" I yell that last part to make sure they hear me.

"Pet, you make my dick so fucking hard with all these suggestions. I didn't think you were into that, but yes, I would love to fuck your asshole while I'm cutting something."

I whip around to find Finn standing behind me, a knife in one hand, a lock of my hair in the other. "Don't even think about it, Number Three."

He drops my hair with an unbothered shrug. "Shouldn't you be up there exerting your will on everyone with your boys?"

"Probably, but I'm having fun back here. Things look different from this angle." He tips his head to the side, checking out my ass.

"You mean in the back of the line?" I ask, the question laced with sarcasm.

"Yes. That. It's been a long time since I've had to do it." He leans his chin on my shoulder. "What do you do while you're waiting?"

"Read a book, listen to music, and *mind my own fucking business.*" I say when the guy in front of me turns around again.

Finn chuckles, eliminating the last bit of space between us. He's standing so close I can feel the heat coming off of him and I get a whiff of metal. It must be the shavings from whetting his knives. "You've got claws, Pet."

"Sure do, and you're crowding my space, so back up before you get scratched up."

His lips tickle my ear, when he says, "Don't tease, Pet. I'm into that. Let's skip lunch and go play."

"Play what?"

"Oh, just a little game I like to call, let's see how many times can I make you scream my name before you lose your voice." His fingers dig into my hip as he grinds against me. My mouth goes dry, and my clit throbs from the way he's holding me and the suggestive nature of his voice. He wraps my ponytail around his fist and tugs. "You like games, don't you, Pet?"

"Only the kind I can win."

He releases my hair and steps back. "You play your cards right with me, and you'll earn more than bragging rights."

He smacks my ass, then steps around me to meet his friends at their table. What the hell just happened? I check for my phone, and wallet. The easiest way to pick somebody's pocket is to do it while they're distracted. Everything's here.

I step forward, order my food, and move to the end of the counter to wait, trying to work out what Finn was up to. LJ's in a study session so I'm eating alone today. We've done some table hopping and finally settled on a spot at the farthest end of the room, by the side door. It's out of the way, of all the other tables. A secluded spot, but it means I have to walk past the red rope section to get to it. I grab my tray and head that way.

I glance over at the legacy table when I walk by. It looks like Finn's already forgotten about wanting me to scratch him. He's sitting with a girl I've seen hanging out with the sorority chicks. I arch a brow as I pass. Busted you on your bullshit buddy.

Once I'm seated, I pull my map out of my bag and put my headphones in, drowning out the noise. I study markings for the parts of town I've already visited. No luck finding a trail yet, but I'm having fun exploring. For the next half hour, I plot a new route, while listening to my tunes and scarfing down my food.

I can't hear anything, but I get the distinct impression I'm being watched. It's hard to explain, but whenever I'm under scrutiny, it feels like the air around me is heavy. I turn my phone camera on, setting it to selfie mode, and raise it up, holding it as if I'm scrolling for something else to listen to. No one's directly behind me. That means whoever's watching me is across the room. Only one table over there ever pays me any attention.

I've been in a good mood today. I aced my ethics test. I'm ahead on my English paper and I shaved forty-five seconds off my run time in Coach Wolfe's class. I refuse to engage with the Coxsuckers. They'll only *try* to ruin my day.

Turning my attention back to my map, I study the side of town I'll be exploring tonight. Canyon Falls is a lot bigger than I thought. I still couldn't tell you what people do for fun around here, but I'm having a blast seeing all the different sides of town.

I finish my lunch and stuff my map back in my bag. I've got six minutes to get to class. The teacher hinted at a pop quiz, and I don't want to be late. I dump my tray and head to the side door. Just as I'm pushing it open, a distinct grumble reaches my ear. "Fucking bitch, why are you always in my goddamn way?"

This door is a little loose, as if maintenance went extra heavy on oiling the hinges. You have to hold the door until the hinges catch to make sure it doesn't swing closed too fast. I push through the door and let it go. Snickering when I hear it make contact. Here's hoping it improves Pax's face.

LJ's waiting for me outside of my last class. There's a mixer at Haven House tonight. Our second stop on the, Get LJ Noticed by a Sorority Tour. We're getting ready at my dorm because I have a private bathroom and more space. And booze. I put my fake ID to good use and stacked up on some wine and liquor when I wasn't eating at The Rock.

I'm going to all these mixers for her, and she's learning to take shots for me. LJ's got the better end of the deal. She's discovering what kind of drinks she likes, and I'm reaffirming my opinion that I hate the idea of joining any clubs.

We ride the elevator in silence. I can tell LJ's nervous about tonight and I'm letting her process it in her own way. There will be plenty of time to get her hyped while we're getting ready.

The doors open, on my floor, and we're treated to the sight of my grumpy asshole neighbor walking down the middle of the hall. Not on one side or the other. Just straight down the middle. His face looks fine. He must've stopped the door with his hand. Next time I'll have to time the momentum of the swing better.

LJ goes to move out of his way but I yank her back up against me. Fuck that. If he needs to get by, he can walk around us or we're all gonna collide. At the last minute Pax shifts to his left. I chuckle when he bumps his shoulder into mine.

"You okay, Thea?" LJ asks

"Yup. Didn't feel a thing." I turn to look at him. "Bet that's not the first time you heard that is it, Tiny Tim?"

"Tiny Tim? What's that?" LJ asks, casting a furtive glance at him.

"Oh he knows exactly what I mean." The elevator doors close before he can say anything.

When I turn back towards my room, I see Finn and Holden standing in the hall. Finn gives me a disapproving look. "Are you poking the bear, Pet?"

"Bear?" I snort. "I think you mean guppy. He's not scaring anyone."

LJ pipes in, "He scares, me."

I shake my head, correcting her. "No, he doesn't. You're not scared of anyone or anything. Don't let them manipulate you into thinking you are." I say as we approach my door.

"Mind over matter, huh?" Finn says with a smile. He's been doing that a lot in public lately. He shouldn't. It's an amazing smile.

Highlighting just how cute he is. Friendly even. And a total and complete lie. I don't trust him any more than I trust his friends.

I press my key fob to the lock and push the door open. "Works for most things." I squint my eyes and give a pointed look at his junk. "Except biology."

His smile falters and I yank LJ into my room before he can say anything else. I dissolve into a fit of giggles thinking of the look on his face. I totally won that round.

Chapter 32
Pax

Fight night at the frat house always draws a crowd. Tonight's entertainment is in the form of girls in bikinis and a kiddie pool full of mud.

Holden and I are talking about Thea. I swear that girl is taking up way too much real estate in our minds lately. So far, our research hasn't turned up anything suspicious.

I'm ready to be rid of my stuck-up bitch of a neighbor. The updates to my father have been surface level, and his response is to keep watching her. I still haven't mentioned that she almost ran Finn over the night he assigned us this task. I had every intention of telling him that night, but as soon as he started with the whole "get me info on the new student" shit, I decided to keep my mouth shut.

My father stresses action over problems. Thea is walking around this campus, defiant at every turn. She's a problem and I can't say anything about it until she's under control.

My dad used to be my hero. When I was little, I did everything he said, everything he asked, because I wanted to make him proud of me. As I got older, I realized that his pride in my accomplishments aren't the same thing as being proud of me. So now my former hero is just the guy whose reputation I want to surpass.

He's a mid-level council member and mom enjoys the perks that position gives her. That means the older I got and as my father climbed the ranks, the less time and attention she had for me.

I don't have any siblings. My mother decided one was enough, and dad was okay with that since I'm a male heir, but I have girl cousins, and Holden has an older sister, while Finn's sister is younger.

Starting in high school, the daughters are paired up with a male heir. They escort him to functions, and go through a type of finishing school to prepare them for helping their future husband's lives run smoothly. Etiquette. Party planning. Smiling.

They learn to obtain information with a laugh and a smile and are told that they must keep their consort happy. In high school the tasks are small. Doing his homework, writing his papers, *wetting his dick.*

It's why we were caught off guard at the social club. We've always been told the women are assets, that they help make good alliances, but we thought that just meant arranged marriages and having children to extend bloodlines. What I saw that night has me rethinking that premise.

High school was fun. The male heirs made it into a game. We all wanted to see how many legacy princesses we could use and abuse before their matches were officially announced. But none of what we were exposed to back then could have prepared us for what we learned when we started college.

It started out small, our senior year of high school. We'd go to functions where we were introduced to representatives from Canyon Falls University and other Ivy League schools. Some of the reps traveled with students who talked to us about campus and fraternity life. Finn, Holden and I always knew we'd pledge Rho Beta Psi. Just like our fathers did.

Then our freshman year of college we started hearing the whispers. The rumors. The hints that there was an even more exclusive group on campus that was harder to join.

We hadn't met any members of that group, and questioning my dad about it, never yielded any answers. The last dinner we had before the start of pledge season each of our fathers finally admitted they were a part of a secret society. The League of the Daggered Ravens.

The brands, rings, and watches we've seen all our lives started to take on new meaning. They told us that getting accepted into the society was hard. We'd be asked to do things that would stretch our moral compass, and even then, there was no guarantee that we would be found worthy.

We all agreed we wanted it, and from that day on, we've done nothing but work our asses off to prove it. I didn't find out about my grandfather's position as a high council member until my application was approved.

So far, the tests we've faced have been easy, but we all know they'll get harder the deeper into initiation we go.

Finn and I got our prospect declaration last year. Holden got his a few months ago. We were worried we'd ascend faster than Holden until Finn's dad let it slip that entering the prospect phase at different times was just another test to see how close we really are.

Any other group would have felt the strain, but the three of us are closer than brothers. There's nothing I won't do for these guys and that they won't do for me. Nothing, not even The League can come between us.

A cheer from the crowd snaps me from my musings. The girls are covered in mud, pushing and pulling at each other. One of them is so drenched her bikini has slipped and her tits are hanging out. Someone pushing through the crowd on the other side of the pit draws my attention. It's Thea. I've seen her at a few other mixers as well.

At parties she dances with plenty of people but when it comes to hanging out, she's always with the same person. The shy girl who's glued to her side. Maybe that's the key. Instead of going directly after Thea, maybe I need to be more subtle about it and target her through her friend.

She notices I'm looking, raises her brow in challenge, then pushes her thumb and pointer finger together.

Fucking bitch needs to quit with the small dick shit. I keep my expression blank. Giving nothing away as a plan finally comes together.

"Okay, I'm here." Eloise huffs, dropping into the seat across from me. She turns her nose up as a bottle girl walks by. "What was so urgent that you wanted to meet here?"

We're at one of the hottest clubs in town. The waiting list to reserve VIP is three months long, and she's acting like it's a cesspool. "I thought you liked it here."

"That was last month. This place has lost its charm."

That means she's no longer the *it* girl among the weekend crowd. I'm shit at making small talk, so I dive into the reason I asked her to meet me here. "How's the review for this year's pledge season coming along?"

"We have a solid list of names. I think the boys will be happy with the final list."

"I need a name added to your roster."

She rolls her eyes at me. "You know our numbers are finite. I can't just make another opening in the house." Tilting her head to the side, sizing me up, she asks, "Who is it?"

She's trying to sound bored, but I'm asking her to do this so she's trying to figure out my angle. "The new girl at the dorms, Thea."

She snorts and shakes her head. "She's already turned down an invite from the Lady Lions, and the Golden Monarchs. She'll never go for it."

I heard she said no to them, but I know a way to get her to say yes. "She will if her friend gets an invite too."

She takes a minute to think. "Who? Layla-Jean? *God.* She's an even worse fit."

"You went to school with her. She knows how this stuff works. It will give your offer to Thea more credibility if she's invited too."

"We went to school together, but she doesn't know shit. Why do you think she's a nobody around here? I'm telling you, Pax, they won't fit in and make it all the way through. Besides, I thought you hated the new bitch. Why are you trying to help her be relevant?"

"I'm not. I just want her to think she is. Give her the invitation, make her initiation hell, and make sure she never makes it to the end."

"You want me to sabotage her?"

"That's, right. Bring her close then make her pledge time so humiliating and unbearable that she leaves school and never even thinks about re-enrolling."

Eloise sits back in her seat. I see the wheels turning. "And what do I get out of this?"

"You get to know you're doing your part to preserve the reputation and rules of all legacy students."

She gives me a look that implies it's not good enough. I knew it would come to this. She's an opportunistic cunt. "Fine. What do you want?"

"Finn."

"You already have him."

"Finn's running around campus getting his dick sucked by every blushing bimbo he smiles at. I want his attention back on me, and I want your support and you encouraging him to focus on me. *Only* me."

"And?" I ask, because I can tell it's not enough.

"And you three boys start showing me the respect I deserve. You need to stop pretending I'm insignificant. I'm in charge of the Future Wives table, but I shouldn't be eating there unless I want to. I've already been matched. The Trium needs to treat me like the queen I am. Acknowledge me. Keep me satisfied and happy, in and out of public."

"You want us all to fuck you?" I snort. "That's not happening."

It's not that we're above sharing. Everyone knows we've done it. But Eloise is tied in first place with Thea as the last person I'd ever want to fuck, and Holden wouldn't even make it in the same room with her without snapping her neck.

It's a wonder Finn even deals with her basic bedroom ass. If it weren't for their arrangement, he wouldn't. She's about to tell me no again, so I say, "But I *can* push Finn your way a little more."

"A *lot* more. I want his dick in his pants, unless I'm around. He can't keep making a fool of me, Pax. Using me, to make his flings jealous then discarding me when he's ready for a new skank to get him off."

I roll my eyes at her version of events. He wouldn't be using other women if Eloise would just try something more exciting than reverse cowgirl. Hell, a quick fuck behind the bleachers would probably get him to act right for three or four days.

"Save the bullshit for your followers Eloise. You've been playing just as hard as he has."

"Well, right now I'm not. I'm done with other guys. Finn is my future husband and I refuse to go through the next two years like this. He's had his fun, now he needs to heel."

I've never told my friends what to do when it comes to hooking up. Frankly, I like when Finn's ignoring Eloise because she's annoying as hell. She thinks she's hot shit because she's already been matched to Finn and is guaranteed a ring.

But this might work in my favor. Finn's interested in Thea. He's trying to hide it under the guise of finding out her secrets for this assignment, but I can tell it's more.

I don't need him going off the rails and getting fixated on her. This is the least complicated way to shut that down too.

"Done."

I slip from my chair and melt into the crowd on the dance floor. I don't trust Eloise, but when it comes to being the queen bitch, I know she plays that role with Oscar winning accuracy. Now, all I have to do is sit back and watch Thea get her ass handed to her over and over again.

By the time the sorority chews her up and tosses her out, she'll be broken and humbled, no one will come anywhere near her, and she'll have no choice but to crawl back to her designated place in this world.

Which is nowhere near my school or town.

Chapter 33
Thea

I stare at the pink embossed lettering on ivory parchment paper longer than I probably should. It's an invitation, that much is clear, but why I received one is the part that has me confused. I've never done or said anything that could make them think I'd be interested in spending the night in a room with any of them.

Uncle Scott only seems to speak to me when he's pissed off at something I've said, but he hit the nail on the head when he told me to keep my focus on my studies and stay away from these entitled pricks on campus.

I close my mailbox and walk towards the side exit. From the squeaks and squeals filling the hallway, I'd say I'm the only one who *doesn't* think getting invited to party with the Prissy, missy, and simpy, is a dream come true.

I got an invitation from three other sororities last week. Who knew there were so many clubs interested in transfer students with alcoholic moms?

I turned them all down. I have LJ to thank for helping me draft the responses. I was going to just throw them in the trash when she explained a formal denial is expected.

It's how other sororities know you're still available to pledge. My insistence that I didn't care about the process fell on deaf ears. LJ's such a rule follower.

I trudge over to her dorm so she can help me turn these people down, too. I could totally draft the reply myself, but I don't actually know which glittery castle sent it to me. There's no name on the envelope or the invite. Just some weird symbol. I figure if anybody knows who it's from, it's my personal pledge season tour guide.

I've barely finished knocking on her door when she yanks it open. I hold up the card. My ears split from the squeal of excitement she lets out. She pulls me into the room and hurries over to her desk to pick up a matching invitation.

It takes a while for her to calm down enough to actually explain why she seems more excited about this invitation than she was the other ones I got. She tells me the Pepto Bismol society is Nu Nu Zeta Nu. She's already making plans for what to wear to the party. I roll my eyes when she throws around words like *exclusive* and *the best*.

I've tried to get out of it. It's been a week since LJ and I got those invitations in the mail. I had to listen to her going on and on about it every day. I finally limited her to one meal only. She chose breakfast and let the joy and excitement carry her through the day. That worked for me too, because we got it over with and then I had the rest of the day to pretend the invite never happened.

But it did happen, and here I am at the address that was messaged to us on our Prospectus accounts this morning. The *only* reason I'm here is because of LJ. She was excited about coming to the kickoff meeting, but also afraid to come to this empty old house alone. So here I am as backup to scare the shadows away.

The abandoned house is on the farthest end of Canyon Falls,

behind the old ice cream factory. The railroad tracks I crossed when I pulled into town are a few blocks from here. I didn't realize what a wasteland this place was, because the other parts of town are thriving.

Even the boardwalk enterprises are clean and comforting. This side of Canyon Falls reminds me of the seventh ward in Nags Creek. There's not much over here. Just dirt, weeds, and sticks, which I guess makes it the perfect place to lure unsuspecting people into some kind of fuckery.

LJ talked my ear off the whole way here, saying that if things go well tonight, we might get invites to pledge the sorority. I didn't have the heart to tell her that I couldn't care less about that shit. Cause, you know, I'm being a good friend.

I roll my eyes at myself. Layla-Jean Breland has wormed her way into my life and under my skin enough that I'm going to endure this night for her.

I even dressed up. I'm in a dress, wearing heels instead of my boots or sneakers. I'm not interested in whatever they're selling, and this is a one night only occasion for me. I'll get LJ through it and then offer my final fuck off in person.

The door to the house creaks open, and we step inside into the dimly lit foyer. I look around the entryway in morbid fascination, still not sure why the fancy invitation directed us here.

They went all out with the creep factor on this. I step further into the residence, heading towards the only room that seems to have working lights, with LJ following closely behind.

We enter what I guess you'd call a drawing room. It's devoid of furniture, with the exception of an elaborately adorned, pink coffee table with a folded place card on it.

As I get closer, I see my name printed on it. The sound LJ makes lets me know she's found one with her name on it, too. I pick it up to read it.

. . .

Dakota Lee

And so it begins...

What begins? Cause there ain't shit happening here. I study the notecard, trying to pick up clues about what we're supposed to do next. It's hard to focus. My fingers tingle. I lose my grip on the card, watching it fall to the ground. Something's wrong. I make my way to the door, calling for LJ to follow me. Just as I step through the doorway, everything goes hazy, then black.

A beeping sound and low chatter cuts through the fog in my brain. Did I leave a tv on? Why is my head pounding? I ignore the pain and peel my eyes open. The first thing I see is that I'm not in my room.

I close my eyes, trying to regain my equilibrium and figure out where I am. Everything comes rushing back. The abandoned house, and feeling like I was losing control of my body. Somebody gassed us and took us.

I sit upright; the movement makes my head swim. I scan the room for an exit. I'm in fight-or-flight mode. More fight than flight. *Shit,* I knew I should've worn my boots, but I guess the heel will make an effective weapon.

My rage simmers down to an irritating hum when I realize I haven't been trafficked. I'm not the only one in this room- and judging by the looks on everyone else's face, they're happy to be here- so I'm going to assume I'm not in any immediate danger. I wasn't in that building alone. I count twenty girls, none of them are LJ.

A voice pipes through a PA system, cutting through the chatter. "You're all awake. Perfect. Welcome to the meet and greet."

Meet and greet? Whatever this is, it's not a friendly tea party like the other things LJ dragged me to. The voice continues talking. "You have all been invited to apply to the most prestigious sisterhood there is. We've reviewed your grades and your extra-curricular activities, and deemed you interesting enough to apply. But unlike the other organizations on campus, your interview is about more than telling us how great a fit for us you'll be. You have to show us that the clever quips, perseverance and poise, the quick thinking and strength you all say you have is real. We're Nu Nu Zeta Nu, the sister sorority of Rho Beta Psi, and unlike our rivals, we're not coddled and merely hanging on the sidelines. We are an important part of Beta Psi's winning strategies. We have to be as fearless and as cunning as they are. We're winners. We're the best. Tonight is the first of many nights where we determine if you have what it truly takes to join us."

The lights go out, plunging us into darkness. I know before I see or hear anything that we're no longer alone in the room. A silk bag is shoved over my head and I'm hoisted off my feet and thrown over someone's shoulder.

I'm all for being manhandled when I want to be, but I didn't give this fucker permission to touch me. He carries me along with his hand on my ass. He's obviously used to these screeching, squealing chicks, but he's got me all the way fucked up. I swing, punching him in his ear. My attack catches him by surprise. His grip loosens and I tumble to the ground.

"What the fuck, man?" Someone yells. I guess dropping the merchandise is a big no, no.

"That bitch just hit me."

He's lucky I don't have my knife to puncture his ear drum. Though my heel might work. I'm pulled up to my feet again, as I'm working to get the bag off my head. An arm bands around me, keeping my arms at my side so I can't swing again.

"Easy. This is just part of the interview process. Nobody's gonna hurt you."

I'm lowered onto something hard, then music starts piping through the bag, cutting off the surrounding sounds. I reach up and discover headphones are built into the covering. After a few minutes, my body sways and an engine rumbles beneath me. I'm in some kind of vehicle.

I sit back trying to count the turns or approximate the distance, but it's hard to do with the music distracting me. Once again, I'm hauled to my feet. I feel a draft seconds before I'm pushed from the moving vehicle, landing on my hands and knees.

I scramble to my feet and work at the ropes around the hood. A voice cuts through the music.

"Home. It's the centralized area encompassing all that we are, from birth until now. The one place we can always return to, even when we're lost. You've all been driven to a location away from campus. We have your cell phones, and tablets or any other electrical items that help with navigation. Your first interview item is to find your way back to campus before sunrise. Good luck."

I finally free the knot, yanking the bag off my head, and look around. The first thing I notice is that I'm the only one out here. Wherever *here* is. The second thing I notice, is that she's right. My wristlet with my phone is missing. The worst part of this is, I'm still wearing these fucking heels.

I don't know how long I was out of it, but I know it was around seven when LJ and I got to that house. The stars are still out, the moon high in the sky. I estimate I have a good five or six hours before sunrise. Now, the question is, how far did we go from the house? That's a problem I'll deal with as soon as I figure out where I am in relation to campus. I look up, scanning my eyes across the constellations, slowly turning in a circle, until I find what I'm looking for.

Hello Polaris, my old friend. I imagine standing on my balcony, looking at the stars. My dorm is always east of Polaris, which means wherever I am, I need to travel in that direction. I'll work out if I'm south or north of campus when I get closer to town. Assuming there is a town close by, seeing how right now I'm in the middle of a road with no signs.

I won't make it far in these heels. I'm not even gonna try. I pull my shoes off and walk barefoot. Promising my feet a nice long soak in the tub when I get back.

I estimate I've been walking about thirty minutes when a highway sign comes into view. I let out a snort. I know exactly where

I am. I make my way down the offramp and walk the two miles to town. When I reach my destination, I dust off my feet, slip my shoes on and strut into the bar. Fucking ironic as hell that I wind up in the place I met Deacon. Er *Coach Wolfe*.

I sidle up to the bar and wait. It's not long before someone walks over and offers to buy me a drink, which I happily accept. On the other side of the room, a group of girls are laughing and wildly gesturing around the room.

One of the girls is wearing a Kiss the Bride sash. A bachelorette party, usually means there's a designated driver or a party bus. I turn back to the guy who brought me a drink and suggest his buddies should buy the girls at the table a drink, too. They agree and I help them carry them over.

As a thank you, the party insists I sit and join in on the fun, and when they're trying to figure out what to do next, I offer my help, suggesting another bar in a different location, and some food at a restaurant that has the best pie in the state.

An hour later, the party bus pulls up in front of Mel's diner. We tumble down the steps of the bus, and pile inside the doorway of the diner waiting to be seated.

I stick around long enough to have some food and take a slice of pie to go, before slipping next door to see if the shuttle driver has to make a run near campus.

I'm told he's already off for the night. One of the maintenance guys hears my request and tells me he's a student at Canyon Falls, too, and offers to give me a ride when his shift is over. I agree, and plop down on the patio furniture overlooking the beach, basking in my buzz while I wait. Forty minutes later, we're on our way.

He unlocks the car and starts apologizing about the condition of his used Mitsubishi Lancer Evolution. I have no idea why. It's old, but it runs and I can see he's putting some time and effort into fixing it up. He tries to pretend he doesn't know what I'm talking about, when I say his car will be badass when it's finally race ready.

"Dude, this car was made for racing. If that's not your end game, then this beauty is suffering in your hands."

He chuckles. "Okay, you got me. I'm fixing it up, and I might be trying to find a way to make it faster. I'm actually an aeronautical engineering major, and this is going to be my end-of-year project."

"There's a big difference between cars and planes."

"Yup, but I'm trying to figure out how to merge the two. Make this car faster, and ride so smooth, like it's flying."

"And the body work?"

"That's a bit of a hobby. Me and my buddy are doing it. That's why I'm working at the hotel. My old man isn't exactly supportive of this, so I earn my own money to pay for parts and supplies." He pulls up to the gate just outside of campus and turns to look at me. "And speaking of which, I'd appreciate if you don't mention it."

"The car or the job?"

"The job. And the car."

I arch a brow. "Should I just forget I ever met you, too?"

"Nope. That part I want everyone to know about."

My lips twitch, but I refrain from commenting.

"The car thing, like I said, it's my end-of-year project and I don't want people getting wind of it. As for the job…"

"Hey whatever reason you don't want people knowing, it's your business." I pull the door handle to let myself out. "Thanks for the ride."

I walk over to the Zeta Nu house to find my shit. It better be there. I let myself inside and spot the table right away. Snatching my purse off of it and checking to make sure my phone, ID and cash are still inside. I have a missed text from LJ asking where I am. It was sent hours ago, meaning she got back before me. Good for her. I shoot off a response, letting her know I'm just getting back and heading to my dorm and will call her tomorrow.

Once I reach Vale Tower, I kick off my shoes again. I promised my feet a soak, but I'm too tired tonight. It'll have to wait until morning.

Chapter 34
Pax

"Zeta Nu had their meet and greet last night." Finn says, sliding into the chair beside me. They're always the last sorority to do a meet and greet, and what happens is a well kept secret. Unless you're us. Finn always finds out what the houses are doing.

"How did it go?"

"They dropped everyone off at different parts of town and took their shit. They had to find their way back to campus before sunrise. Three of the invitees cried and refused to participate."

"Anyone important?" We always take note of who's being weeded out. Legacies that can't cut it find their status plummets pretty quickly. It's hard to rebuild your reputation when you're labeled weak and a quitter.

"Nobody of any relevance, though I saw an interesting name on the list."

"Who was that?"

"Thea."

Holden looks up from his tablet and says, "She doesn't strike me as a sorority girl."

"Her little friend is on the list, too. They've been going to all the mixers together. I guess they've been waiting for this. Zeta Nu is the best sorority on campus."

I look back down at my phone and chuckle. "Let me guess. They didn't make it back?"

"Oh, they did. Thea was dumped further away than anyone. Out in Palisades Shores and got back to campus before the deadline. She's currently ranked as number twenty out of forty-seven remaining girls."

That means nothing. If they had to make their way back to campus without money or a phone, and she came in twenty-seventh, that means she hitchhiked. Stupid and dangerous, and one more reason to suspect she's here on a job. Normal girls don't put themselves and their families at risk like that.

Finn's looking at me, like he knows I had something to do with her pledging. "You know what's funny? There were only supposed to be forty-eight invitees, and Layla-Jean and Thea are not the type of girls the Zeta's usually court."

Holden flips the cover of his tablet closed. "Their Prospectus ranks say they're worthy pledges. My guess is Zeta Nu had similar complaints to the ones we saw on the survey, and invited them to pledge to show the application process is fair, even though the selection committee have already picked their ideal pledges."

I nod. "I'm sure they have, too. I doubt Thea and her friend are resourceful enough or strong enough to make it to the end. But it'll be fun watching them try, don't you think?"

Finn pins me with his gaze. "You don't usually care about pledge season. I'm the one who keeps track of the rankings."

"Well, this year I think I'll watch too. I'll even enter the bracket and put my money on who I think the top ten girls will be."

They both nod, and we get up from our seats, heading to our frat house to enter our names in the pool. This is perfect. I get to watch Thea get trampled by the other pledges, and make some money when she doesn't make it through.

Plus, her going through the pledge process puts an extra set of eyes on her. Zeta Nu pledge masters watch their pledges like hawks. Making sure their rituals and initiation tests are protected from the other sororities. I want a hand at making the bitch miserable. I shoot Eloise a text.

> PAX
>
> I want in on Thea's chastity vow night.

We're not supposed to know what the pledges actually go through and their ranks are posted on the leader board, which only the leadership of Rho Beta Psi has access to. But nobody can keep a secret from us and the chastity vow ceremony is a long standing Zeta Nu tradition.

> ELOISE
>
> I've already done you a favor.

> PAX
>
> This is still a part of that. I have an idea on how to make the chastity vow more interesting.

> ELOISE
>
> You want to participate, then you know what you have to do

Finn. I have to convince him to spend more time with her, without being obvious about it.

> PAX
>
> I'll make sure Finn's on his best behavior when it comes to you

> ELOISE
>
> I want Finn by my side for Hell Week and Mayhem Night

Hell week is the lead up to Mayhem Night, when we celebrate

the end of pledge season. We work in groups or teams to pull our pranks around campus and participate in challenges against the other fraternities and sororities.

A lot of times, the teams wind up bunking together to minimize the chances of getting caught alone by their opponents. That week, Finn will be more compliant about doing what she wants. Destruction and booze usually puts him in a good mood. As long as she's not being a raging cunt.

PAX

Done

ELOISE

Her chastity vow ceremony is two weeks from Thurs. I'll give you the location when Finn confirms he's teaming up with me

We find Garrett in the business center with our recruitment roster and initiation schedule on the screen. He's trying to pair up our pledges with Zeta Nu's for some of the joint activities.

"Are we really doing the obstacle course this year?" Finn asks, staring at the screen. It's been cancelled for the last two years, because the Zeta Nu pledges act like they're too delicate to go through it.

"It's happening." Garrett assures us. "We gave in to Zeta Nu's demands for the last two years. This is our year to get what we want. If they back out of this, then the alternative is a lot worse."

"What can be worse?" I ask.

Holden answers before Garett can. "Camping."

Garrett nods, a mischievous glint in his eyes. "We get our twenty-four-hour amazing race style scavenger hunt and obstacle course or three days camping in the canyons. Which one do you really think the Nu's will pick?"

It's genius, and another way I can get Eloise and Finn to spend time together. Nothing says togetherness like a two-man team. I hate having to force Finn to spend time with her, but a deal is a deal. I pat

Garrett on the shoulder. "You might as well match Finn with Eloise."

Finn sputters, "Say what?"

I ignore the look on his face. "You're the only one who can deal with her. You know how she gets and if we have any chance of this event being successful, we need her to make sure everyone's excited about participating. The two of you teamed up this season is the logical answer."

He doesn't like the idea, but he doesn't fight me on it. Good. That's one hurdle down. Now, I just have to figure out how to get Holden on board with this whole treat Eloise like a queen business she's insisting on. None of us know how to do all that extra sweet shit that girls like. We never have to. We unbuckle our pants and women happily fall to their knees with their mouths gaping open, spread their legs, or their ass cheeks.

These days, the first and last options are my preferred methods for getting off. A fucking pregnancy scam near the end of my freshman year turned me off from pussy. I used a condom, but I know that's not 100% effective, so I had to sit through my father telling me how disappointed he was in my lack of vigilance, until the girl finally retracted her claim.

I kept insisting on a paternity test and she couldn't agree to one, because she was never really pregnant. Turns out she used her roommate's pregnancy test to try to get money out of me. I have no idea how long she thought she'd be able to keep up the sham.

That, and the side jobs I do, have soured me on sex. When I get the urge to fuck, I prefer to find my relief in a mouth or ass, instead of from someone's lying, deceitful cunt.

Thea

I shuffle through my note cards as I walk to my dorm. I just spent two hours in the library studying with classmates, but they were too easily distracted for the group session to be effective.

"Theeeonaaa."

I bite back a growl of annoyance when Michael steps into my path. What is this dude's problem? Why is he always hiding in the goddamn shadows?

"Can I help you?"

He hooks his arm across my shoulder and tucks me against his side. "What's with the hostility? I'm just here to escort you back to Vale Tower. It's pledge season. Not the ideal time for a lady to be out here alone at night."

I shake his arm off and roll my eyes at the obvious lie. I'm not alone. There are plenty of other people out here, and tons in the library. "I'll take my chances, thanks."

"Don't be a bitch, Theona."

"Why not? Because you've already got that title on lock?"

"Here's the thing. We need to settle our unfinished business. You cost me some challenge points for that shit in the alley, and you're going to repay me everything I lost with interest."

"You cost yourself challenge points. Instead of trying to get your micro peen sucked, you should've been safeguarding your treasure and getting the hell out of there."

"I was fine until you showed up, and the more I think about it, the more I think it was a setup. We have rules about that, and since you broke them, I'm owed repayment in any way I want."

I'm done listening. I hasten my pace to get away from him. He grabs my arm, pulling me up short, turning me to face him, his grip tight enough to leave bruises. Time to see Coach Wolfe's teachings in action.

"Get. Your. Hands. Off. Me." I say it as a courtesy because fighting is a last resource. A defense if all other options fail. Or whatever that shit is, Coach said.

"Mikey, Mikey, Mikey. When are you going to get your hearing checked? I can recommend someone if you'd like."

I cringe. This guy is here too? He's another one popping out of nowhere all the damn time.

"I hear just fine, Finn."

"No, I don't believe you do. I was hundreds of feet away and I heard her say remove your hands. Plus, I walked up on this little party and you never heard me coming." He taps a finger against his chin. "Unless you're saying you heard me and didn't care that you were engaging in an activity which would upset me."

Mike's hold on me tightens, like he knows I'm about to slip away. "This has nothing to do with you, Finn."

"Everything that happens on this campus has to do with me. You're manhandling a Zeta Nu pledge without any witnesses present, which is in direct violation of the rules of pledge season."

Michael drops his hands and takes a step back. I don't remember reading any rules prohibiting interactions between other frats and pledges, but what Finn's saying must be true, because Michael starts backpedaling.

"It wasn't like that. I just needed to talk to her about something, and was trying to keep her from walking off."

"Was the *something* an apology for what happened before?"

"No."

Finn's knife makes an appearance. He twirls the blade, digging the tip into his finger. "Then you have nothing to say to her. Even if it *was* an apology, you don't say it with your hands on her in a dark corner of campus alone. You don't speak to her or look at her without my permission. Are we clear?" Finn turns his back on Mike and walks over to me. "You're dismissed."

Mike scurries off, but the look in his eyes tells me this isn't over. I've just been the catalyst for Finn embarrassing him and disrupting his plans for the second time. Not sure how it's my fault, but I need to be prepared for anything.

Finn uses the flat of his blade to tip my chin up, forcing me to look at him. "You okay, Pet?"

I slap his hands away. "Don't paw at me."

"I'm checking for injuries."

I shove him away, pulling Clint out of my back pocket, pressing it against his carotid. "I don't need you jumping in like some knight in shining armor. I can fight my own battles."

"It's not about you fighting your battles, it's about putting him in his place. Mikey thinks because he runs his own team for his frat and they're halfway decent, that they can just challenge us for power. I had to remind him he's beneath us, and will always be looking up at us from his place on the ground. If I have to threaten to spill a little blood, so be it."

I'm not about to let Finn pull me into his little turf war or whatever, so I give him one final warning. "Stay away from me, and stay the hell out of my business, Number Three, or the next person's whose blood will be spilled is yours."

He grabs the blade of my knife. This isn't a butter knife. Clint's blade is sharp enough to slice through an aluminum can with ease. Blood rolls down the knife edge. It'll cut deeper if I try to pull it away. Finn's got his own love affair with sharp weapons, so he knows this.

I guess we've entered into another game of chicken. How long can he stand there holding onto the blade and how long will I let him until I get queasy at the sight of his blood. Jokes on him, it's not queasiness I feel. It's satisfaction that it's my knife making him bleed. Even if I didn't actually do the slicing.

He releases his grip but doesn't back up, and flips his palm over, showing me his hand. "First blood's been spilled, Pet. Now your business is my business. I'll be watching you so closely, you won't be able to sneeze without me knowing about it."

He swipes a bloody finger across my lips before turning and walking away. "Be good, Pet."

Chapter 35
Thea

I'm wound up tighter than I've ever been in my life. It's a combination of things. The incident with Michael in the alley, the bullshit with the pledge invitation, and being left stranded on the side of the road, Finn making me look weak with his odd savior complex, and the uphill climb I have in Physical Enhancement class, since Coach Wolfe still has me doing basic blocks with the other girls.

I've had enough of misogynistic men. We won't even discuss the drought I'm going through with no new dick to play with. I need to burn off this excess energy before I seriously hurt someone.

I bounce on my feet, waiting to enter the warehouse. I hope the vibe in this place is enough to ground me. The bouncer checks me for weapons (they never think to check inside my boot), then tells me the cover charge is thirty bucks. That's pretty steep. This place better be worth it.

Once inside, I travel a long hallway, which empties into a room that definitely tells me the cost is worth it. *Club Dredd* isn't a club at all. Not the kind you dance at, anyway. It's an underground fighting arena. If I were a squealer, I'd squeal. I've found my happy place.

I scan the room, taking in everything. I see people placing bets, folks huddled in corners with fighters, and couples making out. They've even got a bar and concession stand. I don't care about any of those things. I'm looking for one guy. The promoter, because he'll know how I can get my name on a ticket.

I ask a few people and of course they don't want to answer thinking I might be a narc. Finally, I make my way towards the locker room and spot someone who can give me answers. "Hey. I was wondering if you can point me towards whoever can put me on a ticket."

I give the guy with a towel draped over his neck and clipboard in his hand time to look me over. I'm not exactly dressed like a potential fighter but, his shirt says he's a trainer. If he's any good, he'll be able to tell I'm not bullshitting him.

He calls out, "Syl!"

A woman with flaming red hair and leather everything saunters over to us on five-inch heels. "What's up?"

"Little girl here wants to know how she can get on a ticket."

Syl sizes me up, just like he did. "You ever thrown a punch before?"

"Once or twice."

"We do amateur night once a month, and it's first come, first serve. If you lose, you get ten percent of the purse."

"So, when's the next one?"

"In two weeks."

"Boss, we got a problem." A guy wearing a junk yard dog chain around his neck says, hurrying over to us.

"What is it?"

"Crusher can't fight tonight."

"And why the hell not? He's been scheduled for this fight for months."

"His wife just went into labor."

"Dammit." Syl mutters to herself. "He was the underdog, but people are looking forward to this fight after all that IG beef." She scans the list in her hand. "Who do we know that we can pull off standby?"

The guy shakes his head and says, "Nobody who'll get here in time."

Syl doesn't like that answer. The scowl on her face says he better come up with a better one. "There's a lotta folks out there. I'm not interested in refunding any money."

Somebody up there loves me today. They're rewarding me for not cutting anyone since I've been here. That shit with Finn doesn't count. He cut himself. No way am I gonna stand here and miss out, and ignore the gift they're giving me. "I can do it."

They all turn towards me. The trainer chuckles. The guy with the chain looks at me like I've lost my mind. Syl has a glint in her eyes.

The chain guy says, "Not to be sexist or anything, doll, but Crusher was scheduled to fight Big Jim. They're evenly matched in size and he was still heavily favored to lose. You wouldn't last a round with him, with one hand tied behind his back."

He totally sounds sexist. "One round? I'd last more than that, and he can keep both his hands free." I turn to Syl. "Listen, put me in. If I get pummeled, you can keep your money. If I last three rounds, I get whatever Crusher's purse was, and a guaranteed spot on the next fight night. I'm not talking about the amateur ring, either."

Syl's a businesswoman. I'm sure she can see how this benefits her, either way, it ends. She keeps her money, or she gets a new fighter.

"Fine. The fight is in ten minutes, but I can push it back thirty minutes and give you time to change your mind, or get ready."

I shake my head, and let her know I don't need any time. "I'm ready now."

"Syl..." the trainer finally speaks. "She's not even dressed for a fight. Are you sure you wanna do this?"

"You know my rules. They sign up to fight. It's on them." The trainer walks off, shaking his head. To the guy with the chain, she says, "Toro, send out a notice that the betting window will be open for another eight minutes, allowing a onetime change of bets." She hands me a piece of paper. "Sign this waiver. And you're all set."

I give it a quick once over. It's a standard liability waiver and NDA. I scribble my name and hand it back.

She points over her shoulder. "You can purchase a mouth guard at the window. There will be some tape ringside, and we have lockers back there if you wanna hang your purse up and wait."

"I'm good with keeping it ring side." I don't know her or anyone else here and won't trust my shit in their lockers. This way, if someone comes by the ring and steals shit, I'll have a good idea who it was, and enjoy getting it back.

"Okay, then. You're up in ten." Syl walks off leaving me alone with Toro.

"Anything you wanna tell me about this Big Jim guy?"

"I already did. He's huge."

"I'm asking about his fighting style. Does he favor any particular side?"

He walks off looking butt hurt without answering me. Okay, guess it's safe to assume Crusher was his guy and he's about to lose out on money.

I'm glad I opted for the sports bra and jeans look tonight, I muse, as I pull off my shoes, jeans, and shirt and tape my hands, before climbing into the ring. I swing my arms back and forth to loosen up my shoulders and roll my neck from side to side.

I know most fighters would have taken the time to get ready mentally before stepping into the ring. But that shit doesn't happen in the real world. Back home, you don't get ready. You stay ready. You never know when you're gonna find yourself in a brawl just because you walked on the wrong side of the street.

I tune out the announcer as he lists Big Jim's stats. They're just numbers and words used to hype up the crowd. Instead, I assess his build. The way he's standing. I look for scars that hint at old injuries. Anything that might help me gain an advantage.

He's checking me out too, but where I see how hard I'm gonna work to knock him on his ass, he's just seeing a girl with tits and ass. I even hear his trainer say, "This is a joke, right?"

No buddy, it's not a joke. This is really happening. And you're welcome. An excited zing zips through my skin, adrenaline kicking in. This is the feeling I've been missing, by being sidelined in class. This is what I've wanted since the first day I walked into the gym. I might be about to get my ass kicked, but I'm gonna have a lot of fun while it happens.

The bell rings, and I step to the middle of the ring. I can see Big Jim is taking this as the joke his trainer says it is. He's not even interested in swinging for me. More's the pity that I don't have those same reservations.

I clock him three times. Upper cut, upper cut, left cross. I step back, arching my brow in challenge. Do you wanna be my punching bag or are you gonna fight back?

It doesn't take him long to decide, but he still wants to go soft on me. I reward his consideration by kneeing him in the ribs, and when he hunches over, I introduce my knee to his face.

The bell rings ending the round and I back up to my empty corner. His trainer's no longer being loud and obnoxious, so I can't hear what he's saying. Hopefully, he's telling him to fight back. I didn't come here to do all the work myself.

I decide to give Big Jim a little motivation. "I heard you were the best. Obviously that's just internet hype. I guess that's why Crusher didn't show. He said you weren't even worth his time, and let me have the spot instead."

That seems to get his attention. "I can't wait to see what they post tomorrow after everyone uploads video of you getting owned by a girl." I chuckle and say, "I'll be taking your followers and your money and you'll be known as the guy that talked shit and couldn't back it up, in and out of the ring."

His face morphs. That's the magic ticket. His money, his reputation, and his *dick*. Men are so easy to rile up. The minute the break is over I'm back in the middle of the ring, waiting for Jimbo to do something.

He comes at me, slamming his fist into my gut. I expected that's what he'd do. A hit to knock the wind out of me without doing any serious damage. I tense taking the blow, but it still hurts like a sonofabitch. I straighten and smile, letting him know I can take a punch.

He swings again, and this time I duck out of the way, forcing us to change positions. I swing next and he parries away, but instead of giving him a chance to reset his feet, I go for his exposed side. Jim's a fighter. He's trained for this. Instinct kicks in. He recovers from my hit and slams his fist into my jaw.

My ears ring, but I hit him again, opening a gash under his left eye. We trade blows, each of his getting harder, more serious. It's a rush. Three minutes go by fast. The bell rings, ending the round. One more round and I'm guaranteed my purse and a spot for the next fight night. But it's not enough to survive the round. I wanna take this dude down.

I pull out my mouth guard and start talking shit again. "Damn, dude. You look a little out of breath. I guess the air up there is kinda thin. Need more than sixty-seconds to recover?"

"You talk a lot of shit, little girl. Let's see how much you can talk when I have you on your back, submitting."

He's delusional if he thinks that's gonna happen. I don't give a shit how big he thinks his dick is. Mine is bigger and if anybody's gonna tap out, it'll be him.

Break time's over. I spit the blood pooling in my mouth in the bucket at my feet, reposition my mouth guard and return to the center of the ring, assuming my defensive stance. My lip is split, and my eye is nearly closed shut, but those are minor annoyances, and so is the crowd screaming for him to finish me off.

I know the crowd is feeding off of each other's bloodlust, getting more dangerous the longer the fight goes on. I hope security's had their spinach today. Pretty soon, they're gonna have a vicious mob on their hands. Big Jim was already the heavy favor to win. I'm sure everyone else swapped their bets to him as soon as they found out Crusher wasn't fighting.

Not because I'm a woman, but because I'm new, and they'd want to protect their earnings. I'm about to be the one laughing all the way to the bank.

Jim comes at me again and this time I stop playing with him. I dip down and punch him in the junk, since he was too stupid to wear a cup. When he hunches over, I jump on his shoulders, wrapping my legs around his throat.

He straightens, though I'm sure the dick punch still has him in pain, and tries to shake me off. I shove my hands under his chin, lacing my fingers together to tighten my grip and squeeze his throat as hard as I can.

He swings left and right, trying to throw me. It's not gonna happen. I train my legs to be powerful just so I can successfully suffocate a man between them. I might've been doing it for when my pussy is getting eaten, but it works for this, too.

His knees buckle and I know he's gonna try to shift and slam me into the mat. Sucker. He should've stayed standing up, because if he's on the ground, I have better leverage.

Down, down we go, his hand flailing about, trying to grab me. I release his chin and wrap my arm around his arm, pulling hard like it's a rein, taking away that last inch between my thighs and his neck. I keep squeezing. He'll either pass out or tap out. The decision is all his. It's just a matter of what ending to this fight will embarrass him the least.

His pride won't let him concede defeat, so I just keep squeezing, tensing my muscles, making sure there's no space between his neck and my thighs. He's sweating, the tips of his ears go from red to a ruddy purple. His trainer is the one who decides enough is enough and throws the towel in the ring, telling the ref to call it. That's not how this works.

I don't let up until the bell rings, then I take Jimbo's hand and tap it against the mat three times for good measure. I release my hold and crab walk away from him before getting to my feet, and keep my eyes on him as I slip out of the ring. You never know how someone will process a loss. I've had opponents try to come after me when my back was turned.

I grab my stuff and walk over to where Syl is standing. She leads me to a door and down a hallway to her office. When we get inside, she hands me a stack of cash and her phone. "Put your number in. We'll text you about the next fight."

"Thanks." I shove my arms through my shirt and slip my pants on, before typing in my number. I put the cash in my boot before putting them on. When I'm done, I take in the pictures and trophies on the shelf behind her desk.

"Is there a back way out of here?" I made a nice chunk of cash, and have no intention of walking out the front door with it. I'd be a target for sure.

"Out the door and to the left."

I nod and make my getaway. I'm on alert, but silently humming to myself. This was a great way to end my day.

Deacon

The class is having a hard time settling down. The extra chatter is thanks to Michael Pearse and his buddies. I hear the words *fight* and *bet* and tune out the rest of the conversation. I know all about the underground fight club in Red Canyon. I've found some of my best fighters there. Syl's not big on letting unproven people in the ring on a major purse night, but if I'm understanding correctly, that's exactly what happened two nights ago.

I walk to the front of the class, my feet grinding to a halt. Thea's standing against the wall, sporting a pretty nasty bruise on her left cheek. I'm used to the students showing up with minor scrapes and scratches when they're going through their pledge season, which I was surprised to hear she's a part of, but the shiner she's sporting is something different. "LaReaux! My office."

I storm off ahead of her, trying to get my feelings under control before confronting her. I know she's following. She might still have too much attitude for her own good, but she's disciplined when it comes to following direct orders.

"What?" She huffs as soon as she steps into the room.

I close the door behind her to give us some privacy and force myself to ignore the sass in her voice and the ways she's glaring at me. Moving to stand in front of her, I tilt her face to the side so I can get a better look at her eye. Her lip is split, too. "Wanna' tell me how this happened?"

"There's nothing to tell. It was an accident."

Hearing that excuse does nothing to quell the anger I'm feeling. "Don't give me that shit. There is no accident that results in a black eye and busted lip. Someone did this to you. Who was it?"

"I did it to myself."

I scrub a hand across my face. I'm not a counselor and I'm not equipped to have this conversation, but as her *teacher,* I'm obligated to ask and point her to the right resources. "We both know you didn't, and making excuses for your asshole boyfriend or girlfriend isn't going to change their behavior. The school has resources you can use, people you can talk to…"

"What part of 'did it to myself' don't you get? There is no boyfriend or girlfriend knocking me around." She points to her face. "And how I got this was purely consensual. I enjoyed every single minute of it, gave as good as I got, and I can't wait to do it again."

That's the most twisted shit I've ever heard. She's standing here telling me she's proud of these bruises?

"So if we're done here..." She crosses her arms, drawing my attention to her hands.

Her knuckles are bruised like she went a few rounds against a wall. She put up a fight. Good for her. But no, we're not done. "I understand if confiding in me is awkward considering our history, but-"

"We don't have a history. We fucked. *One time.* I didn't know you. You didn't know me. And that's still the case. We're not friends. You're not an acquaintance. You're just my asshole instructor, nosing around in my business. I said I'm good. Either you believe me or don't. I really don't give a shit. Can I get back to class now, *sir?*"

She's not gonna to tell me what happened but I'm not letting this go. I'm gonna find out who the asshole is that put his hands on her and make him wish he could travel back in time and erase the day he ever met her.

I tip my chin to the door. "Go."

She swings around and opens the door with more force than necessary. Her ponytail swishing from side to side as she walks away. A text alert buzzes on my phone. It's an offer to get into the ring at Club Dredd. I rarely do these days, unless I'm testing a new fighter, but after seeing Thea's bruises, I need an outlet. I respond, letting Syl's organizer know I'm in.

I take another second to get my anger under control before going back out to conduct today's lesson. Thea's refusal to give me answers has me feeling quite sadistic.

It's gonna be a brutal training day for the class.

Chapter 36
Finn

Another day, another trip to the library. Once again I try to make the most of my time here and be productive, but Thea, with that thick dark blue hair that fades into purple tips, begging you to pull it. Fuck me lips, and an ass made for smacking, is temptingly distracting.

I bet those big blue eyes would look like shimmering waterfalls if they were wet from her strangling on my dick, too.

I'm on the floor above her, watching her study, and imagining all the things we could do in the dark corners. From my spot, I also see a couple of guys from Lowell House walk into one of the private study rooms. No books or backpacks. They're definitely not here for studying, which means this is a planning session.

A few minutes later, another set of guys from Alpha Mu Xi go into the same room. Now this just got interesting. Those two groups shouldn't be interacting, not when we're just kicking off pledge season.

I send off a text, letting Pax and Holden know about the two frats meeting up and turn my attention back to my pet. Pax is still of the mindset that getting closer to her is a waste of time. He just wants us to follow her and get some dirt we can use against her.

I had to sit through another one of his "She's on our shit list" rants. I get it. We're planning to annihilate her in public fashion, but that doesn't mean I can't have some fun along the way.

I've shadowed her enough to know that watching from a distance won't reveal anything. All she does is go to classes and take long walks. I don't mind when she goes to the beach, but I draw the line when she's off traipsing through the woods. I leave getting bitten by fleas and wood ticks to Holden.

Thankfully, Pax was outvoted. Sometimes coming right out and asking people questions gets better results, and since I'm not studying, now's a good time to start the interview process.

I gather up my things and slide down the railing to the first level. I smile at a few people I recognize before slipping into the spot across from Thea. She drops her head lower, trying to ignore me. It's ok. I don't mind waiting. She'll talk eventually. At the four minute fifty-seven second mark, she looks up and scowls at me.

"What do you want?"

"A lot, Pet. I have dreams and ambitions in abundance. How much time do you have to listen to my list?"

"None."

"Okay, so shall I just give you my top three? A new set of pointys, a nap, and watching you smile."

"Just like I thought." She grumbles. "You're here to waste my time and yours, because I can't help with any of those things."

Sliding my gaze along her body, I say, "I disagree. I think you're the perfect candidate for all three."

Initially, it was a joke but now that I'm thinking about it, she absolutely *can* help fulfill my daydreams. Her tits are pointing at me. I can do delicious things to them to make her smile, and afterwards I'll be ready for a nap. Besides, experience has taught me that a little pillow talk is a great way to get a woman to lower her defenses and spill all her or her husband's secrets.

I give her my most charming smile. Any second now, she'll start blushing. Any second. I scan her neck for that first hint of a flush, a pounding pulse. *Anything.*

"What are you doing?"

"What?" I'm still watching, waiting for her skin to pink up. Did she not get embarrassed about me giving her the full weight of my stare? She should be squirming in her seat by now. Maybe I should pull out some French.

"Why are you staring at my throat? Are you one of those vampire people or something?"

Vampire? "I don't mind blood or getting it on my hands and clothes, but I don't drink it, if that's what you mean. Do you know people who really do that? Wow. Yeah. Not my thing."

"Okay, so same question. Why are you fixated on my neck?"

Maybe she didn't catch my flirty banter before. I try again, adding an obvious compliment to the mix. "It's a pretty neck."

"Thank you."

"It'll look even prettier with some nibbles on it."

"I thought you just said you're not into biting."

Awe. She's trying to catch me in a lie. She'll have to pay better attention to my words to do that.

"No, Pet. What I said was I don't *drink* blood, though I'm happy to lick it off of the right object. But now, we're talking about biting and other markings I'm into."

She drops her head back down and flicks her finger across her phone screen, ignoring the very obvious meaning to my words. "What about you?"

She sighs, like I'm bothering her. "Me, what?"

I ignore the whole dramatic sighing thing. She's not annoyed. She likes spending time with me. Our bonding time just keeps getting interrupted. "Do you chomp on necks?"

She lifts her head and looks me dead in the eyes. I like that she makes eye contact with me. Most people have a problem doing that. Like staring at one of The Trium is a bad omen or something.

"Not in a fanged way, but yeah, I'll wrap my teeth around some flesh when warranted."

She gnashes her teeth together, trying to intimidate me. It's the cutest thing I've ever seen. Nobody ever tries to scare us off. They just fall at our feet. This is new. Her scowling and slamming doors in our faces. Calling us names. *Out loud.* I think I like this game.

I go to pull her phone over to see what she's reading. A flash of steel embeds itself between my fingers.

"Don't touch my shit."

I look down at my hand and back up at her, processing what just happened. "You almost stabbed me."

"I *did* stab you and it's barely a scratch." She snorts and flicks her wrist as if I'm being melodramatic.

I look down again and see the tiny prick mark. I can't look away from the little bubble of blood pooling on my skin.

Thea lets out a sigh and says, "Look, I don't want any trouble, okay? I'm sorry about the knick. I don't like people touching my stuff without permission, and I just reacted. If you wanna scratch me back to make us even, I'll let you."

She holds out her hand like she's really expecting me to do it. It's reasonable to think I want payback, but she has no idea what this is really doing to me or the thoughts her offer has conjured up in my head.

Plus, I've already bled for her the night Mikey grabbed her on campus. This is nothing. But the idea of playing with my knife on her skin? How can I turn that down? She might as well have said she wants to blow me right here and now. It's basically the same thing.

Just thinking about it, my blade juxtaposed against her flesh, makes my dick hard. But now is not the time or place for us to continue our foreplay.

"We definitely need to make this square, Pet, but I don't wanna scratch you back." I say, sliding from my chair. *Lie.* I totally wanna mark her up, but that's jumping ahead too many steps.

She blinks up at me, a wary look on her face. "Then what?"

"I'll think of something." I lick my injury, then walk off, humming to myself. What an unexpected twist. I sat down to play with Thea, trying to find out what game *she's* playing at.

There are a lot of unanswered questions surrounding her appearance in town. Plus, she's a little too cozy with Austin Kincaid for my liking. Everyone knows he'd do anything to make us look bad. I can't think of a better way to have someone spy on The Trium and Rho Beta Psi, then to have an asset living across the hall from us.

I can admit I have more than a passing interest in her. She makes me smile a lot more than I have in a while. But I'm not an idiot, blinded by a fat ass and luscious tits. I'm not about to lose my shit and disregard my suspicions. I'll play this cool until we get answers.

Is she Kincaid's spy, or a league plant? Someone sent to test us on our ability to recognize a Trojan horse? And if that's the case, then why does Malcolm want us all up in her shit? Is that part of the test too?

Out of the three of us, I'm the best person to get those answers. One on one time with me usually reveals people's motives. A little smiling, a lot of flirting, and then they're confessing everything in exchange for me fucking them in the stacks.

I'll flirt and tease the truth out of Thea, too, and if I find out she's here to fuck with our ranks and chances of advancing with The League, I'll make her wish she'd never left that little town in Nevada.

For her sake, I hope there's nothing to find.

Pax

I give a courtesy knock on Holden's door before letting myself in. We all have access to each other's rooms and come and go as we please. This is the second time this week he hasn't come to my room first.

Since Holden never gets more than a few hours of sleep, he usually wakes up Finn and waits in my room for me to come back from the gym. He pokes his head out of his bedroom door, then disappears from sight again. I walk over to his kitchen and note the empty counter. He hasn't even brewed his coffee yet.

"Please tell me you haven't been staring at your computer screens all night." That would explain why he's running behind schedule. If he's in front of his computers, coding or researching, he loses track of time.

"I'll just be a second."

I walk over to his pantry to grab his coffee beans to make him a cup, and fix myself one too. It's a bit of work, but if it's between Holden's blend and the one in the dining hall, I choose this one every time. He's faster at grinding the beans than I am, but soon I have the machine percolating and spitting out dark liquid. I even remember to froth the milk like he taught us. It's not a half bad job. I won't tell anyone, but I like when he makes it. His always has little designs in it. I pour the liquid into a disposable travel cup and set it on the counter while I fix mine.

Just as I'm finishing up, my phone rings with a message. It's Finn wanting to know how long before we're ready to go down for the lingerie show. Holden answers that we're ready now. I look up just as he's coming out of his room, fully dressed, with his book bag slung over his shoulder. I point to his coffee, grab mine and head towards the door.

When we get to the elevator, I bring up the subject of him pulling an all nighter, again. "You know, if you need help getting to sleep, the doc should be able to get you something."

He pinches the bridge of his nose. "I know. I have a prescription, I just don't like how it makes me feel when I take it. I can't be in a deep sleep. You know?"

I do know. Holden's hyper vigilant. Always on edge. The only things that calm him are reading, school work and his computers. I know how vulnerable he'd feel if he was in a chemically induced sleep.

I also know how dangerous it is for him to go without sleep. It's important he keeps his emotions on an even keel. When he's going through these extreme bouts of insomnia, he loses control, and the last time he did that, he beat the shit out of some kid he caught slapping his girlfriend around.

Nobody said anything. The incident was written off as a non-investigative event, because it fell under the rules and secrecy surrounding Mayhem Night, but it was bad. We don't need another incident like that happening. Especially not now when we're prospects.

The elevator stops at the lobby. I hear the girlish shrieks before the doors even open. They run around like they're trying to be modest, when the whole point of these mornings is so we see them.

I glance over at Holden. He's unimpressed with the amount of flesh walking around here.

Maybe Finn and I need to schedule something for him. We keep a copy of an NDA ready to go just in case things go off the rails, but Finn and I never leave him alone, so we can make sure that doesn't happen.

I trail him to the lounge area and sit down on the couch facing the hall. Holden's on my right, and Finn's sitting with his legs draped over the arm of the accent chair on my left.

Today, he's dressed like he's in prep school. White shirt, navy blue blazer, black slacks, a striped silver and blue tie, hanging loosely around his neck, and his ever present beanie on his head.

I take in the girls drifting past, giving a knowing smirk to the one who didn't even bother to tie her robe. A blatant invite if I've ever seen one. She takes a step towards me.

"What the fuck do you think you're doing?" My eyes flick to the left where Eloise is standing. She must've just gotten off the elevator.

She moves closer, getting in the girl's face. "I asked what you think you're doing?"

The girl doesn't answer. She pulls her robe closed, holding it with one hand, as she tries to step away. Eloise grabs her by the robe, tearing it open further.

"Oh, no you don't, you sneaky little bitch. You came to my dorm trying to catch the eye of The Trium. Now you've got it, but you'll walk out of here with your bloated belly and every inch of your cellulite on display."

Eloise's friends step closer, grabbing at the girl too, like they're the evil step-sisters. Seconds later, her robe is ripped in several places, barely covering anything.

The girl's gaze swings to me before she lowers her head and runs out the front door. She doesn't live in this dorm? I guess that explains why I didn't recognize her from any of the other mornings. It's a shame that I didn't get her details.

My phone pings with a message from Holden. I look over at him and meet his knowing gaze. He's sent me a copy of the girl's Prospectus profile. I check her stats. I can work with it. "Thanks, man."

I put my phone away when I see Eloise walking towards us, and grab my coffee from the table in front of me, taking a leisurely sip. She greets me and Holden.

I give a half hearted chin tip, but Holden doesn't even look up to acknowledge she spoke to him. Finn has this weary look on his face as she squeezes into the small space beside him on the chair.

"Can you believe her, babe? Coming over here trying to blend in? As if I don't know each and every person that's housed here. And she was wearing a robe that went out of style two years ago. Nobody's wearing Keiko Couture's winter 2019 line anymore."

"Pajama's go out of style?" Finn asks, deciding to humor her for a few minutes.

"Of course. Sometimes faster than clothes. She really thought one of you was going to think she looked sexy in that?"

He and I share a look. We both thought she looked hot. Guys are easy. Show some skin, smile and let us know you want us and we can make it happen.

I'm just about to say that when the elevator arrives again. Thea walks out, and I lose my train of thought. Now here's a girl that needs to be humiliated and chased away. No matter how we've come for her, she's found a way to adjust and come out unscathed. Unbothered.

That's the part that's pissing me off the most. The chip on her shoulder. The I don't give a fuck attitude. Her willfully and blatantly challenging us at every turn. The longer she walks around here with her nose in the air like she's made of teflon, the more people talk about us losing our edge. I can't let anyone at this school think The Trium aren't the scariest people on campus. Her behavior will not go unpunished.

She sees me looking at her and sticks her tongue out like she's a five-year-old. It's all a game to her. Holden's hand on my arm is the only thing keeping me from launching out of my chair.

I turn to tell him I'm good so he can release my arm. His attention is on Thea, too. Darkness dancing in his gaze. Checking my right, I see Finn's eyes following her out the door as well.

He's looking at her like she's his favorite chew toy, locked behind a glass case. I know he's been playing this weird little game with her, but I can't just come right out and tell him to put an end to it.

Finn will need a reason why he can't have fun with her, and I can't exactly tell him that she might be here to compromise a future member of the league.

His eyes sweep around the room before settling on me. He gives me a cocky grin, acknowledging that he knows I caught him looking. It doesn't matter if he's hot for Thea. Nothing can ever come of it. None of us are capable of having more than flings. We can't afford to get attached to anyone or anything that jeopardizes the blood oath we made to each other. It's us, The Trium, above everyone and anything else.

Chapter 37
Pax

While Finn was tailing Theona around school the other day, Holden was installing a security camera outside her door. This way, we'll be able to see who's coming and going from her room.

A whistle blows, intruding on my thoughts. We're in the back of one of the freshman dorms watching a flag football game. Finn's sitting on a picnic table swiping his thumb across his phone, and Holden's fiddling with his tablet.

"Anything else from your dad about Thea?" Finn asks, taking a break from whatever he's typing.

I turn away from the game to look at him. So far, none of us have had anything interesting to report about the bitch.

"My dad's been silent so far. He was barely interested when I gave him a copy of her schedule and the background information we have on her."

Holden looks up from his tablet. "So, can we back off?"

I know he's worried about the potential fallout from what we're doing. This favor certainly seems to fall into the gray area of what the bylaws allow.

"You know my father. He won't let us off the hook until he feels like he's gotten something useful out of it."

Useful in this case means tying her back to whoever is trying to infiltrate The League and putting an end to the threat. But I've been ordered not to say anything about that until I'm sure that's what's happening.

Holden steps closer, holding out his tablet after launching his drone in the air. We all watch the feed. The drone is tracking the guys from Lowell House across campus. They're so obvious. They're the only frat that's not out here playing in this flag football tournament, so of course we want to know what they're up to.

This is why they'll never be on our level. They don't even know how to conduct a stealth mission without rousing suspicion.

I pull my gaze away from the screen to look over at the sidelines. The sororities have sent members to cheer and to provide water and snacks for their brother frats. The wannabe cheerleaders scream and yell their encouragement.

I spot Eloise sitting in a lawn chair inside a tent, with a fan, like she's too delicate to stand in the heat and yell. That doesn't stop her from wearing the skimpy little cheerleader outfit, though.

The game ends, and it's our turn to take the field. Holden will stay and track Lowell House while Finn and I crash into people. Eloise pretends not to notice us. But I don't miss the way her eyes take us in. Finn's already got his t-shirt tucked into the waistband of his shorts. I'm keeping mine on. I just got a new tat and need to keep it covered for a few more days.

The other team is already on the field talking shit. Austin's staring at the sidelines, casually tossing a football in the air. I see the wheels spinning in his head.

"Which one?"

He drags his attention to me, like it's the last thing he wants to do. "Okay, I'll bite. Which one, what?"

"Which one did you convince to suck you off if you win?"

He smirks, pointing the football at me. "What's it matter? You trying to spin it into a consolation prize when you lose?"

I shake my head. "Your father should just rip the bandaid off and tell you there's no chance of you ever marrying into a legacy family."

He averts his gaze. His attention snagged by something over my shoulder. I turn to see what he's staring at. Thea's standing against the wall watching Austin's team stretch.

Half of the players are on the football team. Coach will have their asses if they get injured with a hamstring or pulled groin injury. When Thea finally notices Austin, she tips her chin, then sinks down to the ground, her back braced against the wall. She's here to watch him play. Or should I say, watch him lose.

Austin's captain of his team, so when the ref calls five minutes to the start of the game, he goes off to gather his squad together.

Finn and I fall in with our captain to get our positions. From where I'm standing, I see Thea still has Austin's attention. I chastise myself for using that name, but I grudgingly admit I like the way it sounds better than Theona. Finn tips his head in the other team's direction. He must notice Austin's interest in her, too.

We come to the line of scrimmage and one of Austin's teammates says something stupid about us, finally knowing what it feels like to be dominated. It's a taunt carried over from high school. When all the fragile girls complained, we were too rough. They cried about how we held them down and wouldn't let them touch us.

That was well before we earned our reputations and were officially declared our generation's Triumvirate. Before the girls learned, it's better to keep their mouths shut.

My gaze flicks to Holden. He's still watching his tablet. That means Lowell House hasn't finished whatever they're doing yet. He'll come onto the field when Finn or I need a break.

I meet Finn's gaze on my right. He has this wild look in his eyes. I silently communicate what I'm thinking. He tips his head in agreement. Today is a great day to slam these fuckers into the ground.

Thea

I walk down the path towards the back of the dorm, hoping I'll find a good spot to sit and watch the game. I saw a bunch of girls heading this way a while ago with umbrellas, tents and chairs. I won't be sitting anywhere near them.

The idea of being that close to all that glitter makes me itch. But this is a Zeta Nu supported event, and all pledges were told to be here or helping to set up for tonight's party. LJ is on party detail and I signed up to come out here.

It's some kind of battle of the frats going on, but Austin is who I'm here to support. I spot him right away and find a spot in the shade against the building that gives me a good view of both sides of the field.

When he mentioned he'd be playing flag football today, I didn't believe him. Not because I didn't think he can play the sport. I've heard all about him being the school's star quarterback. I just couldn't picture him playing without all the protective gear. But here he is. Not a helmet or shoulder pad in sight.

I get settled and the first ten minutes of the game goes by pretty fast. I'm invested in the outcome. This is the first activity I've seen on campus that feels raw and real. A reminder of home.

Austin's team has possession of the ball. He takes the snap, falls back and releases a perfect spiral before anyone can touch him. The wide receiver catches it and runs into the end zone. Austin throws his fist in the air, all smiles, and high fives his teammates.

The little clock on the table flips over to show we're at the start of the second quarter. The score is twenty-one-zip. Austin's team is annihilating the competition. Pax and Finn are on the other team, so I'm enjoying their defeat a little more than I probably should.

Pax's team gets the ball, and it's a quick fourth down. They barely get any field coverage. Grumpy guppy isn't too happy with being on the losing team. He's talking to the guy I assume is the team captain. Whatever the topic is, has him pissed. He's waving his hands in the air and giving his patented mean-face.

Finally, the captain nods his head and Pax jogs over to the picnic bench on the other end of the field. When he comes back, Holden is behind him. He doesn't look happy about having to join the game.

Pax is such a dick. There had to have been someone else he could have swapped that other player with.

Holden lines up as a defensive end on the right, Pax takes the left and Finn drops back to play corner back. Austin gets the snap. In a flurry of movement, Holden breaks through the O-line and knocks him on his ass, but not before Austin has a chance to release the ball. It's airborne, on a crazy trajectory, on its way to the designated man.

Before it reaches the intended receiver, Finn plucks it out of the air, and runs upfield, shuffling by players, leaping over others. Just when it looks like he's going to be stopped, he dives headfirst into a tuck over the guy's back, and lands in the end zone.

Pax's team is now on offense, and once again, Holden is like a blur. Blocking, creating an opening. Giving Finn the opportunity to run. And just like that, after two plays, it's a ballgame.

The girls on the sidelines are screaming Pax and Finn's name at the top of their voices. Fuck that noise. They're cheering for the wrong dude. Holden is the play maker on this field.

I'm transfixed, watching as he runs down the player on the other team. I think he's gonna miss him, leaving room for the other guy to score, but Holden anticipates the guy's gonna try to cut left and he's there, slamming into him. I jump to my feet, yelling, "That's what the fuck I'm talking about. Good hit, defense."

Austin gives me a look, and I shrug. So what? I momentarily

forgot that I'm supposed to be cheering for his team. It was a damn good hit. I'm here for the violence.

The score's tied up and right before the snap, phone alarms and chimes start going off. The girls on the sideline squeal and the guys start cursing. One of them runs over to show Pax his phone. I'm confused about what's going on.

I look at my phone. I don't have any alerts. When I look back up, people are running off the field. Austin jogs over to me. His shirt's plastered to his chest. He runs a hand through his wet hair. "What's going on?" I ask, taking in the chaos around me.

"Frat business. I can't go into any details."

"Because I'm a girl?"

"Because you're a Zeta Nu pledge."

"So the game's just over? At a tied score?"

His friend jogs over to us, carrying his bag. "Look, Thea. I'll catch up to you later. Thanks for coming out to support."

"Yeah. It was a great game."

He smiles again and winks at me. "Call you later."

Before I can respond, he's jogging towards the other end of the field. I turn around to take the path I used to get here. Holden, Finn and Pax are standing off to the side just staring at me.

Holden lifts his shirt to wipe the sweat from his face, and I damn near swallow my tongue. *Fuck.* LJ's, right, he's jacked. Holden sees me staring and drops his shirt. He doesn't smirk like most guys would do if they caught me eye fucking them. He just stares back, as if trying to decipher my thoughts. I hold his gaze, unashamed that I was checking him out. He should be proud of his body. From what I've seen of his abs, they're totally lick worthy.

Like they share some kind of hive mind, the Coxsuckers turn as one, and walk off, melting into the trees.

Chapter 38
Finn

I slide the balcony door open, toe off my muddy shoes, and put my socks in them before stepping inside. We were tied up at the football game, but got called away for a new fraternity challenge. Which we *killed*.

Everyone is still out in the woods partying. I should be there enjoying myself, but I found the whole thing just blah, so I dipped out early.

I strip off my shirt and pants as I walk across the living room towards Thea's open bedroom door. I stroll right in, quietly making my way over to her bed, easing myself onto the mattress beside her, and pull out my toy, ready to play. Her eyes pop open before I even settle my weight on the bed.

"Don't move, Pet." Her eyes drop to what I'm holding between her tits.

"You don't move."

I feel the sting of something digging into my hip. Shit, I should have expected she had a knife somewhere close by.

"Why the hell are you in my bed, Number Three?" Her eyes drop to my chest. "Naked?"

That's a good question. Why *am* I here? I'm a little drunk. I was thinking about coming here as I walked across campus, but I hadn't meant to. Then I did. I guess between the lobby and my room, I made a decision. Once I came through the door, it just made sense to take my clothes off and climb into bed with her. So, Voila. I'm here with my dick in one hand, my blade in the other.

"I think I'm gonna cum on your tits."

"Is that so?" She drags her blade closer to my belly button.

"Mmm."

"And I'm supposed to be okay with you breaking in and doing that?"

"It's late. I didn't want to wake you." I drag the flat end of my blade back and forth across her nipple.

"Are you alone?"

"Yes." The creek of the floorboards has her arching a brow. "I *was*, alone." Did she invite someone here? He's about to be bleeding out at my feet.

She leans up and looks towards the door. "Whoever's lurking around out there should come in, too."

Holden steps from the shadows and leans up against the wall next to the door.

"Now, do one of you wanna tell me what the fuck is really going on?"

"I told you, Pet. I wanna cum on your tits." I flick her nipple with the tip of my blade. It doesn't even bother her.

"And you? What are you doing here, Holden?"

"He's here to-"

She clamps her hand across my mouth. I swipe my tongue across her palm when she says, "I'm asking, *Holden*." She turns her attention back to him. "Why are you here?"

"I came to get Finn." He shifts his gaze to me, like he's unsure why he came here, too. It's a lot of that going around buddy.

There was a lot of hooking up happening at the party. Holden's probably feeling more unfulfilled than I am, since he has a very specific kind of thing that truly gets him off. I don't care about him standing there. I'm gonna shoot my load on Thea's amazing tits. He's free to watch.

Thea moves even though I told her not to, causing the tip of my blade to dig into her tanned skin. A pebble of blood marks the area where I cut her. I suppress a shiver at how good it looks, forcing myself not to lean forward and have a taste.

"Really? Collecting Finn is the only reason you're here? Because you keep staring at my tits."

Holden cocks his head to the side and states the obvious. "They're out and your nipples are hard."

"That's because I'm in *my* room, and I was asleep, until you two broke in. Since hard nipples offend you, maybe next time don't let yourself in, perv."

"They don't offend me."

They don't offend me either. Damn, I want to lap that blood up and swirl my tongue around her nipple. Before I can, she moves my hand aside, swipes the blood away, and settles back in bed.

"What are you doing?" I ask, closing my blade and tucking it into the waistband of my boxer briefs.

"What does it look like I'm doing? I'm going back to sleep. Let yourselves out the same way you got in."

Holden gives her a quizzical look. "You don't care that Finn cut you?"

With her eyes closed, she says, "It's barely a scratch."

"Or that he said he wants to cum on your tits?"

"Nope."

"What if I said I wanted to kiss you?" He asks, taking a step closer. She waves her hand, dismissing us. "With my hand around your throat?"

Her body stiffens. She slowly rolls over in bed and peels one eye open. *Dammit.* Just when I was thinking of all the ways tonight could go. I prepare myself for what's coming next. Once she opens her mouth, I'll have to cut out her tongue, so she never speaks to Holden again. I pull my blade back out, snapping it open.

Thea sits up in bed and scoots back until her back is against the headboard. "For how long?"

Okay. Wasn't expecting that. Neither was Holden. Her scratch is still bleeding. This time I don't hesitate. I lean down and lap it up, savoring the coppery taste on my tongue. Thea flicks me on the ear. I look up and see Holden's still considering her question. He asks, "How long can you hold your breath underwater?"

"Uh... I'm not sure. I've never timed it."

That makes sense. Most people who aren't training to be underwater divers don't time it. We have because survival camp made us do it. The camp counselors Said we should know in case we're ever in a car or aircraft that crashes in the ocean.

"I'll just squeeze until you feel the need to come up for air."

"Do you wanna completely constrict my air or just hold your hand there with a little pressure?" She asks, really giving this some thought.

Holden mulls that over too, before replying, "I'd try it both ways to see which one I find more pleasurable."

"Have you done it before?"

Am I drunk and high and hallucinating? Are they really sitting here discussing breath play like it's a homework assignment?

"Several times." He cuts his eyes at me. "But the experiments were inconclusive."

"I see." The room is quiet except for the thundering of my heart as I wait for her to freak out. After a few minutes, she says, "Okay."

"Okay?" I choke the word out. I know I'm ogling her. But shit, is she serious right now, or is she fucking with him?

She's looking at Holden without a trace of fear when she says, "I'm willing to help you with your little experiment."

"When?" I can tell from his tone that he doesn't think she'll go through with it either.

"Now works for me. Or do you need time to prepare?" Holden

shakes his head. "Okay then, Pretty Boy." She pats the space beside her. "Let's go."

I arch a brow. Did Holden notice she gave him a nickname? He walks forward and settles onto the bed next to her. I move closer to make sure she's not about to stab him with the knife I now know is hidden under her pillow.

Holden is wary of her too, but he leans forward and kisses her. A peck. Then another. When she doesn't pull away or grimace at the feel of his mouth on hers, he finally dives in, committing to his research.

Chapter 39
Thea

These yahoos broke in and disrupted my sleep. It's only been a few hours since I drifted off. I'm already sleep deprived from studying. That must be the reason I haven't kicked them out, and agreed to help Holden with his little experiment.

His lips are soft. Gentle, like he's not sure about this kiss. I open my mouth and sweep my tongue across his lips. He stiffens and I give him a second before doing it again. He finally opens for me, and I slide my tongue against his. He tastes like my favorite coffee from the dining hall and Peppermint Patties.

Slowly, his hand closes around my throat and squeezes. It's just enough pressure so I can feel it. My pussy throbs and I shift, exposing my neck a little more. He leans into the kiss, pressing his chest against mine for just a second, before pulling away.

"You, um." I lick my lips, still tasting him on my tongue. "You still wanna do the other way?"

"Yes." His voice is dark, with a hint of something I can't quite name.

I scoot down a little more to get comfy. "I'm ready when you are."

This time, he doesn't hesitate to kiss me. Just like last time, we kiss for a bit before his hand reaches up. He deepens the kiss, one hand braced against my neck, the other on the side of my head. He climbs fully onto the bed and pins my hands above me with one hand, squeezing my throat with the other.

I'm being kissed breathless and choked at the same time. My clit throbs with need and I grind against him, desperate for friction. He pulls away and releases my neck, staring down at me.

"Oh, shit." Finn says from the other side of the room. I hadn't even noticed he'd moved off the bed. I turn to ask what he's talking about, but Holden pulls my face back to look at him. "Eyes on me," he growls before slamming his mouth against mine.

He settles his body between my thighs and grinds against me. I've been teasing them about having small penises, but it's such a lie. Holden's thickness presses against my center, and all I want to do is hold it and see how girthy it is.

His hand finds my neck again, and he alternates between cutting off my air and holding me in place. I'm drenched and whimpering like a thirsty bitch.

This dude. This quiet dude with the big ass brain is kissing me like a goddamn pro. His tongue teasing and demanding. His hard body holding me in place. My air cuts off again, and Holden breaks our kiss to look at me. He doesn't stop moving against me, though. The sweatpants he's wearing do nothing to conceal how hard he is.

Oh, fuck, this feels *good*. Fucking would probably feel better, but he's who he is, and that's out of the question. Holden releases my hand to twist my nipples and I moan. Now that I can use my hands, I slip them under his shirt to drag my hands across his back. The minute I make contact, he stiffens and flies off the bed. He doesn't stop backing away until he's standing on the other side of the room next to Finn.

"Don't touch me." He hisses.

I sit up, taking less than a second to process what he said. "Don't touch you? Dude, you just had your tongue in my mouth, your hand around my neck and were sliding between my legs like you were a skating pro at the Ice Capades. But touching you is your hard limit?"

I click my tongue against my teeth. "I don't know what fucking game you're playing, but it's over. Get the hell out of my room."

Holden storms off, not needing to be told twice. I glare at Finn, who's giving me puppy dog eyes. "If you're about to ask to cum on my tits, the answer is, Hell. Fucking. No."

His shoulders deflate. Then he brightens up again. "You're right. You're dealing. Processing what just happened between you and Holden. I'll give you a few days to get over it."

He walks out of my bedroom calling out, "Sweet dreams, Pet."

Sweet dreams? After Holden got me all hot and horny? Not likely.

I check the time on my phone. It's almost three am. I need to call Sasha when the sun comes up. Maybe she has some advice on what I can do to get laid, because there's an unending supply of cunt teases in this town.

Coach Wolfe is being dismissive of me. I'm positive I'm being singled out because he's answering everyone else's questions like he's got some sense. When it comes to me, he's barking out his responses and gritting his teeth. My questions aren't stupid either.

If he doesn't know how much I need to rotate my hips to toss a two hundred pound gorilla of a man across the ring, he should just say that.

I've had enough of his shit attitude, so today when he asks for volunteers to demonstrate a new move with Roy Youngblood, the biggest guy in class, I jump to my feet instead of raising my hand, waiting to *not* be picked.

Michael crosses the floor and climbs onto the mats. "Sit down, Theona, and watch the real fighters in action."

"Sure. Who are these *real* fighters? Because I know you don't mean you."

He looks down at me, infusing extra bass in his voice. "Go on, little girl. The adults are working."

He's staring at my tits. After our run-in, in the alley, I already know what he thinks I'm good for. I fluff them, just because he's a piece of shit, and to let him know I see him looking.

"LaReaux, have a seat." Coach Wolfe yells from his spot against the wall.

"Coach, far be it from me to tell you how to run your class, but you said you're teaching real world training scenarios. In what real world will I always be evenly matched against an opponent every time? As a woman, shouldn't I know how to protect myself from an attack by a man that on the outside appears to be physically stronger than me?"

"This move takes practice, and I'm not looking to send anyone to the infirmary today, or field phone calls from daddy's lawyers about why their little princess got injured."

Jokes on him. I don't have a daddy. "I signed the liability waiver just like everyone else, and if you're this much of a chauvinist, maybe somebody's lawyer should be coming after you for gender discrimination."

I ignore the *oohs and aahs* and whispers about me talking back to the Big Bad Wolfe. Because yes, that's exactly what the students call him. There's a recurring question that always seems to pop into my head. How many of these girls know that his mouth definitely lives up to the *better to eat you with,* part of the story?

"I don't mind working with her, coach." Roy says, giving me a quick once over. I can see it in his eyes. If Coach Wolfe agrees, he's gonna take it easy on me. Not exactly what I was going for, but I'm not gonna let my ego get in the way. I want to learn and train.

I've called two other gyms in the area and they both said the same thing. I have to get a signed permission slip from my coach *at school* to train in their gyms. What kind of bullshit is that? I've asked other students, and it really is a rule.

So I stand in front of the class, waiting for a decision to be made. If they want me off the training mat, they'll have to physically move me, and the minute someone touches me, it's on.

I eye Coach Wolfe, waiting for him to say something. It doesn't take long. "LaReaux, I didn't call you up to demonstrate, so sit your ass back down."

Michael takes that moment to walk over to me. I guess he thinks he's about to help me to my seat. Yahtzee. That's just what I wanted to happen. As soon as his hand lands on my shoulder, I duck under his arm, pulling it with me to wrench it behind his back, before putting my foot to his ass and sending him stumbling forward. I don't even put a lot of energy into it, since he wasn't prepared for it to happen. He turns to look at me with a smirk on his face. He thinks I got lucky.

I signal for him to come at me again. He hesitates for a second before deciding to humor me. He lunges, trying to fake me out, and I pretend to fall for it. When he goes to grab me, I slip out of the way and shuffle to the side. He's fast on his feet and adjusts quickly, grabbing me around my waist, pulling me against his chest.

With my arms pinned to my side, there are only a few options I have to break free. Before I can decide on one, Coach Wolfe blows his whistle, and storms over to us, yelling, "LaReaux, my office! Everyone else, go over the moves we learned last session."

He stalks towards his office door, and I follow behind, taking my sweet ass time to get there. When I do, he's standing behind his desk, with his palms flat against it.

He's pissed. I'm fixated on the way his chest is heaving. It reminds me of the way he was huffing against my ear the night we met. The way he's gripping the desk sends my thoughts into overdrive. I know what he can do against a wall, but is he as talented on a flat surface? I force that imagery out of my head. He's my teacher, and he's nothing like the guy he pretended to be the night we met. That guy was a sexy hottie. This dude is a condescending prick.

"You wanted to see me, coach?" I ask, infusing all kinds of sweetness I don't feel into my voice.

"Close the fucking door."

I do as he says. I don't need an audience for this and fold my arms across my chest. He's staring at me as if trying to decide where to start. I stare right back. He told me to come in here. Clearly, he wants to chew my ass out. I'll just stand here and wait until he musters up the balls to do it.

I think I know why he can't. He'd have to admit that this attitude towards me is personal, probably stemming back to our hookup. Well, suck that shit up. It happened. It's over. If he's secretly got a wife or girlfriend or something, he's being really stupid about how he's handling things. Treating me like shit might be the wrong way to go about getting me to agree to keep my mouth closed. Not that I'd track this person down and tell them what happened. I'm not into causing drama like that.

Maybe if I tell him that, he'll start acting human, or showing some sense of decency like he did when he wrongly assumed I was being abused. I'm willing to give it a go.

"Look, I think I know what's going on here. So let's clear the air. I assumed you were single. If I had known you weren't, I never would've sent you that drink. But you can relax. I'm not here to fuck your shit up or anything. And before you say I joined this class to blackmail you, I didn't. I just moved here, and if you remember, we didn't share any details about ourselves that night. I'm good for continuing to pretend it didn't happen. So you can drop the crappy attitude now and treat me like everyone else."

Chapter 40
Deacon

I realize my mistake the minute Thea closes the door. I have a decent sized office, but suddenly it feels like a coffin with the two of us in here.

That suffocating feeling does nothing to ease my temper, and neither does that little speech she just gave. Pretend it didn't happen? That's the part I focus on, because all that other shit about being married or having a girlfriend is unimportant.

I don't have one and it honestly never crossed my mind to think she was here to fuck with me or blackmail me. But she's obviously given it some thought. That's a different type of conversation that we'd need to have if there was something going on between us. There's not. There can't be.

I brought her in here, because I have a point to make. I keep my anger pulled around me, and inflect every bit of the emotion into what I'm about to say. "Are you hard of hearing or just too stupid to value your own safety?"

"All my senses operate perfectly well, so let's go with stupid, since I was dumb enough to think I'd get a fair shot in this class."

She actually has the nerve to look down her nose at me, and finishes with, "Among other reasons."

I get the hint, hooking up with me is now considered a stupid mistake. I don't disagree with that assessment. It's turning out to be one of the worst decisions I ever made, but not for the same reason, she thinks.

"LaReaux, that remark you made about discrimination was way off base. If I didn't think women could handle this class, they wouldn't be in it."

"You can't segregate based on gender. The school would get in trouble."

"It's a private university. We can make boys and girl fitness training separate if we want. Most of these students are used to it."

I straighten to my full height. "Now if you read the class rules, you'd know disrespect of one's self, the class, or the teacher is a disciplinary offense."

Her gaze never leaves mine as I stalk around the front of the desk. "In case you're not sure what your crime is, I'll lay it out for you. You disrespected the class by interrupting their training when I called another student to demonstrate. You disrespected me by arguing with me and accusing me of being gender biased."

I'm standing right in front of her now. I lean closer, putting my face close to her ear. "And can you tell me how you disrespected yourself?"

"Is it when I let Michael get me in a bear hold from behind?" She says with too much sass, letting me know she's still not taking this seriously.

I clench my teeth. That's not where I was going, but yeah, I'm pissed about that part, too. I would have let them go for a few more minutes just to see what she'd do, but when he was pressed against her, I could tell he wasn't thinking about any holds and escapes.

He was thinking he had a hot body in his hands. I wanted to rip his arms off and beat him with them.

"You disrespected yourself by putting yourself in harm's way. I asked for people to demonstrate the moves. I picked two students that I knew could do them correctly, because they have wrestling experience. You just jumped up there with no regard for your safety, and *then* you got trapped in a hold that you had no chance of escaping."

"You didn't give me a chance to show I could escape it. Why am I in here, anyway, and not Michael? He didn't even do the move you told him to. He was too busy tryna put this *little girl* on her back."

He was definitely trying to do that. I plan to deal with him later. Right now, she's the one in front of me.

"You owe me five push-ups for every minute you disrupted class, and five for every minute you were in the ring. That was a total of ten minutes of my class you wasted."

"Push-ups?"

"That's right. You'll do them military style, not on your knees. I wanna hear you count them off, and those arms better be parallel to the floor. If you break form, you'll start over again from one." I point towards the floor. "Get to it."

She stretches out into a plank, eyes trained on me, and lowers. "One."

"It's one, sir."

Her eyes flash with a challenge. She wanted training. This is only a taste of what she'd get in my gym.

"One, sir. Two, sir."

I go to sit behind my desk, leaning forward on my elbows. She's still looking me in the eye, back straight.

"Six, sir."

Usually, by the time the girls who aren't in the MISTIC program get to ten, their arms are shaking and they're ready to quit. They break form and have to start again. But she's still cruising along. "Twelve, sir."

Up and down she goes. Those damn big blue eyes drinking me in. I imagine they're as wide as they'd be if she were looking up at me from her knees. "Twenty, sir."

She doesn't break her rhythm, but she's a little winded. "Twenty-four, sir." Her face is flushed, her glutes locked tight as she maintains her form. "Thirty..." I arch a brow, the sir, comes out on a puff of air.

My fingers are linked together, pressed against my mouth, to hold back the groan that's threatening to escape. I'm supposed to be punishing her, but I'm the one suffering. There's a soft sheen of sweat on her arms, and the flush on her skin extends down to her neck. "Thirty-three, sir."

I shift in my seat, discreetly readjusting myself, as she pants for air. "Thirty-four, sir."

She's doing better than I expected, but I can see fatigue is setting in. Her arms are shaking. If she breaks form, she'll have to start all over. "Thirty-five, sir." I say to keep her moving.

She lowers and repeats it. "Fifteen more, LaReaux."

"Thirty-six, sir."

I stand to my feet and walk back around the desk, leaning against it with my arms folded across my chest. "That's it. Give me one more."

"Thirty, se-ven, sir."

"Don't you dare quit. Show me what you're made of."

"Thirty... eight, sir. Thirty-nine, sir. Forty, sir."

She's paused in a plank. "Ten more. Right now. Perfect form." I drop to the floor right in front of her. "Eyes on me."

She lifts her gaze to mine. "Good, girl. Give me ten. *Now.*"

"Forty-one, sir."

"Forty, two sir."

We go rep for rep together, her eyes never leaving mine. "Forty-seven, sir."

"Give me three. Fucking *more,* Sweetness, and I wanna hear that goddamn, count."

"Forty-eight, sir. Forty-nine, sir."

She lowers herself parallel to the floor and pushes up. "Fifty, sir!"

We pause at the top, staring at each other. I see the hint of pride in her eyes that she finished. She should be proud of herself. I know I am.

I get to my feet first, breaking eye contact as she lowers and pushes back on her knees. She's rubbing her arms, trying to loosen up the muscles. I look at a spot on the wall, instead of fixating on the way her breasts are heaving up and down. From her position on the floor, she's eye level with my dick. I turn away, so she can't see how fucking hard I am right now, and move back behind my desk to hide the bulge in my pants.

"Get back to class, LaReaux, and remember what I said. The next time, I won't be so lenient on you."

When the door closes behind her, I drop down in my chair, squeezing my dick for some relief. *Fuck*, that was the hardest workout I've supervised all week.

Chapter 41
Thea

I'm running late for class again. I was up late talking to Sasha, catching her up on all the bullshit I've had to deal with since I moved here. She's the only one who'd understand the aggression and frustration I've been feeling.

I thought I could work through some of it in gym class, but of course, that didn't end so well.

Coach Wolfe's torture pushups tired me out, but they came with a side of sexual tension. He had me call him, *sir*, to put me in my place. But all I could do was think of other scenarios where I could use that word.

They all included smacks to my ass. When he dropped to the floor and coached me through those last ten pushups, it reminded me of the way he coaxed me through my orgasms. I was sure I was gonna come on the spot.

I'm trying to convince Sasha to come for a visit. Talking on the phone is nice, and now that I have this fancy phone, we can video chat, but there's no substitute for being able to see her face in person. I slip into class and head towards my usual seat when an arm drops across my shoulder.

"What the-"

"You're sitting next to me today." Finn says, steering me towards the other side of the room.

"Why would I want to do that?"

"All the other girls want to."

"Good." I slip from under his arm. "Then pick one of them."

He grabs my ponytail and yanks on it, using it to drag me towards his desk. "No can do, Pet. I choose you."

I flick my blade open, ready to sever his hand from his wrist, but the teacher comes in before I can. "Okay class, in your seats, we have a lot to go over today."

Professor Roberts gives me a pointed look, like I'm holding up the class. I can feel everyone's eyes on me. I don't give a shit about their stares, but the idea of getting on Rickalishious' bad side doesn't sit well with me. The little geek inside of me is still crushing on him and I want him to like me.

I slip into the seat next to Finn. Hopefully, today's lesson won't be a group assignment, so I can ignore him. Roberts begins his lecture and I allow myself to get lost in his words. Finn nudges my shoulder, breaking my concentration.

My fingers itch to spill his blood. I turn, scowling at him. "What?"

"There's this thing this weekend, I'm going."

"Good for you."

"We should go together."

"No." I hiss, turning back to the front of the class.

That was weird. Why on earth would he think I'd want to go out with him? He's hot and all, but he's also got zero respect for boundaries and thinks it's totally acceptable to let himself into my room and declare he wants to paint my tits with his seed.

Basically, he's giving off unhinged behavior and no girl in her right mind would volunteer to be around someone like that. We'll just call me not gutting him that night, a momentary lapse in judgement.

"What do you mean, no? Don't you realize how much clout you'd get going with me?"

"That may sound great for clout chasers, but I'm cool with my current level of unpopularity."

He looks like he's having a hard time figuring me out. Good. I'd hate to be so predictable or easily readable. It ups my survival chances when dealing with sickos.

"Look, I know I may have overstepped by crawling into bed with you without calling first, but before that, I thought we had a moment."

"What moment?"

"Pick one. There was the time in the alley when I saved you, and then there was the campus rescue, and of course we can't forget all the times we went to the movies together."

"Is that how you remember it? Because both of those times you say you rescued me, I was doing just fine on my own."

"Did I read the situation wrong, Pet? Were you looking forward to sucking off Mikey and his buddies?"

I can't hold back the sound of disgust.

"That's what I thought." He's smiling, happier than he was a second ago. "Now that we've established that, my dick is the only one you want to lick."

"Whoa, back up!" My outburst draws the teacher's attention. I slouch down in my seat a little, but I need to disabuse Finn of this stupid idea. Right now. "I didn't say that."

"Sure you did. You didn't want Mikey's raggedy little pencil dick. You were anxiously waiting to see mine in front of Vale Tower before we were interrupted, and I was in your bed, which you didn't seem to mind. Now we're going to the party together this weekend, and we can finish what we started. This time, don't wipe the blood away. That's my job."

"Are you hard of hearing? I'm not going to any party with some basic fuckboy."

He leans closer and nibbles my ear lobe. Why does he keep doing that? And why does it feel so good? His breath sends a chill down my spine.

"Lady, I will touch you with my mind. Touch you and touch and touch until you give me suddenly a smile, shyly obscene."

My head snaps up. My eyes flicking from his lips to his eyes. I'm staring, and my mouth is probably open. Am I drooling? Shit, I think I'm a little wet too. Did Finn just quote E. E. Cummings to me? I shake my head to clear the fog his melodic voice put me in, and take a deep breath, calming my raging heart.

Every time I settle on an opinion about him, he changes tactics. Quoting *poetry*... now that shit's just not fair.

Thankfully, he's quiet for the rest of the lesson. Not that I'm paying much attention because I keep sneaking glances at him.

I'm still not interested in going to a party with him. I haven't forgotten he and his buddies were fucking with my student accounts a few weeks ago. So this new level of interest and niceness has me suspicious as hell. What are they up to?

When class ends, Finn gets to his feet at the same time I do, as if he's expecting me to make a run for it. I'm not running. I'm walking. But I'm definitely trying to put some space between us.

The math genius is blocking the door. My mouth goes dry as I remember the way his lips felt against mine. The way his tongue explored my mouth. How he tasted. How it felt having him rub the evidence of his arousal against me, and his hand at my throat.

They box me in. I've got Finn pressing against my back and Holden in front, making me the thirsty hoe in the middle of a hot-boy sandwich. I wonder if they could handle me together. *No, Thea!* Holden is Coxsucker number two. Abort, abort.

I force my mind to focus on the other time they crowded me. The first time I saw them in the hallway after Pax knocked me over. I also think of how this is reminiscent of the way Mike and his buddies crowded me in that alley.

Is that what this is? Finn said he thinks I owe him for showing up and *saving* me. His version of events and mine differ drastically. I was prepared to deal with those idiots that night and I can deal with the ones boxing me in right now.

I crack my neck, prepared to fight my way out of here if either of them touch me. I hold Holden's gaze, silently daring him to make a move and subtly looking for a weak spot. Fuck, he's like a wall. I'll have to go with the element of surprise.

He stares at me, his brows pinching together, his jaw clenching. *Bring it, asshole.* I ball my fists, prepared to punch him in the dick. We're locked in a stare off, then he steps aside. Giving me barely enough room to walk by without touching him.

Austin's waiting for me in the hall. I look over my shoulder, making sure Holden and Finn aren't trying to sneak up on me. It would be just like them since that's the bitch ass move that started this feud.

They're still standing in the doorway of the classroom, watching me. I don't trust them. I need to make sure my car is in the same spot, my meal card is activated and my mail is still being delivered.

As Austin and I exit the building, I see Pax standing off to the side, which puts me further on edge. I know for a fact he never stands out here. Finn and Holden usually meet him at The Circle. People of habit that deter from those habits are always a red flag to me.

Finn and Holden push through the door, stepping around me to join Pax. That in sync mind meld bullshit happens as they fall into step and walk away in the direction of the parking lot.

Okay, so maybe I misread things, and he wasn't here to try to intimidate me after all. This building is in closer proximity to the parking lot than The Circle is. I guess if they're leaving campus; it makes more sense for them to meet here.

I turn to smile at Austin, who's been talking this whole time, unaware that I was distracted by the enemy. My shoulders relax and I tease him about the disastrous date he had while he walks me to my next class.

Chapter 42
Thea

I climb out of the cab and walk across the street to the place I heard about at one of the fight nights. It's a club where everyone comes for the after party.

I have class in the morning and maybe a pop quiz. Staying out late and drinking when I should be in the dorms studying is reckless, but you only live once, right?

Considering the shit I've been dealing with, I'm overdue for some recklessness in my life.

The club looks unassuming from the outside, even though the entrance is in the middle of an alley. I step through the doors of Pyro-Tech, and just like the sign outside suggests, I quickly check my expectations at the door. The club entrance is on the top level. I'm standing on a balcony peering down over what looks like a three-ring circus.

The DJ is in the middle ring on a raised platform with neon lights that look like flames swirling around her. She's wearing leather hot pants and a black bra, her green hair slicked up into a spiky Mohawk.

While I'm watching, the second ring lowers about twenty feet, and the outside of it erupts in flames. Turning my head to the third ring, I watch as it lifts to a few feet below where I'm standing.

A collective gasp and applause breaks out on my right. I watch as dancers unfurl themselves from the curtains suspended from the ceiling.

They drop down onto the first level, then dive forward, grabbing another set of curtains before twirling and spinning down to the second, and again to the last, level. Once they hit the bottom, the silken fabric pulls them all the way back to the top, to start again.

It truly is like a circus in here. My laughter bubbles over as I watch the dancers in action. I would love to go spinning through the air like that. I wonder if they'd let me.

I'm sure there's more to see, so after a few minutes of gawking at their aerial skills, I walk down the steps to the second level. I find a bar, order my drink, and listen to the conversations going on around me.

Someone mentioning a mask gets my attention, because I saw people in masks when I came in. I finish my drink, order a second and take that with me as I move down to the last level, which leads me deeper into the club.

The further down I go, the darker the lighting gets. As for the masks, there are people sitting at tables wearing them, but the majority of the masked patrons seem to be heading in the same direc-tion. To a curtained off area in the back of the room.

I head that way too. When I reach the curtain, a woman standing at a maître d' stand, greets me. "Hello there, beautiful."

"Hey, yourself." I try to see through the curtain, but it's impos-sibly thick and no gaps show. "Is there a separate cover charge to get back there?"

She looks me up and down and gives me a knowing smile. "The cover is the mask we require our friends to wear. The charge is what-ever spark you choose to ignite. But the windows to the soul aren't the only thing keeping record of tonight's darkly delicious delights."

She reaches underneath the stand and pulls out a red face mask with jewels around the eyehole. It's a partial mask, created to cover one half of your face.

"Do you wish entrance, beautiful?" She's smirking at me like she expects me to say no. I grab the mask and tie it on. My answering smirk letting her know I'm ready to see what's behind the door.

She stands and pulls back the curtain. She places a hand on my shoulder right before I step through. "I hope you have a fabulous time."

"Thank you."

"And if you don't, come see me and we'll see what we can do to make it better for you next time."

"You assume I'll want a next time."

"Beautiful, our friends *always* want a next time."

I step through the heavy brocade curtain, passing from the club into a long hallway. I walk until I reach a dead end, then look left and right to see which way to go. There's a wall to the right, so I turn left and pass several rooms. The doors are closed, to most of them, so I walk into the first one I reach with an open door.

The room is outfitted with couches along the walls and chairs interspersed between them. There's a weird shaped chair in the middle of the room. The slides slope down, forming a deep groove in the middle.

I turn to look back at the door I just came through. Above it, there's a neon sign that says, "On Air". It's off. Right above it is a camera with several more mounted in the corners where the ceiling meets the wall. That must be what the hostess meant by keeping records. The club is recording whatever happens in this room.

I spot a beverage cart over in the corner. I snag a bottle of water off of it and walk towards the open doors on the other side of this room, wondering if they somehow connect to the other rooms down the hall. They don't. Each door leads to a room with a partition set up in the middle of it, cutting the space in half, but the only way in or out is through the door I used.

When I come out of the last room, a guy with a jester mask

approaches me. "Have you selected your entertainment for the evening?" I'm not sure how to answer that, so I give him a blank look.

"You don't have to say it. I'm good at guessing." He takes in my mask and my outfit. "Belt?"

"Excuse me?"

"You're going for brat, right? Daddy's gonna punish you with a belt."

"I'm not participating. I just came to check things out. But you enjoy your evening."

He cocks his head to the side. "There is no 'just came to see'. This place has one rule. And tonight, we test your limits and ability to follow rules."

"Like I said, I'm not participating."

He chuckles. "Refusing to participate isn't an option, *pledge.*"

He hands me an envelope and walks out the door, pulling it closed behind him. I follow him to the door, but when I turn the handle, nothing happens. It's locked from the outside. I pull the note-card from the envelope to see just what kind of bullshit I can expect to go down tonight.

A lady of Zeta Nu Theta is distinguished. An upstanding woman of moral superiority. An ethereal beauty beyond reproach. Her asset is her wit, intelligence, compassion, and body. A Zeta Nu knows when and how to correctly wield each one. As part of the transition from the old life into the new, a Zeta Nu Pledge is honored to publicly declare a vow of chastity that extends through the end of the second semester after they cross over. We look forward to celebrating you.

Cruel Legacy

.   .   .

Strong of mind, kind of heart, pure of body.

I read the words again. Seriously? A vow of chastity? There's no date when this *celebration* is supposed to take place. If I'm supposed to turn down dick just because they say so, they should at least provide a countdown clock or something, so I know how many days I have left to get my kitty licked.

I have to laugh at myself. Even if I had a date, I don't have any prospects I can use to help me get off. I've been hesitant about going out and picking someone up after the last guy turned out to be my teacher. With my luck, the odds of that happening again are like seventy percent.

I look around the room, trying to figure out why they had this delivered to me tonight. Here. I already knew the pledges were being watched, but this is a little too much.

I blink, and rub my eyes, which are suddenly feeling irritated for no reason. I look down and see smoke swirling around the floor. A look towards the ceiling shows it's coming from the vents up there too.

I'm familiar with the sensation I'm feeling. The weird taste in my mouth. They're filling this room with whatever gas they used to knock us out the night of the meet and greet. This time, I lower myself to the floor. I'd rather not do the whole falling down on my face thing again.

My ears are ringing. I lift my hands to plug my ears and find them chained together in front of me. What the fuck?

My breath fans back at me. I reach up and find they've placed another silk bag over my head. I focus on the static that I know is external to the pounding in my head.

The pledge master's voice plays from a recording. "A Zeta Nu's journey from their old life to the new symbolizes an awakening to the true strength of woman kind. There is no greater or more important choice than to accept a vow of purity, but the journey to the decision is a personal one. Tonight, you will decide. You must freely and willingly choose to leave behind the dark and enticing delights that men seek to enslave us in. Your vow to be a true lady means bringing them into the light. A Zeta Nu does not engage in carnal pleasures for pleasure's sake. The secrets of her enticements remain behind closed bedroom doors. A lady always, in and out of the public eye."

I mull over what she's saying, and it sounds an awful lot like the opposite of a lady in the streets, a freak in the sheets. I'd have to play Pious Pam for three more months, *after* I cross over. I wanna say fuck no, but I'm doing this for LJ. She needs my support and if intentionally swearing off dick makes me a good friend, I'll do it. I'm not getting any action anyway, so I can deal with it.

"Do you accept this most solemn vow? Pure of mind, pure of heart, pure of body. Speak now, pledge, verbally making your intentions clear."

I wait to see if anyone else speaks. I don't hear anything, so I assume I'm the only person in this room. I take a deep breath and say, "I accept, Sovereign Sister."

A gong sounds, and the voice says, "Let the test begin."

Test? Before I can work through that, the slack in the chain tightens. I'm hoisted off my feet, then yanked hard enough to pull my arms out of their sockets. I walk across the room to keep that from happening, praying I'm not about to run into anything.

The ambient temperature in the room changes, and I can make out a glow. That's the only reason I can tell I'm in a different room. Someone grabs the chains, yanking my hands over my head. They pull hard enough that I'm wrenched off my feet. Someone else grabs my legs, and together they carry me forward.

My back hits something cold. The chains are readjusted, and

something's cuffed around my ankles. I'm spread eagled on a flat surface.

A voice on my left says, "I wouldn't get too close until she's compliant. She likes to hit."

I remember that voice. It's the guy that slapped my ass the night I was dropped on the side of the road. "You're not still pissed about that little tiny tap, are you?"

The person who answers makes my stomach flip, a wave of unease crawling up my spine. "It's okay. She won't be getting much use out of her arms or legs tonight."

I feel the jab of a needle in my neck and a burning sensation as something is pushed into my veins. "What the fuck did you just give me?"

"Just a little something to make sure you can't cheat on your test."

The pledge master's voice comes again. "All proctors are on hand. You may now commence with the test. Good luck, Pledge."

The bag is still over my head. I can't see anything through it, so I use my hearing, trying to gauge how many people are in the room with me.

"Do you know what the chastity vow is, Pledge Thea?"

"Sure do. It's a pledge's promise that they'll be fingering themselves for twelve weeks after pledge season is over."

"It's a series of progressively more difficult questions or scenarios used to determine if you're smart enough, brave enough and pure enough to get yourself free without compromising your vow, and embarrassing your sorority. There are no limits to how far a proctor can go to administer the test."

Sounds perfect to me. Once the idiot behind me lets go of my arms, I'm putting him and his other *proctors* on their asses. I'm working out the sequence of events while he drones on.

"First question."

I wait for him to say something, but he doesn't. Instead, I feel someone's fingers ghosting over my face. They stop against my collar-bone. The touch is soft against the silkiness of the bag.

"Second question."

What I think is the same hand picks up where it left off, continuing south and slowly circling my breasts.

I fake a yawn because it's obvious these *questions* are designed to arouse and titillate. They've gotta do better than some nipple play to get me horny. With the third question, I hear the soft snip of scissors and my shirt falls open. "That shirt was vintage. Somebody's gonna buy me a new one."

I shift, trying to ward off the stiffness in my shoulders. The fourth question is actually a question. "Do you like having your tits played with Thea?"

"Do you?"

Someone squeezes my tit. I tilt my head to say something smart, but a jolt of electricity shoots through me. "What the fuck?" I pant when my body stops seizing.

The person asking the questions says, "Strong of mind, kind of heart, pure of body."

The next question is a kiss on my bare midriff. I hollow out my belly to get away from the person's lips. I'm met with another shock. My pants are yanked off, and I'm asked a riddle.

"What has a big top and three circles that never meet?"

My smart ass says a woman's body, and I'm rewarded with another zap. Turns out the answer was a circus.

They go on and on. Asking questions and zapping me when I get them wrong. Or they pepper my skin with touches that I'm not supposed to react to. Although when I don't react, I get zapped for that, too. It's hard to tell what they want from me, other than to torture me, which isn't working. I laugh after our latest round. My skin burns everywhere from the repeated shocks, but the sting is keeping me focused.

They take a break and I strain my ears, trying to hear what's happening around me. I can't make out anything, their voices low and coming from the other side of the room.

The pledge master's voice announces. "Section one complete. Commence section two."

Section two? How many sections are there to this *test?*

The restraints around my legs are removed. I wiggle my ankle and point my toes, stretching my calves. A hand grabs my ankle and lifts it high. I've had my legs elevated and pushed back enough to recognize the lump they're now resting on is somebody's shoulders. With the way there spread wide, I'd say it's two different people spreading me open.

The only thing hiding my vag from them are the panties they didn't cut off. I was rolling with this little game, but now I'm pissed.

"What kind of stupid ass initiation test is this? Is this how you get your shit off and pass it off as a sorority thing? You can't get a woman, so you and your buddies pin her down while you push your useless dick in her? Why don't you tell me who else is here, Paxton? One of the pledges from Rho your boat house or one of the full-fledged members?"

My legs are lowered, and the bag comes off. I smirk as Pax leans forward, glowering at me. "I wouldn't put my dick in you if it was on fire and your cunt was the only way to extinguish the flames."

If Pax is here, that means his bosom buddies can't be too far away. "Then what are we doing this little wrestling hold for?"

I turn my head as much as I can, spotting Finn over against the wall. His eyes are glued to the top of my tits, that they pulled out of my bra. I can't tip my head back, but odds are good Holden's the one yanking on my chains. I knew this had to be another combined pledge event. I just don't know why I've got these three here when they're full members already. Maybe this is another one of their stupid fraternity games.

"If phase two gives you and your deranged little team points for fucking someone with a witness present, switch places with the psycho. At least I won't be throwing up the whole time."

Finn smirks at me and steps closer. "Awe Pet, you think I'm hot?"

"That's not what I said."

"You called me psycho and said my face doesn't make you wanna vomit."

"That's not the same thing, Number Three."

"Sure it is."

I wish I could wave my hand in his face to get his attention, since he's basically holding this conversation with my left tit. I whistle, "Hey, eyes up here, buddy."

He finally looks up, and I'm almost sorry I told him to. Finn looks slightly unhinged. More than usual. Before I can ask what he's thinking, my head's wrenched back. It's an awkward angle since I'm laying flat.

"You're not scared." It's a statement, not a question. I swear Holden is too perceptive for his own good. Out of the three of them, he's the one I think sees me the clearest, and that freaks the hell out of me and pisses me off at the same time. Because how dare he try to dissect me.

"Of you Coxsuckers?" I scoff and roll my eyes. "The only reason none of you are bleeding on the floor is because you jumped me, drugged me and have me at a disadvantage. Why would I be scared of you when I can kick your asses in a fair fight?"

"You should be thanking me for the drugs." Holden says, as if he did me a favor.

"Thank you for shooting poison in my veins?"

"It's not poison, it's a pain reliever. It's helping to take the edge off the taser. Trust me, if we didn't give it to you, it would've hurt a lot worse."

I bat my eyes and in a sickeningly sweet voice say, "If you untie me, I'll show you *my* worse. I promise to make it hurt."

"You think so, Pet?" Finn asks, drawing my attention back to him. "Because there are grown men who can't."

"Pussies. They're probably afraid of your reputations so they're unable to do what it takes to win."

Pax steps closer, trying to intimidate me. "And what is it that you think it takes to win against us?"

I smirk at him because he's the first person I'd best in a fight. He's seventy-four inches of pure muscle, and too cocky. That'll be his downfall. "I know what it takes. You have to risk it all and fight like you have nothing left to lose, because when you do, that's when you find that thing you need to win."

Holden comes around to the edge of the table, to stand shoulder to shoulder with Pax. "You're looking for that thing right now."

"Maybe I already found it, Pretty Boy."

Pax's patience is wearing thin. He scrubs a hand through his hair. "Stop trying to stall. You can't talk your way out of phase two. You're gonna break before this night is over with."

I smile brightly at him. He's already told me his goal. What he hopes to accomplish tonight and I'll never give him the win. "Am I though?"

"This is your chastity vow. We're about to see how far you'd go to keep it or how quickly you'd break it." His cold eyes meet mine. "Phase one proved you're strong of mind. Phase two, we prove you're no different from every other pledge that's come through Zeta Nu's doors, and that's a slut who would do anything for Trium cock."

"I thought you said you'd rather burn your dick than let me put out the flames."

He grabs my chin, forcing me to look at him and see all the hate he has for me. "I would. But I never said other things wouldn't be used."

And with that statement hanging in the air, he slides a tray closer and produces something I wasn't expecting. "What the hell are you gonna do with that?"

"You ask too many questions. How about I just show you?"

He wrenches my panties to the side and impales me with the crystal phallic shaped tool. No lube, no warm up. I burn at the bite of pain. I know there's a tear at my opening. The wand is ice cold, like it's been in a freezer, sending a shiver through me.

"Get this thing out of me." I dig my heals into the table trying to push away from it.

Pax orders the other two, "Blindfold her, then hold her legs."

"Don't you dare." Of course knife boy dares. He whips a blindfold out of his pocket with a flourish of his wrist.

"We might have to gag her, too." Finn says leaning forward. He's gonna have to let go of my leg to wrap the cloth around my eyes. This is my chance to make my move.

Faster than anything I've ever seen, he's on top of the table with me, both of his knees pressing into my thighs, making it impossible for me to move. Holden takes over, holding my legs, and Finn moves up my chest. His crotch is at eye level, and there's a noticeable bulge.

"Yeah." Finn rasps, eyeing my mouth. "We should totally gag her."

I read the intent in his eye. "Try it, and whatever appendage is close to my mouth is getting bitten off."

He shifts and palms his dick as if the idea turns him on. He leans forward, swiping his mouth against mine. I go to bite his lips, but he backs away before I can. Leveling him with a glare, I warn, "If you ever do that again, I'll make you regret it."

He leans forward, grazing his lips against my ear. "Empty threats are a waste of time, Pet. I'll kiss you whenever I want."

"They're not empty."

He ties the gag around my mouth. "They are until we're done with you, and that won't be until you're begging us to give you relief with our cocks. So the sooner you say, 'Fill me with your big juicy cock, Finn', the sooner we'll let you go."

I get the impression he's hoping I won't be that easy to break. He's about to get his wish because I'll never give them the satisfaction of hearing me ask them for anything.

They're used to being the most desired and most feared people on campus. I'm about to show them just how unimpressed I truly am.

Chapter 43
Holden

She's covered in sweat. Strands of hair stick to her face from her thrashing about. Thea's chastity vow has a hidden purpose. We're trying to get answers out of her about the night she drove into town and what she heard when she stumbled across Michael and his friends, completing their frat challenge.

It's been an hour since we started the test and we're no closer to finding answers than we were when we walked in.

This may seem like an extreme way to get answers, but I've seen the look in Thea's eyes. She gets off on fighting. Coming straight out and questioning her was never gonna work. Pax's suggestion that we administer her test was the perfect solution.

The shot I gave her was a beta blocker for the pain, but there was also a touch of Thiopental to heighten her state of suggestibility. What better way to get her to lower her defenses than a little truth serum and orgasmic release? Or in her case, repeated denial of that release, until she's ready to cave.

We've brought her to the edge over and over. I'm watching. Waiting for the sign that she's finally breaking. Needy. Begging for relief and willing to give up every secret she's ever held.

She's endured the electric shocks, and now the edging and she hasn't broken yet. Questioning aside, she should definitely be begging to get fucked by now. Maybe I got the dosing wrong for the nerve blocker and gave her too much.

I steal a look at her while she's busy glaring at Pax. She's gorgeous like this. She's mumbling something over the gag. Okay, so maybe she can't exactly beg with words since her mouth is stuffed.

"What's that?" Finn teases. "You want to come, Pet?"

He lowers the gag, and she hisses, "I'm. Not. Your. *Pet.*"

Finn rolls his eyes, as if he doesn't believe her. "And yet you're purring whenever we resume our little chat."

"It's a snarl, you asshole."

"Either way, it's sexy as fuck. Shall we start again?"

He looks over at me, giving me the sign to move on to the next and final phase. I step forward and yank her bra down, placing silver clamps on her pert nipples.

"Oh, fuck." She pants. Her back arches off the table. Good thing her arms are strapped above her head. She's been clenching her fists this whole time like she's desperate to punch someone. Pax is standing in the corner like an annoyed bouncer.

He shoved the dildo in her, then backed off to let me and Finn do the hands on portion, while he lobbed question after question, getting angrier by the second.

We're close. I can feel it. Finn wasn't lying when he said she's purring. We just need to press her a little more. I just can't tell if we should be adding pain or pleasure to the mix.

Finn darts his tongue out, wetting his bottom lip, as he stares at her tits. "What were you doing in the alley, the night Mikey and his friends found you, Thea?"

"Minding my own fucking business."

"And what did you see?"

"Three idiots in the middle of a circle jerk."

She stiffens slightly. It's the first hint that she's hiding something. I look over at Finn. Did he notice it too? My hands trace down her thighs as I drag the feather I'm holding back and forth across her thigh. Down to her ankle, then back up to her hip, before starting the process all over again.

I could make her tell the truth. Inflict fear upon her like she's never felt before. The little experiment in her bedroom was nothing. I could literally choke the life out of her.

There's nothing like the fear of death to make a person compliant. But we're confined to the guidelines of the test. We don't physically harm the pledges.

"Just one honest answer, Thea, and this will all be over."

"I'm answering. You just don't like the words I'm using." She pants, trying to twist away from my touch.

"This is ridiculous." Pax storms over to us, murder in his eyes. "Let's just beat the answers out of her."

And just like that, whatever progress we've made goes up in smoke, as I watch Thea close herself off. I can see her going through the steps. Her jaw clenches, her eyes go blank, and then her face is eerily serene. She's tucking her emotions and responses back into their boxes, ready to fight.

Going on instinct, I grab one of the toys off the table and shove into her cunt. The shock of the action and the relief of finally having something inside her, is too much for her to ignore.

She moans, and I add my finger along with it, because I can't pass up the chance to finally feel her pussy. She whimpers, the sound going straight to my cock. I hold her gaze as I move the toy and my fingers in and out. It's almost imperceptible, but I feel it. Her body moves against my hand.

I have one last chance to get our question answered. I remove my finger and shove it in her mouth as I fuck her with the crystal wand. The thing is no bigger than my finger, but she doesn't care. She braces her feet against the table, rocking her hips up to meet it.

I lean closer and drop my voice. "I've been thinking about that night we came to your room. And how I should have choked you harder."

Her eyes flutter closed.

"Thea, you want to share your secret, don't you?" I ask, working her pussy over.

"Yes. God, yes."

"Go ahead." I lean closer. "It's just me and you. Tell me everything, and I promise to wrap my hand around your throat while I make you come so fucking hard, you'll float among the stars."

"I heard, I heard." I stroke the toy in and out, letting my thumb brush across her clit. Finn leans over and sucks a nipple into his mouth. "Oh fuck, I heard someone say…"

"Yes?"

We all wait with breathless anticipation for what she's about to say. She takes a shuddering breath. *"Fuck you."*

She laughs. She laughs so hard tears pool in the corner of her starless night eyes. Pax throws a chair and storms out of the room. I look at Finn, who just shrugs. Our time is up. We'll have to find another way to get the answers we want.

I remove the wand and shove it in her mouth, then Finn walks over and jolts her clit with the Taser. Her eyes flash with lust and anger. He smirks at her and says, "Congratulations, Pet. You made it through your ceremony. Too bad you'll be spending the next six months sexually frustrated."

He laughs as we walk out of the room.

Pax ordered the Beta Psi pledges to drop Thea off just outside the gates to campus, telling them we didn't care about if she made it back to the dorm or not. Or rather, Finn and Pax said they didn't care. I didn't say anything. I never do, which they took as my agreement.

After we parked our cars, I made an excuse about needing to go to the library. As soon as Finn and Pax were out of sight, I walked back toward the gate to keep an eye on her. Instead of heading to the dorm, she turned towards the thicket of trees that leads to the stream.

Pure of body. That part of the chastity vow doesn't mean what people think it does. It really means mastery of your body, and Thea showed that. She took all that sexual energy and frustration and somehow tamped it down. Never asking for release. When her test was over, I felt like I was the one strapped to the table.

The chastity vow rankings won't post until every girl goes through it, but I think it's safe to say Thea got top marks.

We all had different reactions to her playing us. Finn was amused and horny, Pax angry, and I'm more curious than ever to see just how much pressure she can really take.

Chapter 44
Thea

"Hello, Pet."

I'm sitting at a picnic bench on the outer ring of The Circle, enjoying time alone. Or I was, until he walked up.

I look up from my book, leveling a glare at him. How many damn times do I need to tell him not to call me that? My chastity vow ceremony was three nights ago. I haven't seen much of my neighbors since then. Finn and Holden even skipped class.

I guess they were off licking their wounds since they didn't break me. Their pity party must be over.

"Number three." I look around for the other Coxsuckers. "Does your daddy know you snuck out of the house?"

"My father? What's he got to do with anything?" He scrunches his nose, then groans. "You're talking about Pax, aren't you?"

"Sure am." The way he keeps chastising Finn whenever it looks like he's having fun with me definitely gives off stuffy old father vibes.

"Pax is not my daddy."

"You sure? He certainly seems to be in charge of your play dates."

Last week, I heard him tell Finn that he'd be taking Eloise to dinner. It was supposedly already arranged, and all Finn had to do was show up. That's daddy vibes or pimp vibes and I'm guessing none of them are getting paid to have sex.

Finn swings my legs around so I'm facing him and braces his hands on the table, leaning close. He drops his voice like he's letting me in on a secret, dragging his eyes along the length of my body. "I'd like to schedule another play date. With you. In your bed. With us both naked."

"We weren't naked."

"Your tits were out. My chest was out. We only had our underwear on. Things were definitely heading in that direction before Holden pushed me out of the way with his little experiment."

"Uh, no. They weren't."

He reaches out and grabs my left tit. "What the hell are you doing?" I grab his hand, squeezing it hard enough to break, and shove him away.

"Gauging how big your breasts are."

"You should've written the measurements down during my sexual assault ceremony, and don't you think you should ask before touching me?"

"No."

No? Did he really just say that? "And why the hell not?"

"Because if I ask, you'll tell me no, and sometimes it's better to ask forgiveness than permission."

"Not where touching someone else's body is concerned."

He's back in my personal space. "Facts. But in this instance, you want me touching your body. You like the naughty little thrill you get from doing something so private in public."

I go to protest, but I can't. I sort of do. Finn hovering over me like this is messing with my head. I can't stand him and his friends because of the way they act and the shit they've been doing to me, but when Finn's attention is on me like this, and he's staring down at me with those sweet puppy dog eyes, that don't quite hide the cunning and mischief, I feel a little tug. Like I want to hold my hand out and invite him to go do something reckless with me, and *that's* the problem.

I'm always willing to do reckless, but I'm supposed to be maturing. Surrounding myself with friends who are a good influence on me. Staying out of trouble and all that. Right now, this smug fucker has me questioning why.

"You're gonna beg me to suck those nipples one day soon, Pet."

"Keep dreaming."

"As we lie side by side, my little breasts become two sharp delightful towers and I shove hotly the lovingness of my belly against you."

I'm fixated on the way his mouth moves as he recites Cumming's words. Shit, why is poetry so hot?

His tongue darts out to wet his lips, and he asks, "You wanna kiss me right now, don't you?"

Finn's always talking, giving his mouth and tongue a workout. Is he a good kisser? What am I thinking? Kissing him falls firmly in the reckless column.

I beat that urge back and stare up at him, pretending to be bored out of my mind. Ignoring the butterflies in my stomach and that heady feeling I get when I experience that pull of attraction to somebody. I snort derisively. Hiding the fact that, yup, I was thinking about kissing him.

Instead, I say, "Let's hold off on that until you become someone I actually like."

"If you don't like me now, it'll never happen, so why don't I just skip the useless waiting and kiss you, anyway?"

He's being intentionally difficult, and yet his question makes so much sense. "Besides the fact that I'm not interested?"

"Aren't you?"

He's staring at my chest. Thank god for the sports bra I'm wearing. It does a great job at hiding my nipples. He won't be able to tell they're hard unless he touches me again.

He wedges his knee between my legs. It takes everything in me not to react. I arch a brow and take a deep breath, hold it and let it out slowly, releasing the tension in my body. That cools me down. A little.

His smile widens. "I like this game."

I hold his gaze, waiting for him to elaborate on the game he thinks we're playing. He leans over again, his warm breath fans my ear as he whispers something in what I think is Japanese. I have no clue what he's saying, but I'm guessing it's vulgar. Then he licks up the side of my face.

"Did you just lick me?"

He looks happy as fuck about it, too. "Don't even think about washing it off."

I get to my feet, shoving against his chest to put some space between us. "Oh buddy... not only am I gonna wash it off, but I'm gonna scrub the skin until it's raw."

I grab my book and march into the closest building to do just that. It's a five-minute walk from where I was sitting, but at least I looked fierce, strutting away.

I stomp down the hallway, cursing the traffic pattern the students are forced to use, and finally reach the bathroom. When I get to the sink, I turn on the water and nothing happens. I try the next one and still no water. All the sinks are out of commission.

I find another bathroom on the second floor. Those sinks aren't working either. Shouldn't there be a sign posted that the water is off in this building?

I head to the gym and push my way into the girls' locker room. How the hell isn't there any water in here too? As I'm trying to figure out where to go next, a campus alert rings on my phone.

I pull my phone out to read it. Great. The water is off on campus while unscheduled repairs are being conducted and there are only two bathrooms available. One for guys, the other for girls.

Water conservation is imperative. So unless you have to use it to take a shit, they're off limits. An attendant is assigned to each bathroom to ensure compliance. Oh, and ladies can go to the infirmary if they're bleeding through their tampons and need a little extra clean up.

I'm in my next class, fuming. I can't believe I have to sit through this entire day with Finn's spit on my cheek. This is... *his* fault. *Sonofabitch.* I told him I was scrubbing my face and somehow he's made it impossible for me to do it. I don't know how he got the water turned off so fast, but I know it's him.

My class ends and I head to The Rock, which is just as busy as it usually is. I'm looking for a quick pre-packaged meal, but I hear the hospitality manager telling someone that the water works fine in the dining hall.

I guess Finn wouldn't dare eat pre-packaged food, so he's graciously decided to keep potable water on in here. I order a Grilled Chicken Caesar Wrap. I'm told it's a five-minute wait for the chicken to be ready, then grab a parfait with strawberries and extra whipped cream for dessert and go to my table to wait for my number to be called.

I give a tight smile to my table mates and casually scan the dining hall. Austin walks by, heading to his usual spot. I reach out to grab his hand, giving it a little squeeze.

"Damn, Thea." He says, grinning down at me. "You look good enough to eat."

I smile at him, and start to brush off his compliment, but then I come up with an idea. When genius and inspiration strike, you have to roll with it. I wish I had time to loop Austin in, but I don't. Hopefully, this doesn't backfire on me.

"Oh really? Prove it."

I make a production of smearing the whipped cream along my cheek, where Finn licked me. Austin wastes no time leaning forward, kissing and licking from the tip of my chin to the top of my cheekbone. I meet Finn's gaze over his shoulder. *Take that mother fucker.*

When Austin's gotten as much of it off me as he can, he presses his lips against mine. Shit. I wasn't expecting that, but I go along with it, kissing him back, earning double points, since Finn was going on about kissing me earlier.

Austin pulls away with a laugh when his buddies start whistling and cheering.

"I'll catch you later, beautiful." He walks away with a satisfied smirk on his lips.

I'm sure I'm sporting one too.

Chapter 45
Holden

Finn's upset. I caught the flash of emotion on his face before he hid it away behind his mask. It's not hard to guess that Thea is the reason behind it.

He was happy as hell when he walked into the dining hall. But he's twitchy now after watching Austin maul her like a banana split. He's been flipping his knife around for the last few minutes. I don't know what it is about this girl, but she stokes his crazy in a way nobody else ever has.

The way she's looking at him tells me she knows it, too. I don't like the murderous look in his eye, and scan the table for someone else to direct his attention to. Not that I care if he stabs the football jock. But we really don't need to be dealing with that shit right now. Not when we're a just two weeks out from Mayhem Night. There will be a lot of alumni on campus for these next fourteen days. Including Finn's father.

"Be right back." Finn says, climbing to his feet.

I watch him walk towards the kitchen. Seconds later, an alert goes off, informing us the water has been restored to campus. A cheer goes up in the dining hall. When Finn sits back down, he's smiling again. To anyone else, this is Finn's M.O. He doesn't stay upset long. But as his best friend, I know the change in attitude is because he's up to something.

"The water issue was you?"

"Yup."

And now it's back on. Glancing back over at Thea, I deduce that whatever is going on has to do with her. "Are you sure you don't still need it off?" I'm glad it's on. I wasn't looking forward to having to go to the frat house to shower. But if he's gonna play with the plumbing again, I'd like a heads up.

"Nah. I've taken care of the issue."

He's smiling as he eats. Totally at ease and in a playful mood. He's even smiling at Eloise, which I personally think is a bad idea. Giving that shrew attention affects us all. Come to think of it, why is she sitting here with us instead of at the future wives' table?

I feel my sandwich turn over in my stomach when he lets Eloise kiss his cheek. He doesn't even flinch. That means he's heavily into plotting mode, and whatever he has planned is more sneaky and devious than turning off the water.

We run into Thea when we're entering the dorm. She looks freshly showered and dressed like she's going out.

"Did you enjoy your lunch, Thea?" Finn purrs.

"I did. I enjoyed the dessert even more." She's trying to get a rise out of him, throwing that stunt with Austin in his face. "Next time, try harder, Number Three."

"Oh, Pet. You think you won this round? That's cute."

"I did win. I got your saliva off my face while the water was off, didn't I?"

He rolls his eyes and drawls, "Yes. I bet Austin felt like a big man, with that dry ass kiss."

"At least he got a kiss."

"So did I."

She chuckles. "Licking me, unwillingly, is not a kiss."

"Pet. You very willingly swallowed my spit."

"No, I didn't. Never even came close."

Finn smiles, and I pinch the bridge of my nose. I have an idea where this is going.

"Oh but you did, Pet. Complete with a little happy dance in your seat."

Thea takes a step forward, her eyes flashing with anger. "What did you do to my drink? Did you spit in it?"

"No, Pet. I would never." He says as if that's the most absurd thing in the world, when we both know he totally has and would. "But I did lick around the rim of the glass, your utensils and your sandwich."

She turns red and looks like she's about to scratch his eyes out. But that doesn't stop Finn. He likes pushing people's buttons.

"I was so fucking hard watching you devour your food."

"You sick fuck! Why the hell would you think it's alright to do something like that?"

He shrugs like it's perfectly acceptable to lick people's shit. "You let Austin lick my scent off of you after I told you I wanted you to carry my spit on you all day. What else was I supposed to do?"

It's a genuine question. Crazy as it sounds, Finn really wants her to tell him what other recourse she thinks he had.

"Look here, little psycho. You can't just go putting your bodily fluids into people without their permission. It's wrong and depraved, disgusting and-"

He cuts off her tirade. "Not people. Just you."

"What?"

"I'm not gonna put my bodily fluids in people without permission. Just you. You're the only person."

"And that's supposed to make me feel what?"

"Happy."

She looks to me for help, but I've got nothing because a part of me understands exactly what Finn is saying. I want to do shit to her without permission, too. I *have* been doing things to her without permission. She just doesn't know it. I'm not like that with anyone else. I don't even think about doing it to someone else. It's just her.

"I don't..." She shakes her head at the insanity of it.

Finn steps closer and grabs her hand. "Why are you upset, Pet? I did something for you I won't do to other girls."

Her mouth gapes open like he's really flipped his lid. "Number Three, this isn't like giving me flowers."

He rolls his eyes. "Of course it's not. I don't do that flowers shit. Holden's the plant guy. You like flowers? Tell him and he'll plant some."

I cut my eyes at him. Why's he bringing me into this shit? She's probably gonna start screaming any minute now. Or go back into her dorm and throw up. Or something else uncalled for and dramatic.

It's not like he held her mouth open and spat in it. Although I can definitely see an appeal to doing that. I can picture it so clearly. Her mouth slack as I squeeze the air out of her delicate little throat. Me hovering over her, collecting saliva in the back of my mouth then passing it into hers.

Thea licks her lips and bites down on her bottom lip hard enough to leave dents. "Licked my utensils, huh?" She nods and walks away. That's it. No temper tantrum. No freak out.

When she reaches the end of the path, Finn and I walk into the building. I wait until we're in the elevator before asking, "What the hell is going on with you?"

"Nothing."

"We're not supposed to be making nice and romantic gestures to her."

Though the idea of nice where any of us are concerned is all a matter of perspective. Most people would definitely not categorize turning off the water on campus, so they're forced to walk around with spit on their face, or licking their food and utensils as nice or romantic. But for Finn. This is him being sweet and attentive in a hyperactive puppy kind of way.

"Pax says we fuck with her. That's what I'm doing."

"It looked an awful lot like flirting to me."

"He didn't say we couldn't have fun with it. She's just not supposed to be enjoying it." He bumps my shoulder. "Besides, you're one to talk. You were the one who kissed her."

Being forced to take part in that fuck fest at the social club and then the adrenaline rush I got from knocking into people on the football field had me on edge. We had to stop the game before I tired myself out. I still needed an outlet.

I caught Finn on the security camera climbing onto her balcony. I wanted to see what he was up to, and used his balcony the same way he did, to keep the existence of the access panel a secret.

I hadn't planned on kissing her. But I'm not sorry that I did. I liked the way her lips felt on mine. The taste of her tongue in my mouth. It felt good rubbing my dick between her thighs. I'm not sorry for anything I've done afterwards, either.

Thea is the perfect little toy and for as long as she's here, I'll continue to play with her.

It's been two days since lick-gate, and two days of Pax and I having to listen to Finn say he has to find something else to do to Thea, because she's not playing the game like she's supposed to.

Finn and I have just come back from the gym. Pax is still there, and I'm ready to go back and join him. I think we're all a little on edge and Finn's complaining isn't helping.

I want her to act right, whatever that means, just so he'll stop obsessing about her and focus on pledge season and everything else we need to do.

His laundry bag is sitting in front of his door. He grabs it and unlocks his door, heading straight for the couch to dump the bag on it like he always does. As soon as he opens it, we're hit with the most obnoxious smell.

"Finn, carry that rancid shit outside." I say, pointing to the patio.

He does and I follow him, only to find some kind of laundry line rigged across his balcony. There are clothes hanging on it, and they smell like ass. Okay, not literal ass, but sweat. And lots of it. He pulls a pair of his boxers off the line.

"It's wet." He touches the hoodie that's next to it. "All of it's wet, but why doesn't it smell like it's been washed?"

Better question is why did the laundry girl take his stuff and bring it back wet instead of drying it? Both of our gazes drift to the balcony across from us. He says, "This has to be Thea's doing."

"If it was, how did she get in to raid your closet? Did you forget to lock the balcony door?"

"No. All of this stuff was together. I sent it out to be laundered so I could wear it tonight."

It would be one thing for it to be just wet. We could throw it in a dryer. But it all needs to be rewashed.

"At least she didn't fuck with my favorite beanie." He says, pulling it off the line. It's his favorite because it converts into a ski mask. He says it makes him feel like a ninja. That comes in handy when an impromptu prank falls into our laps.

"Why do you think the clothes smell so bad?" He asks, turning the beanie over in his hand.

"My guess? She used them to mop the football team's locker room, had the team wipe off with them, or dumped them in dirty mop water. If not all the above."

He nods, heading to his bathroom. I hear him turn on the shower. "I'll meet you out front in an hour." He says over the spray of water.

"Since when do you need an hour to get ready?"

"Since I have to plot my revenge on Thea."

All signs point to this being payback, but I try to be thorough. I don't want to falsely accuse her of anything. She's got a big enough target on her back. "You're sure this was her doing?"

"Oh yeah. I'm sure." He comes back out wearing a towel. "Clearly she had help, because someone had to climb over here and rig the line on this side. It was probably that fucker, Austin. But this was definitely her way of getting back at me."

I leave him to shower and go to my room to pull up the camera feeds on my laptop. Finn's front door remains unopened, and the only person I see on our floor getting off the elevator is Thea, and the laundry attendant dropping off the bag.

Yesterday was Finn's massage day, and I haven't had a chance to turn the balcony cameras back on yet. There's nothing to suggest Thea touched Finn's laundry bag. But the footage from the hallway could be a looped feed. I'll have to do a little more digging to see if it is.

Ninety minutes later, we walk into Zeta Nu's house for this week's pledge dinner. I'm immediately put on edge. There's too much noise and the overly excited squeals of the pledges make me want to dig my eyes out.

I know they're just expressing their joy at making it through another week and being one step closer to crossing the line, but do they have to express their joy in that overly chirpy way?

Eloise walks up to us with a smile on her face. "Evening boys, glad you could make it."

We would've skipped, but Pax is all about a show of support this season. The girls did their best on last week's obstacle course. This is us acknowledging that. It's also one of the last chances they'll have to really mingle with our pledges because next week the final group of girls will face their chastity vow challenge.

When it's over, some of them won't be looked at or treated the same. It's not as simple as how the guys will perceive them after it's over, it's about the girls confronting how they truly feel about themselves. Thea seems to have recovered well from her vow. Then again, she never broke, so why wouldn't she be okay with how things went?

Eloise walks her fingers up Finn's chest, bringing her hand to rest on his shoulder. "Finney, did you really have to wear your hat tonight? This is a semi-formal event."

"I have on shoes and slacks, so I'm in compliance with the dress code."

His attention is on the room. He's looking for someone. I can guess who.

"I know, but the hat doesn't really fit."

"It's my favorite hat." He says in a tone that suggests she's supposed to know this. As his *fiancé*, she *should* know this.

"But babe, couldn't you have just left it home tonight?" She pouts.

He drags his attention from the room and focuses it on her. A hard glint in his eyes. "You don't want me wearing it tonight?"

"It doesn't match your outfit or the theme we have going on."

"I'd be willing to take it off, but you'll have to take something off for me, too." He caresses her cheek and her eyes go all soft and dewey. A little gasp slipping through her lips when he brushes his mouth against hers.

Finn has been playing these games with Eloise for years and she still hasn't learned there's no way to get him to do what she wants without giving up something in return.

"Will you take off something for me, Ellie?"

"Of course. My watch, the necklace. Anything you want."

"Good." He leans closer, lowering his voice so only the two of us can hear. "I'll take off my hat right here and now, if you take off your panties."

I chuckle at the horrified expression on her face. This is why Eloise will never win against Finn. She's too worried about her reputation, putting on this act of being such a perfect legacy daughter.

I don't know when she's going to wise up and realize that what Finn wants right now is the opposite of perfect. He's rebelling against his future and will continue to do so for as long as he can.

His request serves its purpose. Eloise stops asking him to take off his hat and when he doesn't give her the attention she's craving, she stalks off in search of something else to complain about.

Finn and I mingle with the pledges and try to get to know some of the girls better. Or rather, he mingles. I'm just standing around with them, silently watching. I spot Pax off in the corner with Eloise. She's gesturing around and looks pissed. I guess she's got an issue with what he's wearing, too. She's probably telling him his tattoos on display are not formal enough.

When he catches me looking, I walk over to rescue him. None of us can stand to be in Eloise's company for long, although he's been spending more time with her lately because of our combined pledge events.

Before I reach where they're standing, he pulls out his phone and steps out of the room to answer the call. Rescue mission aborted, I go back to the other side of the room, in search of Finn. When I find him, he has Thea in a corner.

As I get closer, I hear him say, "Nice try, Pet."

I step up beside them to watch their interaction. She flicks her eyes over at me, then shifts to the left before addressing Finn. "With what?"

"Making my clothes smell like swamp water. I don't know how you managed to do that, but I'm impressed. I'm also pissed that I have to toss out half a wardrobe, but impressed all the same."

"I don't know what you're talking about."

"Is that really how you wanna play this?" Finn gives her a look that says he's being generous about letting her reconsider her answer.

"I'm not playing anything. I didn't mess with any clothes."

I'm watching her micro expressions as she talks. She's a helluva actress. It's hard to pick out anything that suggests she's lying, but we all know she is. I just wanna know how she got Austin on our floor without being caught by the cameras.

I say, "Look. We don't care that you did it. But there's a breach in our security and we need to know how Austin bypassed it."

Finn adds, "And how you got into my room."

"I wasn't in your room."

"You weren't?"

Just so she gets an idea of how bad an idea it is to continue lying to us, I warn, "Be very careful about how you answer next. Ask around and they'll tell you how we deal with liars."

"I wasn't in your room."

Finn and I share a look. I guess she wants to find out firsthand what happens when you lie to a Trium.

He points to his head and asks, "Then how did you get my beanie?"

"That thing? Oh, your little girlfriend had it. She was in the laundry room bragging about it, so I swiped it from her when she wasn't looking."

Is she talking about Eloise? I doubt it. She doesn't do her own laundry, so it must've been someone else.

"So you admit you swiped my hat and then broke into my room to destroy my clothes. It's a bit extreme since I only licked your stuff, but okay."

Finn's face screws up. "Oh god. Did you lick all those things? Is that rancid smell your dragon breath?"

I snort. Nobody does dramatic comedy like Finn.

She glares at him. "Listen Coxsucker. I didn't destroy your clothes. I wouldn't do that. I swiped your hat and... and that's it." She eyes the hat sitting on his head before averting her gaze.

I step forward and tip her head back around, not letting her hide from this, letting her know I see the truth. "That's a lie, and that is certainly *not* it."

She pulls her chin from my grip, backing up a step. "I'm gonna go find my friends."

I step in front of her, blocking her exit. "If you're so innocent, why are you running?"

"The two of you are standing here accusing me of vandalism. I might have caught a case or five, in my past, but clothes are expensive and I wouldn't do something like cut up your shit or whatever."

It's not cut up and if she did it, then why is she alluding to that being what we mean by destroyed?

"Okay, do you admit you were on Finn's balcony?"

"Yup. Sure was."

"So, how did you get inside his place? The door was locked when we came home."

She throws her hands up, and huffs, "I didn't enter his room. I climbed over the railing."

That makes sense. That's how Finn got into her place, but I'm having a hard time imagining her being able to make the jump. It's not a tiny gap between their railings. "You rigged the clothesline, so how did you get his hoodie and boxers if you weren't in his dorm room?"

"Your friend likes to take his clothes off in the open air. The hoodie was in the hammock. His boxers were on the patio table." She narrows her gaze, taking in Finn's reaction to what she's saying. "You know, you really should be thanking me for returning your beanie. I hear it's your favorite and you hardly ever leave home without it."

Finn's still going off about his clothes, but I'm listening to her words. "What did you do to his beanie?"

I expect her to lie and deflect, but she doesn't. "I did the only thing I could do, considering what he did to me."

I cast a glance at Finn, choking back the laugh that wants to escape. "You spit in it?"

He pulls the hat off and sniffs, and shrugs, before he shoves it back on his head. "Doesn't smell like spit."

I study people all the time and try to duplicate their mannerisms in social settings. That's how I've gotten so good at reading people. "It's not spit you put in it, is it?"

"Nope." She pops her P, a smile tugging at her lips as she snags a drink from a passing waiter.

"What do you mean, no?" Finn's eyes dart from her to me as if I might have some insight on this. I don't. "Pet, you can't go changing the rules. Our game is to outdo the other and I have spit inside you... I..."

I narrow my gaze at her. She barely contains her laughter. Her eyes twinkling with whatever her secret is. Finn pulls his mask down. His eyes widen as she casually sips her drink.

"You didn't." He sniffs again, then shakes his head.

"Didn't what?" I ask, since he seems to think he's on to something.

"Did you..." He flips the hat over and brings it back to his nose. "Oh, Pet, you naughty, naughty girl."

I move closer, ready to force the secret out of her. "What did you do with his beanie?"

She doesn't answer. She just winks at Finn and walks away. His hand clamps down on my shoulder, preventing me from going after her.

I look over at my friend, wondering why he's okay with her walking away with this secret. "We need to bag it up and find out what she did. It could be poisoned."

He shakes his head, dismissing my concern. "Only the best kind of poison."

"You recognize the smell?" I reach out and check his pulse with one hand, pulling my phone out with the other to call 9-1-1.

"Oh yeah. It's called Fragrance Du Pussy."

My head whips around. "Huh?"

He's got the biggest grin on his face when he says, "She wiped her pussy with my hat."

Instead of shoving the damned thing in his pocket, he slips it back on his head, unrolling it so it's a full mask, and wears it down for the rest of the night.

Chapter 46
Deacon

I disconnect my call and scrub my hand through my hair. I've been fielding calls for two weeks about new prospects for the guardianship program at MISTIC.

The League lost two guardian trainees in the past month. One to rehab, the other to pregnancy, and they're desperate to replace them.

MISTIC has mandatory drug testing, so I have no idea how the guy showed clean all this time. I even heard him say he was set up and that there's no way it wasn't a clean sample.

As for the female candidate. There's no mandatory birth control policy. That would sort of defeat the purpose of spawning the next generation of guardians, but the timing is less than ideal. Once she has the baby, she can restart training.

My relationship with The League of the Daggered Ravens is a complicated one. My family's been involved with the organization since its inception.

There are two branches to the society. You have the legacies who run it, taking full advantage of all it has to offer. Then there are the families whose duty it is to protect the legacies as well as their assets, monetary and physical, at all costs, The Guardians.

Cruel Legacy

Some guardians work their way through the government so they'll be in a position to protect the legacy members who are politicians. Others become leaders in national defense, and then you have the basic body guard types. At any rate, a guardian's family and descendants are all assigned to a legacy line. They protect each generation of that family until they die off or fail to take their place within The League.

That's what happened to my family. The line we swore our allegiance to died off when my grandfather attended CFU. The heir died in a car accident.

My grandfather wasn't officially assigned as the heir's guardian yet and he wasn't there when tragedy stuck, but he carried the weight of that accident for years.

It changed the trajectory of our family. With no line to protect, my grandfather went to work with a private security firm. My father joined the intel community. Me, I wanted nothing to do with any of it.

I was great at sports, and in high school, baseball had my heart. I thought I'd go pro, until I realized that what I loved was the physicality of working out, and admitted that I didn't want to spend my life traveling for games, getting traded, making others rich.

I did my time in school, focused on health, nutrition, and body mechanics. Then, I discovered Mixed Martial Arts. I started training, started winning, and I never looked back.

Eventually, I realized I had a good eye for talent and started training others. I figured The League would leave me alone since all my time was spent helping people become better at beating the shit out of each other.

It turns out someone thinks that's a useful skill set and now I'm here, tangled up with them, because opening a gym wasn't cheap and there's really no such thing as getting out of The League. I made a deal with them. Not that I had a choice.

I got to open my gym, and they agreed for the most part to leave me alone. All it cost me was a huge chunk of my soul. I'm a small fish in their pond and I'm happy they don't force me to participate in the marriage games or whatever else the council comes up with to amuse themselves. But fringe living doesn't mean invisible. The council has decided training others to be in top physical condition is a useful skill set and they've found a way to monetize it to their benefit.

The League is connected to sponsors for some of the biggest names in the boxing world and the UFC, and they help fund lots of fights around the world.

My Physical Enhancement classes help prepare students to face the grueling conditions of MISTIC.

At first, it was simple. Train the children of the guardian lines. But when enrollment at CFU started dwindling, when there were less male heirs from guardian families to tap for protective details, they decided all MISTIC students and lower legacy families could do the job. With no real power or contribution to the council, those families are expendable.

Protecting the top of the food chain is imperative. Every student I push towards MISTIC is just one more person who'll never get the chance to decide what they want for themselves. I guess that's true of all league members.

I laugh to myself. The kids on campus think they're such hot shit, pledging fraternities and sororities, going through their little challenges. They have no idea that the little tasks they're given don't even come close to the things they'll be expected to do when they progress from Wren to Sparrow, which is the next level in The League.

If you can't handle crossing lines and getting your hands dirty, you'll never be more than a grunt. A foot soldier. That's a life I'd never want.

I've heard people whisper about it over the years. How I was supposed to be my family's ticket back into the fold. I was supposed to be the one to get us out of banishment and reassigned to a high level legacy line. I refuse to do what it takes for that to happen, choosing to earn the council's scorn and derision every chance I get.

At any rate, I owe them names and I've been dragging my feet about providing them. I know I can't keep putting it off. They've been hearing rumors, just as I have, about this new fighter everyone's obsessed with. I can't keep telling them, "I don't know who it is," because it's my job to know.

The thing is, I've been trying to get answers, but every time I ask someone in the fight circuit if they know who he is, they clam up. It's more than them not wanting to admit they go to underground fights. It's like Syl's got a gag order on them that surpasses her usual NDA.

I open my anonymous account on a social media site I rarely use. Syl doesn't allow cameras and recordings at her fights, but I know a guy that always seems to sneak a device in. He's uploaded a clip of a fight last month, but he's sitting too far away to really show who's fighting.

I can make out enough to see it's a woman going up against Big Jim. She's fast, but speed won't be enough. Jim's a beast. One blow at half power will send that girl flying. This must've been some kind of promo thing Syl had going. I wonder how much it cost the girl to get five minutes in the ring with him.

The swing of her ponytail niggles at me. Like it's tickling a memory, but I'm not sure why. I click out of the video, because I don't need to see the fight to know how it ends, and pull up another one. I watch this one all the way through as well as the next two, jotting down the names of the fighters I want to do more research on.

Big Jim would be an ideal guardian candidate, but he's already made a name for himself in the underground fight club and is gaining traction on the amateur circuit. He'll never be able to blend in on a guardian detail.

I bang twice on the back door of the warehouse. The minutes tick by while I wait for someone to answer. The camera mounted in the doorway will let them know I'm authorized access. My picture should already be in an envelope on the table inside the door, since I'm on the ticket to fight.

Syl doesn't trust IDs because they can be faked. She has current pictures of her fighters, taken within forty-eight hours of their fight night. When Syl says you need to look the way you'll look the day of your fight, she means it. I've seen the guards turn someone away because they cut and dyed their hair to match their fighting shorts the day of the match-up.

The door opens, and I walk through the X-ray scanner to make sure there's nothing that can be considered a weapon on me. With the increased use of polymer and ceramic knives and 3D printing, Syl takes no chances.

The final security check-point is for surveillance devices, and a doctor checks my teeth, under my tongue and between my nails for razor blades, stick pins, and pills that can be discreetly hidden and used on an opponent.

I don't take offense to the invasive checks. I might not be desperate enough to cheat, but that doesn't mean no one else would. The amount of money you can make here is insane and egos are fragile. Some people will do whatever it takes to win the cash or protect the latter.

I'm one of the last fights of the evening. I drop my stuff in the locker room, securing my bag in a locker with the lock I brought, then head out to the main area.

I stop in front of the betting table, even though I'm not wagering money, but I like to see the point spreads. I don't recognize any of the names on the lower end of the board. They have the smallest bets assigned to their fights. They must be newcomers. "Looks like the fourth fight's gonna be cancelled, huh?"

The guy clicks his mouse as he studies something on his computer screen. "Nope. Both fighters for the fourth bout are here."

"You don't have a name in the opponent section."

He shrugs. "That's how they want it and Syl said it's fine."

"So how do people know who they're betting for?"

"As you can see, most of them bet on the name that's posted. They know him, and his stats. They just have to hope they picked the right fighter when it's over with."

I move out of the way so the people behind me can place their bets. I find a seat close enough to the ring to watch the fight and far enough away to blend into the crowd to avoid being spotted by any fans.

Right now, I'd be miserable company. Thea's still showing up to class with bruises. I've been following her around campus, trying to see who she meets up with. So far, the only guy I've seen her with is Austin Kincaid. His face is just as annoyingly chiseled and clean as it's always been, and I've seen him shirtless in the gym. He's not the guy knocking her around.

I also called around to see if she's joined any of the local gyms, thinking maybe the boyfriend is a muscle head at one of them, but she's not. None of the owners have gone against school policy and signed her up, and I sure as hell haven't signed a permission slip. They could be lying, but if they are and I find out, that'll be the end of them running a gym in Canyon Falls.

They know what's at stake and it's not worth the lie or the hassle to try to get around me.

I switch my mind to scouting mode and tune out the people around me. I'll be in a better headspace to deal with socializing after my fight. Then, I'll be ready for the smiles and compliments. The attention from willing women who can't wait to congratulate me on my win.

We're coming up on the third round of the third fight, and I've seen enough. Both fighters are untrained, and taking sloppy shots at each other. Whoever comes out as the winner will literally have lucked out on this win, because there's no skill or fight plan involved.

The lights in the building flash twice, then plunge us into darkness. I know what that means. I jump out of my seat, making my way to the floor. When the lights come back on, I'm in front of the ring, facing the locker room. I stop dead in my tracks, trying to make sense of what I'm seeing.

People cross in front of me, running for the exit. When there's finally a gap, the person I was staring at is gone. I look around and spot a swinging ponytail with purple fucking tips. I ignore the screams and yells from everyone trying to get out of the building before the cops descend. The problem is, they're running towards the door the police are probably coming thru. I run back up the bleachers and run along the length of it, since everyone else is heading towards the floor.

I jump down when I get to the end and cut Thea off at the betting table. I grab her arm and drag her into the locker room. The lights are still off, but it's fine. I know this place like the back of my hand and always use the same locker. I have my lock undone and my gym bag in my hand, in under a minute, then I'm dragging her back out the door and deeper into the building.

What the other guests and fighters don't know is this warehouse used to be an art gallery with a passageway that connected to the restaurant next door. I pull her through the door that leads to the hallway where the restaurant bathrooms are, then over to the stairs that lead to the roof of the building. Once we exit the roof, we cross over two more buildings before taking the fire escape down to the streets.

"Wolfe. Wolfe!"

"What?"

"Where are we going?"

I don't have an answer for that. My only goal was to get us to safety and make sure we didn't get arrested. I've already accomplished that. We're away from Club Dredd and nobody will suspect we were at the fight. I slow down, but I don't let her hand go. Something tells me if I do, she's gonna take off and I need answers. Like what the hell was she even doing there?

Red Cliffs is a long forgotten town, with one working gas station - convenience store combo. Nobody comes here unless they're coming to Club Dredd or in a pinch for gas on their way to Palisades Shores. It's depressing. I walk us another few blocks before stopping in front of a closed down comic book store. "You wanna tell me what the hell you're doing out here?"

"Nature walk."

"Don't start with your shit, LaReaux. Do you have any idea how dangerous it is for you to be at Club Dredd? What am I saying? Of course you don't. Pampered princesses just want the excitement of doing something dangerous." I spit out, "Your boyfriend didn't even wait around for you to make sure you got out safely, and that's the guy you're protecting. If there's any justice in the world, he got caught up in the sweep."

She asks, "How did the cops even know there was a fight going on tonight?"

"Someone snitched. We made it almost halfway through the night before the raid, so it was probably someone who lost a lot of money."

I take in what she's wearing, and slowly, the pieces slot into place. The reason the ponytail on that grainy ass video seemed so familiar is because I watch it swish and sway away from me all the fucking time. Like some goddamn pendulum keeping time with the rhythm of her hips as she walks.

"You're the girl who fought Big Jim."

She gifts me with a smirk. "No, Wolfe. I'm the girl who *beat* Big Jim."

Chapter 47
Finn

I'm bored. It doesn't take much to make me feel that way, and it's getting harder to find ways to entertain myself. I'm in the eighth-floor lounge, scrolling through my phone, trying to find someone who might be able to distract me for a few hours. The elevator doors slide open and Thea walks out carrying a bag.

I get to my feet and follow her. I usually avoid the laundry area. It's too hot and too crowded. I don't need to go in there, because I have a roster of people who fold and fluff my towels. But today I do. By the time I get to the door, she's leaning over, pulling things out of her laundry bag.

I hop onto a table behind her, taking in the view. God, she's got an amazing ass. She's got her headphones in and is dancing around as she sorts her clothes.

I groan as her ass wiggles back and forth, begging me to touch it. She turns her head to look at me, then goes back to what she's doing. Ass wiggle and all.

I hop off the table and walk over to the machine she's using and stand in front of it to make her acknowledge me.

"Move."

"I don't think I will, Pet."

"I'm using that machine, Finley. Move!"

"This one? So it's yours?"

"For now."

I bless her with a smile. "Then I really don't think I'm gonna move. This one has a good view of the tv. I think I'll just take it for myself."

"Oh, really?" She looks around the room. "Where's your laundry?"

I shrug because I don't know. I leave my bag outside my door and someone takes it away dirty. Two days later it's back, clean.

"Do you even know how to do laundry?"

"I understand the principles of it."

Her mouth gapes open. "Seriously? You've never done your own laundry?"

"We've got staff at home that does it or takes it to the cleaners, and I've got girls here to do the same."

"That's how I was able to mess with your shit, Number Three. Doesn't it worry you to give people access to your clothes?"

I pick up a bra and twirl it around my finger.

"Why are you playing with my dirty underwear?"

"You want me to play with the clean ones instead?"

"No, Finn, I don't want you touching them at all."

"Because they're dirty?"

"Because they're mine and I already told you I don't like people touching my shit."

Her fingers are twitchy. She's getting ready to snatch them back, or maybe... "What if I let you touch my dirty clothes, too?"

She elbows me out of the way and turns on the washer. "I'm not doing your laundry." She drops the lid and looks at me. "And you shouldn't want random chicks doing your laundry, either. It's why your shit keeps coming up missing."

"I'm not missing anything." She arches a brow, then shakes her head like I'm pathetic. "Did you take something, Pet?"

"Not me. Not this time. But if you're sure you're not missing anything, maybe I got it wrong."

I rack my brain for if I am or not. I have a lot of clothes and I'm a mood dresser. I don't keep an inventory of what I have, and I've been known to just go out and buy shit when I'm too tired to check my closet. Other than my favorite beanie, I don't put too much attention on any other article of clothing.

"What do you know, Pet?"

"Nothing." She moves over to another machine, prepping it for another load of clothes.

"Yeah, you do. Spill."

She glares at me. "I don't know shit. I was just making an observation, because in my experience, whenever guys let women have access to their clothes, shit comes up missing. Women claim clothes as a sense of ownership of the guy they belong to. It's a status thing. So my guess is, if you're letting people do your laundry, they're walking around in it or sleeping in it, and bragging to their friends about it belonging to you."

"Girls brag about their affiliation with me all the time."

"I'm sure. But if they're bragging about owning a piece of your clothing, that says they're more *affiliated* than everyone else. You strike me as the kind of guy that goes to her place and barely undresses. The shove your pants down to fuck and bounce as soon as you've bust a nut, type. There's no chance of you leaving your clothes behind, so your conquests would have to resort to stealing them."

She's right. I don't need to get naked to get a blow job or fuck. She also makes a good point about guys giving girls their clothes. It's a way to show how serious things are. A public claiming.

I've never given a girl my clothes to wear and I certainly haven't given permission for them to help themselves to clothes as payment for doing my laundry.

"You sure you don't have any names you wanna give me?"

"Nope. Don't know shit."

"Would you tell me if you did?"

"Nope."

"Why not?"

"Because what goes on between your clothes and your little fan club is none of my fucking business."

Yet she mentioned it, so on some level she wanted me to be aware that it's happening. I walk around the room and spot my bag in the corner. Whoever is on schedule to do my laundry this week picked the bag up this morning. Do they always just leave it out like this?

I drag it over to where Thea's standing and watch what she's doing. "Wanna help me out?"

"I already said no to doing your laundry." She looks over at me. "But I will teach how to do it yourself, because you don't need bitches using you like this to elevate their status."

"You've got it wrong, Pet. I'm using them." When she laughs, I ask, "What's so funny?"

"What's funny is you're supposed to be this larger-than-life entity on campus. Bullying and torturing people into submission, and yet you have no idea that the people you should pay attention to are the randoms who you have no connection or established relationship with. The ones who are happy to do you favors without asking for anything in return. Especially if they're women."

Someone comes in and takes their clothes from the machine to the right. I ignore the look I get when I stand in front of it and start fiddling with the knobs. "Okay, show me what to do."

Pax is waiting in my room when I get back. He looks at me when I walk in, and says, "I thought we were heading off campus for drinks."

I forgot I asked him to hang. Holden's working on a paper, and we won't see him for the next few days. "My bad, man. I lost track of time."

"Doing who?"

"Laundry."

"No seriously. What's her name?"

"I *am* serious. I was doing my laundry. Did you know fabric softener is how you get the towels fluffy?"

"Why would I know some shit like that?"

I pull out one of my fluffy towels and rub it against my face. It's soft and smells amazing. Pax goes through a ton of workout clothes and does his own laundry, but his towels have never felt like this. "I'm just saying. It'll change your life." I toss it at him so he can see what he's missing out on. He throws it right back.

"Are we going out or what?"

I no longer need the outlet, but since he's here I say, "Yeah. Lemme get changed real quick."

Chapter 48
Thea

I step out of my bathroom with my towel held up to my chest as I hurry across the floor to grab my phone off my bed. I reach it too late to answer, and check the number. It's from an unknown caller. When the voicemail chime dings, I put it on speaker to listen to the message while I dry off and get dressed.

I might not know the number, but I know the voice on the other end of the line, and the words she says lets me know she's in trouble. I'm gonna kill whoever came up with these fucking initiation tasks.

But first, I need to go rescue LJ from her chastity vow ceremony.

I already knew that each pledge's experience would be different. I'm just glad that wherever they dropped her had a phone available for her to use. It's one thing for the Coxsuckers to try to seduce me into submission, but LJ is sweet. She's innocent. She's what the Zeta Nu's are looking for. I don't want her first sexual experience to be like this.

I replay the message. Thankful she wasn't blindfolded and was able to give me the cross streets to where she is. A quick search tells me it's in Red Cliff. I call a cab. This place is on the other side of town from where Club Dredd is. There's no way I'm driving my car there.

The rundown neighborhood brings back so many memories of Nags Creek. Memories I'd rather avoid. Still, I push my shoulders back and slap on my "don't fuck with me face". No matter how far you move away, you never forget how to operate in these types of spaces. Sliding into that role comes easily.

As soon as I approach the back of the boarded up house, an acidic taste hits the back of my throat. Chills slide down my spine. I know that taste. I know that smell. It makes my stomach turn and my blood boil, knowing my friend is in here. Knowing some asshole brought her here.

I approach the cracked stairs, and take shallow breaths. The air is permeated with the smell of excrement, and body funk. There are people hanging out on the porch and in the living room when I enter the house.

Nobody cares that they're sprawling across discarded furniture covered in piss, shit or vomit. It doesn't bother them that the stiff substance they're rolling around on is probably someone else's cum.

I avoid eye contact. I don't have time to deal with tweekers offering to eat me out for five dollars. I didn't even bring a wallet with me, my money is hidden in my phone case which is stuffed in my bra, held there by tape. Carrying anything else is the fastest way to get robbed.

I find LJ in the back of the house. She's in the corner against a wall, doing her best not to look at all the fuckery going on around her. If she wasn't squeamish about sex before, this will definitely convince her to never do it.

"What do you want?"

I dart my eyes away from her to glance at the guy who walks up to me. This is his show. He's got that vibe about him that screams pimp. When I find the guy who brought her here...

I jut my chin towards LJ. "I came for my girl."

"Your girl?"

"That's right."

"What do you mean, your girl?"

I toss the question right back at him. "What would you mean if you said she was *your* girl?"

He smirks at me, like he's caught me in a lie. "Nice try. I know where this fancy bitch goes to school. She and I already had a nice chat."

"That's right, I go to that fancy ass school too." I give him a smile that subtly relays what I'm doing at the school. He looks me up and down, not sure if he should believe me. I squint my eyes and ask, "Don't I know you?"

The question catches him off guard just as I expected it to, but he recovers quickly. "No."

I nod, like I'm puzzling it over. "You sure? Could've sworn I've seen you around before." I position myself directly in front of him to get a better look, while slowly backing up towards LJ. If some shit is about to pop off I want her safely behind me.

"I told you, you don't know me bitch."

"Thea." LJ calling my name puts his attention back on her. I hate what I'm about to do. "Don't you fucking see me talking?" I whirl around and shove her against the wall, snarling, "Shut the fuck up, before I consider trading him for someone who knows her fucking place."

Her head pops back. The look of panic on her face is real. Not wanting to keep my back to him for too long, I turn back and say, "See what I'm dealing with? Fucking socialites wanna stick it to daddy, and walk on the wild side, but they've spent all their lives being pampered and got no fucking respect."

I hook my thumb at LJ. "This one is new and thought she'd take a job without my permission and keep the cash."

I look around the room trying to see if any other pledges are here that I'm gonna have to save. It's one thing to get one person out safely.

It'll be harder convincing him I have a whole stable of idiots. "She come in with one of yours?"

He shakes his head. "I found her near the club a few blocks over."

"So how did she wind up here?"

He shrugs, like girls like LJ wind up here all the time. If they're lost and don't know the dangers lurking around, they probably do. "She asked to use my phone and I had some business to take care of."

And of course that request was gonna cost her. Shit. I give him another look over. "Are you absolutely positive I've never seen you before? Because I never forget a face."

He advances on me. I get a better look at his tattoo when he steps closer into the light.

"Does your boss know about your side hustle?"

"What?" He backs up a step.

"I'm thinking he put you over at the club as a pharmaceutical rep. He know you trading in flesh too? I won't knock your hustle. But if you worked for me, I'd want my cut."

"You don't know what you're talking about little girl."

"No?" I hold out my hand. "Lemme use your phone. I'll call and see if I've got it all wrong."

He sneers at me. "That's how your bitch got here. Using my phone."

"Yup." I pop the p, totally unperturbed by his threat. "And if I'm off, then you get to party tonight." His eyes light up, knowing exactly what I mean. "Of course I get to sit in. She's still my investment."

I look at the room, letting the disgust show on my face, "And we don't do this mattress on the floor shit. You'd need to take her back to the club or to your spot for a high-end client." I hold out my hand. "Your phone, so I can make a call."

"I'm not giving you my phone, so you can call the cops."

He wants to call my bluff. I'm good with that. "Fine. Then you dial the number and I'll talk. Or better yet. Snap a picture and send it to the number I give you, and I guarantee your boss will be calling to tell you I'm legit." I give him a smug look, communicating that this is only gonna end one way. "And if not. We go have a party."

It's too good a deal for him to pass up. Especially since he knows he doesn't know me. I recite the number I want him to call, and he snaps and uploads my picture. Now we wait. He keeps checking his watch.

I told him five minutes and since the number wasn't one he has saved as a contact, he's thinking he's home free. The countdown on his alarm ends and he smiles like a predator about to pounce. "Like I said. Full of shit."

He nods his head toward the door and I grab LJ's hand pulling her behind me. He directs us to his car, and we climb in. I see him on the phone. Probably calling someone with a little cash to burn.

LJ whispers, "I can't believe this is happening."

"Nothings gonna happen."

"You bet him and lost."

"Yeah. Looks like. But trust me LJ, I'm not gonna let him hurt you." I turn to face her. The stress and fear mar her cute little face. I get it. I just took her from one bad situation to another. She probably can't tell, but being out of that house is a win. He's taking us to a place with more controlled variables, and that means I can get us out of this. Safely.

A tear slips down her face. "I don't want my first time to be me turning tricks."

I squeeze her hand. "I promise you babe, you won't be getting anywhere near a dick tonight."

We drive in silence for thirty minutes. We're still in Red Cliff, but at least now I recognize the area. He pulls behind a building, opens the back door, and points a gun at us, motioning for us to get out. "The gun is unnecessary."

"Yeah, cause no bitch has ever lied or backed out of a deal before."

I'm a woman of my word, we're definitely gonna party. It just won't include the type of touches and moans he's expecting.

He leads us down an alley and towards the front door of a club, tipping his chin to the guard at the door and sliding him some cash.

We're ushered inside and taken to the back. Nobody looks twice at him, which means they're not looking twice at us. My ball cap hides my hair, so that's one less identifiable marker.

I try to think of what else I can do so this doesn't blow back on us. I can get through being incarcerated, but LJ would never survive it.

We walk into the room and the difficulty level increases. His boys are already here. Their eyes brighten as they slide over LJ. I push her into the corner. Looks like I won't even get any foreplay out of the deal. He's strutting around making a big production of things, and I go old school. The guy at the table has a teardrop tattoo on his face. I pick up the bottle of Jack off the table and smash it against his skull. He slumps down in the chair.

LJ screams. I ignore the sound. I need to incapacitate these other dudes first, before dealing with the one who brought us here. I launch myself at the second guy just as he's trying to get to his feet and dig my fingers into his eyes. You can't fight if you can't see.

He stumbles, knocking me backwards. I lift my foot and kick into the side of his knee. It doesn't break, but he falls. When he's down, I stomp on his dick. Before I can reposition, the third guy knocks me across my face. A full fisted punch.

The blow leaves me reeling. I stagger and regain my bearings. Okay. That's how he wants to play this. I launch at him like I'm in the ring. LJ's cries filter to my ears, but I can't help her. She's crying. She's fine. She's still in the room. That's good enough for me. If I keep these assholes busy, they'll be too battered to go after her. I hope.

Except for the one in the corner. He looks like he's high enough to try to fuck her while his boys are fighting me.

The guy whose dick I stomped drags himself to his feet. The one who punched me, pushes me towards the guy in the corner.

Clint's stuffed in my bra, next to my phone. I was hoping to do this without bloodshed, but that plan has clearly gone to hell. I pull out my knife and slash the leg of the guy who punched me. It'll take him a minute to drag across the floor.

The guy we came with rushes at me. He slams me against the wall and wraps his hands around my throat.

The door slams open, and I make use of the distraction. I slam my elbow into his nose. He's done with me kicking their asses and pulls out his gun and pushes it into my forehead. *Bitch move.*

"Enough!" The command comes from behind him, but he ignores it. The hammer cocking next to his ear finally gets his attention. "You know I don't like repeating myself."

The gun pointed at me lowers, but he doesn't move away.

"Care to tell me what the fuck is going on here?" The guy who I guess just saved my life asks.

"Just about to teach this bitch some respect."

The guy with the gun spares a look at me, his eyes widening. Yeah. I'm sure I look like shit. But, *whatever.* I still look better than his friends. He asks, "Why aren't you picking up your phone?"

"I told you, I'm busy." The pimp turns and glowers at the guy. "Now get your fucking gun out of my face."

"No can do, Brick."

"I outrank you." He spits out, infusing more venom into his voice. "Lower your gun."

The guy holds it steady and before I can try to come up with a reason for this turn of events; the door opens again. From the way everyone straightens up, I know I'm looking at the boss. His gaze slides around the room before settling on me. Then he does some-thing un-boss like. He starts shaking his head and paces back and forth.

His phone is ringing. The look on his face says he's afraid to answer it. But he does. "Sir? Yes. I'm here now." He listens, his eyes going wide. "Yes sir. I'll take care of it."

He looks to me, his eyes not warm or friendly, or cold or menacing. They're just. Resigned.

"Thea LaReaux. On behalf of the Inferno Skullz, I would like to apologize for my lieutenant's behavior, and in accordance with our code, you may select the punishment up to and including his death."

Everyone holds a collective breath and the guy that started this party looks at me again. "You're kidding. Right? I tuned her up a bit. But look what she did to slim." He points to the guy I cut.

"Slim is lucky he's bleeding out over there. Had he been with you when this fuckery started an hour ago, he'd be in the same boat."

"An hour?"

"That's right. A mother fucking *hour,* I've been calling you. An hour I've been hunting your ass across this city. If Jonah hadn't spotted you rolling up, I'd still be looking for your ass."

"Boss. I didn't hear my phone ringing."

"Maybe because you turned it off? But I bet you kept that second burner on so you can throw this little party." He tsks, disapprovingly. "And didn't even invite me."

"I was gonna. Just as soon as I got them started." Brick chuckles, and so does the boss. The guy with the gun is the only one who looks nervous.

"Get them started, huh?"

"That's right, boss. Give 'em a little X. Stretch those jaws out a bit."

The boss nods. That's obviously how things go around here, so he's not surprised to hear the plan. "Right. And they were down for it?"

"Yeah."

The boss sweeps his gaze across the room. "And the ass whipping I walked in on?"

Brick shrugs. "No biggie. Things were under control. They're new to the game."

"Right. One question, who put them in the game?"

That's not the question he was expecting, he answers honestly. "We had an agreement."

"Which was?"

I look over Brick's shoulder at the guy with the gun, but he's avoiding eye contact. Something is happening here. If I were in a helpful mood, I'd warn Brick to stop talking. But I'm not feeling helpful. I'm still trying to make sure LJ and I get out of here.

"I sent her picture to a number and if I didn't get a call from you within five minutes, it was party time."

"And then you turned your phone off?" The boss says with a laugh.

The idiot smirks, proud of his treachery. "Easiest deal I ever made, boss. We've never seen this bitch before, so I knew you wouldn't be calling."

They laugh again, and the hairs stand up on the back of my neck. I take a step closer to LJ. He's clueless. His boss' laugh isn't friendly. There are deadly undertones to it. He called. And the idiot had his phone. Turned. Off.

The boss stops laughing. "I called."

"No boss. You didn't."

"Check your phone."

He pulls it out, and powers it on. It sounds like a Vegas casino with all the pings and dings going off. He shrugs again, still too stupid to realize that shit's about to hit the fan. "Nope. No missed calls from you."

"But there is one from a 725 area code. Isn't it?"

"Yeah. I don't even recognize that number, and they didn't leave a message."

The boss's shoulders slump, because his second in command is still not getting it even though he's leaving breadcrumbs for him to follow. If Brick's this dumb, how did he even get the position? The boss' face hardens, and he says, "I *am* the message." Looking at me, he asks, "How do you want to handle this?"

Well, shit, this took a turn. Brick's eyes widen, and he finally looks at me. "B-Boss." He stutters the word, as the truth sets in. I wasn't bluffing about my pull. I mean, *I know* I was telling the truth, but I figured that favor I was owed had expired. I hate that I used it on this. But, I guess I can make another deal. I'm sure there's something they could need help with.

"What's going on, Dante? Did you smash this bitch or something? And who was on the phone?"

The look on Dante's face turns deadly. Is he insulted at the idea of fucking me? That's cute. He's not exactly my type, but I'm a good fucking lay. I finally decide to be helpful and offer an explanation of what I think is going on. "My guess is the person on the phone from the 725 area code was from the regional office. You know, the folks in the Vegas chapter."

I leave it at that. I don't need to go into detail about how me and some of the Skullz moved in the same circles and that I earned a favor. Which brings us to now. It's up to me what happens with Brick, but I don't have time or want to get in the middle of Skullz's politics. To Dante, I say, "All I want is for me and my girl to walk out that door, and have all of you forget you ever met us."

"That's it?" Dante stares at my face. Yeah, I'm sure I look a hot mess, but I've had worse beatings. Not my problem if he has to explain what happened.

"Hey, I'm alive and breathing. I'm not here to get in the middle of your politics. I was only at that flop house to get my girl. Wouldn't have involved you at all, except negotiations stalled early on in the process." I point to the door. "I just wanna walk out of here."

"And what are you gonna say when *he* calls you?"

I'm hoping he won't call. "I'll say that it's all good."

"You'd do that?" Dante cocks his head to the side, trying to decide if I'm trustworthy. I can see how much of a jam he's in.

If I say his lieutenant went off book and damn near killed me, he'll be short a guy. It's hard enough to find people you can trust. I think that's even more true for him. I don't know the dynamics of their relationship, but the look on his face when he first came in makes me think it was more than business.

"It's already done." I drag LJ towards the door and shove her through it ahead of me. I don't stop to look around. I grab her hand and pull her through the crowd and out onto the street. I keep a hold of her until we're out of the club and in the back of one of the cabs that was idling at the curb.

I keep watch over LJ as she sleeps. I'm having trouble wrapping my head around everything that happened tonight and how she wound up in that situation.

Stupid pranks and initiation tasks are one thing, but intentionally putting people in harm's way. I can't let that slide. How did the pledge masters even know to take her to that sort of place, and why were they okay with leaving her there?

I'm mad at myself too. I hate the way I talked to her when I was trying to get us out of that house. She hasn't said it, but I could see she was actually afraid that I was gonna let them touch her.

"I'm sorry, LJ." I lean forward, pecking her cheek in a goodbye, before letting myself out of her room. I rub at the ache I feel building in my chest. I didn't set out to care about her. I tried not to let her get attached. This is why. I'm a terrible friend and hardly ever make decisions that don't involve fighting back against someone. I know I didn't select this challenge for her, but I definitely made the experience worse.

I refuse to let any tears fall as I accept the truth. She's never gonna wanna be my friend again.

Chapter 49
Thea

Eloise is a dead woman walking. I storm into Zeta Nu house, letting the doors bang open, announcing my arrival. It's one thing to plan pranks your initiates have to do to prove they're worthy to join this psycho slumber party. But actually putting people in danger, that's just evil.

I'm not even all that mad about what I went through with the Coxsuckers. It was irritating. The pain reliever Holden pumped through my veins definitely numbed the taser, and the attempt to drive me crazy by edging, well that sucked but it was also a little fun. Especially when I refused to cave to their demands and sounded off a final, fuck you, right before the bell rang, ending my test. The look on Pax's face was priceless. I'd go through it all, just to see it again.

But LJ's experience wasn't fun. If she hadn't been able to call me, then who knows what would have happened. Actually, *I* know what would have happened.

The Infernal Skullz isn't some wimpy little boys' club pretending to be tough. They're the real deal. With chapters in various parts of the Western United States. Different chapters focus on different things as their primary source of income, but they *all* dabble in drugs, prostitution, and gambling.

Unlike the Nevada Chapter, the guys here aren't above forcing someone into it.

I get angry all over again, and let it fuel me as I march towards the back of the house to the little throne room Eloise likes to bark out her shitty orders from. She's here just like I knew she'd be with her so-called pledge masters. Madison scowls at me, and before she can even ask why I'm not doing the little sorority pledge dance, I cock my hand back and smack Eloise like the bitch she is. The chair rocks sideways, dumping her on the floor.

Madison shrieks, "What the hell do you think you're doing, pledge? Violence against a Sovereign Sister will cost you twenty pledge points."

Twenty? That's it? I could beat the shit out of all of them and still have points to spare. I smile at the thought, but that's not why I'm here. I whip around to face Eloise.

She gets to her feet, holding her palm against her cheek. I hear the other members and pledges whispering behind me, and saying how much I'm gonna regret my actions.

I have to refrain from jumping on Eloise again, reminding myself this isn't Nags Creek, and I don't have to fight dirty to win. Nobody here is jumping in, and I'm going to give her the chance to fight back. *Please* let her fight back.

She doesn't, because of course whatever supernatural entity created me doesn't like me. "Why are you all standing there? Do something." Eloise points to Madison, indicating she should jump into the fray. Okay, so maybe they like me a little today, because Sovereign Sister Madison is second on my list of people whose ass I wanna kick.

She doesn't move toward me, though. Not until Eloise literally shoves her at me like some kind of shield. I guess Madison does the math and decides fighting me is easier than dealing with Eloise.

"She attacked a Sovereign Sister. We have to do something about it. As your pledge master, I order you to defend."

Oh great. Putting the peons in the way. I didn't sign up for that and neither did they, but if they want any chance of crossing over, they have to do what Madison says.

I give them all one warning. "Don't involve yourselves in this. I'm airing my grievance with the Sovereign Sister with witnesses present as outlined in the pledge handbook."

"The handbook doesn't give you permission to physically assault anyone."

"It says equal and just manner. Since you guys let several *someone's* put their hands all over my body, and inflict a measure of pain, I'm returning it in kind. The fear and confusion you feel is equal to my experience at someone else's mercy while strapped to that table. So you see, I'm being more than fair. I don't have anyone holding Eloise down, preventing her from fighting back."

I cup my fingers toward myself, telling her to bring it on. Madison backs up. She can't exactly say I'm wrong. The pledges do too. It's clear Eloise isn't about to engage in this. It's fine, I have one more trick up my sleeve. There's something she's always talking about. Bragging, really, and I'm about to use it against her.

"I move to have Eloise removed as Zeta Nu Interim President and propose a new leader be chosen in accordance with the sorority's bylaws."

"You can't do that!"

The bylaws say as Interim President she has to be able to meet all the requirements of the current pledge year. That means all tasks, games and expectations. If she can't cut it, then she's tossed out.

I look over at Madison, who would be filling in for her. I don't think she deserves a promotion, but just the fact that Eloise has to step down until it's over makes that bearable. I put a motion on the floor and I wait for someone to say something.

Eloise snickers, "Your motion is-"

"I second the motion."

I turn around, looking for the person who has the balls to speak up against Eloise. I can't tell who said it, and by the ways she's squinting, she can't either. The sorors move into the room, pushing the pledges out of the way.

Another person adds their vote. Eloise's face turns beet red. I only need one more member of the pledge committee to agree and it's a done deal. I'm sure there're some loopholes Eloise will be free to exploit, but at least she has to put herself out there.

"I join with the motion."

My eyes bug out as the treasurer steps forward. She's one of the most brutal committee members and has thrown more than a few evil eyes my way. With her vote, Eloise is about to enter a fight for her life period in her sorority memoirs.

"I'm going to make you pay for this, Pledge." Eloise hisses at me.

Oh, this is good. This is even better than I could have hoped. "Me? No, boo, you can't make me do another motherfucking thing in this pink taffeta hell hole. Consider this my official resignation. I quit."

"Quit?" Madison asks, clearly never having heard those words before.

"That's right. You can take this pledge pin and your unicorn sparkles and shove them up your ass. I'm too fucking awesome to be a Zeta Nu." I pull the pin off the underside of my shirt where it's hidden and slap it into the treasurer's palm on my way out the door. I wouldn't want her to have to write that expense off.

Two days ago I went all rage queen on Eloise and her sister bitches. I'm glad I quit. Sorority life was never gonna be a good fit for me. I'm just sorry that LJ will have to deal with them without me.

I don't trust those vindictive cunts not to try to make her redo her chastity vow night, but she's a grown woman, and I can't make her quit. This sorority is her dream, and I'd be an even crappier person if I tried to make her give it up.

I finish my last lap on the track before walking over to the stands to stretch. I've been upping my cardio and hitting the heavy bags in the gym after hours. I still haven't found a trainer willing to take me on, so I'm reading books and watching videos on the internet trying to learn some new moves. I have a fight coming up and I need to be ready for it.

After a quick stop at my dorm to shower and change, I head out for dinner, checking my phone on the way. No new messages. Not that I expected any, but I kinda' hoped there would be. I ignore the looks I'm getting when I step into The Rock.

Everyone knows I went bat shit crazy and caused a power vacuum in Zeta Nu house, even if they don't know why. They're talking about me, but I don't care.

I'm not the only one who thinks it was long passed time Eloise got called out on her shit. Hence the reason the committee voted for her to re-qualify as a Zeta Nu. I'm just the only one who had the balls to say something about it.

I grab my food and eat quickly. I might not care about the whispers, but that doesn't mean I have to sit around and listen to them. I'm almost done with my meal when LJ comes in. I swallow my last bite and screw the cap back on my water bottle. Time to go. I dump my tray and walk towards the exit, so she can enjoy her meal without having to look at me.

I'm almost to the door when she calls out to me. "Thea."

"Yeah?" I stop, half facing her, half facing the door.

"Are you avoiding me?"

I wouldn't call it avoidance. I'd say I'm being respectful of her space, not wanting to add to her trauma. "No."

"It feels like you are. We haven't talked all week and you keep rushing off when I get close to you." She drops her voice. "Is it because I wasn't helpful?"

I frown at her question and shift around to face her. "What do you mean?"

"That night. I was in the corner crying and screaming when you were fighting those guys. If you're mad at me about that, I get it." Her eyes glisten with unshed tears. Shit, this is why I've been keeping my distance. I didn't want her having to see me and think about *them*. "I'm not tough like you and you could've been killed. Because of me."

The tears slip free. No. Na, ah. Not fucking happening. She has nothing to feel guilty about. "LJ, none of that was your fault."

"You told me you didn't think I should go out with the pledges that night. That you had a bad feeling, and I didn't listen."

I did say that, and I hate that my gut feeling was right, but this isn't her fault. She should be allowed to hang out and not worry about the pledge masters putting her in a fucked up situation like that.

The other pledges have been tight-lipped about their chastity vows, but I get the feeling LJ and I got the extreme version of the test. I just can't figure out why.

"There's nothing wrong with wanting to be part of a group or club. I was wrong for letting you go alone. If I had been there... Look, if anything, you shouldn't want to be around *me*, after the way I talked to you and let that bastard think you were my bitch."

She steps closer, grabbing my hands, her eyes wide and clear. "I would be your bitch every day, Thea. If you hadn't of shown up I'd have been forced to..."

I pull her in for a hug. I know what she's thinking, and that's what scares me, too. She's saying she forgives me. I don't think I deserve it, but I'll never make her sorry for giving it to me. I know how hard it is to forgive. I struggle with it. What am I saying? There is no struggle. I hold on to a grudge the way a dog holds onto his favorite chew toy.

"I'm gonna teach you how to fight, so you don't have to feel like that again. I can't promise you'll always win, but you'll learn enough to temporarily disarm your attacker and have a better chance at getting away. And I'm getting you a knife. They say diamonds are a girl's best friend. I call bullshit. Knives are. Don't fight me on this, LJ."

She wraps her arms around me and sniffles into my neck. "I won't."

Pax

"Do you have an update?"

I muffle my groan. This is what I get for not looking at the Caller ID before answering my phone. I've been avoiding my father just because I knew this would be the first question he'd ask. No, I *do not* have an update. My plan has gone to shit since Thea dropped out of pledge season after her chastity vow.

If someone's trying to reshape alliances, it might be time to bring it up with the high council. We still haven't found anything useful on her.

If she's a threat, like he suspects, whoever she's working with has covered her tracks well. This might be above my pay grade. It's definitely a fucking waste of my time and talents, and boring as hell. We're back to following her around. I've been letting Finn take my turns.

I'm probably gonna have to jump back into the rotation. Every day it becomes more clear that he's taken more than a casual interest in her.

I can't deny that she's a hot piece of ass, and ordinarily I'd tell him to go for it, but if dad's intel is correct, this girl's existence here could signal trouble for us and the other prospects. No matter how much I hate this assignment, it's my job to make sure we're protected.

"Actually sir, I was gonna contact you about this, to request permission to expand my search into the people who pay her tuition."

"Why would that be of any interest to you?"

"You always say follow the money. The background data we have on Thea is slim. There's no record that she had connections to anyone in Canyon Falls until she moved here. Whoever she's working for is probably using this so-called aunt and uncle to cover their tracks."

He doesn't answer. After a few seconds, I press the issue. "Dad?"

"Make quiet inquiries only. You know how tricky it is when it comes to the residents of Canyon Falls."

A lot of the residents get alert notifications to warn them when someone submits a public records search on them. It's a more secure way to control the information that's available to the public and protect their privacy. I already know to proceed carefully, but I acknowledge my father's warning, knowing he sees it as a sign of respect.

We end the call, and I lean back, finally settling myself more comfortably on the couch. I hate that I'm on edge, even when he can't see me. I'm a grown ass man, but my father has a way of making me feel like an uptight teenager, still trying to earn his approval.

Today's call couldn't have come at a worse time. It's all over Greek Row how disrespectful Thea was at Zeta Nu. She went off the rails, and I have to scrap the plan I worked out with Eloise. I pinch the bridge of my nose. I'll think of something else, but first, I need to get Holden on this new task.

My phone chimes. This time, it's the proximity alert in front of the elevator. I pull up the surveillance app on my phone and watch as Thea's friend walks toward her room. She dropped out of initiation season too.

One person quitting on their own is relatively unheard of. Pledges usually fail out, but Thea could be explained away. Two people dropping from the same pledge roster, and leaving leadership in chaos, now *that's* catastrophic and an attention grabber. Eloise and the ladies of Zeta Nu are gonna need to get their shit together before their house rank plummets.

As their partner organization, Rho Beta Psi is at risk of being dragged down with them. We'll have to play this carefully. If we back away from the Zeta Nus while they clean up this mess, we'll alienate the sisterhood who are integral to how we operate on campus.

If we come out and openly support one nominee over another while they're in chaos, and that person loses, we risk pissing off the incoming leadership.

My mind is going a million miles a minute, with possibilities and what ifs. No answers are readily available. I need an outlet. I drag myself off the couch and scoop my keys up from the side table where I dropped them. There's only one thing that'll settle me right now, and that's going for a drive.

Chapter 50
Thea

I did an extra circuit on the track today. It's been raining all week, and I couldn't go on my usual walk. I should probably start using the indoor gym at the dorm, but I hate being cooped up inside.

The locker room is empty by the time I'm finished. Perfect. I can take as long as I want.

The lightbulb between the locker area and the showers flickers, like it's ready to die out. I just hope it lasts until I'm done. It would suck ass to have to shower in the dark.

I pin my hair up to keep it from getting wet and lather my body, leisurely rubbing the soap against my skin. I rinse off and turn off the shower, giving myself a little shake to get some of the water drops off of me, before grabbing my towel, tucking it loosely around me.

I make it to the locker area right before the light flickers again. This time, it blinks out for several long seconds before turning back on again. I pull my locker open and place my bag on the bench then, sit down on my towel while I apply lotion to my skin. The light flicks again. It's definitely on its last leg.

It blinks off a third time just as I'm standing up to slide my pants up over my hips. This time it's out longer than before. Just as it comes back on, I'm grabbed from behind and shoved against a locker. I rear my head back to slam into whoever is behind me, but they manage to avoid the contact, and wrap their hand around my mouth so I can't scream for help. Not that I would.

"Hey, there, Pet."

A little of the fight leaves me when I realize it's Finn. His hand slips, and I open my mouth to bite down on his fingers. He groans, pressing against me, before moving his hand down to caress my breast.

"What are you doing, asshole?"

"You know what I'm doing. I'm here to continue our game."

I grab his hand and bend his fingers backwards. "The game is over creep. I won."

"You don't win until one of us begs for mercy. I think it's time you learned that."

"The only person who'll be begging is you, when I gut you, if you don't get your hands off me." I try to buck him off. "Seriously Finn, quit it. I'm not interested in playing with you. I won, you lost, deal with it."

His arousal presses against my ass. "No, no, no. Bad, Pet." He drawls against my ear. "You don't get to say you won and end the game. You have to actually best me, which you haven't. You tempted me with that little stunt with my hat. I've had just a hint of your essence. Now I need a proper taste."

He said the game is about one-upmanship. I balk at what he'll have to do to get one up on me. "I'm not fucking you."

"Who said anything about that?"

He shoves his fingers into my pants and has no issue getting them under the thin side strap of my panties. Now I'm wishing I'd have worn my thick cotton ones. The shocked gasp that tumbles from my lips when he brushes his fingers through my folds is the only sound I let escape.

I clench my walls to prevent him access. It does little to stop his intrusion, adding a bite of pain when he rams his finger inside me, slowly moving it in and out. I clench again, an involuntary flutter of my inner walls.

"That's it." He rasps against my ear. His voice sounding as sinful as molten chocolate. "Wet it up for me, Pet. I want you dripping like you were at the chastity vow ceremony, so I get the full flavor." He moves his finger in and out, going a little deeper each time, before finally removing his hand. Heavens knows why I'm wet. Finn's the absolute last person I'd ever want to get with. He lets me go and I gather my indignation around me like a cloak. When I turn around, I'm gonna unleash the fury of hell on him.

I think I must be imaging things when I feel a prick on my neck, but then his finger swipes over the area. When I turn to face him, I spot the blood on his finger. He sticks that one and the one he had inside me in his mouth. Sucking the opposing fluids off.

My mouth gapes open, while his eyes flash with mirth and hunger.

"So good." He groans, licking between the digits like he did the night in the movie theater with the extra buttery popcorn. When his fingers are clean, he eyes me like he's thinking of coming back for seconds.

"Don't even try it." I warn, fully prepared to leave him bleeding on the locker room floor.

He just smiles, like there's nothing I could possibly do to stop him from coming at me again. He caught me off guard the first time. He won't get a second. "Oh, Thea, Thea, Thea. Haven't I already proven that there's nothing you can do to stop me?" His eyes drag down my body, his lips twisting into a cocky smirk. "Unless you weren't trying to stop me."

I cross my arms over my chest. I'm in a bra and jeans, but I feel utterly exposed right now and it's not the outfit I'm wearing. I've been around men in less than this. It's him and the way he's staring at me like he's just peeled back a layer and found out something no one else knows.

The thing is, he has. I wasn't trying all that hard to fight him off. Of course, I didn't think he'd actually finger me, but then it was happening and my stupid vag decided it wasn't the worst thing to happen to it.

That's it. I need to get laid. I've gone too long. That's the only explanation for why I'd be getting even the slightest bit turned on by Finley Jefferson Rhodes, the Third.

Chapter 51
Thea

A shadow appears on the sidewalk ahead of me. I slow my steps, looking to make sure no one's behind me, too. It could be nothing, or it could be someone looking to snatch a purse or grab a person off the street.

I slide Clint out of my pocket in case I need it. The person steps out of the alley when I get closer. I keep Clint out because I haven't decided yet if I'll use it. "Why the fuck are you hiding in an alley, Finley?"

"I'm waiting, Pet. Not hiding."

"Waiting for what? The alley to become less pissy smelling?"

"No, silly. I was waiting for you to catch up." He looks down the street. "You took the long way around. It's way faster if you just take Carsello and the field behind the houses."

"That street's blocked off for construction."

"It's an old barricade. They didn't finish the work. It's overrun with grass and weeds now, but it's useable."

I squint my eyes. "How did you know I'd come by here?"

"I heard you tell Austin you were coming to check out Graffiti Warehouse."

"And thought you'd spend the afternoon waiting in an alley for me to pass by?"

He holds out his hand. I glance down at what he's holding. "I uh, I got you tickets."

They're first come, first served. Everyone wants a chance to go inside for the nighttime viewing. "Why?" I ask, holding Clint in front of me. I smell a trap.

He looks and sounds sincere when he says, "Because you needed tickets and they were gonna be sold out before you got here."

Every time I think I have Finn figured out, he does something unpredictable. Like this. It makes me feel weird. Kinda warm and a little tingly. Sensations that I only ever embrace when I'm fucking. We're not fucking, and that's what makes it weird.

"I mean, why is it any of your business? I didn't ask you to do this." Reaching into my pocket, I ask, "How much do I owe you?"

"It's a gift, Thea."

"I don't take gifts from men, so what do I owe you?"

He runs a hand through his hair, messing it up worse than it already was. His curls just refuse to be tamed. "Consider it a thank you for helping with my laundry situation."

"Figured out what you were missing, huh?"

He scowls at me. "You could've just told me it was my Die Bloody and Screaming T-Shirt, and special edition Tamahagane Steel jersey."

I guess that means he didn't get his hoodie back yet. Should I tell him? *Nah.* It's not my business. He figured those two shirts out, he can figure the rest out too.

"How did you even know those things were mine?"

Because he's wearing them in his social media pictures, but there's no way I'm confessing to looking at his profile in a moment of weakness when I was slightly curious about him.

"You're not gonna tell me, are you?"

"I can't tell what I don't know."

He smiles. "Fine, Pet. Keep your secrets. But one day you're gonna tell me everything." He turns and starts walking. I fall into step beside him. He's got the tickets and I want to see this show. I'll reimburse him, of course.

"The day I tell you anything is the day you fall to your feet in a crowd and publicly pledge your undying love and devotion to me, and we both know that'll never happen."

The actual exhibit doesn't open until after sunset. I was coming early to get tickets, but since I don't need to, I have a few hours to kill. I hope I'm not about to make a huge mistake. "Look, I, um, appreciate you getting in line early to get me a ticket. I guess the least I can do is feed you before you head back to campus."

"I didn't just get you a ticket, Pet." He holds up his hand and fans the ticket out, showing there's two of them. "Why do you look so surprised?"

I'm here alone, because LJ had to cancel and Austin wasn't interested. "I didn't think this was your kind of thing."

"Ask anyone who was here for my skateboard era. They'll tell you this is totally my kind of thing."

"You had a skateboard?"

"Still do. I just don't use it anymore."

This is the first time Finn and I have actually ever talked, and I admit I'm curious about him. "Why not?"

He shrugs. "Because it was time to grow up."

"I don't think there's an age limit on skateboarding. The X games let you compete forever." We dart across the street, trying to outrun a car. When we get to the other side, I say, "I never quite got into any forms of skating. I was more of a bicycle and motorcycle kind of girl. But if I knew how, I'd be using it to get around campus."

"When we first moved back from Europe, I was really into skate culture. Going down the hills felt like flying. Then I started learning and mastering flip tricks. Canyon Falls doesn't have a skate park or ramp, so I was using any structure I could to get those same angles and heights."

Those are the same things we did to make bike ramps.

"Eventually, my dad had enough with the broken bones and convinced me to find a hobby where I'd land on my feet. That's when I started taking my Parkour training seriously, and I never looked back." He looks over at me. "That's how I know Carsello is passable. I used the buildings on that street to get here."

I gape at him. "You did not."

"I did. It's how I get around most of the time when I don't have my car. I'd do the same thing on campus, but there's some liability issues associated with that."

Nothing about Finn says rule follower. I noted that character trait the first day we met. "So you're saying you've never done it?"

He grabs my arm, pulling me up to face him. "You want me to tell you all my dirty little secrets, Pet?"

"I don't know. How dirty are they?"

"Absolutely filthy."

I chuckle. That's doubtful.

"You don't believe me?"

"I can't say one way or the other. Filth is in the eyes of the listener."

His thumb strokes cross my shoulder. "I'll share something with you, but you'll have to do the same."

I back away and resume our journey towards our destination in search of food. "I don't wanna know anything about you."

"What if I say I'll tell you a secret about the campus?"

I pivot around and walk back towards him. "Keep talking."

"I'll tell you a little known secret about the campus and you'll have to tell me something about yourself."

I take a minute to think about it. "This secret. It can't be something I can look up and research on my own."

"It won't be."

"And I reserve the right to ask a follow up question about this secret if I need clarification."

"One follow up question and I get the same."

I arch a brow. This negotiation is going too smoothly. I don't trust him. "You'll answer honestly?"

"Only if you do."

Fair enough. "Okay. Let's hear it."

"Why do I have to go first?"

"Because, Number Three, my secret will depend on your secret."

He shakes his head and scolds, "Nice try, Pet. I know you just wanna blow me off."

Geez. He's just as distrustful as I am. But he has a point. Him going first leaves me a lot of wiggle room. I hold out my hand. "We'll shake on it. I promise I'll hold up my end of the deal."

He slides his hand in mine and tugs me closer. "And if you break it, Pet, I promise to make your life hell." He pulls away and starts walking again. "Parts of the campus used to be connected to the old mine."

"That's something I can look up. Try again."

"The secret is that some of those tunnels are still accessible."

I hurry to catch up to him. "You're kidding."

"Nope."

"And you know where they all are?"

"I know where some are. There are also ones that used to connect to town."

I file that info away. I haven't found a walking trail above ground. What if it's because it's below ground? Damn, I've already used up my follow up question. I'll have to agree to another round to get Finn to give more details. I'm not ready to do that yet. He's waiting for me to take my turn. What can I say that's equivalent to this without giving too much about me away?

"I never learned to skate because it wasn't something we did where I lived. Nobody had the money to go to the rink, and even if you owned your own skates, using them outside wasn't even possible. Anything with wheels was subject to be stolen."

Out the corner of my eye, I see his lip turn down. He asks, "Did they steal your stuff a lot?"

I pull out Clint and flick it open, waving it back and forth. "My knife is the only thing I had worth stealing, and nobody wanted to lose a finger trying to do that."

Graffiti Warehouse is actually three warehouses right next to each other, with scaffolding erected to serve as tunnels to transit between them.

The walls inside are painted completely black. The ink from the tags glow in the dark, lighting our journey from room to room, each floor and then on to the next exhibit.

Our tour takes a little over two hours, and ends on the roof of the final building, which has been converted to a rooftop bar with a tapas menu. We sit around the gas fire pit. I'm mesmerized at the way the flames jump off the fire glass. It's hauntingly beautiful and deadly all at the same time.

Finn tries to steal my food even though he's got twice as much food as I do in front of him. I pull my plate away. "We just looked at the same menu. Why didn't you just order your own?"

"Because then we'd have the same thing, and that's no fun."

"Yeah, but we'd have our own portions. You don't see me trying to swipe food off your plate."

He sips his drink, and says, "I wouldn't mind. That's kinda how it's done everywhere I lived overseas. You sit at the table and big bowls of food are put out and we pass them around."

I try to imagine what that would be like to sit at a table with everyone just eating everything. I'm used to food rations because there was barely enough for everyone in the house.

Foster parents get paid to keep kids, but it's not enough to live off of. Some work, so the payment is additional income, and other parents take in extra kids. Either way, the amount they get doesn't add up to much, when you factor in groceries and household expenses. That means a lot of times there was no such thing as second portions and snacking on left overs.

It was worse in the last few group homes I stayed in. We were older. Outside of school and curfew, we had less supervision. You had to protect your food or someone would steal your plate.

Since living on my own, I've gotten used to the ideas of left overs and having more than enough, but that doesn't mean I just want people reaching into my food.

Finn cocks his head to the side. "You've never shared food before?"

"I have. I shared my booze with you, and didn't decapitate you for stealing my popcorn."

"I mean willingly."

"Sure. I just cook or order extra and give it to whoever I'm sharing with."

Shaking his head, he says, "Try it this way, Pet. I have some of yours and you have some of my mine. It saves time and money, and I bet you'll like it."

"I'm fine with my Swedish meatballs and shrimp. You have fun with your croquettes, steamed cod, and squid puffs."

"Espencat, and Pulpo a la gallega."

The words sound smooth, coming off his tongue. "Just because you make it sound all fancy doesn't change that it's a squid puff."

"Is that why you're saying no? You grossed out by squid?"

"Not at all. I just prefer it breaded and fried."

"Try it Pet. I promise you'll like it."

"You can't promise that, Number Three. We have different taste buds."

He scoots closer. "How about this? You try it, and if you don't like it, I'll tell you another secret."

I shift, angling my body towards him. "What if I do like it?"

"Then you'll share your plates with me."

"Fine." I lean over to grab one, but he pops my hand before I can.

"The fuck, Finn?"

He picks ups a squid puff and says, "Close your eyes, and open your mouth."

"I can feed myself."

"We're gonna do it this way. Close your eyes. That way you're not looking at it and you can just focus on the taste."

"I can taste fine with my eyes open."

He bites his lip and shakes his head. "Trust me when I say some things taste so much more decadent when you savor it with your eyes closed."

His gaze rakes down my body, and I'm rocked with a memory of him sucking on my nipple at my chastity vow celebration. His voice is huskier when he says, "Close your eyes and open wide."

I do. Not because I'm having a reaction to his voice and how it sounds like sex. Or because my body is warm, imagining him saying those words as I'm on my knees. Nope. I do it, because I want another secret.

His finger skates across my lower lip, then dips inside. I crack an eye open, because that's not food. "Don't peek. Just roll with this."

"It better be an astronomical secret for dealing with this."

I close my eyes and open my mouth again. This time I keep them closed when he puts his finger in my mouth again. "Suck."

I do. Tasting the filling from his squid puff. I swallow while his finger is still in my mouth. He slowly retracts it, then tells me to open it again. This time when I do, he puts the entire thing in my mouth. I bite down and chew. "Tell me what you taste."

"Squid. I taste squid."

"What else?"

"It's um. Kinda sweet but peppery too."

"That's the Sweet Paprika. What else?"

"I can taste the potato and herbs, and nuts?"

"Olive oil. Now open again and this time chew slowly. Let the flavors melt onto your tongue."

I comply, and when I'm done with the second bite, he tells me to open again. This time, he tilts my chin back and puts a glass to my lip. I drink, shocked at the dark hint of wine.

I moan as the wine accents the flavors lingering on my tongue.

Before I can finish swallowing, Finn's mouth is on mine. Pushing his tongue inside. Our tongues swipe around each other, sharing the fluid. I almost moan again, as I get a double hit of the food and drink from his tongue.

We break apart, and my eyes open. He's still close. His eyes hooded as he looks at me. "Well, what do you think?"

I swipe my thumb over my lip, catching a stray drop of wine. He grabs my hand, sucking my thumb into his mouth. My core clenches. Fuck, that feels good.

First, he fingers me in the locker room, now he's stealing kisses, and I didn't stab him or punch him, which would be totally justified after the shit at my chastity vow. I don't know why it's so easy to let my guard down around him.

I murmur, "I think you get to keep your secret, Number Three."

LJ flops down on my bed, a dramatic sigh falling from her lips. I roll my eyes at her antics. She obviously wants to talk about something, but she's waiting for me to ask what's wrong.

This is why I'm shit at this normal friendship thing. I don't ask what's wrong. I expect people to put on their big girl or boy panties and just say what's on their mind. The silence stretches on and when it becomes too much for her, she finally says something.

"You know, when people walk in and sigh real loud and don't say anything, you're supposed to stop what you're doing and ask what's wrong."

I look up from the notes I'm reading and say, "Or you could just come in and say, 'I've had a fucked up day' and tell me whose ass I need to kick to make it better."

She opens and closes her mouth. Then repeats the action two more times, but no sounds come out. I think I broke her.

"You would do that? Just go around kicking ass, because I said someone upset me?"

"Of course. That's the kind of friend I am. Not the sit around and talk all about feelings all the time type. We can do it sometimes. But I find a good ass kicking can do wonders for a mood." That puts a smile on her beautiful face, and I say, "Go on and vent now. I'm listening."

"I don't need to."

"Why not? I thought you were upset."

"I was, but you've made me feel better."

"How? I haven't spilled any blood yet."

She looks away and I know she's embarrassed about whatever she's about to say. "Eloise was talking in class about organizing a luncheon and made a comment that I wasn't included because I'm not one of them. You know, because I'm no longer a pledge and don't have friends."

I jump to my feet and stomp over to my closet to put my shoes on. Bitchy Beat Down the Sequel coming right up.

"Hey, where are you going?"

"Babe. You just gave me my marching orders."

LJ rushes up to me and drags me over to my desk. "No, I didn't. Sit down. I don't need you to beat up Eloise for me." My lips twitch. She heard all about me going Mata Hari on those Zeta Nu cunts, but I never told her I did it for her. That's not a burden I wanted to put on her.

"Oh, you wanna do it yourself? Cool, I got your back. I'll hold back the other plastic bitches so they don't jump in."

"Thea, we're not fighting anyone. Shit, I don't even know how to throw a decent punch yet."

I shrug, dismissing her negative talk. "You're learning, and with the proper motivation and me restraining your victim, I know you can get two good shots off."

"Hush. Just let me finish."

"Okay."

"So anyway, I was thinking about what she said all day, and was feeling kind of down when I saw all the groups of people and pledges out at the mall. She's right, you know. I'm alone. I've been an outsider to those girls for a long time now. But then, I came here tonight, and you said you'd kick ass for me. You were immediately on my side and didn't even ask why or what I did wrong. So I know Eloise is wrong. I have a friend. A better one than I could ever have imagined."

"Of course you have a friend, LJ. I'm not warm and fuzzy like you, but I let you talk my ear off. I cook for you, and I tell you stuff. The only other person I talk to like that is Sasha."

"I know. It's just taking some getting used to."

"What is?"

"That our friendship isn't like everyone else's." When I give her my 'I don't know what that means, look,' she explains, "You know, going shopping and doing trips and lunches and all that other stuff you don't do."

"Just because people do lunch and spend their daddy's money together doesn't make them friends. Eloise and her group aren't on equal footing. There's a power dynamic, and she only likes them as long as she's the one on top. You and me, we're equals LJ, and I love doing lunch and shopping. I just prefer vintage or thrift stores and mom and pop restaurants on the boardwalk over fancy Rodeo Drive shit."

"I don't know how you can say we're on equal footing when you do more stuff than me."

Ah… so now we've hit the real reason for her melancholy. Her virgin status. God, why is so much emphasis put on it? You're not cool enough if you're still a virgin after a certain age, or you're some type of unicorn prize to be won if you are.

Both viewpoints reduce women to the sum of a hole with a fold of skin around it. Provided you haven't actually broken your hymen some other way.

"LJ, it might seem like I've done all this cool shit, but in the grand scheme of things, I haven't. I grew up different from you and certain things were a matter of influence and survival. I learned how to fight for survival, and I had sex, just to see what all the damn fuss was about. When I got tired of hearing the older guys talking about my virginity and the plans they had for me, I took matters into my own hands. But I told you, sex isn't some great equalizer. Once you have it, what you enjoy will be totally different from me. My kinks won't be your kinks and it's doubtful we're even attracted to the same types of guys. Carrying a weapon doesn't make me special either. I did it out of necessity. Now it's as much a part of my signature style as high-top sneakers, band tees, cropped tops, and ripped jeans. If you wanna learn to fight, I'm happy to show you moves. You want a blade of your own, we can go shopping for one. As for sex..."

"You wanna be my first?"

"You're a sexy bitch. But hard pass, babe. You lack the equipment I like to play with." That makes her laugh, easing more of the tension in her face. "I was gonna say, if you're really serious about losing your virginity, just pick some random guy at a party and do it."

"I couldn't do that. I want my first time to be special."

"Special is a state of mind. You can wait until you're dating a seemingly perfect guy, who takes you to a hotel room decked out in roses and candles and he can be a shitty lay, who talks shit about you afterward, making you regret wasting your first on him. Or you could meet a hot guy at a bar and the two of you have an understanding. No words. Just passion. He rocks your world, you never hear from him again, and at night when you're alone and frisky you pull that material from your memory and let your imagination and hands roam free."

"That's a very specific analogy." She snorts.

She's got no idea. "My point is. Special is however you want to define it and it might change many times before and after you actually lose your V-card."

"So, which experience did you have when you lost yours?"

"The kind where I was in the backseat of somebody's car and he was finished before the pain of my broken hymen even receded. It was perfect."

She scrunches her nose. "Doesn't sound perfect."

"It was for me. It was my choice, with a guy I liked, and he was sweet."

"So he didn't talk shit about you afterwards?"

"Nope. That was the second guy I slept with. *The asshole.* The one who *thought* he was my first. Jokes on him."

"Uh oh. What did he say when he found out?"

I smile fondly at my subterfuge. "Nothing. I never told him. It was my secret, and a cherished memory. Like I said. I was happy with my choice."

She shakes her head. "How do you do that?"

"Do what?"

"Always be so confident in your skin?"

"I'm not. I fake it a lot of times until I feel it." Flicking my gaze to hers, I warn, "And if you ever tell anyone, I'll gut you."

I'm not going to get any more homework done, so I scribble one last note, then close my books. "Now, would you like to go do something with me?"

She jumps off the bed. "Sure. I'll meet you back here after I get changed."

I shake my head and say, "You don't need to change. What you're wearing is perfect."

She takes in her outfit and quirks a brow at me. "It's just jeans and a tank."

"Yup. Like I said, it's perfect for where we're going."

Chapter 52
Holden

Idon't make a habit of keeping tabs on my friends, but the proximity sensor for the secret passage in the hallway went off hours ago. I checked the camera feeds and saw Finn running through the underground tunnel towards the garage.

He was in a hurry, but clearly not in any danger. Now I'm waiting for him to get back to find out what's going on.

The knock on my door signals his return. I open it to let him in, and go to grab a bottle of water from the fridge. "You want something to drink?"

"Yeah, a drink will be good."

I grab a second water for him. It's late. Too late to give him a beer, especially when I don't know if he's already been drinking. I hand him the water and sit in my bean bag chair. "You set off the proximity sensor when you took off today."

"My bad, dude. I was in a hurry."

"I could see that. Where was the emergency?"

"Thea was heading out, so I went, too."

Finn and I took on the bulk of shadowing Thea. Neither of us were all that upset that Pax found reasons to get out of his turn. He and Thea are like oil and water. Whenever they get anywhere near each other, they're at each other's throats.

My guess is Pax wouldn't be able to keep his distance and just watch her the way Finn and I can. He's too in your face with everything. Their altercation would probably end in bloodshed.

"Did she meet up with Kincaid again?" I try not to sound too interested in the answer. None of us likes that guy, so of course he's the one who's spending time with her.

Finn shakes his head. "She and her friend, that LJ girl, were hanging out in some rundown strip mall out by the crater."

"Doing what? Driving through a ghost town and taking selfies?"

"Watching a fight."

"Who was in a fight, and why didn't we know anything about it?" We've got our finger on the pulse of everything that happens on campus, so a dispute we knew nothing about is troubling.

My ears ring as I filter this information into my already over-loaded brain. I feel like there are too many things happening at once.

Our pledge schedules, prospect challenges and this thing with Thea. Not to mention trying to figure out if she's funneling information to Austin now that she's no longer pledging Zeta Nu.

I'm glad Finn was tailing her tonight. I had a lot of studying to do and my focus would've been on my assignments instead of paying attention to what she was doing. "So, the fight?" I prompt, forcing my brain to focus on one thing.

"Oh, yeah. It wasn't a dispute, it was a brutal display of athleticism and endurance."

"Doesn't that apply to all fights on some level or another?"

"Not like this. It was a MMA battle. A UFC event. A bloodsport reenactment."

Wherever he was, and whatever he was watching, is still sitting with him. He's basically vibrating with excitement. That's Finn.

I like to inflict pain, but he gets off on violence, and no matter how polished he is on the outside, he's got that bloodlust thing always simmering under the surface.

Some people do yoga or meditate to recenter themselves. Like me. I'm people. But Finn is all about the action and thrill. Jumping off buildings and bloodshed. The more vicious the battle, the more blood he sees, the better he feels.

As for Pax, he's into speed. The faster he's going, the happier he is. If he's racing against an opponent, that's even better. None of our hobbies are what I'd call league approved. Nothing that puts an heir in mortal danger will ever be, but there's not much they can say or do about it until we're full-fledged members.

We received our preliminary acceptance letters last Christmas. Our father's never once mentioned that there were hoops to jump through *before* we could receive our prospect badges. Then we got our official documents listing us as first year prospects, and another set of orders were issued.

There are secrets on top of secrets within The League of the Daggered Ravens. Sometimes I wonder how the members keep them all straight.

The good thing is I can go to my dad with questions. He's assured me that once we're official members, the council will start being more forthcoming, within reason. Our access to information will be commensurate with our level within The League. Because we're legacies, we'll start with a higher rank inside the organization than someone recruited off the streets, but we'll still have to work our way up.

The guys and I have a plan. We'll be mid-level council men, overseeing The next generation of prospects and recruits by the time we hit our thirties.

That'll be younger than our parents were when they ascended. We'll be sitting on top of the world, and living the rest of our lives in financial security, shuffling powerful people around the chess board of our world.

Or at least that's the plan for Finn and Pax. My involvement won't be as big as all that. I'll probably be sitting behind a desk at a law firm, making problems go away with legal briefs, bored out of my mind.

That's my father's plan for me. It's all he's ever talked about since I was a kid. My hobby of software design is just that. A hobby.

I hate that he's planned my life out for me and that there's not much I can do to change his mind.

I guess that's why I turned to piercings and tattoos. They're the only things I could control in my life. My parents flipped when I came home with my first tat, until I promised to never get them in places that can't be covered up by long sleeve button ups and expensive sports coats.

A tattooed lawyer would be okay for the mafia, but not someone representing a league member. As for my visible piercings, I can take out my eyebrow, lip and tongue rings during working hours.

I click my tongue ring against my teeth. I don't even have as much ink as Pax. He's got a full frontal, sleeves, and half his back and entire neck. The bottom half of his back is blank, for now.

We both pick out tattoos to make a statement or to showcase something of significance in our lives. He just has more to say with his.

Finn and I hang out for a little while longer before he heads across the hall to his room. I complete a few more assignments, then make my way to my spare bedroom.

I take calming breaths as I wait for the faint click that locks me in the space within the wall before lifting my palm to the panel that gives me access to Thea's room.

I keep to the darkest part of the closet, watching as she discards her clothes, getting ready for bed, and wait until she falls asleep before stepping into the room.

I pull the syringe from my pocket, and lean over her, watching the shadows dance across her face as she sleeps, smiling at the cute pinch of her brow when the needle penetrates her skin. Then I go to search the rest of her dorm room while waiting for the sleeping aid to take effect.

I know I shouldn't be in here and if Finn or Pax find out, I'll never hear the end of it. But it's do *this* or do something that will really bring disgrace to our team. Something like grab her on her way back from the library or to class, shove her to knees, pry her mouth open and shove my cock down her throat.

I'm snooping for information I can use to help my research, but her place is just as empty as when I checked the first time. Her breathing's evened out by the time I get back to her bedroom. I discard my clothes, and crawl into bed, naked beside her.

I lay on my side, and reach out to stroke the side of her breast, enjoying the feel of her skin under my calloused fingers. My hand drifts down to the side of her ribcage to the little scar there.

Her skin is a tapestry of small nicks and marks. I want to know the story behind each and every one. I trail my hand down a little further to her knee, then drag it back up to her hip where I started, before repeating its path.

My dick is so goddamn hard right now, throbbing with the need to play with her. I could do whatever I want to her for the next few hours, but I won't do more than this. I grip her throat, pulling her against me, and close my eyes, taking calming breaths, trying to ease the tension from my body and quiet my mind even though I know I won't be able to sleep.

Tonight isn't about sex, or satisfying my darkness. It's a social experiment, and since she helped out with the last one, I see no reason why she shouldn't be my science partner for this one too.

I settle in close, with her body curled into mine, and close my eyes, mentally documenting what it feels like to lie in bed next to a woman.

Chapter 53
Thea

My backpack sprouted legs while I was in class. My gym locker was jimmied open, and filing a police report was just as effective this time as it was when I went in about my car.

The cops on this campus are a waste of fucking resources. The officer tried to make is seem like I lost my bag, forgot my combo and ripped the locker open on my own.

I spent the last hour at the residence hall administration building waiting for them to issue me a new key fob, since mine was in my bag.

I drag myself off the elevator on my floor, coming to a stop in front of my door. Somebody's been here. The clear tape I keep on the door is no longer laying flush against it. I push into my room, knowing I'm about to see some shit to set me off.

The destruction is worse than I imagined. The floor is littered with pages from my textbooks, broken dishes, and my snacks are floating in the sink.

I move to my bedroom, where things only get worse. My clothes are in tatters all over the place. In the bathroom, I find the tub filled with hair dye and my shoes soaking in the solution. My empty backpack is discarded on top of my shredded comforter.

And just in case I have any question about who did this, my phone chimes with a video of Eloise and the Zeta Nu pledges playing in my room. I ignore the video and get to cleaning up the mess.

I missed two days of classes trying to put my room put back together, and received a warning from the RA about the excessive bags of trash I hauled down to the dumpster. I'm walking across The Circle when Eloise comes up to me and says, "I'm surprised you're still showing your face around here."

"Why wouldn't I be?"

"Because you've been wearing the same clothes for three days."

She turns her nose up as if I smell. I don't. I am wearing the same clothes, but I've washed them every night. This isn't the first time I've only had one decent outfit to wear.

"I am?" I look down at myself like I hadn't realized. "Shit, I guess I am."

I know what this is all about. This is her retaliation for fucking with her leadership position in the house. There's a crowd gathered around, as if she sent out an invitation to watch our interaction.

I see *them* standing apart from the crowd. The Triums. They say they run the dorms, so this has their names written all over it. It's laughable. They couldn't break me with messing with my accounts, so now they've moved onto my personal belongings.

They're all watching me. Waiting for me to crumble and cry because the clothes Moira bought are ruined. Jokes on them. I've lived without fancy shit all my life. It's no big deal to me that they're destroyed now, except for the absolute waste of money.

This must be the things the girls they deal with care about, so they thought it would apply to me too.

Eloise steps closer. "Whatever will you do, now that you can't dress like you come from money? Now that everyone will see you in the tatters you were born to wear?"

I throw my head back and laugh. Then laugh even harder as the sneer slips from her face when I step closer. "You think you're intimidating me? Walking around here calling out my clothes with your nose in the air like you're some kind of queen? Bitch please, you're just The Trium's pawn. Doing whatever they say, because they're a bunch of pussies, too afraid to get their hands dirty. Well, I've got a message for them. Tell them if they wanna break me, they'll have to try harder than this."

I shove past her to make my way to The Rock.

"You look like her in that outfit, you know."

I pause and turn to ask, "Like who?" She's staring down at a picture. I know exactly which one it is. I watch as if in slow motion as Eloise rips it down the middle.

I don't even remember the day it was taken, but my mom's in it. She's smiling, and she looks happy. It's also the only photo I have of her. It's the only way to hold on to any sort of memory of her being someone other than the alcoholic I remember.

My vision turns red, as the sound rents the air, and I feel myself lose control. I launch at her, determined to do more than smack her this time. She's going to get every single punch I held back at the sorority house.

A set of arms band around my waist, catching me mid leap, and hauls me back against a strong, muscular chest. I struggle against the person holding me. I reach my arms up, searching for their eyes. A forearm locks around my throat.

A familiar voice breathes against my ear, "Attempting to attack a faculty member is a serious offense, LaReaux."

Coach Wolfe's still holding me when he barks out, "You all have thirty-seconds to disperse or I'll be writing you up."

"For what?" Someone yells.

"I don't know yet. But whatever it is will be creative and expensive."

Eloise walks off smiling like she's won something. She hasn't. Wolfe's interference has only delayed the inevitable. He's on to something, though. I'll have to come up with a creative punishment.

"You shouldn't be jumping into my fights, Coach. It could be dangerous."

"I'm not jumping in." He releases me and moves in front of me. "I'm preventing them, and you shouldn't be fighting on campus, LaReaux."

"Yeah, but something tells me I'll never get her in the ring, so I have to bring the ring to her."

He stares down at me, and I straighten to make myself taller. His lips twitch like he's amused. Fuck him. I know I'm intimidating.

"Which brings me to the next point. You're done fighting for Syl."

I laugh at the absurdity. I'm gonna take on more fights so I can replace the shit those pink sparkling bitches destroyed.

He tips my chin up to look at him. "Wipe that look off your face."

"What look?" I blink innocently up at him.

"The one that says you're planning to break my rules again."

"I'm not..." He gives me a look that makes me wanna punch him in his stupidly handsome face. Why are all the assholes so fucking panty meltingly hot, and off limits?

He's still gripping my chin when he asks, "The rules, Thea. What are they?"

"Those bullshit rules only apply in class."

"For you, they apply, *always*."

I'm not going for that shit. He's not gonna control my life in and out of class. "Sorry, Wolfie. I don't agree to those terms and you can't enforce that shit."

"Thea, if you're fighting for Syl on one of the later fights, I already know what you're capable of. To let you fight a student on campus would be irresponsible of me."

"You don't know shit. You have me doing catfights and slap boxes in class." I demonstrate a move by slapping at his hand. It doesn't phase him.

"I know Syl, and I know how she operates her business."

I shrug. Maybe he does. He was there the night the cops raided Club Dredd. They didn't stop anything. Syl just moved locations, and I'm still on the roster. I'm done with this conversation and after my run in with Eloise, going to The Rock has lost its appeal. Maybe I'll go to the boardwalk and eat at the diner.

"You will not be fighting on campus, or for Syl. It's done Thea."

Now he's pissing me off. "Who the hell are you to tell me what I can and can't do? Fuck you, Deacon."

Instead of getting mad, he smiles at me. "You're gonna do exactly what I say. You know why?" He doesn't wait for me to answer. "Because it's what *I* want and you doing what I want, gets you what *you* want."

What is it with all the men thinking they can boss me around and make me comply with their idea of who I should be and what I should do?

"What is it that you *think* I want?"

"A trainer."

Okay, now he's got my attention. "You'll sign my recommendation so I can train at a gym off campus?"

"No, LaReaux. I'll train you myself."

I did my research. His is the best gym in town. He turns out top-notch athletes. Winners. The best.

I have to give up fighting for Syl, and lose out on all that cash, but I get to train and maybe he'll set up some legitimate bouts for me. At a minimum, I'll get to scrimmage against some amazing fighters. Shit, he's got me.

The look in his eyes says he knows I'm about to cave. No self-respecting woman caves this fast. I'm gonna hold out, maybe get him to sweeten the deal.

"Don't fight it, sweetness. You know you want to get all hot and sweaty with me. I'll give you everything you want, and all you have to do is promise no more fights."

"You'll train me like you train professionals? None of those basic bitch moves you have me doing in class? You'll let me punch and take a punch, and let me fight professionals in my weight class?"

"No."

"Then, no deal. Now if you'll excuse me, there's a bitch that needs slapping, and I need to call Syl to see if I can get a second fight this week." I just make it past him when he yanks my collar, pulling me back.

"Fine. I'll set you up for a fight, but only when I determine you're ready. But that means I don't want to see any more bruises on your body unless I'm the one who put them there."

I hold out my hand, waiting for him to take it to seal our deal. "Then I agree that as long as you hold up your end of this deal, I won't engage in any physical altercations of the fighting variety unless I'm being forced to defend myself."

He presses his palm against mine and tugs me forward until I'm pressed against his chest, his thumb grazing against the back of my hand, igniting sparks along my skin.

His warm breath fans across my ear. "Good, girl."

I settle into my chair for another family dinner. This is like the fifth one I've been to. They haven't been all that bad. The conversation is still awkward if we talk about anything other than school and whatever thing Aunt Moira is working on at her marketing firm. She's actually pretty good with social media layouts, and I've given her a few ideas for where she can go to get some cool landscape scenes.

We're falling into a comfortable sort of existence, so when they ask about school I tell them about my attempt at joining a sorority, but leave out the fight, the pledge initiations, and the fact that psycho barbie destroyed my shit.

"Zeta Nu?" Moira chuckles, but it's a strained sound. Like she can't imagine it. Neither can I, yet for five hellish weeks I was a fucking *pledge,* sporting a glitter pink pledge pin.

"I know. I'm just as surprised as you are, but LJ wanted to pledge, so I did it to support her."

"How does Layla-Jean feel since you dropped out? She's not worried that the sorority will put a wedge between the two of you?"

"LJ resigned from pledge season, too. We both realized the Nus weren't a good fit for us."

Scott gives a little shake of his head. "You know your aunt was a Zeta Nu, right?"

"Uh." I look over at Moira. "No, I had no idea. Her face isn't on any of the walls."

"She was. Your aunt and I are extremely private people, so you wouldn't find her picture in any of the common areas, but she's in her pledge photo over in Founder's Hall. If we had known you were pledging, we could have attended some of the family events with you."

I chew and swallow the broccoli spear in my mouth before replying. "I'm actually glad you didn't know. The introductory parties and family days were a drag. Just a bunch of people standing around acting stiff and boring and the pledges were on the serving committees. No offense, but being your servant for the day sounds about as appealing as a root canal."

"Serving? That's not what the pledges are supposed to be doing. When I was a Zeta Nu, family day was a chance for the alumni members to come and impose some wisdom over lunch and participate in a few games. It was a bonding experience."

"Then maybe I *should* have said something, because the people in charge now had us running around with trays in our hands and bowing and scraping every time an alumni squealed, Nu Nu Nu. The realest thing I heard was only the strong survive pledge season."

I aim my fork at them. "My quitting isn't a sign of weakness, it was an act of mercy. Towards them. I was never gonna turn into the cheerful drone they wanted."

"How were your scores?"

I shrug, digging into my lobster tail. "Top five." When I look up to grab the butter sauce, Moira has a big ass smile on her face. "What?"

"Top five, that's an amazing rank. I was top five as well."

Scott arches a brow. "Your aunt is being modest. She was the number one pledge, her year."

I nod. I can see it. She's sweet and sophisticated. "Must've been easy when all you had to do was know how to pick the right color concealer. I kept losing points because of that."

She squints and throws a roll at me. The action catching us both off guard. But she presses on, her cheeks stained pink. "Hush, I'm sure the physical aspect of pledge season is the same. I remember the crap we had to endure."

"Ri-ight."

"I'll show you some pictures sometime. I've got them in the room in the back. Oh, that reminds me. The insurance adjuster called. He's finished going through the storage unit, and will be sending a delivery of stuff here in a few days. I figured it would be easier to have it here than to ship it to the dorm."

"Thanks, yeah. That's fine."

"Great, you just come home and go through it whenever you want."

Scott segues the conversation into some party his old college buddies are throwing and I zone out while he and Moira discuss coordinating outfits.

My stuff arriving from storage is perfect timing. Hopefully, some of my clothes survived.

Chapter 54
Deacon

Thea strolls into my gym like she owns the place. I get her to sign the liability and membership forms then walk her over to the ring to meet two of my best fighters. She hasn't been here for more than five minutes and I already know I've made the worst mistake of my life. Being her trainer is gonna end in disaster and tears. Theirs and hers.

I slip my jacket on but leave it unzipped. I have rules about everything being covered on campus, but here, I encourage my fighters to wear fitted, comfortable and breathable clothing here, so I can see their form.

Thea strips out of her t-shirt as she walks towards me and that's what starts me plotting a mass murder in my head.

I give the guys a few seconds to get their comments out of the way. "Alright, stuff it. This is Thea. She's here to train."

She stares up at me. "They know my name. Aren't you going to tell me theirs?"

"Their names aren't important."

"But mine was?"

"Yes, because it lets them know you're serious about being here, and puts them in the right mindset."

"Which is?"

"That you're a teammate. A sparring partner. Someone who's going to work hard to put them on their asses."

"Shouldn't I know the same thing about them?"

"When you actually succeed in knocking them down, they'll give you their names."

"So I have to earn it?"

"That's right. Now go warm up. Ten minutes on the treadmill, incline at five, then ten on the heavy bag so I can see your form."

She gives me a two-finger salute. "Aye, aye, *sir*."

While she's warming up, I go over to the ring to watch Tank and Colton spar. "Where'd you find her?" Tank asks, before putting his mouthpiece back in.

"She's a student."

"High School?"

"College, asshole. But she's still off limits. Now stop talking and start swinging."

Ten minutes pass and Thea climbs off the treadmill and walks over to the bag. I stay by the ring but watch her set her feet and start punching.

She's fast and strong, but I can already see areas where I'll need to push her. The first is her endurance. Ten minutes on a five incline should not have her breathing as hard as she is.

The fight rounds at the matches we participate in are five minutes, but I train my fighters to be able to go longer.

Higher endurance levels mean their blows stay powerful and consistent. I'm gonna have to push her hard and get her to a breaking point. Push her to a level of bone heavy exhaustion that makes her feel like she can't stand on her feet a second longer, then make her hit the same spots on the bag with perfect power and accuracy over and over again.

"I'm not training quitters, LaReaux."

"This isn't training. It's me punching the heavy bag."

"That's right, and you're gonna punch it a hundred more times, and then give me fifty push-ups for your back talk."

I chuckle, because push-ups are her favorite exercise. *Not.* "If you miss a punch, or swing too wide, you'll start again."

She growls, but has enough sense to say whatever she's thinking under her breath. She finishes her 100 adequate jabs, then drops to the floor.

I sit down in front of her, with my legs crossed, and lean my elbows on my knees. "Sing to me, LaReaux."

She lowers her body and pushes up. We've done these enough time as punishment in class that she already knows what I want. Her sounding off, calling me *sir-* is one of my favorite things to hear. She infuses every bit of anger she feels toward me into that one word.

I'm an equal opportunity asshole, but I give Thea more shit than I do any of the other girls in class, because when she hits the point where others would have given up, she grits her teeth and tells me to fuck off.

It's inappropriate, but that shit gets me hard. Maybe our initial meeting has something to do with it. Maybe a part of my punishing her is to punish myself, because I want her and can't have her. It's why I refused to train her.

But now, here we are. I asked Syl about her and she told me Thea's win over Big Jim wasn't a fluke, and showed me her fighting stats for her other matches. So when I walked up on her about to go full on UFC on Eloise, I jumped in.

I was trying to diffuse the situation, but I knew the minute she had a chance she'd go after her again.

Fights between students don't mean shit to me, but Thea's skills would draw attention. The kind of attention she doesn't need.

With her being a new student, no ties to the legacy side of The League, she'd be a perfect recruit for MISTIC and the guardian program.

I watch Thea on campus. I've heard her talking in the halls with her friend and Austin Kincaid.

She wants to be an archaeologist. Travel the world and study lost civilizations. If she gets on The League's radar, her dreams will be over. They have ways of making you bow to their demands.

So I'll train her, and the rules are clear. No fighting outside of this gym. I promised to set her up with a fight, but that'll be a long time coming and it won't be one that gets a lot of media coverage.

I flick my gaze around the rest of the gym. I've got a great group of people, all training to be the best on the court, on the field, in the ring, on the track, or in the dojo. I'm proud of the training program I've built here.

"Forty-five, sir."

I drop my attention back to the woman in front of me. Perfectly straight back. Ass muscles clenched. I wonder if she'd clench around my cock, if it were buried between those sweet cheeks.

It's the last thing I need to be thinking about, but now that I am, I can't seem to switch the imagery off. Count this as reason number two, why training Thea is a horrible idea. I want this girl when I know I shouldn't. I'm disciplined, but I'm a man and knowing what she tastes like... this is gonna be torture.

I climb to my feet before the last number falls from her lips. "Decent effort. I'll see you tomorrow."

I stalk off towards the ring without looking back at her. No more delays, no more excuses. I need to find someone to hook up with, before I do something stupid, like breaking mine and the school's rules by fucking Thea over the desk in one of my offices.

Chapter 55
Thea

Deacon Wolfe, the teacher, and Deacon Wolfe, the trainer, are not the same. I didn't know what I was asking for when I told him to go as hard on me as he does with everyone else.

I'm sore and exhausted, and happy. My mind has been clearer than it's been in weeks, and I have a way forward with the Eloise situation.

There's no way I can let what she did to my picture slide. The bitch didn't even have the decency to drop the photo so I could tape it back together. She took it with her like some sort of souvenir.

In the two weeks since our encounter, I've noticed some things. I don't even know how I missed it before. I guess because I was trying to keep my head down. But now it's up and I know the one prize she wants more than anything. A prize I'm about to snatch right out from under her.

I drop into the seat next to Finn, placing my new laptop on the desk. It's the same model as the one Uncle Scott got me and is the biggest purchase I've made with my winnings.

\Replacing my wardrobe is gonna take a while. I'll get a few things Aunt Moira brought, but other than the underwear, everything else will be department store or thrift store finds.

Turns out I like lacy bras and panties, and don't hate that sometimes they come from expensive stores.

I still haven't gone through the stuff from the storage unit yet. School, working at the hotel, and training with Deacon haven't left me much free time.

Finn glances over at me. He's sporting a different beanie today than the one I tainted. "Pet?" His greeting comes out as a question.

"Number three."

"What brings you to this neck of the classroom?"

I look over to where I usually sit. "It's a little boring in the front."

"Oh, Pet, say less." He leans in close, his voice dropping to a seductive purr. "You wanna resume our games?"

"Do you? I'm in the lead. You'd have to come up with something huge to top my last move."

He licks his thumb, then rubs it over my bottom lip. "I think you mean *I'm* in the lead. I had you juicing all over my fingers, remember?"

"I remember you ambushed me and couldn't follow through, and if I was wet, it was from my shower and had nothing to do with you."

"Ask anybody, Pet. I'm a master orator and skilled piano player. I'm good with my hands and tongue. If I wanted you creaming my hand, you would have been."

I can't believe he took the bait. Oh wait, yes I can. His ego is as big as this room. "Care to put a wager on it?"

"What are the terms?"

"We each get five minutes to make the other cum. If I win, I get to hold that cute little knife you keep in your pocket."

"For how long?"

I have to play this carefully. His knife is his precious. If I push too hard, he'll back out. "Five days."

"One."

"Four."

"Two, but I reserve the right to request proof that you didn't pawn it."

"Deal."

He lifts a lock of hair from my shoulder and tugs on it. "What do I get when I win?"

"What do you want, *if* you win?"

The answer he gives isn't the one I was expecting. "For twenty-four hours you'll answer any question I have, truthfully."

It's risky. I hate answering questions. My present and past are my business. I share with LJ, but she's learned not to ask a million questions about everything. She lets me tell her when and what I want.

He's asking a lot. I guess this would be the emotional equivalent of giving up his knife. Good thing he won't be winning. It's gonna take longer than five minutes to get me off.

"Agreed. Do we need to schedule a date and time to execute this bet, or are you game to go at any time?"

He leans close, his lips just a hair's breath away from mine. "Pet, you should know by now that I live for spontaneity."

I don't back away. I'm not about to let him think I'm scared to engage with him. I tip my head, letting our lips brush together.

"Okay, then, good luck." I gather up my things and move back to my usual seat.

Finn cornered me two days ago and went to town on my clit. The boy is indeed talented with his tongue and fingers. In my head, I was begging for more, *and* thinking of the least flattering things I could to make sure I didn't combust too soon.

I tried to think of the way my arms burn when I do pushups, but Deacon's face kept popping up. Those bedroom eyes, his lopsided grin and pussy pleasing lips are the opposite of a lady boner killer.

So I thought of Ms. Mercer's hawkish nose and cold eyes. That helped. So did thinking of the second guy I ever had sex with, Terry, and his dry ass kisses. He didn't do shit to support his claim of being phenomenal in bed, but the memory of his lackluster performance was helpful in my time of need.

Finn was on his knees for almost eight minutes. I admire a man who doesn't quit. But the bet isn't about who can work their jaw the longest, it's who can make the other explode in five minutes or less.

I like the whole catch you by surprise thing, and that's exactly what I'm about to do to Finn.

I'm standing in the hallway next to a door that leads to a faculty only stairwell. When he passes by, I grab his hand and pull him through the door. I have to make this fast and make it count, so I've brought something along to the party.

Wasting no time, I sink to my knees and pull his cock from his jeans. I give it an introductory pet, because I'm a lady, sometimes, then do my best to swallow the entire thing. I can't. I know my strengths and weakness. I'll never be able to deep throat a dick without gagging and I lean into that.

Sometimes you go for finesse and other times you go for mess. I choose messy and enthusiastic. It helps that Finn doesn't smell like putrid ball sweat. I'd have to forfeit this bet if he did, because do-overs never came up in our negotiations.

"Oh, Pet, that feels incredible." I look up at him through my lashes. "Look at you, making all my wet dreams come true."

I slurp loudly, knowing the sound effects are gonna help. "That's it, slurp on me, Pet. I'm your favorite blow pop."

He does taste good, but I don't have time to savor this. I fondle his balls, making sure he's good and distracted, before slipping the toy around the base of his cock. He grunts as I snap it closed.

His hands try to push me away, but it's too late. I flick the button on the remote -putting it on a medium setting- then shove it back in my pocket, using my mouth and hands, adding to the friction.

"*Pet.*" He groans, fisting my hair. "Oh god. No fair, no *fair.*"

He's pulling me closer and pushing me away, trying to fight how good it feels. I lean down, sucking his balls into my mouth, then push my head further between his legs, flicking my tongue across his perineum.

"Fuck, girl, you. Oh, my *god.* Yes. That's it, Pet." He lets go of my hair and reaches back to spread his ass cheeks. I blow against his perineum, letting the cold air add to the sensation of my tongue, then move back to his dripping cock. My tongue swirls around the swollen tip, lapping up the moisture.

I try to swallow him down again, before pulling back. My hands keep rhythm as my mouth pistons up and down his shaft. He grabs the side of my face, holding me steady, and bucks wildly into my mouth. I massage his balls like I'm rubbing dice.

He thrusts once. Twice. Then holds himself still. I gag as he invades the back of my throat. I push against his thighs, giving myself a little room, then hum around his cock, which pushes him over the edge. His groan echoes through the stairwell. "Fuuu-ck."

His tastes explodes on the back of my tongue. Salty and thick. The timer goes off as I'm climbing to my feet. I swipe a residual drop of his seed off my lip and suck my finger into my mouth. His hooded gaze tracks the movement, his tongue darts out like he wants to sample his taste on my tongue.

"I win."

His gaze meets mine, and he pulls me into a hug, a husky chuckle falling from his lips. "You certainly did, Pet."

He steps back and looks down at the cock ring. "Do I even want to know how many people you've used this on?"

"That one is brand new. Got it just for you." Holding out my hand, I remind him of the reason I just blew him. "Now I think you have something for me?"

With his dick still hanging out, he slips his hand into his pocket and pulls out his knife, reluctantly placing it in my hand. I peck his lips, and promise, "Don't worry, Number Three, I'm gonna take real good care of it, like I took good care of you."

Finn's knife is a thing of beauty, but I didn't want it just to admire the gentle way it flips open or the detailed etchings on the handle. I need it to make a statement and to do that, I'll have to flash it around.

I order a big juicy T-bone steak so I can do just that. One day would have been plenty of time to send my message, but I couldn't help giving Finn shit about it. This thing is his baby, the way Clint is mine. He probably feels naked without it. I can relate. I'll give it a nice sharpening and polish before I give it back.

My food arrives, and I pull the knife out with a flourish. I admire the light glinting off the metal, then lower it to my plate to cut into my steak. LJ eyes the knife but doesn't ask any questions. This knife is distinct, and Finn flashes it *a lot*. Everyone knows who it belongs to.

I'm about halfway through my food when the murmuring starts. Somebody with a big mouth has finally gotten up the balls to comment on my fancy new utensil. I hear the uptick in voices and the commotion coming from the roped-off section of the room.

Eloise's voice is louder than everyone else's. "What!"

I slip another piece of steak between my lips. The mouth watering morsel basically melts on my tongue. Canyon Falls as a whole is shit, but they've got quality chefs in this town.

The shrieking shrew lands at the end of the table, squawking, "Where the hell did you get that?"

I finish chewing my bite, then lift the knife to check my teeth in its reflection.

"I asked you a question."

I slowly drag my gaze away from my image to look at her. She's got her supreme bitch face on. The one that says I should be cowering after what she did to my room. If I gave a shit about her, maybe I would be. "This? Oh, I got it from Finn."

"You mean you stole it from him."

Her deranged clown posse falls in behind her and nods. I wonder what it's like to travel with your own fan club and have them mindlessly agree to whatever you say. I try to imagine it and grimace. I'd be pissed off and freaked out. I'm not cut out for minions.

"I mean, I held out my hand and asked nicely. He was happy to comply."

"Finn would *never*. He doesn't let anyone hold his knife or his favorite beanie."

"And yet..." I tap my chin. "I've played with both."

"That's impossible."

I give her an understanding smile. Sympathetic even, as the man of the five minutes comes through the door. "Here he comes now. Why don't you ask him?"

She rushes over to Finn, then has to backtrack, because he doesn't stop walking until he's level with my table.

"Tell me Finney. Tell me she's a lying, whoring thief."

I snort a laugh because I am a thief, or have been when a situation calls for it, but I never whored myself out. Any and all sexual encounters were consensual, and no money was exchanged. Even this little bet I made with Finn had a dual purpose. I wanted him to give me permission to use his knife, and I needed an orgasm.

My gaze connects with his. "Go on, Number Three. Clear up the confusion."

I hold the knife by the tip with one hand and rub the other back and forth across the handle, the way I did his shaft.

"Did I steal this exquisite blade, or did you hand over your favorite knife to me when I asked you to?"

He confirms, "I gave it up when you asked."

"And were you under duress when you did it?"

"Not in the least." He drawls. "I was in a very *giving* kind of mood."

His eyes darken, and my stomach clenches as I see the lust in his eyes. I get it. When we're being flirty, I can totally see the appeal with

Finn. He's yum and sweet and oozing sexy fun. He might just be my new favorite thing to play with. We'll see. He has potential.

"How. How did this happen?" Eloise stabs her finger towards his head, breaking our stare off. I flip the knife around, catching it by the handle. LJ's gasp gets my attention, and I lower my hand.

I glance around the table. Nobody else seems to have noticed what I was about to do. He's not mine. There's no reason why I should be itching to cut this bitch for pointing her finger in his face, but dammit, I almost did.

"She said she's played with your beanie too. Is she drugging you, Finn? Is that it? Is she your supplier, and this is payment?"

His what? I supplied him with an orgasm, but that's not what she means. "Drugs? Bitch, really? Because the only way he can be nice to me or part with things is if I'm his drug dealer?"

She links her arm through his and pulls on him as if trying to shield him from me and my illicit wares. The urge to cut her rises up in me again. What the hell is with that? It's her. I don't want to defend him. I just hate her.

"That *is* what girls *like you* do where you come from, isn't it?"

Finn shrugs her off. "I'm not on drugs, Eloise. Thea asked to use my knife, and I let her. What I want to know is why the hell you think who I loan my shit to is any of your business?"

"Because it is, Finn." She stomps her foot. "I'm your future wife. I have the right to know where our future combined assets are going."

Oh, this is too funny. I don't keep it in. I throw my head back and laugh. The sound draws her attention back towards me. "What the hell are you laughing at?"

"You. Oh Sovereignly Stupid One. I'm laughing at *you*. You're all up in arms about this materialistic shit."

I wave the knife around. "How would you feel if I told you that some of your future went right down my throat?"

I let the weight of my implication set in and watch her face morph into shock, anger, embarrassment, and then back to anger, again. *Bullseye.*

I turn back to my food. I cut into the steak and stab it with the tip of the knife, and raise it, holding it out to share with Finn. He leans down, accepting it. His mouth near my ear when he asks, "Oh, Pet, was this the whole purpose of our little wager? So you could throw it in Eloise's face?"

I turn my head. Our faces are close, and for a moment it's like we're the only two people in this room. That's a dangerous feeling to have around him, because he's here and his buddies are never far behind. I haven't forgotten the shit they've done to me, and after this showdown with Eloise, it'll be even more important for me to watch my back. But I can't help teasing him, "Now if you had won, I'd have to answer that question, truthfully. But since you didn't..." I turn back to my food.

"Finn, I demand to know what's going on."

I make the mistake of looking over at Eloise, and damn near ruin my appetite. Holden and Pax have joined the little party at my table, along with a few more of Eloise's followers.

"Trouble?" Pax asks, as he glares down at me. "What am I asking? It's her. There's always trouble. His attention settles on the knife I'm wielding. "And why the hell is she using your blade like it's a run-of-the-mill steak knife?"

I hate this jerk. Always implying I'm the problem. Who asked him to come over here? Uh, no fucking body.

Finn tells him, "We made a bet, and it appears the odds were *not* in my favor."

"How did you lose a bet to her?" The way Pax poses the questions says it all. He's insinuating I cheated. I'm about to knock his ass down a peg, too. I exaggerate my wink, cocking my finger like a pistol at dumb and dumber and say, "Easy come. Easy blow."

Finn throws his head back and laughs. The warm, carefree sound rolls through me like a gentle wave. Definitely dangerous if we weren't on the opposite side of things.

"Touchè, Pet. Touchè". He walks backwards toward his table

with a smile on his face and I blow him a little kiss, to take the sting out of him having to leave his knife behind.

Eloise immediately runs after him. Holden scratches his neck, studying me like I'm a problem he'd like to dissect and solve, before moving away, and Pax, well fuck that asshole. I don't know what he's doing because I've given him my back. Risky, I know, since all signs point to him wanting to stab me in it.

Chapter 56
Holden

Something happened between Finn and Thea, and whatever it was, was different from the usual trysts he has with girls on campus.

None of them have ever walked away with his knife and afterwards he's never looked at them with the same hunger he still has on his face.

This thing barely scratched his itch. I hate that I don't know why he can't stop thinking about her. I can't either.

That's why I'm hovering in the space between our rooms again. I want to see her. No, that's not right. I *need* to see her. I've been dosing her and crawling into bed with her almost every night.

When I lay down next to her, my body relaxes and I'm able to sleep, and I can't explain why. It's not like she's always in a peaceful sleep.

She tosses and turns a lot and fights in her sleep, but it doesn't bother me. It's like her little cries soothe me. I wish I could see what she's dreaming about. Who's in her head upsetting her. Then I'd like to go find them and make them hurt.

They don't deserve to take up space in her head and dreams.

They don't deserve her fight. The only one who should ever bring her pain and torment is me.

I'm already stripped down. No need to pretend I'm not going to do exactly what I'm about to do. I waste no time jabbing the needle into her neck. There's really no way to be slow about it, then slide under the covers.

I've stopped caring about her waking up and seeing me before the drugs take effect. She won't remember me as more than a dream, anyway.

"How was your day, Rey?" I always ask her about her day, then tell her about mine. In these moments, I can be completely honest with Thea about my thoughts and feelings, and she doesn't judge me. She can't because she's unconscious.

I tell the guys a lot, but there are still some things I hold back. Things that most people would find abnormal. I don't need the judgement. I don't need the concern or pity. I just want to be, me.

"My day started off great, you know, after a quick sun salutation and coffee. I got an, A on my English paper. Of course, Dr. Murray still found things to critique. The last two pages are all inked up, but I decided not to make a big fuss about the six point deduction. It's a matter of opinion if my conclusion was an accurate summation of the body of the paper."

I slip my hand around her, pulling her head to my chest and massage the back of her neck. She likes when I do that.

"Then you know what happened at lunch. What was Eloise even upset about? She hates that Finn is so into knives and she's always telling him to stop wearing his beanies. But today, all of a sudden, she's mad about him letting someone hold his stuff? I heard her accuse you of giving Finn drugs. Maybe she's the one on drugs. It would explain the mood swings."

I look down at her. "For the record, I'm opposed to drug use. This little sleeping aide doesn't quite count, because we need this so we can be together, but anything else, you're not allowed to touch anything other than alcohol and I guess pain relievers if holistic means don't work. Everything else is off limits."

She snuggles against me, and I take that as her agreeing. "I talked to my dad, and he said he's worried about me. As a first year prospect, now is the time when fathers should be ready to entertain the idea of matching me with their daughters, and nobody's made any overtures. It seems I don't fake normal as convincingly as I thought I was doing."

She mumbles something in her sleep that sounds a lot like, *fuck normal.*

"Thanks, Rey. It means a lot to me that you said that."

I roll us so she's on her back and settle myself between her thighs. My dick nestled between the cleft of her legs.

"I see you, you know. Looking at me. I think you know I watch you too. But I try not to be obvious about it. Not let you know just how much I wanna crawl inside your head and pick it apart. To know everything there is to know about you. You're dangerous, Rey. I knew it the first time I saw you at my oasis. You have the power to make everything we're building come crashing down around us. I see it in the way Finn laughs when you play your games with him. It's not the fake laugh he gives to everyone else. I feel it, right now when my brain is yelling at me so loudly to do what I want to you. I think that's the real reason Pax dislikes you so much. Because you bring out the things in us that we try to hide from everyone else. You make us want to let down our guard."

I rock back and forth, teasing myself against the juncture of her thighs and bury my nose in her hair, filling my lungs with her scent.

"God, Rey. You always smell so damn good. I wish we could play the way I want to."

I scoot down a little, brushing my lips across her nipples. Peeking up at her, I say, "Just a little nibble." I clamp down on it, then lave it with my tongue. I give the other one the same attention. Alternating between each one, until her breath hitches. She likes a little pain. I could push her, help her find out just how much pain she can take.

The taser we used at her chasity vow ceremony was on a low

setting and she had pain meds in her system, but I could see her eyes shining every time I zapped her. She wasn't afraid. She was getting off on it.

"You're such a pain slut." I stroke myself as I love on her nipples, sliding my hand back and forth, until I'm on the edge, then pull back. "You know the rules. I don't cum unless you do."

I roll off of her and prop myself on my side, so I can watch her. I put her hand between her legs. "Show me how you like it. Rub that greedy pussy, Thea."

I help her along until she takes over. She looks so beautiful when she cums in her sleep. One day soon I'm gonna be inside her when it happens.

Soon, she's panting and whispering. The sounds she makes are addicting. "There you go, being a cock tease again. I've warned you what those noises do to me."

I move to straddle her body, resting on my knees, working my dick in time with her fingers. "We're gonna try something new tonight."

I study her face, watching for the signs that she's close. I know her so well from our nights together. She bites down on her bottom lip, the sign she's about to crash over in waves of pleasure. I pinch her nostrils closed, stealing her air.

"You're such a fucking brat, Thea. I warned you about teasing me. It's like you want me to use your body as my personal playground. You want me working my issues out on your skin. You like me in control of every breath you take."

The way her body seizes. *Fuck,* it's glorious. I release her nose, letting her get a bit of air, then constrict it again. I repeat it in time with the movement of my hand on my dick, dragging my pleasure out.

Her fingers never stop moving. She's as addicted to our time together as I am. Even if she doesn't know what's happening in the waking world, her body likes it.

Her mouth parts in a silent cry. "Yes, Rey. Fuck, I'm cumming too."

I lean over, slamming my mouth against hers, giving in to this pull I have towards her, and the pleasure winding through my body. It seems like I always have an endless supply of cum shooting from my sack. I don't even jack off alone any more. I save it all for her.

I reach down, smoothing my hand across the expanse of skin showing above her panties.

"Do you have any idea how much I want to pump you full of my cum?" I lift her damp fingers to my mouth, a contented hum spilling from my lips as I lick them clean.

When I'm done, I climb out of bed and walk over to the bathroom to get a washcloth to clean her up. I hate removing our combined scents from her skin, but I don't want to risk her discomfort or breaking out in a rash from sleeping with my seed on her all night. When she's clean, I get back in bed, finally ready to sleep. I check again to make sure my alarm is set. I'll be leaving before the drug wears off.

I pull my girl back into my arms. "Soon, Thea. I'm gonna have you soon."

She mumbles and sighs, "K."

Who knows what she's dreaming about? I'm practical. I don't daydream like everyone else. I work on facts. But for now, I let myself pretend that she's agreeing to be mine.

Pax

I shove my laptop into my bag and walk towards the exit of my Organizational Behavior class. I should be getting an A in this class, but I'm not because the real world study of my organization is going to hell, and it all rolls back to Theona LaReaux.

That girl is incapable of staying out of trouble. Whatever shit she did at Zeta Nu house has painted an even bigger target on her back with Eloise. I know her room was ransacked and her shit destroyed.

She should've let it go, but she didn't. She came back swinging and somehow roped Finn in on this shit. He gave up his knife to her and seemed happy about it, but it angered Eloise in the process.

The only people who have ever held that knife are me, Holden, and members of his family, and he's there watching everyone like a hawk until he gets it back. But Thea had it and was cutting her medium rare steak with it.

Easy come, easy blow. It doesn't take a genius to figure out what she meant by that. All you have to do is look at how calm and relaxed Finn has been the last couple of days. I'd almost thank her for finally giving him some ass, but it's hard to celebrate your friend getting laid when the bitch is someone you're trying to get dirt on.

Maybe now that Finn's succeeded in his quest, he'll get his head back in the game. I stifle a groan when I see Eloise waiting for me outside of class. I don't have time for her shit today.

"Pax, I know you see me standing here."

I keep walking. If she has something to say to me, that's not the way to get me to listen. All the bitches in this school are going crazy. No one would dare speak to me like that before Thea came here.

"Pax!"

In the blink of an eye, I'm on her, slamming her into a wall.

"The only time I wanna hear a walking cum box yell my name like that is if I'm pumping my dick into said cum box. If you need an audience with me, act like you've got some fucking sense."

She nods her understanding, but I slam her against the wall once more for good measure. It's not even her I'm upset with, she's just here. "Now what do you want, Eloise?"

I loosen my grip, and she straightens, smoothing out the wrinkles in her shirt. "We need to discuss how to move forward with our agreement."

"What agreement?"

"I take care of your Thea problem and you take care of my Finn problem. I don't feel like you're holding up your end of the deal."

"Our deal was for her to be thoroughly and completely humiliated, so she'd learn her place. She dropped out of pledge season, and appears to be standing taller than ever."

"Her quitting pledge season doesn't change our terms. I'm still holding up my end of the bargain. She *will* be on her knees, crying and begging for mercy."

She points to me. "I don't know what kind of shit operation you're running, but if you don't get Finn back on track, Zeta Nu just might have to wonder if Rho Beta Psi is worthy of our time and support."

"You're threatening me?"

"I'm reminding you that everything here is built on tradition. It would be a shame if the current Trium was the reason those traditions were no longer upheld."

It would signal to the council that we're inadequate leaders. Zeta Nu is made up of more than thirty percent of legacy daughters. Their mothers, grandmothers, aunts, were all members, just like the brothers of Beta Psi.

"It doesn't matter what I say to Finn if you're walking around being confrontational with him all the damn time."

"I'm not confrontational. I'm demanding respect for my status. I'm not some common skank. I told you, the three of you need to show me more respect."

I owe her nothing, but the frat needs her support. She's still going through her re-qualification and if she wins, we can't afford to have alienated her. I can't make an official stand as a Beta Psi member, but my public treatment of her will go a long way.

"I don't know what any of us have done that can be considered disrespectful."

"That bitch being close enough to Finn to wager anything, for one. How did that even happen?"

"They're in a class together. You know Finn, he's a jokester. This one obviously backfired on him. It's no big deal."

"I don't want them friendly and dealing. I don't want her near him in class or anywhere else. Finn's, *mine*."

"Maybe you should focus less on him being yours, and more on you being his."

"What the hell does that even mean? I'm his. I'm his future wife."

"It means if you don't give Finn a reason to want to publicly claim you as his, nothing I say or do will matter."

I step away, done with this conversation. This is ridiculous. I didn't sign up to be a fucking relationship counselor. I suck at it because I don't do relationships. None of us do, but Finn would be good at it.

Eloise just tries too damn hard on some things and not enough on others. Finn's bored, and she needs to figure out how to combat that. I have a few ideas, but I doubt she'd take advice from me.

Holden texted that they're already heading to The Rock. I'm just crossing The Circle when my grandfather steps out of the alcove on the side of the Admin Building.

As a legacy and alumnus, he knows where all the tunnels are. The alumni often make use of them for meetings, or in his case, to catch me off guard.

"This is a surprise." I keep my tone neutral and my face devoid of any emotion, since I don't know if he's here on legacy business, regular business, or simply as a former student and my grandfather. Either way, I can't give him anything he could use against me.

"I thought we'd have lunch."

There's a place all alumni like to eat at just outside of campus. "Very well. I'll meet you at the restaurant."

He holds out his cane. He doesn't need it. It's a prop and a weapon. I've been on the receiving end of his love taps before and learned not to flinch.

"I thought we'd eat here. In the dining hall."

This is bad. Like really fucking awful. He's not here to see his grandson. He wants to see how well we're running things. He knows our schedules, so it's not like I can sneak away or send an alert to the guys to stay away. I have no choice but to follow him down the path, and pray to whatever entity is listening that everyone is on their best behavior.

Chapter 57
Thea

There's a weird type of heaviness in the air when I walk into the dining hall. It's like everyone's on edge. Out of habit, my gaze darts to the off limit area.

The Coxsuckers are in their seats like always, but today they have a guest. I ask LJ, "Did someone finally end up with a parole officer?" I do nothing to hide the giddy look on my face.

She looks over at the table. "Uh, no. That's Malcolm Cox, Senior. We just call him Mr. Malcolm. He's Pax's grandfather, and easily one of the biggest alumni and donors to the school. I heard a rumor that he employs like thirty percent of Canyon Falls. "

"Is that right?" I catalog his face and tuck that information away for later. "I guess I should go say hello."

She snags my arm before I can. "I wouldn't."

"Why not? If he employs so many people, he might be my boss one day." Mostly, I just wanna get a closer look at the old man, and the way The Trium are actively avoiding looking my way just screams, come over and fuck with us.

"I don't know, Thea. The few times I've been around him, he didn't give off the nicest vibes."

"So he's basically an asshole. A real life image of what Pax is gonna be like when he grows up to be a bitter old man."

I look over at the table again. "You sure you don't wanna go over there? It's like time travel without all the quantum entanglement stuff getting in the way."

She ducks her head. "Shit. They're looking at us."

"That's never worried you before."

"Well, it worries me today. Look around, Thea. Do you notice anything different?"

"You mean besides the pussy brigade not doing their strut walk back and forth in front of the table, you acting weird, and grandpa Pax being over there?"

"Uh. Yeah. That's exactly what I mean. The fan girls aren't over there today."

"For those of us who are new, wanna explain why that's significant? After that whole production at the beginning of the year, I kinda figured this was another instance when other folks get called up off the bench, or they finally grew some brain cells and are now firmly on team, fuck those dudes."

She shakes her head like I'm too much for her sometimes. It's fair. I am.

"The only person saying 'fuck those dudes' is you. Everyone else wants a piece of The Trium. But, with Mr. Malcolm here, only the top tier girls will approach the guys. Not even the idiots who are usually bitching about Vale Tower's morning lingerie show are saying anything."

I snort at the lingerie show comment. A bunch of chicks walking back and forth in their underwear for those jokers is one of the funniest things I've ever seen. Like landing a man while you're just in your panties is such a great achievement.

I take my time to really look around the room and shrug. "There's nothing *to* say. Seems to me that for however long this mood lasts, the second and third strings get what they want. Ass by the handfuls."

Slinging my arm over her shoulder and pulling her towards the line, I say, "I can see you're on edge. I don't understand why, but I see it, so I won't go offer my customary fuck you to the dastardly dudes of Canyon Falls."

She relaxes into me. "Thank you."

We get our food and go to our usual table. Things over here haven't changed. Nobody new wants to sit with us. No sooner than I add ketchup to my fries, a shadow passes and settles on my right. The smell of Axe body wash and mint lets me know who it is.

"Afternoon, beautiful."

I said I wouldn't go over there and start any shit, but that doesn't mean I can't enjoy this time away from their smothering scrutiny and petty jabs. I lean into Austin's side and slide a fry through the ketchup and cheese before popping it in my mouth. I chuckle at his strangled gasp when I suck the ketchup off my thumb.

The conversation flows freely around the table and I relax more than usual, since I'm not on guard for an attack from one of the pussy posse members.

I've been here for nearly three months, and today is the first day I feel like I'm having a normal college lunch experience. Not including my momentary psychotic break when I was a *pledge*.

In fact, I'm feeling so chill that I don't complain when LJ agrees for us to watch Austin's teammate Oscar, pull some random stunt on Friday night, or when Oscar reaches down to hold LJ's hand as he walks her to class. She tosses a look at me over her shoulder. We have a silent conversation with our eyes. She's okay with it, then I am too.

But if not, in the immortal words of Mrs. Sprout, I'll cut a bitch.

My peace and reprieve are over when I finally get back to my dorm. The Coxsuckers are parked outside the building, arms folded across their chests like gang enforcers. Their entertainment is back in its usual form, too, but all the tits in the world aren't enough for them to miss my approach.

Conversely, I don't miss that they're scowling at Austin over my shoulder. There's a scowl meter and Pax is usually at the top of the grid, but today, the math genius might be winning.

He usually looks at me with indifference or curiosity, but today, I'm getting a full on scowl. His grey eyes are dark like an impending storm. When they sweep over me, I no shit feel a chill in my bones. I don't know what I did to earn this reaction.

We've been doing great with our passive animosity towards each other. If he wants to ramp it up to active animosity, I'm happy to add him to the list. "Problem, Pretty Boy?"

I ignore the way Finn's brows jump to the top of his forehead. This has nothing to do with him.

I see Eloise and her shadows moving closer. I ignore them too. It's Holden glaring at me like he wants to rip my head off, so he can damn well explain why he's suddenly decided to go full asshole. Or maybe I already know the answer.

"Awe, do you boys have indigestion? Did sitting around with future Pax give you a glimpse into just how much of an uptight prick he's gonna be in old age? All anti-fun and shit, and now you're mad at me, because I've been right about him all this time?"

I step closer. "It's not too late to change teams. Come over to the dark side."

I'm close enough to touch him and for some reason- okay, not just some reason, it's because I've thought about doing it once or twice since the night he freaked out on me- I actually reach out and do it.

Resting my hand on his shoulder, I stand up on my toes and coo... "Come on, Pretty Boy, let loose for once in your life."

I can't even describe what happens to his eyes. I don't have time to process any of it, because someone from the bitch brigade takes it upon themselves to put their hands on me.

What happens next is crazy as shit. I turn around and push her off of me. She stumbles into some dude I've seen hanging around Michael, and he steps around her to confront me. Like it's my fault the bitch wobbled in her heels.

I'm in the middle of reminding myself about Deacon's no fighting rule when the guy grabs me. This is where it gets crazy. Holden snatches me backward and he, Finn and Pax create a wall between me and the guy.

Like I said, crazy as shit, because there's no way these three are trying to protect me. For one, I don't need it, and two, Holden and Pax can't stand me. But holy shit.

I keep trying to squeeze between them, but they're so fucking wide I can't find an opening, and when I try to dart around them, Austin is there, blocking my way.

"Is there a problem?" I recognize the tone of Finn's voice. He's probably got his blade out, ready to play.

"I'd say. That bitch pushed me."

I might not be able to get around them, but my mouth still works. "The bitch pushed someone else. *She* fell into you, and *you're* the one acting like a pussy about it."

"Come say that shit to my face."

"I'm trying, you fucking cry baby. Stop hiding behind the Coxsuckers and come face me like a man."

Holden is the one who speaks next. "You will not be getting around us to confront her. What you will be doing is brushing this shit off and walking away with your balls intact."

He cracks this neck, making his words sound more ominous.

"Or," Finn says, "We can go with option two."

I'm just spit balling here, but I think I want option two. If it's Holden tackling folks like he did on the football field. I'm all for option two. But if option two is them fucking with this dude's accounts, I'll pass. I know how much of a pain and bore that option actually is.

I don't know why I'm asking, but I say, "Number Three, does option two include bloodshed?"

"Some."

Good enough for me. "Come on crybaby, pick door number two. Show me how much of a man you really are." I say, heckling the guy.

Pax mumbles, "She's like a female Finn."

I'll take that as a semi-compliment. When he's not being a total dick, and we're playing our little one-upmanship games, I'm a knife boy fan.

The wall of muscle parts and I push my way to the front in time to see the guy walking away. *Dammit.* No bloodshed.

A hand lands on my arm and spins me around, dipping me backward. I clutch onto Finn's arms to keep from falling over.

"Pet, what have I told you about that mouth?"

"I don't know. Which time do you mean, Number Three? Is it the time you told me how good it felt?"

Finn growls, straightens up, lifts me up by my ass and turns towards the building. I yell over his shoulder. "Austin, I can't believe you're letting him manhandle me like this. What happened to all that protection from a few minutes ago?"

He chuckles and shakes his head. "I'm not sure you mind him manhandling you right now. If I thought you did, I'd flatten his ass."

I nod once. That's good enough for me. I wrap my legs around Finn's waist while he walks. I don't know what the hell has gotten into these guys today, but I'm amused enough to let it all play out. When we get inside, Finn lowers me to the ground and points to the elevator. "Go to your room, Pet, and stay the fuck out of trouble."

Why does he keep saying that? I don't go out looking for trouble, trouble looks for me. He walks out of the building and leaves me standing here like he expects me to obey.

I'm going to my room because that's where I was headed before all this happened, and not because he told me to.

The Sovereign Shrew enters the lobby seconds after Finn exits. "I told you to keep your grubby fingers away from my man."

I rub my eyes, tired of the drama. "I touched a lot of guys today. You'll have to be more specific about which one belongs to you."

"Them." She hooks her thumb towards the door. "The Trium. Finn, Pax and Holden are legacy heirs. They don't fuck commoners."

"Right, and which one is yours?"

"The one you touched."

"Well, today, I touched Holden, and the last time I *touched* Finn. Does your ownership shift from one day to the next? Or do they share you?"

Her mouth gapes open.

"Hey. I'm not kink shaming. I mean, go girl. If I had to pick between them, I'm not sure I'd be able to either."

That last part has someone else speaking up. "You wouldn't pick Finn over, Holden?"

Why's she saying it like it's the dumbest thing she's ever heard? "No, I would. Not. Just like I wouldn't pick Holden over Finn. They'd have to get in the ring and fight it out. The last man standing gets me."

Eloise taunts, "They wouldn't fight over you. They wouldn't even want you."

"Is that supposed to hurt my feelings? Because it doesn't. It's not about what they want. It's about what *I* want, and if I wanted them, I'd have them. Keep that in mind the next time you want to order me to stay away from someone."

I flick my fingers. "Now run along and wax something painful, will you?"

The doors slide open again. Eloise looks over to see Finn staring at us. She hisses, "Watch your back, bitch," then pivots around and walks away.

I head over to the elevator, laughing my ass off at her threat. Watching my back is the story of my life.

Chapter 58
Pax

I shut the door to the classroom and pull the shade. There are a lot of rumors circulating around campus about us and I need to squash that shit.

I can't go to every person on campus, so I've called a meeting with the leaders of each of the organizations. We're making an official statement here and now. They can pass the information down to their members.

I don't even know how the situation got out of hand. One minute I'm minding my business, the next I'm facing off with Stefan Pollack. One of Michael's frat brothers.

We try not to mix it up with them because out of every other group on campus, they're the ones with a chip on their shoulder big enough to think they can take us on for the number one spot.

The Trium and legacies are number one on campus, but tradition only gets us so far. We have to fight to defend our spot. We can't afford to let our ranking slip, because if we do, Michael and his frat are definitely waiting to fill the void.

Getting into a pissing contest with them was never the plan, but we also couldn't let them stand outside of our dorm and disrespect a resident. Why the hell did that resident have to be Thea? *Always* fucking Thea.

I agree with her on one point. She's got balls of steel to call Stefan Pollack a pussy. They're bigger than his too, because nobody gets in Holden's face and teases him the way she did. I meet Finn's gaze across the room and nod. We're ready to start the meeting.

He whistles to get everyone's attention, and I walk to the front of the room.

"I know you've all heard about the altercation in front of Vale Tower." I look directly at Michael when I say the next part. "We're here to clear up any misinformation that may be floating around campus and hope that you'll pass along the information to your respective groups."

Michael, ever the hothead, blurts out, "We know what happened. You threatened a member of my house."

"A member of your house walked into the middle of a disagreement between two residents of Vale Tower. He was an innocent bystander until he decided to get upset about a nudge and threatened my resident."

"You had no right to jump in. It would've been a fair fight."

"*Perhaps*, if a fair fight is a five eleven man going up against a five and a half foot woman, that's half his body weight. I know Coach Wolfe trains for these types of events, but those match ups are supposed to be in the ring, under his supervision, are they not?"

"The smart mouthed bitch was asking for it." Stefan says from the back of the room.

He's here because it's his right to give his side of the story, but Michael is the one we're really concerned about. Whatever decision he makes, the rest of his frat will abide by it.

Michael asks, "Which girl was it?" I'm surprised he doesn't already know. Or if he does, he just wants us to say it so everyone hears it.

"Theona LaReaux."

He locks eyes with Stefan. "I agree, she's mouthy." He turns back to me and says, "She's no wilting flower. She comes hard at the guys in class, trying to knock us around. You should've let Stefan handle her. I'm sure he'd have done a better job than what you're doing."

I share a look with Finn. I already know about him intervening between them. There's a lot of bad blood there. Finn's knife flicks out. "I already told you, Mikey. If anybody's gonna declaw her, it's gonna be me."

This is not the way this meeting is supposed to go, but what did I expect? Finn's got an attachment to this girl and nobody gets between him and his toys.

"Now are you challenging me for possession of my, Pet, Mikey? If so, I'll happily discuss the terms."

"That conversation was between us, Finn, and Stefan didn't know." Mike flicks his eyes at me. "That still doesn't explain why the other two jumped in."

"Doesn't it?" Finn hops down off the table and stalks around the room trailing his knife blade along the desks.

"Bow down and plead
    Before those who lead
    Leave your will and moral compass at the door
    Bleed and Cower. Our rival devoured.
    The Triumvirate. Legacy Born"

He reaches the back of the room as he finishes reciting the last line.

"We're The Trium. We're one. My word is theirs and their word is mine. Theona LaReaux lives in Vale Tower. She is mine. She is *ours*."

He taps his knife against his chin. "Now I'm not unsympathetic to the embarrassment Stefan experienced at Thea's hands. Just as you've both already mentioned, she's mouthy as fuck. Makes you wanna cut out her tongue."

He stares off into space as if imagining what that would look and sound like. Whatever he's thinking is enough to put a smile on his face. Sick fuck.

I redirect this conversation to try to find a resolution. "Finn, what are you thinking is compensable?"

"I say we deduct house points from Rho Beta Psi and allocate them to Ironside."

I hate the idea, but it's also the easiest path to take with zero bloodshed. I look at Holden, who agrees.

Turning my attention to the rest of the room, I say, "Now, to make sure we're on the same page. The Trium acknowledges the role our resident played in the altercation and will take appropriate action to make sure something like this doesn't happen again. However, if it does," I make eye contact with each and every one of them. "Theona LaReaux is a Trium matter to deal with. From here on out, any correction or embarrassment that needs to occur will come from us. If we need to delegate the tasks, we have no problem reaching out for assistance."

It's not even like I care that Michael and his goons want to make an example out of her, but they were stupid to try to do it in front of our building, and that's the point we're making here.

We adjourned our meeting after settling on a reduction of twenty house points. We had to promise our frat that we'd participate in the next three house selected challenges in order to get them to agree.

I haven't checked the calendar but if we haven't signed up already, that means they're boring, easy, or both.

Finn thinks it's a small price to pay for maintaining order. I agree. I'm just pissed we have to deal with this shit at all because of her.

This should have been an easy task. Watch her. Report back. All this bullshit we're dealing with and I'm supposed to believe she's a nobody? There's definitely something off with this girl.

"Keeping an eye on this girl is turning out to be more trouble than it needs to be." I walk over to my fridge to get us all drinks. "She's gotta be a league plant. There's no other explanation for it, which means from here on out we have to make sure we're always in game mode. We can't leave any room for them to doubt that we deserve to be league members."

"She's not a plant." Finn says from his place on the couch.

"Do you have proof that she's not? Because the lack of evidence proving her *innocence* is pretty damning, if you ask me."

"Since when does no proof, prove anything?"

"Since Holden hasn't been able to dig up a single lead on this girl outside of the paperwork, we initially found. It's a professional level black out."

Holden's nodding his agreement. It's not this hard to dig up information on normal people.

Finn's fun is in jeopardy, so he's in argument mode. "Maybe what we found is all there is. Or do you think her foster care and juvie records are a deep fake?"

"I think none of us know anything about this girl to make a decision one way or another, and I don't like not having answers."

What I like even less than no answers is having to deal with this drama with the other houses right after my grandfather spent the afternoon on campus.

I guess I should be happy nobody acted an ass until after he left. I'm sure he has spies around to keep an eye on things, just like all the other council members do. Anyone could be a spy. That's why I only trust the people in this room.

"I hear what you're saying, Pax, and you know I'll go along with whatever the two of you decide, but I think Thea's harmless. If her records are lost or locked or whatever, it doesn't matter. I know who she is now, and she's not some secret league asset. Everything that happened the night she came into town was just a coincidence."

"Did she tell you that when she was winning that knife off of you?" He still hasn't explained what the fuck they bet. Finn never loses a bet, so if she knew how to win, that's another check mark in the column, for she's specifically here to ruin us.

"I've watched her. Followed her around, and spent time with her. She's never once gone near anyone from The League. The only Wrens she's come into contact with are the ones on campus, but we're the only ones she's ever interacted with."

"It could all be electronic communication." Holden says without looking up from his tablet. "She hardly uses her Prospectus account and isn't all that active on any other social media platforms, either. That means she's probably got a ghost account. I could get into her phone and laptop, if you want."

I haven't asked him to do it before now. He's got rules about who he hacks and why. It's never just arbitrary, or to simply spy on people out of boredom. They have to be a target and I've been hesitant to make her an official target, even though my father has given me a reason to. Why is that?

I look over at Finn. He's kicked back on the couch, hat in his lap, a stupid smile on his face as he stares at his phone. If there's something to find, we need to do it before he gets any more attached to her. I nod my head, giving Holden permission to break into her electronics.

"We might need to install a tracker on her phone too..."

Finn's head pops up. "Why would we do that?"

"Just because we've seen her go into buildings doesn't mean she doesn't slip out another way. We all know this town and campus are full of secrets. How to make your way around and through it undetected is one of the biggest ones."

Finn shakes his head. "Now you're reaching."

"No, you're ignoring the facts and acting pussy whipped."

"What facts? We don't have any, unless you count the fact that you're being a secretive asshole, just like your father."

I thought I was hiding it better, but I should have known they'd see through me. Holden lowers his tablet and says, "Pax, now might be the time to tell us if there's something else going on here."

Thea

I chuckle at the message on my phone. Finn's been contacting me on the school's social app all week. He wants me to promise to show up at the movie theater tonight. I'm training with Wolfe and don't know if I'm gonna have enough energy to sit through a late night screening. Of course I didn't tell him that. I just said I'm on my way to let a man get me all hot and sweaty, and let him infer what he wants from that.

He's inferred that means sex and is now demanding to know who I'm fucking.

Since my sex life is none of his business, I've been refusing to answer.

KNIFE BOY

Whoever he is, Pet. You don't need him

I can do all kinds of delicious things to you.

We can skip the movie, and I'll show you

ME

I like the way he works me over

Whatever you're offering can't even come close

KNIFE BOY

You need to tell me who this dead man is

If I have to hunt down the answer myself,

You won't like the consequences.

ME

Bring it on, Knife Boy

When I look up from my phone, I spot Pax leaning against my car. I scan the parking lot for signs of Finn. If he sent this lug to follow me, we need to have a talk about stealth. Pax is a walking billboard. His ink, his height, and his perma-scowl, makes it impossible for him to blend in.

I plaster a smile on my face. "Oh my god, are you here to wash and detail my car? Make sure you get the tires with your toothbrush and I'll give you a nice tip."

"Here's a tip. Whatever you think you're doing with Finn, knock it off."

"Or... whatever your friend thinks he's doing with me... is none of your fucking business."

"That's where you're wrong. Everything on this campus is my business."

I pluck imaginary lint off my shirt. "Only the people trying to suck up to your overbearing ass are stupid enough to pretend to believe that. Since I don't fit into either of those camps, I'm happy to tell you to fuck off."

"And I'm happy to tell you that Finn only sees you as a challenge. You've got him so twisted up for your loose ass cunt that he's running after you. But just as soon as he nuts down your throat, he'll be over it. Enjoy his attention while it lasts."

I gasp in mock horror. "He didn't tell you? I swallowed his cock in a stairwell in Briar Hall, weeks ago."

I give him a pitying look. "If he's stopped gossiping about girls with you, I guess that means the two of you are no longer as close as you think."

One minute I'm laughing up at him, the next my back slams against my car. His fist rams into the door. I'm pretty sure he's left a dent in it.

He's got me caged in, his chest heaving as he fights to regain control. This brutish display would probably send people running in tears. I guess if I grew up differently, I'd be running too. But I learned the hard way not to back down from bullies.

"Come on, big guy. Whatchu wanna do?"

He looks torn, like he doesn't know how to answer.

"Do you want me on my knees, showing you just how good I made your friend feel? Give you a little taste of why he's so obsessed with me?"

"Shut up."

"I had him speaking in Latin, you know. Sucked his soul right out of his cock."

"I said shut up!" He slams his hand against the door two more times.

Pax is just too damn easy to rile up. "Make me."

I bite down on my lip. My clit is tingling and I know my nipples are probably hard. I'm still in my dick-less phase. Finn's all fun to play with, but we haven't crossed into boning territory yet. I doubt we will.

"Why can't you just keep your mouth shut? Do you get off on

pissing people off? Pushing them to the point where all they want to do is choke the fuck out of you to get one goddamn second of peace?"

I tap my chin as if I'm considering his question. "Am I the problem? Or is it everyone else? Perhaps you and these people you're referring to have unrealistic expectations for how I should act. You know, with the whole 'I'm a legacy, you're not. Now bow down, bitch.'"

His jaw tenses as I make fun of his status. "That's what's really eating at you, isn't Pax? That all these months you've been trying to crush me. Embarrass me. Hurt me, and I'm still standing."

I cock my head to the side. "Or is it because something else lurks underneath all that misplaced hate you have for me? Are you really just mad at yourself for wanting someone you've convinced yourself is trash?" I drag my eyes down his body, then back up. "What do you say, Pax? You want a taste of my dripping cunt?"

"Not even if it was going to be the last cunt I'd be offered for the rest of my life."

"What's wrong? Afraid you'll get addicted?"

He leans down. "More like I'll catch something."

What a typical basic comeback. When faced with a woman confident in their sexuality, what do you do? Try to slut shame them.

I heft a shoulder, completely unbothered. "Then might I suggest you back up? Wouldn't want any of my cooties to get on you."

Laughter from the other side of the parking lot cuts through the tension in the air. He jumps away from me like he really is afraid of catching something. I roll my eyes and open the door to the car, shoving my bag in the back seat.

I'm behind the wheel, car in motion, before he can say anything else. I don't even give a courtesy beep as I back out of my spot. He catches on pretty quick and jumps out of the way so he doesn't get run over.

Chapter 59
Thea

What have I gotten myself into? I've been asking myself that question all day, as one person after another plucked, pinched and waxed areas of my skin that usually go untouched. It's all thanks to LJ. My dear sweet LJ.

Her parents are having an anniversary party and I've agreed to go as her plus one. The problem is, I mentioned this party to Aunt Moira, and she decided to turn it into a bonding moment. Her torture team is at the house getting us ready.

LJ snorts when I glare at the woman with the tweezers. "I think my brows are fine."

"They're still just a little thick. You want them thin so they look smooth when we paint them on."

I push her hand away from my face. "Here's a thought. If we don't pluck them like the feathers off a chicken, you don't have to paint them back on."

"And your bikini area? Did you want the Brazilian?"

My eyes snap to Moira's, who gives me a reassuring smile. "It's not as bad as you may have heard when they hold the skin correctly."

I've had a Brazilian before. Sasha and I found a Groupon. It was cool and all, but I also remember how sensitive I was afterwards. I'm just shocked she put it on our schedule. LJ hops up on the table and says, "Do me. I've been neglecting my maintenance."

"LJ, you are not about to spread your legs with me sitting here."

She laughs at me. "They have a rolling curtain, silly."

The ladies bring in two more tables and rolling dividers. Moira grabs a table and I climb onto the last one.

"Know what this reminds me of?" LJ giggles. I should probably cut off her mimosa consumption. "It reminds me of the day The Trium was naked on your balcony."

Moira screeches. "They were what?"

Moira and Scott haven't exactly expressed their views on dating. Not that I would listen, but I get the impression they'd pick out a nice, sweet, safe boy. Somebody from Scott's office, to bore me to death.

"Relax, Aunt Moira. LJ's a little tipsy. They weren't naked on my balcony."

"Oh, okay."

My lips twitch. "They were naked on Finn's balcony."

She makes a sound like she's choking on her spit. "Was this, um, a fraternity prank?"

"Nope. It was Finn's weekly rub and tug and they did it exhibitionist style."

"Do the boys often just sit on the balcony with their parts out for the world to see?"

She sounds more concerned with each question. I'd draw the curtain back to look at her, if someone wasn't situated around my lady bits with wax and tape.

"Only when they want to annoy me."

LJ sighs. "They don't annoy me when they're like that. Those men are yummy. Too bad they only pay Thea any attention."

"Is this true, Thea? Have you caught one of the Trium's eyes?" I recognize the lead up to a lecture when I hear it. I'm a little old for the sex talk and I'm not having it with my aunt.

"Like I told you before, Aunt Moira, they're a bunch of jerks. Finn and I have a neighborly feud going on. It's nothing more than that."

"Okay, but if they're a problem, you have to let us know. We'll take steps."

"It's fine. Nothing I can't handle."

She doesn't say anything else after the technician tells her to keep still.

LJ's house is bigger than my aunt and uncle's. That's saying a lot because that place is massive. She lives ten minutes away, her neighborhood the middle divide between Moira and Scott's level of wealth and where she told me The Coxsuckers live.

LJ's dad's in tech, and developed some kind of micro mini processing circuit that electronic companies were willing to pay big money to use. He licensed it to a company, catapulting their lifestyle to this. Her mother wanted big and fancy, her father wanted quaint and comfy. This was the compromise. LJ got the wrong end of the deal, since Eloise lives across the street.

"I can't believe in a couple of weeks it'll be Christmas break and I'll have to deal with that all day."

She waves her hand at the line of cars in Eloise's driveway. Since their parents are all friendly, Eloise and the plastics posse will be at the party tonight, too. I'm thinking of going back to Nags Creek to hang with Sasha for the holidays. Maybe I should drag LJ with me to save her from having to deal with them.

I step out of the car, hyperaware of how sensitive I am in my freshly waxed areas. I knew I would be, but it was fun being pampered and just hanging out with LJ and Moira. It reminded me of the times Sasha and I would do mani pedis and each other's hair.

Speaking of, I've got my color touched up. The bottom layer of my hair is full ombre, but the rest is a dark chocolate with ombre strands serving as highlights, adding random pops of color to my hair.

It was Moira's idea to do it this way, and I love it. She also picked out the cut out maxi dress with the criss-cross halter neckline. My stomach is bare, and the slit goes all the way to my left hip. I have Clint strapped on my right thigh. I feel powerful and sexy in this dress.

I don't plan on getting all dolled up like this all the time, but Moira has a good eye and if I had to dress up; between her and LJ, I wouldn't make a total fool of myself.

LJ gives me a quick tour of the foyer, stairs, and second floor as she takes me up to her room to drop her bag off.

I left my stuff in my room at Moira's. She was actually happy that I left dirty clothes behind. I guess it makes the room feel used. I haven't been up there since the weekend I moved here. I go to dinner, and sometime I visit Cora in the kitchen.

That's all the use I have for the place, except now there's also a closet with my stuff from the storage unit that I need to go through.

That house is a building where people I'm related to live. They pay my tuition; I have access to more money than I can do anything with, even though I don't touch their accounts, and they aren't completely unbearable, but that's their home. Not mine. I have no connection to it. I guess that's why I haven't even considered staying here when the semester is over.

We spend time in LJ's room, which is only slightly bigger than mine, without the sitting room attached to it. Hers has a balcony with a set of stairs that leads right down to their pool. "I'll trade you."

"What?" She sips from the champagne glass she's holding. This she can do. Champagne and wine. Anything harder and she's sputtering and spitting. Although she's better than when we first met. If it tastes like punch without a hint of alcohol, she slams them back. Jello shots are her favorite treat.

"I'll trade you the sitting room you're crazy about, for the balcony that goes to the pool."

"Girl, are you nuts? You practically have an entire floor to yourself. Why would you trade?"

"Because your balcony goes to the pool." She has a point. I am on the floor alone, and I even have my own game room, office, library combo.

There's a door in the sitting room that wraps around the wall on the other side of the stairs. LJ and I had fun exploring it together when Moira pointed it out. She was apologetic, assuring me it was an oversight that Mercer forgot to mention it.

The tea cup with the lipstick I saw on the table makes me think it wasn't an oversight but hoarding the knowledge. Somebody in that house is using the space. I don't blame them. It's so comfy, I could spend hours in there reading, or studying or napping. It's got a little chaise lounge and a reading chair just for that purpose.

"A nursery."

I zoned out on what LJ was saying. "Huh?"

"I said the office space, it's so cozy the way it's set up, and how it's situated in the room. It would've been the perfect spot for a nursery. I wish they would've found you sooner. You could've been visiting here as a kid and I would've always had a friend."

"I don't live in what if's. You know that. I'm here now. We're friends now, and I'm glad about it."

She puts her glass down and throws her arms around me. "LJ..."

"Shush. Deal with it."

I hug her back, because I do have to deal with it. I meant every word. I'm glad LJ and I are friends. She's sweet and funny and has a huge heart. "How tipsy are you?"

"A good amount. Have to be, to get through tonight."

"Enough to make some reckless decisions with a hot guy?"

She giggles, pulling back from our embrace. "I wish, but trust me, none of the people here are going to be thinking about being reckless. It's a party, but it's an excuse to network, and talk shit about other people's businesses while trying to boost your own. It's gonna be a complete bore, which is why I invited you to suffer along with me."

I link my arm through hers, and walk her towards the door.

"Boring, you say? We'll just have to see about that."

Chapter 60
Thea

Boring doesn't even begin to cover the mood in this place. The parents in attendance and their offspring are all playing different versions of the same game.

The sons look like they're prepped on what to say to cast their parents in the best light, and the daughters of a certain age have this way of laughing. A combination of sweet and flirtatious, that have the sons making fools of themselves to hear it again.

LJ's mother dragged her away from me a few minutes ago. She's in the corner with her parents chatting up someone who's supposed to be transferring to Canyon Falls next semester. I think her parents volunteered her to show him around.

I help myself to another flute of champagne and turn towards the door at the wrong moment.

The bubbles go up my nose, and the liquid down my air pipe, causing me to sputter.

I compose myself quickly, but the damage is done. I've already embarrassed myself, and it's their fault.

They're late, just like they are for the school parties. But now, I know it's a choice. They like turning heads when they make an entrance. Tonight is no exception.

Usually I ignore their slow-mo walks into a room. That's not happening this time. They're in suits. All three of them.

In a world where they're already too damn attractive, this is just unfair. Finn ditched his beanie, his hair falling in waves against his forehead. The dark blue three-piece suit fits his athletic frame to perfection. He's opted for a crisp white shirt, silver patterned tie and straight fold pocket square.

Holden's in black, his white banded collar unbuttoned at the neck. His hair is styled away from his face, a hint of shadow roughs his jaw. He's also wearing a pocket square, but his is stuffed into the pocket, adding to his deconstructed look.

He's casually formal, and understatedly sexy. I'm fighting the urge to go over and stick my hand through the opening of his shirt to squeeze his pecs.

The lead Coxsucker is leaning heavily into the silver spoon bad boy vibe he always has going on. The cut of his suit accentuates his wide shoulders. He's also foregone the tie and a button, his jacket's open, showing the vest underneath. His hair is slicked back, high-lighting the angles on his face. His tattooed neck on full display. His ink in stark contrast to the formality of the suit.

I'm given different looks by way of greeting. Finn smiles and winks. Holden drags his eyes over every inch of my dress. I cock my hip, showing just how high up the split actually goes. It's not an invite, but if he's gonna check me out like I'm a museum exhibit, he should get the full effect.

Of course, his expression is unreadable and I can't decide if he likes what he sees or not.

Pax is always the easiest to read out of the three of them. He oozes hate and disgust. Dressing up to look like a mafia prince doesn't change that, any more than making me look like a runway model changes me, and in the spirit of being ourselves, I lift my middle finger in greeting.

Before our usual series of glowers and death stares can kick off, Eloise cuts across the floor, heading straight for them. She kisses Finn's cheek, then Pax's and finally Holden's.

Oh, so she can kiss him, but my touch when he was shoving his tongue in my mouth grossed him out? I fight the urge to go over and touch him out of spite.

Instead of moving along, she stands next to Finn, giving me a cruel smile. The possessive stance and grip on his arm, telling me he's off limits. I stare at that hand, and brush my fingers against the side of my thigh, letting Clint comfort and ground me. I will not let this bitch bait me. Not tonight in LJ's home.

She leads Finn to where the other legacies are standing. Pax and Holden follow. My two minutes of excitement are over and now I need something else to do.

"Why is a beautiful girl like you standing over here all by yourself?"

Thank god. Someone I actually like has arrived. I smile up at Austin. He looks good too. Damn, do they teach them how to dress up as GQ models or what? He's in a pale grey suit with a light purple shirt and a dark purple tie.

"I don't know anyone here, other than you and LJ and since my track record with making friends is so bad, I figured it would be safer for the party guests if I stay over here and guard the dessert table."

"And where is Miss Leyla-Jean?"

I point to where she is. Her parents have introduced her to someone else. I'm thinking she won't get free until she's had face time with every guy in here.

I'm happy and horrified on her behalf. Happy, because she needs practice interacting with guys, horrified that her parents are parading her around like this, forcing her to do it.

Turning back to Austin, I ask, "Why aren't you over there being bored by old people like everyone else?"

"Student athlete. Right now, all anyone cares about is if we're selling tickets and winning games. Sports is the biggest revenue stream on campus and in town, so I don't have to smile and nod like an idiot at the alumni. They're happy to donate money to Canyon Falls' Athletic Department."

"Right, but based on what LJ said, the people here are trying to make business connections and the kids are supposed to brag on their parents."

"Shit." He chuckles. "You still don't know, do you?"

"Know what?"

"Who my father is."

"Mr. Kincaid."

Now he outright laughs at me. "*Roger* Kincaid. Owner of the Canyon Falls Coyotes."

I furrow my brows, then the name slots into place. "Wait, what? You're serious?"

"Yup. So, like I said, donating to the athletic department is all I care about. That's what helps my dad. The school can recruit top-notch talent, win games and then he can recruit top-notch talent to his dynasty and win games, and fill stadium seats."

"Why am I just finding out your dad is Roger Kincaid? Four rings, three teams, Roger Kincaid?"

He laughs again. "I kinda thought you knew the first day we met and were just pretending not to, so I'd make an effort. But then when I realized you actually had no clue who I was, I liked that you just wanted to be my friend. I swear I wasn't keeping it from you. I get a lot of flack from the legacies at school, because of him."

"He's a legend. I don't know why they'd bitch about that."

"That's exactly why. He's a legend. His oldest son is carving a path as a coach, and here I am, the football god on campus. I get just as much attention as the legacies, and we both know how much they hate competition."

"Aren't the frat and sorority prank wars and games built on competition?"

"They are, but at some point, every organization needs something from a legacy. A favor. A job. A date. I don't need anything from them. I can use any one of my father's contacts for that."

I raise my glass. "To not needing anything from them."

Austin standing next to me, draws a crowd. Now people who I'm sure were actively avoiding me, walk over to talk to him. He makes a point of introducing me. I'm exhausted from saying hello and explaining that I'm new to town.

It looks like LJ has a break, so I slip away from Austin and his friends to rescue her, ignoring the stares I'm getting from the legacy side of the room. Funny, even at this party there's a divisive line. I, for one, am happy I'm on Austin's side of the snobby divide.

I'm almost to LJ when someone grabs my arm. "Where are you off to in such a hurry, Pet?" Finn smiles down at me. "Lemme guess, Kincaid has bored you to death with his football stats and now you're off in search of more stimulating conversation."

"If I were, this wouldn't be a stop on my route."

"Be honest, Pet. I'd be the only stop you need." He pulls me into his arms and spins us around into a dance.

"There's no music playing."

"When you're around, there's always a song in my head. Most of the time, it's the tune to Mission Impossible or jazz, but given our current surroundings, I think a little waltz is appropriate."

Instead of pointing out we're the only people dancing to his imaginary song, I let him spin me around. "You're pretty graceful, Number Three."

"Dancing is like sex. I've had lots of practice."

"With the dancing or the sex?"

"Both. I'm happy to show you those moves, too. Just say the word." His lips skim my ear. "*Please* say the words." There's a desperate plea to his request.

Pax is staring at us, like always. "I don't think your daddy's gonna approve *that* playdate."

"My dad? Who Pax?"

"Of course. Unless your real father is around here looking at me like I'm trash, too."

He shakes his head. "He couldn't make it, so he sent me, the younger, cooler, sexier Finn, in his place."

I finger the collar of his suit jacket. He's got the sexy part on lock tonight.

"I saw you checking me out when I came in, Pet."

"You clean up nice, number three."

"You know what else I do?"

"What?"

"I fuck, dirty."

I could use a little of that in my life. Pax and Holden walk up. It's like they have a beacon that flashes whenever Finn and I even think about taking our flirtation further. "Finn." Pax says in a disapproving tone.

I pull my hand from his and turn him to face his friends. "Told ya'." Before he can turn back around, I'm back on my mission to rescue LJ. I finally reach her after I'm stopped a few more times.

"Girl, you are working this room tonight." I tease, linking my arm through hers to pull her to the side so we can get a few minutes to talk.

"Blame it on my mom. Every eligible son in attendance warrants an audience. As if I have a dance card that needs to be filled."

"Any of those sons catch your eye?"

She chews her lip. "A few, but it does me no good if they don't live around here, does it?"

"LJ, babe. That's the best-case scenario. To hookup and not have to see them every day?" I wiggle my fingers. "Gimme all the hotties that fit that description."

"More than one?"

"I decided a long time ago that I'm not really into relationships. I already know I suck at them. If you wanna party, have fun, get blown.

I'm good. If you need me to call and text and do all that other couple shit. Pass."

"Have you ever actually tried dating?"

"Once. When I was fifteen."

"And what happened?"

"He got mad when I told him I agreed to go with someone to a wrestling match at the high school. That's when he explained dating meant I couldn't hang out with any guy that wasn't him." I snag a fresh champagne flute from a passing waiter.

"I can't be restricted like that. I've always been a bit of a tomboy and an action geek. The girls in my neighborhood were getting into makeup and stuff and I still wanted to learn how to do wheelies on motorcycles. Telling me no guy friends put an end to my romantic hopes and dreams. Now I can have the fun and the dick. It's perfect."

She shakes her head at me. "Just wait. The right guy's gonna come along and change your mind."

"He'll have to club me over the head and handcuff me first."

She scrunches her nose. "Eeew, girl, I am not drunk enough to hear about your kinks." We cackle, drawing disapproving looks, and laugh even harder.

Just as I'm relaxing, and having fun, with LJ, she's pulled away again for another round of musical sons. I entertain myself by walking around the room, observing the people I recognize from school in their natural habitat.

For the ones that are standing off in corners with their friends, I try to match them with their parents.

Some are easier to figure out than others. Namely, the ones that are dressed like perfect replicas of their fathers or mothers, and some are the spitting image of their parents.

Finn said his father couldn't make it. I wonder if he looks just like the second Finley Jefferson Rhodes, or if he favors his mother. He didn't mention her being here, but that doesn't mean she's not. I scan the crowd again, trying to see if I can pick out the woman who birthed Finley Jefferson Rhodes the Third. Nobody stands out in the looks department, and the older women I've seen him interact with are giggling just as hard as the younger ones.

Holden, on the other hand. His father is here. I heard someone say Mr. Sullivan, and I checked to see who they were talking to. He's just as big and broad as Holden.

His hair is blond, but he has the same stormy grey eyes as his son. He's also a watcher like Holden is, cataloging every move and conversation happening around him, only he's not as obvious about it.

Or as obvious as I was. He caught me watching him and did a very un-Holden like thing. His lips twitched. Not quite a smile, but close enough.

Then, he vanished. Seriously. One minute we're looking at each other, but then a group of servers walked by with huge trays and by the time they moved, he was gone. It's the kind of vanishing in a crowd skill I have yet to perfect. I'm impressed that such a big guy can move so stealthily.

There're tons of food here, but it's basically feed yourself and mingle vibes. I like that there isn't a table and seven course servings happening. That means I can graze as much as I want. I haven't eaten since this morning, and I've been drinking the bubbly, so it's time to put something more in my stomach.

I mentally applaud LJ's parents on the food choices. There's a lot of fancy hors devours, but there are basic foods too. I'm trying to decide between the chicken salad sandwich and turkey pin wheels. It's a tough choice. I should probably stop trying to decide and take both. The way the caterers keep bringing out food, I'm sure there's plenty for everyone.

"How horrifyingly uninteresting."

"It's food. Not too many ways to dress it up." I say without looking up. I finish making my selections and look around for an empty cocktail table. I spot one over on the other side of the room. Hopefully, I can get to it before anyone else does.

"I wasn't talking entirely about the food."

I finally look at the guy who's underwhelmed about the party fare and atmosphere. My breath gets trapped in my chest. I know exactly whose daddy this is. This is the head asshole thirty years in the future.

"As this is my first Canyon Falls anniversary party, I have nothing else to compare it to, Mr. Cox."

"I'm sorry. I've talked to so many of you girls this evening, so forgive me if I don't remember your name." He murmurs, "Though I should definitely remember someone as alluring as you."

"Nothing to forgive. This is our first time meeting." I shift my food to my left hand and hold out my right. "Thea LaReaux."

He takes it, but his attention isn't on my hands and manicure. It's aimed lower. He finally drags his eyes up from my exposed leg to my face. It's taking everything in me to keep the booze down.

"Now that I have your name, it and its owner won't be far from my mind."

His comment is above board, but the icky feeling I get says his true thoughts are anything but. His grip tightens when I try to pull my hand from his. Instead of showing fear or disgust, I do the last thing he thinks a woman would do. I hold his gaze and squeeze his hand right back.

Out of the corner of my eye, I see Pax, Finn, and Holden staring at us. I can feel their anger from here. Tomorrow they'll be some new level of drama and I'm sure I'll hear all about how I had the audacity to talk to a parent above my station.

Malcom Cox just stares down at me the way I do my opponents in the ring. He's looking for a sign of weakness. Waiting for me to act like all these other sycophants and probably ask for a job or offer to blow him. "I've heard interesting things about you. Any truth to the rumors?"

His voice is smooth now, as if my question has opened the door to us flirting. "Depends on what you've heard."

His grip loosens, and he strokes a thumb along the back of my hand. I barely contain my snort. He's delusional if he thinks he's charming my panties off. "Oh, the usual stuff. Your family is a bit of a legend around here. Powerful friends. Owns a lot of businesses. Donates to the school." I say as if it's inconsequential. Because to me, it is.

"You don't sound impressed to be in my presence."

"That's because I'm not."

He loses the jovial smile. "You're not? Might I ask why?"

I shrug. "Unless you've found some way to cure cancer or hangovers or even how to put your pants on two legs at a time, you're just the same as everyone else, except for the extra dollars in your bank account."

I can see he doesn't like the idea that I think he's a basic dick. Like father, like son.

The mayor approaches before he can say anything else. I pull my hand away and dart to the other side of the room to eat my food.

I talk to a few more people who drift by and have another drink, but I keep Daddy Cox in my sights.

Something tells me if he corners me again, our conversation won't be as friendly.

Chapter 61
Thea

I need a break. I've smiled and talked and danced with Austin and his friends, while enduring the whispers and scathing looks from Eloise, her friends and their parents. Now, I'm tapped out.

LJ noticed I'm running on fumes, seconds away from relinquishing the grip on my tongue, so she sent me to get some air. I didn't want to wander around outside her house alone, so I'm wandering around the inside of her house.

I've finally found the room she suggested I use to decompress. As soon as the door closes behind me, some of the pressure in my chest deflates.

I love a good party, but constantly having to answer who I am and where my parents are is wearing on me.

I don't care if people know I grew up in foster care, but the pitying looks I get and the way the women gripped their purses and their husbands tighter grates my nerves. I don't want their diamonds or their old ass men.

I'm standing by the window overlooking the Dahlia garden when the door opens. I turn and see Finn coming into the room. "Naughty, naughty, Pet. Are you snooping through the Breland's home?"

I don't need any new rumors getting started about how I was casing the joint. "I'm taking a break from all the fancy, fancy. LJ told me to use this room."

He reaches up to loosen his tie as he approaches me. "We're hiding out then? I don't blame you. That dress *has* been causing a lot of problems tonight," he says in that voice he uses when he's reciting poetry.

"With who?" I ask, moving over to the bookshelf to read the titles. He steps behind me, his hands latch onto my hips, before sliding under the slit of my dress and resting on my thigh.

"You know, I'm supposed to be out there mingling with my friends, networking for the frat, being a model guest, but all I keep thinking about is how I want to peel this dress off of you and find out if..."

He hisses as his hands drift higher, stopping along the leather pouch strapped to my inner thigh.

"That's so fucking hot." He groans, stroking his fingers over the handle of my blade.

I don't know if I'll ever get used to the idea of a guy thinking me being strapped is hot. I press back against him and find he's hard. How many weeks have we done this dance? Teasing and taunting, and all it's done is give me the worst case of blue bean.

Even now, my clit is throbbing. The way he's stroking the knife and cooing in my ear about the length of my blade is a little unhinged. Yet, I'm a girl who can appreciate his reverence for steel.

He grinds his erection against my ass in slow, lazy circles. His hand moving higher. I part my legs, just in case he wants to be a good boy and touch my clit. The alcohol has me buzzed and the heat in my belly needs somewhere to go.

"You want this?" he rasps against my ear.

"Do you?"

"Oh, Pet. I think we both know that all the games we've been playing have led to this. I knew the inevitability of it from the first moment we met. I'm just glad I get to have you to myself before the other two figure it out too."

Before I can ask him to explain, he pulls me away from the bookshelf, his hands on my waist, as he pushes me towards the middle of the room. My thighs hit the pool table. He places his hand between my shoulder blades and pushes me forward until I'm leaning across it. I feel the cold brush of metal against my thigh, and my heart rate kicks up for another reason. "If you cut me, I'll cut you right back."

"God, yes." He rocks against me and shoves my knife into my hand.

I glance over my shoulder. The look on his face says he's fucking serious. "We've teased this before, Finn. We've even shared some accidental nicks, but are you saying you actually *want* me to cut you?"

He catches his bottom lip between his teeth and nods. That's crazy. Right? That he wants me to actually cut into his flesh. I turn all the way around so I can get a clearer picture of what he's saying.

He steps back, cocking his head to the side. The pose is causal, like he's unbothered about what I'm thinking. But I look closer, and see that there's something else under the surface. He wants to do this, but he's nervous about what *I'm* thinking.

I guess I want this too. Or rather, I want his dick in my vag, so if this is what's gonna get us there, I'm down. "No massive blood loss, nothing that'll leave a scar. Just enough pressure so you feel it."

His face lights up as if it's Christmas and his birthday all rolled into one. He kisses me, pushing that happiness into me, and rubs his cock against me. I spread my legs wider and grab his ass, directing his movements towards my needy clit. *Please don't flake out, please don't fake out.*

Finn slips his hand between us, stroking me through the damp sliver of material covering my pussy. With his other hand, he unhooks the clasp holding my dress up, letting the material fall to my hips, and leans forward, latching onto my nipple. I rock against his hand, desperate for more. *Finally.* It should not have been this damn hard to get laid.

"Number Three, please tell me you have a condom."

He steps back, shrugs out of his suit jacket and vest and unbuttons his shirt, before pulling one out of his pocket. Then shoves his pants down his legs. Half dressed in this suit, with the pants pooling around his knees. *Yes, please.*

Once he gets it rolled on he looks over at me, his eyes widen at the view. I've hiked my dress up, and opened my legs wider, my second knife on display. It's much smaller than the first, but no less lethal when I need it to be. In response to the look on his face, I say, "Like you don't travel with more than one."

He lifts me under my arms, pushing me further back on the pool table and crawls on it with me.

He starts off slow. His calloused fingers tease my nipples, while he drags his length across my core in unhurried strokes, teasing the nerve endings in my body. It's a slow build. The way the pressure builds in a kettle right before it whistles.

I slip my hands inside his shirt, using my blade as an extension of my hand, running the flat side down his spine, before dragging the tip back up like an extra long fingernail.

That little move. Just the threat of it, snaps something inside him. He climbs to his knees, grips my hips, and slams into me. Somehow, I get his shirt off with one hand. I drag the knife down the front of his chest, twirling the tip in the shallow indentation of his belly button. He drags his swollen cock out to the tip, then surges back in.

He picks up speed, tightening his grip on my thigh. "Please, please, please." He whispers as he moves in and out.

I can hear the strain in his voice. Like he's holding back. I dig the knife a little deeper. Just enough to pinch.

He holds me tighter, the sensuous roll of his hips has the tip of his cock hitting different angles inside me on the up and down stroke.

"I wanna explore every single inch of you. Find out what you like." He says as he pounds into me. I tighten around him, lifting my hips to meet him.

"Fuck, Pet. You feel so damn good."

I can't maintain the grip on my knife, my need to grab onto him, overpowering. I pull his hair, biting and kissing whatever parts of his warm skin I can reach.

I'm close. With one final effort, I pick up my knife again, grip his hair, tugging to the sides, exposing his neck, and hold the edge of the blade to his throat.

With a ragged groan, he whips out his knife. I have no idea where he was hiding that thing. He mimics my position, holding his knife to my throat. The sting sends me over the edge. My legs lock around him as my body twitches from my release.

His hand moves from my throat. There's a dull thud somewhere near my head and then the sound of felt ripping as he buries his face in the spot between my shoulder and neck.

"Oh, fuck, Pet. Fuck. Don't stop squeezing me. Take it all."

I contract my Kegel muscles, milking his cock, until his movements slow. His chest heaves against mine.

When he finally lifts his head, his eyes are clearer than I've ever seen them. I don't wanna sound like a cliche or anything, but my heart misses a beat.

I'm seeing Finn up close and personal and without the shadows on his face or the restlessness in his eyes. Without the mask he wears trying to convince people he's always happy.

Right now, he's just raw and real, and breathtakingly beautiful. "Hi, Number Three. It's nice to finally meet you."

His eyes widen, then his face splits into a wide grin. The kind that makes my vag clench around him.

"Shit, Pet. That feels good and too much, all at the same time." His groan is a combination of pleasure and pain, but that doesn't stop him from rocking against me. I can totally go for round two if he can. He places a soft kiss against the corner of my mouth, then pulls away, leaving me to lie on the table with my dress rucked up over my hips.

I lean up on my elbows to watch him sort out the condom and fix his clothes. His neat, pristine suit was nice. Rumpled after sex, it looks even better.

A smile splays over my lips. "Now that we've gotten that out of the way, what should we do next?"

He comes over to help me up off the table and assists with fixing my dress. He brushes his lips over the back of my neck, sending a fresh wave of tingles and desire to my core, and says, "I have a few ideas."

Finn

Holden is sitting at the table nursing a cup of coffee when I finally emerge from my bedroom. I sink down onto the couch next to him and sip the freshly squeezed orange juice he brought over for me. I love a good cup of fresh squeezed before I start my day.

The Breland anniversary party was full of influential people and I think I've gained some good contacts for me and my friends, but I don't remember much about who I talked to or what I talked about before and after my little tryst with Thea.

Before, I was bored like I often am at those things. After? After, I was trapped in a loop. Remembering her words, and the way her body felt under mine. *"Nice to finally meet you."*

She saw something beyond the surface that most people choose to ignore or pretend doesn't exist. So I've learned to pretend it doesn't exist. That night, I couldn't do it. I didn't want to do it. I expected her to bail when I mentioned wanting to play with my knives. But she rolled with it and wielded that blade like a pro. She even recognized when I needed more and gave me the excitement I crave.

Thea's not the first girl I've flashed my knife at during sex. I always give my partners a heads up when I want to play with my blades.

Sometimes girls say yes, not fully understanding what they've agreed to, just so they can brag and say they've fucked me or hoping it leads to some great romance. I let them think what they want just so I can get what I want.

Knives are always *cool* and *awesome* and *no problem* until I make them a part of foreplay and sex. Every time I've allowed myself to let go, it's ended the same way. With me deep in their cunts, working my way to a nut as they moan and groan underneath me. But when I look in their eyes, I see what they really feel. Fear and revulsion. What I enjoy disgusts them. I'm fun. A man to be wanted and desired. A prize to be had until the blood play starts. Then they can no longer pretend that I'm just a normal guy with a knife obsession.

Even the girls from the South side who hang out at the Parkour gym I frequent, stay strapped, but I doubt they want the pointy end anywhere near them when nipples are dangling around. Thea didn't even flinch, and she wasn't holding back the urge to vomit. Her skin was flushed. Her eyes were bright. She was into it.

Fuck, I came so hard I thought my spine was in danger of snapping. When it was over, my soul felt clearer than it has in weeks. I'm not sure how long it'll last though, but that's usual. I do something to lift the cloud, but then it comes back. It always comes back.

Holden looks up from his book. "Where'd you disappear to Saturday night?"

"When?"

He turns the page. "Between the hours of 8:43pm and 10:18pm."

Leave it to this guy to know the exact time I was missing. "I went to shoot some pool."

He looks up at me, looking through my eyes and into my brain, in that way he has. "Interesting."

That could mean so many things with Holden. "What is?"

"You got laid."

Does it show? Thea and I weren't holding back with each other, but nobody came in the room, and I think we were discreet when we were playing hide and seek.

We took turns hiding and every time Thea found me; she dared me to do something risky. Most of my dares involved her letting me give her pleasure or us taking a drink. She was hammered by the time our game ended and LJ dragged her back to the party.

"That's generally what happens at any party we go to."

He's still assessing me, then nods and buries his head back in his book. I think that's the end of the conversation, but then he says, "You weren't with one of your usual girls."

Damn Holden for his astute observations. He's the hardest person to keep a secret from because he notices everything. "You're not gonna ask me who it was?"

"Don't need to."

"You're not even curious?"

He looks up at me again. His answer tumbles out at the end of a disgruntled sigh. I know he's trying to read, but he's the one who started this line of questioning. "If you need to talk about it, then Pax is probably the best person for you to compare notes with."

"I don't wanna compare notes. We're not reading from the same book." I grumble. Pax is the last person I want to discuss Thea with. With Holden, I know he has an interest in her, even if he hasn't actually acknowledged it yet. Pax will just complain that I should have been working the party instead of working my dick inside Thea's sweet pussy.

I look at the time and get to my feet, heading towards my bathroom.

"Where are you going?" Holden eyes me suspiciously. Probably worried I'm going back to bed.

"To shower before we head to class."

"You're never in a hurry to get to class on Monday unless there's a project due or a test."

He's right, I'm not. But I am today, because I'm excited to see my pet.

Chapter 62
Pax

I try to avoid coming home as much as possible when school's in session, but my father's message was clear. It was imperative he talk to me, in person, first thing this morning.

Given the nature of our last conversation, I have some idea what it's about. Even though we just saw each other on Saturday, I know the topic isn't one he'd be willing to bring up with so many unaligned families around.

I'm skipping out on breakfast for this meeting. I had just enough time to shower and get here before he needs to leave for the office, or his business trip or whatever he has going on that meant this couldn't wait until later on today.

The door to his study is open. He calls me in before I can even do a courtesy knock. I step inside, waiting for him to invite me to sit. You always wait for an invitation to sit. He waves his hand and I lower myself into the chair.

"Did you make any new contacts at the Breland's?"

"I believe we have some good leads for next year's freshman class, and a few people to liaison with when we're closer to graduation."

"Leads, and liaisons. Anything more concrete than that?"

"The Breland's themselves."

That catches him by surprise. "They're still relatively new to the area, and have never expressed an interest in doing business with us before."

"The wife, she shared that she's interested in being more involved with various charities around town. Right now, she's only able to write checks and wants to assist with coordinating a few functions in the upcoming season."

There were plenty of lunch plans being made around the party that her daughter was excluded from. It's a glaring reality that they're disconnected from the powerful players in town.

Money can only get you so far. Alliances are important. We're all happy to eat their food, drink their booze, and use the opportunity to make deals for ourselves, but nobody was really there to celebrate the Breland's. Unless you count Thea and Austin who didn't care about working the room.

That doesn't mean they lacked attention. Thea's dress caught all kinds of interest. More than once, I had to nudge a person's attention back to the conversation we were having. And Finn couldn't stop staring at her, no matter where she was in the room. I thought I was gonna have to drag him away when they started dancing. He's fixated on this girl.

"Excellent news about the Brelands. I'll pass it along to the council." He unlocks his desk drawer and puts the folder he was looking at into it. "Now, for the reason, I asked you here." He shuts the drawer and leans back in his chair. "The LaReaux girl. She's a mouthy piece of ass."

I saw him talking to her at the party. She obviously said something disrespectful to him. "She definitely lacks manners."

He makes a derisive sound. "That doesn't seem to stop the interest she was getting from a lot of people. The council noticed Finn was one of those individuals. Shocking, since his life match was in attendance that evening. In fact, he seemed quite distant with Eloise." He arches a brow, "There were some complaints lodged about his behavior. I haven't logged them in yet. I wanted to speak to you first."

There it goes. I should have known Finn's actions wouldn't go unnoticed. "It's nothing."

"I want to believe that. Finley is an outstanding prospect. His ability to get people talking is a skill we admire. He's going to do great things for The League." My father leans forward, resting his elbows on his desk. "We can't afford to have him distracted by this disrespectful ingrate. Does he know what we suspect about her?"

I had to come clean once I mentioned putting the tracker on her phone. Sharing the news with them alleviated some of the weight I was feeling. I hated keeping it a secret. "He does."

"And he's still sniffing around her? That doesn't sound like someone loyal to our cause."

"As I said, it's nothing. We decided Finn's ability to learn secrets was invaluable in finding out more about her. He's pretending to like her, to get close."

"Eloise insinuated it was more than that. That there've been a few altercations because of his involvement with the girl."

"Finn's a Trium. You name me one girl, one woman in town, who hasn't at least thought of going after one of us. Eloise always has competition in that area. The two of them often use other people to make the other jealous."

"You're saying she's lying about the situation?"

"Not at all. She and Thea have a contentious relationship. Part of it is Eloise thinks there's an interest on Finn's part, because we haven't told her he's doing a job." I let the statement hang in the air. Daring him to tell me I'm wrong for not looping her in.

"Of course. Eloise isn't privy to that information. But you said that's a part of it. What's the other part?"

"Eloise was tasked with helping to teach Theona some manners, under the guise of initiating her as a Zeta Nu."

"Smart move."

"Unfortunately, Thea isn't a social creature. Given the way she grew up, it's not surprising that she doesn't play well with others. She reacted badly after her chastity vow ceremony and trashed the Zeta Nu house." I leave out the part where she struck Eloise. If she hasn't told anyone about that, I won't either. "And if I understand correctly, her parting act as a pledge was to put Eloise's status at the house to a vote."

"Ah. I see." He jabs his finger into the desk. "I knew there had to be a more reasonable explanation. Eloise failed to disclose that detail. Did the officers agrees to the vote?"

"They did. And she's re-qualifying."

"Mouthy bitch, disruptive bitch." He works his jaw and exhales sharply. "I can see Eloise wanting to spin this into something it's not. Technically, her entire relationship with Finn could be called into question if she loses her position at Zeta Nu. I thank you for clearing this up for me."

"Will we get a copy of the complaint?"

He waves me off. "I'm not taking this to the council. There's clearly nothing there. We don't get involved in house politics. The by-laws allow any member to be challenged and required to requalify for their spot in the sorority. The LaReaux girl is one of the few people to read the rule book."

"I'm sure she fixated on that part just to create dissension in the house."

"I've only spoken to her for a few minutes, but that is the same conclusion I have." He stands and gathers his keys and wallet off the desk. "Have you made any progress on the other matter?"

"I made the inquiries. I should have a more comprehensive file in a few days."

"I trust you were discreet with the resources you used?"

"Yes, sir."

He walks to the door and holds it open, waiting for me to stand. "Excellent. I'll be out of town for the next few days. Update me as soon as you get something."

"Will do, sir."

He flicks off the light, plunging me into darkness. It's a pretty accurate depiction of how I've felt lately about my relationship with my father. The further along I go in the selection process, the more I realize our relationship is hidden by layers of darkness and shrouded in secrecy.

Chapter 63
Thea

I spent all day on the couch yesterday, nursing a massive hangover. I was already at my drink limit, but then Finn wanted to play.

I couldn't say no to the chance to do something other than stand around and watch other people standing around, so of course I said yes. Who doesn't like hide and seek? I just wish we could have had more people involved.

Maybe I can convince LJ, Austin and some of his buddies to agree to a campus wide hide and seek game.

Fun time plotting has to wait. I'm still trying to piece together everything that happened Saturday night, and make sure I didn't black out at some point. I can think straight now that I'm less dehydrated than I was yesterday.

My brain speeds through the boring parts of the night, recapping all the highlights. It's a short reel. Me and LJ laughing whenever she got a break from her parents. Talking football with Austin. Playing a sexy version of Clue. The killer of my pussy was Finn, in the library, with the knife on the pool table. And then our game of hide and seek game, which included drinking and several more orgasms, when he decided to reward me for being such a good hider.

Looks like all the memories are there. Now I just need to find some energy to go do what I have planned for today. My afternoon classes are canceled, so rather than hang out on campus, I'm finally going to grab some of my stuff from Scott and Moira's.

I stop for a coffee on my way. The caffeine gives me a boost and I'm feeling less zombified when I get to the house. Cora answers the door with a smile that I'm happy to return. "Good Morning, Miss Thea."

"How's it going?"

"Great. Just going over the grocery list for this week. Mrs. Hughes didn't mention you were coming today."

"I had some free time and wanted to go through my stuff from storage. Get an idea of what I have left."

"Oh. Of course. Is there anything in particular you want for dinner this week? Or snacks for school? I'd be happy to add them to my list."

"You're amazing. Can I get those biscuit things we had with the lamb? They would be great for breakfast on the go."

"Of course."

I reach into my back pocket. "How much?"

"Oh, stop. You know I can't take your money." That doesn't stop me from trying to give it to her whenever she adds stuff for me to her list.

"The room with your things is in the alcove just under the stairs. It should already be unlocked."

"Thanks, Cora."

There are two rooms in the alcove which lead to the previously mentioned off limits wing. I turn the knob for the first door. It swings right open, just like Cora said it would. I step inside and roll up my sleeves, ready to get to work.

I've gone through three boxes and I'm starting to think I might be in the wrong room. These boxes are full of high school pictures and trophies for Scott.

I heft the box I just opened into my arms to put it back where I got it from. They're stacked at odd angles, as if someone was in here going through them and couldn't be bothered to straighten them up.

I grab one more box to be sure. The bottom falls out; the contents spilling onto the floor. I re-tuck the flaps at the bottom and drop down onto the floor to pick the stuff up. This one is full of photo albums. I flip through them to get a look at Scott as a kid. A small part of me is hoping I find a picture of my mom, since the only one I had of her is gone.

Unlike the first two boxes, this one has pictures of a girl in it. It's clearly Moira. I stare at the photo, trying to figure out why she looks different, until I see her eyes. Moira has brown eyes, but in this photo they're blue. I guess she went through a colored contact lens phase.

The second album has more pictures of Moira and a few of Scott. The third album is wrapped in tissue paper. I carefully unwrap it, my fingers gliding over the embossed cover. I only make it as far as the second page. My hand is stalls on a picture of Moria. Pregnant. The photo right below it is of her and Scott. He's affectionately cradling her bump.

There are more pictures on the next few pages. Then I come to the last two sleeves that have something in them. There are three documents. A hospital issued birth certificate for baby girl Anotèa Hughes, with inked footprints. It lists Moira and Scott as the parents.

The two documents on the last page are a birth and death certificate for a baby boy Theo born to Hailee Laurent.

The birth certificates are dated within a week of each other. The year after I was born. None of this makes any sense.

My mother's last name is LaReaux, and we lived in Louisiana after I was born, not in Greece, and she definitely wasn't pregnant while I was still a baby. I stand, knocking an envelope over. Pictures tumble onto the floor. The bottom of my stomach drops out as I stare at them. There are dozens of photos of me as a baby.

"Thea, Cora told me..."

I look up to see the shock on Moira's face. I'm furious. They said they didn't know about me. But these are pictures of me and my mom up until I was three. "What is this?" My voice shakes, my mind swirling with the lies I was told. "What the hell is any of this?"

"It's-"

"Been a lie! All this time, bringing me here was based on a lie? Am I a replacement?"

"A replacement? What? Thea, no!"

"Then what the hell is this?" I wave at the photo album.

"Thea. Those documents are fakes."

"Some kind of scam? Do the two of you pretend to be pregnant and then sell babies in an elaborate adoption ring under fake identities, or something? Because my mother's last name isn't Laurent, and I sure as shit don't have a brother."

Scott steps into the room behind her and bellows. "We're not criminals, Theona!"

"Fake birth certificates, fake death certificates. Or maybe not. If these aren't real, then where's your baby, Moira? Because you looked awfully pregnant in those photos. If they're not photoshopped, where's the kid?"

Moira cries, "Oh god, not like this. You weren't supposed to find out like this. I needed more time." She falls into Scott's arms.

I glare at him, daring him to chastise me for making his delicate little wife cry. I'm not sorry. I want some answers before I leave this house of horrors behind.

"Answer me one question. How did you get pictures of me if you didn't know where I was?"

Scott sighs before answering. "I knew where you were up until the time you left Louisiana."

I snatch an envelope off the floor, replaying his words. He knew where I was until we left Louisiana.

He knew where we were, until I was three. A horrible thought crosses my mind. "Shit. Did you? Are you..." I can't even form the words, but it's possible. Right? I mean, people are assaulted by family members all the time, and the checks would make sense if he was trying to buy her silence. "Did you... are you my father?"

"Yes."

I'm gonna be sick. "What kind of fucking monster are you? You raped her?" It makes sense. At first it was a game. We moved to experience new places and cultures. But after the car accident, mom started saying people were after her.

"God, no, Thea. I never attacked Hailee."

I hold up my hand. "If you say your cousin wanted to have sex with you, I'll gut you where you stand."

He pales. "It's not what you think. It's not like that. Hailee and I aren't actually related. She's..." He looks at Moira. "Everything's complicated. If you'll just come down to the living room, we can explain it."

"I'm fine with hearing the rest of the lies you plan to tell me right here. So if you're not related to my mother but you are my father, what does that mean? That you got her pregnant in secret? Because so far all the stories you've told me say you and Moira were together when she was in college."

Another possibility occurs to me. "Did you have an affair with my mother?" I look at Moira. "Did you threaten her when she wouldn't take a payoff?"

"It wasn't like that."

"No? Then were you trying to gain custody of me and she couldn't afford to fight you in court, so she hid me away? I guess you finally got your wish, but I'm almost twenty, so you're late on that end."

"Actually, Thea. You're just eighteen, and nobody was fighting for custody. Moira and I let Hailee take you away."

"Let her? It's not like you could forbid it!"

They share a look, and when I look at Moira again, I'm struck by the color of her eyes. My voice sounds small when I ask, "You're wearing contacts?"

Her hand flies to her face, and my mind goes back over details I ignored when I got here. Her fussing about mom not sticking to the plan, the comment about my bedroom, and LJ saying the library nook looks like a nursery. I stare at Moira's blue eyes, startlingly similar to mine, and ask the question that nobody answered, earlier. "Moira, where's your baby?"

She takes a step toward me, tears running down her cheeks. "I'm looking at her."

"No. No." I shake my head. "No." This can't be happening. How the fuck is this happening?

"Yes, Thea. We're your parents."

It makes no sense, and yet it does. Because that's just how fucked my life has been up to this point. "If that's true, then how did I wind up with mom?"

Moira wrings her hands. "We asked her to take you away. And she agreed, because she's my sister."

Her sister. Moira's. "You're telling me my whole life, everything I knew, everything I went through, was built on a lie? I've had no one for years, because you gave me away to your *sister,* and then you brought me here and still perpetuated the lie!"

"We did what we thought was best for you. You have to understand, we never intended for you to grow up the way you did. We were trying to protect you."

"Newsflash, *Aunt* Moira. You failed."

I run through the house and out the back door, taking the steps down to the beach. I don't know where I'm going. I just need to get away from here.

Chapter 64
Holden

I close my eyes and take a deep breath, letting the soft hum from my computers wash over me.

The search I'm conducting has been running for two weeks. I finally got a hit on it, and I know whatever results came back will either be garbage or life changing.

I unlock my computer and go through the process of searching through the syntax code until I see what I'm looking for.

Three possible matches returned. The first is hospital records from a town in Greece. It's looking like it's a garbage result, but my brain won't let me ignore it. I have to review everything. I click on the file.

I've seen a lot of documents from different places all over the world. There's no mistaking the one page medical record I'm looking at.

I don't speak Greek, so I run it through a translation program. When the words reconstitute it says Moira was admitted for removal of a fibrous cyst.

I pull up the second link. It's a flight manifest for a private jet, with two passengers flying from Greece to New York. The passengers are listed as Hailee and Moira. It's dated the day after the note in the medical records.

I'm no doctor, but I imagine it's not likely that Moira was on an eleven hour flight after having a cyst removed from her uterus. And why was Thea's mother in Greece when she had a one-year-old at home? Was this before Thea's dad took off?

I scan the medical records one more time to make sure the dates are the same. Maybe there was a planned flight, and they had to cancel because of Moira's operation. I click the last document and wish I hadn't.

The record of live birth changes everything. No wonder we couldn't find anything about Thea's family; the history she's concocted is complete bullshit. But this birth certificate I'm looking at, I'm sure it's real.

This has to be the most elaborate scheme I've ever seen. Moira and Scott had a child, but there's no record of it anywhere. Hailee LaReaux's name is on a birth certificate for Theona LaReaux, but there are no hospital records of her ever giving birth in any of the places Thea supposedly lived. If I were planning to infiltrate The League. This is how I'd do it.

The question is, are the Hughes's in on it, or were they the original victims of whatever the hell is going on here? And where is Thea's mother? The part where she fell off the face of the earth, that part's real. I send Pax and Finn a text. Neither of them waste time coming over. I've just finished printing the birth certificate when they come through the door.

"You've got something?"

I hand off the printout, too furious to speak. She's been playing us. Playing Finn this whole time. Likely targeting us just to tear us down and make us look like fools. I know better than to let my guard down around poisonous women.

For weeks now, I've been going into her room. Working up the nerve to finally let her know what I want, and none of it is real. It can never be real.

Finn looks at the document and says, "I don't know what you guys think this means."

Pax answers, a satisfied smirk on his face. "It means your little pet has been lying to us from the start. Just like I said she was."

Finn frowns. "Because she changed her name and pretended to be older than she is?"

"Read it again." Pax urges, knowing Finn only skimmed the document.

"Wait. Why does this list Scott and Moira as the parents?" He looks up at me. "Where did you get this?"

"Dark web." Which is why I wasn't expecting to get any decent search results. Why would a pair of snowflakes like Moira and Scott Hughes have documents buried so deep we can only find them on the dark net?

"Holy shit." He gives me a look. Almost pleading. "She didn't do this herself. Right?"

Pax answers before I get the chance. "She avoids any conversations about her past. Spends a fuck ton of time exploring the town and has a knack for showing up where she shouldn't be. That's all suspect on its own. Together, it paints a pretty clear story. She's definitely here to cause trouble and pick apart the next generation of league members."

"But she hasn't done any of that. Like you said, she keeps to herself."

"Think about it, Finn. How many unaligned families were at the Breland's? How many of those sons hung out with Austin and Thea? And if she would've got you on the hook, how many legacies would have followed? Starting with Eloise and her lackeys?"

"I would never choose anyone over us."

"That's not how it looked to some of the council members at the party. They noticed the attention you were giving Thea."

He scrubs his hand through his hair. "There's no way they can question me or my loyalty. I've never given them a reason to."

"I agree. And that's what I told my father. That your time with her was in line with our plans. And now that we have the information we need, none of us will ever have to see or deal with her again."

It's hard to miss the glee in Pax's voice. "What are you saying, Pax?"

"I'm saying, Theona LaReaux's time living in my tower, on my floor and walking around my school like she belongs here has come to an end. We're gonna expose her and send her back to wherever she came from."

He smiles. "As a bonus, the league will know that we're the ones who protected our brothers from whatever she had planned." His eyes bounce between me and Finn. "No one gets away with trying to make fools of The Trium."

I wish I had more time to sit with the facts, but Pax is right. If she's here to cause a rift in The League, we have to stop her now, before the end of pledge season, when the initiates who don't get selected will be more willing to join a revolt.

Hasn't she already sewn discord at Zeta Nu? And with Austin on her side, it's only a matter of time before she pulls in the jocks.

"What's the play here?" Finn asks, finally over whatever moment of disbelief he was wrestling with.

"It's simple, really. First, we let her know we're on to her. Second, she's no longer under our protection. She'll soon realize that without access to us, through you, there's no way she can move forward with her plans. I'm almost certain she was letting people think you were in on it."

"I wasn't. I was bored and had some fun playing with her, just like I have dozens of times before."

"You fucked her and it's done. Right?"

Finn jerks his head, then walks out the door. Pax says to me, "Time to shut down her accounts and access to the outside world. I want her on a closed loop where we can see and control everything."

"On it."

Chapter 65
Thea

I've never walked across the hall and knocked on Finn's door before, but I'm doing it tonight because I need a distraction. I can't think of a better one than combining booze and dick.

When he opens up the door, I hold up the bottle, giving it a little shake, and push my way inside. "My turn to get you sloppy drunk and have my way with you."

I shove the bottle at him. "Start drinking and stripping."

He takes a sip. A really small one. I tip the bottom of the bottle up, making him take a nice healthy man sized gulp. I snort when he chokes a little, sputtering. A few drops roll down his cheek when he pulls the bottle away.

"What the hell, Thea?"

"What the hell, indeed. That's definitely the question, knife boy." I take back my bottle back and drink as my mind works over that question. It gets stuck in a loop I want no parts of. I force my mind on what I came here for. To forget. He's staring down at me and not in the way he usually does. "You look too serious. You need fun too?" I tap my chest. "I'm your girl." I point at his pants. "Lose those and come over here."

"You need fun, Pet?"

"Yes. And dick." I clarify, not wanting there to be any confusion about why I'm here.

"Mmm. I've got all the dick you need."

I doubt it. He's only got one, but he knows how to work it, and that's all I need right now. I take another swig from the bottle. This time I kiss him, pushing the liquid from my mouth into his. He grips my ass, pulling me close. Our tongues meeting in a vodka drenched kiss. He pulls away, grinding the evidence of his arousal against my center. "This what you want, Pet? My cock in your dripping cunt?"

I slip my hands into his basketball shorts, working my hand up and down his shaft. I tilt my head back, looking up at him through hooded eyes. "You want my dripping cunt around your hard cock?"

He drops his head, pressing his forehead to mine, and slips his hand into my yoga pants, mimicking my actions. "Don't try to turn this around on me. Answer me, Thea. Are you desperate for me?"

I know he can hear the sounds his fingers are making, sliding in and out of my pussy. I'm wet for him. Desperate for a way to forget the shit on my mind. "Yes. Shit." I bite my lip, working myself against his fingers.

"Game time, Pet. One question and you get every inch of me just the way you like it."

"No questions. Just fucking."

"Come on, Pet. You love our games. One question, one truthful answer, and I spend all night making you feel good."

He sinks to his knees, pulling my pants down my legs, and presses them open. They don't move much, the range of motion hindered by the fabric pooled over the top of my sneakers. He slides a finger through my folds again. "You're sloppy wet. I need a closer look." He pulls out his phone, puts it between my legs, and clicks the shutter.

"You better delete that shit as soon as we're done."

He studies the phone screen and says, "I think you dripped a little." With a smile, and that infamous purr of his, he redirects the conversation back to this stupid game he wants to play. "One question. One truthful answer."

I can give that to get orgasms. "One question."

"Shall we do some warmup ones so I can know when you're telling the truth?"

"I'm always truthful."

"You've never lied?"

"Never."

"That's a lie right there. I've never gotten a straight answer out of you."

"Lying and evading aren't the same thing." I reach for him. "You've had your question. Time to let me play with your cock."

"That was a warmup, a causal conversation, Thea."

"Fine. Ask your stupid question. The real one."

"Don't be mad, Pet." He offers me the vodka bottle that I don't remember relinquishing, tipping it over my mouth so I can drink. When he pulls it away, he lowers it between my legs, teasing it against my opening.

"Finn?"

"Mmm?"

"Your question." My pulse is rioting, my core clenching around the bottle, desperately clinging to the feeling of having something inside me. He doesn't answer, working the bottle in and out.

He retracts it. "My question..." He puts the bottle to my mouth. I tip my head back, opening to catch. "Is why the fuck are you here lying about Scott and Moira Hughes?"

I'm shit at controlling the look of surprise on my face.

"That's right. I know. Running around here calling them your aunt and uncle when they're really your parents. Did you really think we wouldn't find out, you duplicitous bitch?"

"It's not like that, I didn't know, I just-"

I don't get to finish what I'm saying. He yanks me forward, shoves the neck of the bottle in my mouth, forcing the liquid down my throat. I try to pull away, but he's holding me by the back of my head to keep me in place. I sputter and gag, trying to swallow the vodka. My stomach roils, ready for it all to come back up. He moves the bottle but clamps his hand over my mouth, forcing me to choke on the combination of alcohol and bile.

"Your time here is done. Your plan here is ruined. I suggest you go back and tell whoever you and the Hughes are working for that they'll never infiltrate The League or cause a rift between The Trium. Get your stupid ass out of my town and school, or the next time I see you, instead of making you choke on this booze or my cock, it'll be your blood blocking your windpipe." He digs the point of his knife into my throat. "You feel me?"

He moves his hand, and before I can recover, he drags me over to his door and pushes me into the hallway, with my pants still down around my ankles. I drag my gaze away from my feet when a door opens behind me. Pax and Holden are standing in their respective doorways, staring at me. The cold, smug look on Pax's face says he knows exactly what happened and is getting off on seeing me in such a humiliated state. When I turn to my room, I see a red X spray painted on the door. "What the fuck is this?"

Pax says, "You've got three days to be out of that room and off this campus."

"Or what?"

"Or you'll find out what really happens to people like you at this school."

"Girl people, or poor people?"

"You're not really poor, are you, Anotèa Hughes?"

"That's not my name."

"Your birth certificate. Your *real* birth certificate says it is. You're already at this school under false pretenses. Nobody else has to know, but if you're still here three days from now, it will become public knowledge. And don't think, for one second, that Finn's gonna jump in and save you. I think he's made it clear how he really feels about you."

He turns to go back into this room. "Three days." He says before the door clicks shut. I make the mistake of looking at Holden. His face is a block of unworked marble. Cold. Detached. Empty. He says his first set of words to me without me speaking first.

"You never should have come here. Be smart, and leave on your own, while you still can."

Chapter 66
Pax

My eyes are burning and I feel a headache coming on. It's because I'm sitting here trying to read this textbook without my glasses. I hate those things, but I need them to read tiny words on a page.

A thud hits the wall behind me. Finn's been tossing his knives all damn day. I know he's working through some shit. He annihilated that girl. It was some of his best work, but he's still gotta deal with the fact that he let her get close enough to be a threat to us. We all have to deal with that. If I would have pushed Holden to find answers, gotten permission for us to dig into the aunt and uncle sooner, we could have avoided the weeks we wasted.

This was an off-the-books mission, so at least we don't have to explain to anyone what took us so long. When my father briefs the league, they'll be singing our praises.

I pick up my phone. Still no response. I texted him days ago to let him know we finally got answers. I know he's on a business trip, and he rarely answers texts from home unless there's an emergency issue only he can deal with. That hardly ever happens. But considering how pressed he was about this, I expected him to take a minute to text back. I'm not expecting a pat on the head or praise, just a simple acknowledgement that he even got my text.

I click over to the group chat.

ME

Dinner?

Finn's response is immediate.

FINN

Not hungry.

Holden's always the voice of reason, says,

HOLDEN

It's not about being hungry. We're days away from Mayhem Night. We have to show.

For six days, we rile the campus up, our pranks putting everyone on edge, and we let loose on Mayhem Night. It'll look bad if we're MIA this close to the end of pledge season. Plus, I want Thea squirming in her seat every time she sees or hears a whisper about us. I want to watch her crumble under the threat that I'll expose her secret to the entire campus.

Many people want to join The League, but they know it's damn near impossible to do so. Still, they pay their dues, and do what's needed, finding ways to make themselves invaluable.

Thea wasn't here to join us; she wanted to tear us apart. Mess with people's families and positions within our world. If the guardians find out, there *will* be an even bigger target on her head..

I make a quick trip to the bathroom to put some drops in my eyes, then snag my key off the table, and head next door to drag Finn out of his room. He's already dressed, sitting on his couch when I walk in.

"I've got a bad feeling, man." He says in greeting.

"You always have a bad feeling leading up to Mayhem Night. We're good. Holden's good, and as long as nobody takes things too far, we have nothing to worry about."

He barks out a dry laugh. "With the shit that happens, how far is too far?"

I smile, glad he's at least in the mood to joke around. "That's the beauty of us making the rules. Anything goes until we say it doesn't."

"True. So true."

"Now, are you ready to go or not?"

"Yeah, man. Let's go to dinner."

Finn has a bad feeling, but all I feel is excitement. We've put the Rho Beta Psi pledges through a lot of shit this year, and our frat is still on top of the leader board, even after giving twenty points to Ironside. Whatever happens this week will close out this cycle of games. Then a new round starts after winter break. We'll tally them all up at the end of the school year to determine who wins the trophy. It's staying right where it is. In Rho Beta Psi's possession.

The noise level in The Rock quiets when we step through the doors. I don't know why people think they have to go silent when we enter this place. We've never demanded anyone stop eating and stare, but it's been like this almost since the beginning. It doesn't bother me, but I know Holden would prefer if they didn't gawk at us. We cut to the front of the line to place our food orders. Finn may have said he wasn't hungry, but he orders fries and a steak burger with the works. Holden orders a poke bowl, sushi, calamari salad and seaweed salad. I opt for a steak, medium well, potatoes and asparagus.

Of course, we don't wait in line or for our food. Nobody says anything. The one person who would isn't in line. She pretends not to notice us when we walk by her table. I reach out and tip her glass over, giving her a warning. "Two days, left."

We've all seen how stubborn she is, but she'd be stupid to be anywhere near here when my countdown ends.

She looks at Finn like she's expecting him to say something. He does, but I'm sure it's not what she wants to hear.

"What's that I hear? Chaos and despair. I listen closely to the tune. Liars around, muzzle the sound. Tick tock, boom, welcome to your impending doom."

Shit, he's more pissed than I thought. When Finn starts rhyming death limericks, that's how you know you're in trouble. All eyes turn to Thea, but nobody is dumb enough to ask what she did while we're standing here. If they've been paying attention, they know it's not just one thing. This girl has had it coming since day one.

Finn leads the way to our table singing, boom, boom, boom. Each word getting louder and louder until he lets out a wolf howl at the end. He's getting into the spirit. This year's Mayhem Night is gonna be the best one yet.

Our food arrives just as we get to our table. Eloise is already here at the middle of the table, but changes seats when Finn sits down.

"I'm so excited about this year's Mayhem Night and what Zeta Nu has planned. What about you, Finney?"

She meets my eyes, a slight shift to her brows. I made her a promise. I have to honor it. "I think we're all excited to see what the sororities came up with for the joint party this year. The two of you are still linking up for the final pranks and party, right?"

"Of course." Eloise beams up at Finn, waiting for him to answer.

Someone across the table says, "I can't imagine having to go through the chastity vow all over again." That little jab is a reminder to Eloise that she has to remain celibate until spring break.

"It sucks, but it's totally worth it, for Finn to be my first again."

Finn drags her closer and kisses her the way he used to when they first got together. I'm shocked and slightly weirded out about it. I've seen Finn kiss girls before. Seen him fuck them too, but I've never been turned on by Eloise that way.

Even the times we've all been in a room together, I could never bring myself to watch or try to join in. That's how it's been with girls we've shared, too. One of us usually drifts off to the side because we're not into it.

Eloise puts her hand on Finn's chest, breaking their kiss. "What are you doing?" He reaches for her and she shifts away, putting space between them. The smile she gives him doesn't reach her eyes. "Save some for later, babe. We don't need an audience."

"The fuck I care about an audience? Come back over here and work my dick."

"Finn, that's an inappropriate request around our friends."

His jaw clenches. He's unhappy about being chastised like a kid. This is what I was talking about. She needs to loosen up. She knows Finn's not opposed to a little PDA.

He likes being the center of attention and his love language is touch. He made Holden and me take the quiz and learn all about that shit. From what I got out of it, it means if he wants you rubbing his dick in the middle of The Rock; you need to do it or he feels like he's being rejected. Rejected Finn, angry Finn, sad Finn. Dealing with those three emotions always ends in the same way. She's about to wind up in a heap on the floor and he's gonna go find someone else to play with.

I did my part. She's the one about to fuck it up. "Chill out Eloise. Nobody cares if you and Finn suck face at the table. If anyone is saying anything, it's because they're jealous of you. Nobody else has a Trium."

That calms her down a little. She sweeps her gaze around the table and across this side of the dining hall. There are people watching. The looks of envy are obvious. She scoots back over to Finn, kissing him on the cheek.

"I'm sorry I overreacted, babe. It's this vow. That damn bitch really fucked me over voting to have me redo my pledge season. You know I can't resist you, but I have to be strong. I can't fail at any of my challenges." She kisses the corner of his mouth.

He scoops a fry into his mouth, the harsh lines on his face easing, as he asks someone at the table about a video game. I feel someone's eyes on me.

When I look across the room, I see Thea staring at us. I guess she caught the little display with Finn and Eloise. Good. I hope it's sinking in. She's nothing to Finn. She never was.

A guy carrying a large poster board stops right next to Thea's table. I hear him say, "Thank you."

"Excuse me?"

"I said thanks. For the food."

"What food?"

"I got an alert that said the Drop out Pledge of Zeta Nu paid for my dinner." He holds out his phone to show her the message. Other phones start pinging, as every person in the dining hall gets an alert that tonight's dinner's been comped by the dropout pledge from Zeta Nu. Thea's now a nobody. Non existent. Not even worth having her name used. So from now until the day she leaves, she will only be referred to as The Dropout Pledge.

She looks at me, knowing I had something to do with her generosity. I gave her three days. I never said they'd be easy or that I would leave her alone. I hope she's stashed away whatever money she's earned for agreeing to come here to fuck with us, because we're about to bleed every one of her accounts we find, dry.

Chapter 67
Thea

I stumble a little, coming down the side of a hill. I hope I'm heading in the right direction to get back to campus. With everything going through my mind, I lost track of time on my hike and got turned around a few times. I thought the fresh air and walk would help. It didn't. How has my entire life been one big lie?

I've been dealing with abandonment issues for years, so it shouldn't bother me. But it does. I've just found out I'm not wanted all over again. Moira and Scott bringing me here doesn't matter. They did so under false pretenses. I don't think they ever planned to tell me the truth, and were perfectly happy to let me think they're my aunt and uncle.

They even lied about their relationship with my mother. I never questioned the adopted cousin-sister story, because family is what you make of it. I've had plenty of "siblings", growing up in foster care, and Sasha is the sister I would never turn my back on. We have love between us. If she needed me, I'd be there for her no matter what. So when they gave me that elaborate backstory, I believed it. I accepted it. Lies. *All lies.*

How could Moira dress me up and give me her car and not say a word? Well, fuck her. I didn't need her to be my mother before. I damn sure don't want or need it now.

I cross the road, picking my way through the overgrown grass. If my calculations are correct, three quarters of a mile along this route is the property that borders the ice cream factory. I make a mark on my map. I think I'm close to finding the hiking trail that leads all the way to the Hollywood sign.

My feet ache. Earlier, I was stomping and kicking up dirt and rocks as I walked out my anger. The grass gets lower. It's freshly cut. Up ahead are the gates to the cemetery behind campus. The gates are usually closed, but tonight, they're open. I walk through them, ready to make another mark on my map. It's like a maze in here. I carefully pick my way around the headstones. If I had someone who was interned here, I'd probably have a better idea of where I'm going.

Instead, I use my instincts, and keep walking in the direction where I think the back side of the campus is located. I clear the side of a five-foot cross and come to a stop.

The middle of the cemetery is lit up like a Christmas tree, the smell of burning wood hangs in the air. Ahead of me, a robed figure weaves around the plots, carrying a torch. I keep to the shadows, following at a safe distance, to see what kind of stupid fuckery is going on.

Every time the sun goes down, one of these frat boys is vandalizing or stealing something. To have all that money and still not want to pay for shit. Amazing.

The robed figure is heading deeper into the maze of gravestones. I glance down at the dates on the headstones as I walk by. They're rundown, unkept. I guess the families of those buried on this side have long since died off or moved away. I duck behind a tree when he walks behind a mausoleum. Then hurry to the tree directly across from it to get a better look.

I blink twice to make sure my eyes have fully adjusted to the dark. From where I'm hiding, I can make out a group of girls. They're blindfolded, standing in a circle, with people standing behind wearing masks and robes similar to the guy I followed. The mausoleum they're standing behind has structural damage. The front door and back wall are missing, and the roof's collapsed inward. There's a slab of cement in the middle of the floor. On it, a girl lays bound to four fence posts, staked into the ground around all four corners of the stone.

The mask of the person standing at the foot of the stone is a different color than everyone else's, but it's no less creepy. This is clearly the end of whatever ritual they're doing because the guy sounds like he's winding up his speech.

"Do you accept us without reservation? Do you vow to be loyal and obedient? Do you accept this fate?"

Those words are just another variation of what I heard at my chastity vow ceremony. But this is not a Zeta Nu thing. Those prissy bitches wouldn't be caught dead in robes that color. I roll my eyes at the absurdity of it all. They're trying to be all mysterious and shit. After this, they'll just go off to a party, congratulating her on joining whatever weird club they belong to. My guess is it's some kind of gothic thing.

The rest of the people in masks chant in time to the music that's playing. The song and chants reach a crescendo, then stop, plunging the cemetery into absolute silence. Someone from the back of the circle steps forward as a new song begins. This one has a steady drumbeat. It's more basic. More primal than the one before. He drops his cloak, revealing he's naked underneath, and climbs on top of the altar with her. I watch from the shadows as my brain flicks from confusion to understanding. My throat goes dry as he settles between her legs, then drives into her with everyone watching.

Does every club incorporate sex play in their rituals? I guess I should be glad the Zeta Nus encourage you to abstain for as long as you can, because saying no doesn't seem to be the point of this ceremony.

The forceful snap of his hips pushes her against the rough

cement. She'll be walking away with tons of scrapes and bruises, as evidence of this night.

I should be off somewhere getting fucked. But I wasted my time on someone unworthy of it. I was stupid to think that after Finn and I hooked up, we could come to some sort of arrangement. He did exactly what Pax said he'd do. Flaked as soon as we went there.

It doesn't hurt my feelings. It's whatever, but he could've just come right out and said he wanted to fuck, weeks ago, and saved all the games and flirting. Kicking me out of his place with my pants down isn't even the worse thing he did. I had a sweatshirt on. Holden and Finn couldn't see shit, but even if they did, so what? I've gone streaking and skinny dipping plenty of times.

What I'm pissed about is Finn accusing me of lying about my past, and never giving me the chance to talk. I don't owe him my life story, but I've never lied about anything. I omit details or I don't talk at all. That's how you survive in Nags Creek. You don't voluntarily tell anyone shit and if asked a direct question; you don't know shit. That way, you can't get caught in a lie or in the middle of a dispute you really know nothing about. In this instance, even if I wanted to talk about it, I couldn't, because I didn't know Moira and Scott weren't who I thought they were.

Fuck! When did my life become a story arc from a soap opera? Young girl grows up on the wrong side of the tracks, comes to town and finds out she's connected to an established family. The only thing missing was me falling into a star crossed love affair with the cocky rich son of the rival family.

The guy moans, pulling my thoughts from my fucked up reality and back to the action happening in front of me. I feel like a complete perv for watching. But I'm unable to look away from the flex of his hips, the width of his back. More cloaks drop to the ground or fall open, exposing a sea of flesh as the rest of the group moves closer, kissing and sucking each other's body parts.

My gaze flicks back to the center. The guy finishes and another takes his place. I'm looking at the girl on the altar. She hasn't spoken.

Is she even conscious? Her head turns answering that question. Her back arches meeting the new guy's thrusts. He's finished faster than the last guy, and then a third enters her. What the fuck is going on here? And yeah, I'm hating a little cause whatever it is, she's living my dream of having a multi-dick life.

I look down at my phone as it buzzes in my hand and immediately dismiss the text from Moira. I don't have shit to say to her. My eyes snag on the date before I can re-lock my screen. I swipe open my calendar. It's Mayhem Night? I look back over at the scene in front of me. What I'm seeing makes even less sense. I thought this was a major prank night. I guess those are the lies being told, so nobody finds out that *this* is what all the frats and sororities are doing. Having one big outdoor orgy. Thank god LJ and I dropped out of pledge season.

I've seen enough. I slink back into the safety of the trees and hurry back towards the main part of the cemetery. Someone steps in front of me just as I reach the turnoff towards the woods that I'm pretty sure leads to campus.

He's dressed just like the guys in the orgy circle. I can't tell who he is, but from the set of his shoulders, his feet and the tension radiating off of him, I *can* tell I'm in trouble for breaking the rules. Don't come outside during Mayhem Night. I saw the posters, trashed the posters, and deleted the messages from the school administration and campus police. Someone moans, drawing his attention to the action behind me. I take advantage of the distraction and run.

Turns out that's the worst thing for me to do. He yells, alerting everyone to my presence, and an answering cheer follows. The next sounds I hear are the heavy footsteps of him behind me.

I'm running through the trees as fast as I can, but with those long ass legs, he has no problem catching up to me. He laughs, a dark and menacing sound that causes my flesh to break out in goose bumps. I throw on another burst of speed, pushing myself to run faster than I ever have.

The path ahead of me splits. I dart left at the last second, but he doesn't fall for it. He catches me, grabbing me from behind, effortlessly lifting me off my feet. I twist and squirm. His hold on me tightens as I struggle to break free.

He's panting against my ear. I'm glad he had to work to catch me. His menacing growl says, "Here's what's gonna happen. We're gonna play a little game. You like games, don't you?"

He sets me on my feet but maintains his hold on my hip, to keep me in place. "Fighting won't change your fate. I need you to understand from the beginning that you will be punished for being out here. A punishment that includes pain, and whatever else the people lurking in these woods decide to do to you. But I'm willing to give you a chance to save yourself. When I let you go, you run. Run as fast as you can, back to the safety of your dorm. If you make it, I'll forget all about you being out here snooping, but if I catch you..."

I wait for him to finish. My back stiffens when he drags his tongue across my face. "If I catch you, I'll claim my reward, and I won't stop until I've hollowed you out. Eviscerating your soul until there's nothing left but a desolate feeling of emptiness and despair. Do you understand what I'm saying?"

I don't answer. I'm not afraid of him or his macho posturing. Seriously, what can he really do to me? He yanks my hair, tugging my head to the side. "If I win, I'm going to fuck you hard. In every single hole. You'll scream and bleed and I'll bathe in your tears, your fears, and your pain."

I gasp at the image of brutality that conveys. "Does that disgust you, Rey? To hear that I'm going to split you wide open? Guess what? I don't give a shit how you feel about it. I'm gonna hold you down and make your lying lips scream for me to stop. But I won't. I'll keep going until you feel so violated you'll never look at me the same again."

Look at him the same? With this creepy ass mask on, I don't even know who it is. As if reading my thoughts he says, "Don't worry little liar. When I'm inside you, I'll tell you exactly who I am."

He's delusional. Or drunk or high. Maybe a bit of all three. "Whatever you think you're about to do, it's never gonna happen.

Some girls might fall for this Halloween vibe you've got going on, and fall down with their legs open, but I won't. Your putrid dick isn't getting anywhere near me." His hand clenches in a fist. "Awe, does that give you the sads, knowing I'll gut you if you try anything?"

He drags his nose through my hair. "It makes me feel so good, Rey. Tonight, I want you to fight. To draw blood. To make it hard. Because when I finally overpower you and take what I want, it'll be that more satisfying."

What the hell is he on?

"Since you're new to this game, I'll give you a two-minute head start. If you have any sense of self preservation," He grabs my face and squeezes. "You'll run."

He releases me with a shove and steps back, folding his arms across his chest, then starts counting, "One Mississippi, two Mississippi, three Mississippi."

Chapter 68
Thea

I'm a fighter. I have no problem defending myself, but with the number of people out here, and the threat from this guy bouncing around in my head, I decide the best defense I have is to run.

So, I do. I know more than two minutes have passed, but I don't slow down to look behind me. He's coming. I can hear him. My breath comes in heavy pants, my chest is on fire. Coach might need to add a lot more running to my cardio plan. The pace I run for the ten minutes he makes me do on the treadmill isn't shit compared to this full out sprint.

The footsteps behind me quiet down as I break through the trees onto the asphalt parking lot behind the football field. This lot is on the visitor's side of the stadium. To get to the other side, I have to pass through the tunnel that runs underneath the scoreboard. I'm safer than I was under the cover of trees, but I don't stop moving. I still need to make it back to the dorm before anyone else sees me.

I reach the bottom of the tunnel. The pit, the lowest part where the two sides meet, creates a bowl below the line of sight. You don't know anybody's in the middle of the tunnel until you're right in front of them.

I smell the spray paint before I hear the hiss from the can. Then the vandals come into view. There are three of them down here.

One with a ski mask, one with a plastic store bought clown mask, and the third is wearing a ball cap with a scarf tied round the lower part of his face. They all have spray paint cans in their hands.

The guy with the ski mask slips his phone into his pocket and steps away from the wall.

"Well, well, well. Looks like it's my lucky night." I ignore him and walk towards the pink unicorn he was drawing on the wall. "What are you even doing out of your dorm? Are you spying for one of the sororities or frats?"

"Neither." I cock my head to the side. "I gotta say, I'm in awe of your style. I especially love the unicorn fart trail."

"It's a fly and a tail." The guy holding the blue spray paint adds another streak to the tail.

Footsteps pound down the ramp. My head jerks around. Three people in robes and masks are coming towards me. Based on their body shape, I'd say they're women or extremely tiny guys.

"I heard you caught a prize." A feminine voice says, confirming my theory. I'm willing to bed one of them is Eloise. I can smell her cloying perfume.

I cut my eyes to the guy in the ski mask. He must have sent off the text as soon as he saw me. "Awe, did you call back up? Are you afraid of little ole me?"

"I'm not afraid of shit. Someone's offering a reward for anyone caught outside on Mayhem Night, and here you are."

"Do you know what happens when the uninvited turn up at Mayhem Night?" The first girl asks. Her somber tone making the situation sound more ominous than the situation calls for.

I answer, "They get chased through the woods and stumble across emerging artists?"

The guy in the ski mask steps forward. "They become nothing.

No one with a brain, or thought. They have no rights. We get to do whatever we want to them."

The one who was holding the blue spray can says, "I remember you. You're always out where you're not supposed to be. If you're not a frat spy, you must've hunted us down so we could finish what we started the last time? If that's the case, I'll send them away empty handed." He takes a step towards me, palming his dick.

"I don't know what you're talking about, but if you're asking me to castrate you, I'll be happy to do it." I flutter my lashes. "Just step over here where the light is better, so I can cut it off."

"Finn's not here to protect you this time, you mouthy little bitch."

"I never needed his protection before, slim."

"What are you saying about Finn?" The indignant shriek confirms it's Eloise. "What does he have to do with anything?"

"The last time me and this bitch met up in the dark, he came through and dragged her away. A real knight in shining armor for the skank. My guess is he didn't want her sampling anyone else's dick."

Fuck. He's running his mouth like a gossiping teenager. The lower half of his mouth is exposed and twisted into a smirk. He knows he just said the one thing to take this from a friendly little squabble to an all-out brawl. There's no way Eloise isn't gonna wanna to take my head off over this. Her friends too, because they're moving closer to me. Still, I refuse to cower. "Uh, Oh. Sounds like you're jealous. Did you want Finn to drag you off instead?"

The last guy, the one in the clown mask, stalks closer to me. "I'm gonna teach you a lesson tonight, Theona. One you'll never forget."

Only one person calls me Theona with so much derision dripping from their lips. "I doubt it, *Mikey.* Guys like you who talk a lot can rarely back it up."

Eloise tips her chin, and the girls come at me from the right. The guys are still off to my left. The girl directly in front of me pushes me like some chump on the playground, afraid to take a swing. I grab her, slamming the flat of my hand into the bridge of her nose. She goes down, and I stomp on her hand. It'll be awhile before she can push someone again.

Mike grabs my arms, pulling me to him. "It's easy to fight girls with no training, but I get tired of you talking shit all the time. Let's see how tough you are without Coach Wolfe or Finn jumping in to save you."

Works for me. I shoot my hands up and press my arms out. He thinks I'm breaking his hold, but what I'm really doing is getting leverage. I bring my knee up, slamming it into his gut. He shoves me away before I can reset my foot. I fall onto my ass and land on my tailbone. That shit hurts like a motherfucker. I scramble back to my feet just as the second girl comes flying at me. I catch her with a clothesline, then step over her body.

I turn to square off with Mike and his buddies. I'm so focused on them that I don't realize Eloise has moved out of my line of sight until it's too late. Sensing someone behind me, I turn, but before I can complete the movement, a wooden mop handle smashes against the side of my head. I try to shake off the ringing in my ears, but the distraction is all they need to come after me. The blow to my stomach knocks the wind out of me. I drag air through my mouth and look up, earning a smack to my face from the girl whose nose I smashed. I swing, my fist connecting with someone's face. I can't tell who. A hand grabs me and I bend the fingers back with a forceful tug. That earns me a satisfying snap.

I manage to grab Eloise's hair. Fighting against the pull of the people grabbing my arms, I force her backwards, slamming her head into the wall. I wrestle Clint out of my pocket, but before I can use it, someone else hits me with the mop.

The blow lands across the back of my knees and back. My knees buckle, and it's only because I grab somebody to break my fall that I don't end up on the ground. Another fist smashes into my face. I lash out, burying my knife into the stomach of the person in front of me. Warm blood slicks my blade. I pull it out, letting their life force coat my fingers and straighten for the next attack, holding my knife in front of me. This didn't have to turn messy, but instead of fighting one on one, they're coming at me at the same time.

"She's got a knife." Someone yells.

"Get it from her!"

They'll have to pry Clint from my cold, dead hands. Someone runs at me, head on, and another comes at me from the side. They force me backwards. Someone grabs my knife hand, smacking it repeatedly against the cement wall. My knuckles split, but I maintain my grip on the handle.

I'm rewarded with three successive punches to my face. My jaw is on fire, the left side of my face swollen, my nose is definitely out of alignment and my eye is damn near shut. I take another blow to the stomach and double over.

Seconds later, my arms are pinned behind my back. I'm wrenched upright and being used as a punching bag. The ribs on my right side are sore. Someone hits the same spot twice more and I cry out when I feel them crack.

I try to block out the excruciating pain in my side and chest. I stomp on the foot of the guy on my left and donkey-kick the one behind me. He yelps when my heel connects with his dick and shoves me forward.

I land on my hands and knees. Someone stomps on my hand, forcing me to relinquish my grip on my knife. They stomp again, shattering my wrist. The next kick to my stomach makes me wretch. My stomach emptying what little food I had in my system. I'm forced to breathe through my mouth, since my nose is clogged with blood.

Eloise squeals, "Stay down, you stupid cunt!"

I chuckle as I stagger to my feet and spit a wad of blood at her shoes. I put my guard back up and ask, "Who's next?" If they want me to stay down, they're gonna have to put me down hard. I'm unsteady on my feet, but I've been here before.

Michael launches at me, and I weave out of the way. I time it a little too slowly, so his fist grazes my face. With a surge of energy, I kick his ankle as hard as I can, satisfied with the howl of pain I get for my efforts.

They all rush me again, knowing they can't take me one on one even when I'm injured. Someone picks me up from behind, slamming me to the ground.

The back of my head smacks off the concrete. My vision blackens. I feel my clothes being cut, from my body with my own weapon, while someone wrenches my right arm over my head, and spreads my legs apart, just like they were at my chastity vow.

They pull my arms past the natural state. Pain ricochets through me where they dislocated my shoulder. My scream spurs them on. I hate that I gave them that sound, but they won't get any more.

"Let's see how good you scream when I'm fucking you bloody, you little whore."

"Use this in her ass." someone says with a little too much glee.

Ski mask straddles my face and says, "I'm gonna get her mouth." He pries my mouth open. I no longer have my knife, I'll have to go old school. As soon as he puts the tip of his dick in my mouth, I clamp down as hard as I can.

"Agh. Shit. Get her off of me, get her off."

My mouth fills with blood, but I don't let go. Someone kicks me in my vagina. It's probably the one whose dick I kicked in.

My vision goes spotty and I finally release him when I'm kicked in the head. Passing out would be a blessing right now. My body can't stay in this fight and pain state much longer. I know these guys have every intention of finishing what they started, but at least I won't be awake to see it.

My vision fades in and out. I'm on the edge of unconsciousness, but I'm aware of hands pawing at the rest of my clothes, and the weight of a body against me. This is it. This'll be the one thing I've fought to avoid my whole life in group homes, foster homes, and on the streets. Fucking fits that these rich, entitled assholes will take something from me I don't want to give. They take everything else from those weaker or poorer than them. Why not take my body too?

I put my last reserves of energy into staying conscious. I want to be awake for this so I can get as many clues as possible for who to kill when this is over. The dark is winning, though. I claw at the face in front of me, managing to get a hold of the bandana, pulling it off, just as I feel an unwanted touch between my legs. I stare him in the face, committing it and the jagged scar that slashes across the corner of his mouth, to memory. "Shit, shit. What do I do? She's seen my face."

My twisted smile promises retribution. He glares at me. Then blow after blow rain down on my face until the darkness wins.

The soft murmur of voices reaches my ears as I struggle to lift my lids. Did I leave the television on? I move my hand to find the remote, but the comfort of sleep drags me back under. It's fine. The sound's low enough that I can just ignore it.

When I wake again, it feels like a hot box in my room. Is the AC out? I should get up and call maintenance, but I'm too tired, my body doesn't want to cooperate. I'll call in the morning. My eyes drift closed again. Sleepy. I'm so sleepy.

Someone's talking. I try to make out what the voices are saying, but they're muffled, and too far away. One voice gets closer. It has a niggling kind of familiarity, but I don't know where I know it from. "Nobody can know about this. You need to make this problem go away."

Epilogue
Thea

I wouldn't say I'm claustrophobic, but I'm not a fan of extremely small windowless spaces, either. I'm not sure why, but it's always been an issue for me.

It was stupid of me to focus all my attention on *them*, so I never saw what was happening around me. If I get out, no, *when* I get out of here, I'll make them all pay. Starting with her. The bitch that had the balls to look me in the eye as I regained consciousness, then jab a needle in my neck before slamming the coffin shut.

I strain my ears trying to pick up on sounds. Hoping they're still out there. But the longer I listen, the quieter it gets. And the longer I sit, the more it feels like something else is in this box with me.

I try to move only to find I can't. I'm paralyzed. It must be whatever she injected me with. When the smell of smoke reaches me, I know I'm well and truly fucked. This is more than just a silly initiation prank. Beyond bullying the new girl. The threats I took as meaningless. Harmless. *No big deal.* Were real. I'd been getting notes all week. Stupid taunts from the pledges and I dismissed them. Now, the last note flashes through my mind.

Here lies Theona LaReaux. Finally filling the grave she was always meant to.

The coffin fills with smoke, cutting off what little oxygen I have. I take a deep breath, holding it for as long as I can. My chest burns, my eyes water, and finally I have to gulp air. The heat of the flames reach me. My feet literally put to the fire. My mind races over all the things I wanted to do with my life. The missed opportunities.

How did I survive growing up the way I did, fighting and living in the roughest part of town and homes? How did I make it out alive, only to end up like this? Beaten, and buried in a coffin to die. They'll probably get away with it too. Cremation leaves no proof a crime's been committed. That's okay, because I plan to come back and haunt their asses.

The heavy smoke worms its way into my lungs. This is it. I think of Sasha and how I never got to show her my new town. And of LJ. I promised to go with her to her grandmother's birthday party. She's gonna think I flaked.

My last thought is of my mom. I haven't seen or heard from her in years. I never let myself admit it until now, but she's probably dead. With the shit I've done, I'm heading to the same place she is. At least I'll get to see her again.

The tightness in my chest feels like an anvil crushing me. My eyes shut and I drift off again, finally free of everything.

Afterword

Okay, okay, okay.... I know what you're thinking. I'm a Coxsucker. Absolutely vile, for ending the story there. Am I right?

Trust me, I agree with *everything* you're saying right now. I promise I won't leave you hanging for too long. Book two (Twisted Legacy) is in the works, and just as soon as it no longer resembles an unfinished jigsaw puzzle, I'll put it on pre-order.

Join my Newsletter to be among the first to learn about release information for Twisted Legacy, book two in the Heartless Heirs of Canyon Falls saga, or follow one of my social media accounts for updates on my writing status.

About the Author

Dakota Lee is an overworked mom of three human garbage disposals and a dog who thinks she's a wolf.

In the daylight, she loves paranormal/ supernatural books and tv shows, comic book movies, action movies, and the comfort of a good Hallmark movie.

When the sun goes down, she's been known to tune into some after dark deliciousness that she would never tell her co-workers about.

She's here to push boundaries through her words and hopefully take you on a twisty, thorny journey on the way to a happily ever after.

And if you happen to fall for the asshole before he's redeemed, that's okay.

Dakota's got a weakness for the bad boys too.

facebook.com/dakotaleebooks

instagram.com/authordakotalee

tiktok.com/authordakotalee

www.ingramcontent.com/pod-product-compliance
Lightning Source LLC
Chambersburg PA
CBHW061049210726
48294CB00001B/68